Praise for *Shadow Man*

"Few men who write serial-killer novels have created a woman of such depth. . . . [*Shadow Man*] will be among the best crime fiction you will read this year."
—*Washington Post*

"A terrifically good, terrifically scary serial-killer story . . . This one's very hard to put down."
—*San Francisco Chronicle*

"Coldly, stunningly brilliant. Move over, Thomas Harris, McFadyen has brought a new game to town."
—Lisa Gardner, author of *Gone*

"Brisk and fascinating." —*Kirkus Reviews*

"First-time novelist McFadyen writes like an old pro. . . . A series to watch." —*Booklist*

"This disturbing serial-killer drama set in California marks a promising debut for McFadyen, who combines many conventions of the genre but with far more exquisite, intricate results than the norm. . . . [His] writing is crisp and smart, and his scenes pack a visceral punch without being cheap or exploitative. Barrett, for her part, is a memorable protagonist."
—*Publishers Weekly*

SHADOW MAN

Cody McFadyen

BANTAM BOOKS

NEW YORK TORONTO LONDON SYDNEY AUCKLAND

SHADOW MAN
A Bantam Book

PUBLISHING HISTORY
Bantam hardcover edition published June 2006
Bantam mass market export edition / February 2007
Bantam mass market domestic edition / April 2007

Published by
Bantam Dell
A Division of Random House, Inc.
New York, New York

This is a work of fiction. Names, characters, places, and incidents either are the product of the author's imagination or are used fictitiously. Any resemblance to actual persons, living or dead, events, or locales is entirely coincidental.

Bantam Books and the rooster colophon are registered trademarks of Random House, Inc.

ISBN 978-0-553-58993-1

Printed in the United States of America

www.bantamdell.com

OPM   10 9 8 7 6 5 4 3 2 1

To my parents, for encouraging me to take the road less traveled. To my daughter, for giving me the gift of fatherhood. To my wife, for her unshakable belief, her unending inspiration, her eternal love.

ACKNOWLEDGMENTS

Warm thanks to Diane O'Connell for her editorial advice and for her endless encouragement; Frederica Friedman for her invaluable editorial advice; Liza and Havis Dawson for their tireless work on my behalf, including some great editorial assistance and just a thousand other things; Bill Massey, my editor at Bantam; Nick Sayers, my editor at Hodder; Chandler Crawford for her always able and amazing foreign representation; to my wife, family, and friends for supporting me in my desire to write. A final special acknowledgment to Stephen King for the book *On Writing*. It made a difference, and helped tip the scales from thinking about writing to actually doing the deed.

I

DREAMS AND SHADOWS

1

I HAVE ONE of the dreams. There are only three; two are beautiful, one is violent, but all of them leave me shivering and alone.

The one I have tonight is about my husband. It goes something like this:

I could say he kissed my neck, and leave it like that, simplicity. But that would be a lie, in the most basic way that the word was created to mean.

It would be more truthful to say that I yearned for him to kiss my neck, with every molecule of my being, with every last, burning inch of me, and that when he did, his lips were the lips of an angel, sent from heaven to answer my fevered prayers.

I was seventeen then, and so was he. It was a time when there was no blandness or darkness. There was only passion, sharp edges, and a light that burned so hard it hurt the soul.

He leaned forward in the darkness of the movie theater and (*Oh* God) he hesitated for just a moment and (*Oh* God) I quivered on a precipice but pretended to be calm, and *Oh* God *Oh* God *Oh* God he kissed my neck, and it was heaven, and I knew right then and there that I would be with him forever.

He was my one. Most people, I know, never find their one. They read about it, dream about it, or scoff at the idea. But I found mine, I found him when I was seventeen, and I never let him go, not even the day he lay dying in my arms, not even when death ripped him from me as I screamed, not even now.

God's name these days means suffering: Oh *God* Oh *God* Oh *God*—I miss him so.

I wake with the ghost of that kiss on my flushed seventeen-year-old skin, and realize that I am not seventeen, and that he has stopped aging at all. Death has preserved him at the age of thirty-five, forever. To me, he is always seventeen years old, always leaning forward, always brushing my neck in that perfect moment.

I reach over to the spot he should be sleeping in, and I am pierced with a pain so sudden and blinding that I pray as I shiver, pray for death and an end to pain. But of course, I go on breathing, and soon, the pain lessens.

I miss everything about him being in my life. Not just the good things. I miss his flaws as achingly as I miss the beautiful parts of him. I miss his impatience, his anger. I miss the patronizing look he would give me sometimes when I was mad at him. I miss being annoyed by the fact that he'd always forget to fill the gas tank, leaving it near empty when I was ready to go somewhere.

This is the thing, I think often, that never occurs to you when you consider what it would be like to lose someone you love. That you would miss not just the flowers and kisses, but the totality of the experience. You miss the failures and little evils with as much desperation as you miss being held in the middle of the night. I wish he were here now, and I was kissing him. I wish he were here now, and I was betraying him. Either would be fine, so fine, as long as he was here.

People ask sometimes, when they get up the courage, what it's like to lose someone you love. I tell them it's hard, and leave it at that.

I could tell them that it's a crucifixion of the heart. I could say that most days after, I screamed without stopping, even as I moved through the city, even with my mouth closed, even though I didn't make a sound. I could tell them I have this dream, every night, and lose him again, every morning.

But, hey, why ruin their day? So I tell them it's hard. That usually seems to satisfy them.

This is just one of the dreams, and it gets me out of bed, shaking.

I stare at the empty room, and then turn to the mirror. I have learned to hate mirrors. Some would say that this is normal. That all of us do this, put ourselves under the microscope of self-reflection and focus on the flaws. Beautiful women create fret and worry lines by looking for those very things. Teenage girls with beautiful eyes and figures to die for weep because their hair is the wrong color, or they think their nose is too big. The price of judging ourselves through others' eyes, one of the curses of the human race. And I agree.

But most people don't see what I see when I look into the mirror. When I look at myself, what I see is this:

I have a jagged scar, approximately one half inch wide, that begins in the middle of my forehead at my hairline. It shoots straight down, then turns at a near perfect ninety degree angle to the left. I have no left eyebrow; the scar has taken its place. It crosses my temple, where it then makes a lazy loop-de-loop down my cheek. It rips over toward my nose, crosses the bridge of it just barely, and then turns back, slicing in a diagonal across my left nostril and zooming one final time past my jawline, down my neck, ending at my collarbone.

It's quite an effect. If you look at me in right profile only, everything looks normal. You have to stare at me straight on to get the full picture.

Everyone looks in a mirror at least once a day, or sees their reflection in the eyes of others. And they know what to expect. They know what they will see, what will be seen. I no longer see what I expect to see. I have the reflection of a stranger, staring out of a mask I can't take off.

When I stand naked in front of the mirror, as I am now, I can see the rest of it. I have what can only be called a necklace of cigar-sized circular scars, going from under one side of my collarbone to the other. More of the same traverse my breasts, go down across my sternum and stomach, ending just above my pubic hair.

The scars are cigar-sized because a cigar is what made them.

If you can put all of that aside, things look pretty good. I'm small, four foot ten inches tall. I'm not skinny, but I am in shape. My husband used to call it a "lush" figure. After my mind, heart, and soul, he used to say, he married me for my "mouth-sized boobs and my heart-shaped ass." I have long, thick, dark, curly hair that hangs down to just above said ass.

He used to love that too.

It is hard for me to look past those scars. I've seen them a hundred times, maybe a thousand. They are still all I see when I look into the mirror.

They were put there by the man who killed my husband and my daughter. Who was later killed by me.

I feel a broad emptiness rush into me thinking about this. It's huge, dark, and absolutely nerveless. Like sinking into numb Jell-O.

No big deal. I'm used to it.
That's just how my life is now.

I sleep for no more than ten minutes, and I know that I won't be sleeping again tonight.

I remember waking up a few months ago in the middle hours, just like this. That time between 3:30 and 6:00 A.M., when you feel like the only person on earth if you happen to be up then. I'd had one of the dreams, as always, and knew I wasn't going to be getting back to sleep.

I pulled on a T-shirt and some sweatpants, slipped on my battered sneakers, and headed out the door. I ran and ran and ran in the night, ran till my body was slick with sweat, till it soaked my clothes and filled those sneakers, and then I ran some more. I wasn't pacing myself, and my breath was coming out fast. My lungs felt scarred by the coolness of that early-morning air. I didn't stop, though. I ran faster, legs and elbows pumping, running as fast as I could, reckless.

I ended up in front of one of those convenience stores that fill the Valley, over by the curb, gagging and hacking up stomach acid. A couple of other early-morning ghosts looked over at me, then looked away. I stood up, wiped my mouth, and slammed through the front door of the store.

"I want a pack of cigarettes," I said to the proprietor, still gulping in air.

He was an older man, in his fifties, who looked Indian to me.

"What kind do you want?"

The question startled me. I hadn't smoked in years. I looked at the rows behind him, my eyes catching the once-beloved Marlboros.

"Marlboros. Reds."

He got me the pack and rang it up. Which is when I realized I was in sweats and had no money. Instead of being embarrassed, I was, of course, angry.

"I forgot my purse." I said it with my chin jutted out, defiant. Daring him to not give me the cigarettes or to make me feel ridiculous in any way.

He looked at me for a moment. It was, I guess, what writers would call a "pregnant pause." He relaxed.

"You've been running?" he asked.

"Yeah—running from my dead husband. Better than killing yourself, I guess, ha ha!"

The words came out sounding funny to my ears. A little loud, a little strangled. I suppose I was a little crazy. But instead of getting the flinch or look of discomfort I so wanted from him at that moment, his eyes went soft. Not with pity, but with understanding. He nodded. He reached across the counter, holding the pack of cigarettes out for me to take.

"My wife died in India. One week before we were supposed to come to America. You take the cigarettes, pay me next time."

I stood there for a moment, staring at him. And then I snatched those cigarettes and ran out of there as fast as I could, before the tears started rolling down my cheeks. I clutched that pack of cigarettes and ran home weeping.

The place is a little out of my way, but I never go anywhere else now when I want to smoke.

I sit up now and smile a little as I find the pack of cigarettes on the nightstand, and think of the guy at the store as I light up. I guess a part of me loves that little man, in the way you can only love a stranger who shows you a kindness so perfect at a time when you need it the most. It's a deep love, a pang in the heart, and I know that even if I never know his name, I'll remember him till the day I die.

I inhale, a nice deep lungful, and regard the cigarette, its perfect cherry tip as it glows in the dark of my bedroom. This, I think, is the insidiousness of the cursed things. Not the nicotine addiction, though that's surely bad enough. But the way a cigarette just fits in certain places. Morning dawns with a steaming cup of coffee. Or lonely nights in a house filled with ghosts. I know I should give them up again, before they get their claws all the way back into me, but I also know I won't. They are all I have right now, a reminder of a kindness, a comfort and a source of strength, all rolled into one.

I exhale and watch the smoke billow, caught here and there by little currents of air, floating and then disappearing. Like life, I think. Life is smoke, plain and simple; we just fool ourselves that it's otherwise. All it takes is one good gust and we float away and disappear, leaving behind only the scent of our passing in the form of memories.

I cough suddenly, laughing at all the connections. I'm smoking, life is smoke, and my name is Smoky. Smoky Barrett. My real name, given to me because my mother thought it "sounded cool." This makes me cackle in the dark, in my empty house, and I think as I laugh (as I have before) just how crazy laughter sounds when you're laughing alone.

This gives me something to think about for the next three or four hours. Being crazy, I mean. Tomorrow is the day, after all.

The day when I decide if I go back to work for the FBI or come home, put a gun in my mouth, and blow my brains out.

2

ARE YOU STILL having the same three dreams?"

This is one of the reasons I trust my appointed shrink. He doesn't play mind games, dance around things, or try to sneak up and flank me. He goes straight for the heart of it, a direct attack. As much as I complain, and struggle against his attempts to heal me, I respect this.

Peter Hillstead is his name, and he's about as far from the Freud-appearance stereotype as you can get. He stands just under six feet tall, with dark hair, a model-handsome face, and a body I wondered about when I first met him. His eyes are the most striking thing about him, though. They are an electric blue I've never seen on a brunette before.

Despite his movie-star looks, I cannot imagine transference happening with this man. When you are with him, you do not think about sex. You think about you. He is one of those rare people who truly care about those they deal with, and you cannot doubt this when you are with him. You never feel, when you talk to him, that his mind is roaming elsewhere. He gives you his full attention. He makes you feel like you are the only thing that matters inside his small office. This is what, to me, precludes having a crush on this hunky therapist. When you are with him, you don't think of him as a man, but as something far more valuable: a mirror of the soul.

"The same three," I respond.

"Which one did you have last night?"

I shift a little, uncomfortable. I know that he notices this, wonder what he's decided it means. I'm always calculating and weighing. I can't help it.

"The one about Matt kissing me."

He nods. "Were you able to go back to sleep afterward?"

"No." I stare at him, not saying anything more, while he waits. This is not one of my cooperative days.

Dr. Hillstead looks at me, chin in his hand. He seems to be contemplating something, a man at a crossroads. Knowing that whatever path he chooses will be one he can't take back. Almost a minute goes by before he leans back and sighs, pinching the bridge of his nose.

"Smoky, did you know that within the ranks of my fellow practitioners, I'm not all that well thought of?"

I start at this, both at the idea of it as well as the fact that he is telling me at all. "Uh, no. I didn't."

He smiles. "It's true. I have some controversial views about my profession. The primary one being that I feel we have no real scientific solution to the problems of the mind."

How the hell am I supposed to respond to that? My shrink telling me that his chosen profession doesn't have any solutions to mental problems? Not exactly confidence-inspiring. "I can see how that might not be appreciated."

It's the best response I can muster on short notice.

"Don't get me wrong. I'm not saying that I think my profession contains *no* solutions to mental problems."

And that, I think, is one of the other reasons I trust this therapist of mine. He is knife-edge sharp, to the point of clairvoyance. It doesn't spook me. I understand it—any truly gifted interrogator has this ability. To anticipate what the other person is thinking in response to what you are saying.

"No. What I mean is this: Science is science. It is exact. Gravity means when you drop something, it will always fall. Two plus two is always four. Nonvariance is the essence of science."

I think about this, nod.

"That being the case, what my profession does?" He gestures. "Our approach to the problems of the mind? Not a science. Not yet, at least. We haven't arrived at two plus two. If we had, I would solve every case that walked in that door. I would know, in case of depression, do A, B, C, and it would always work. There would be laws that never changed, and that would be science." He smiles now, a wry smile. Maybe a little sad. "But I don't solve every case. Not even half." He is silent a moment, then shakes his head. "What I do, my profession? It's not a science. It's a collection of things you can try, most of which have worked before more than once, and, having worked in more than one case, are worth trying again. But that's about it. I've stated this view in public, so . . . I don't have the greatest rep among many of my peers."

I give this some thought while he waits. "I think I can see why," I say. "Things become more about image, less about results, in some parts of the Bureau. It's probably the same deal for the shrinks that don't like you."

He smiles again, a tired kind of smile. "Right to the pragmatic center of it as always, Smoky. At least, in things that don't involve yourself."

I wince inside at this. This is one of Dr. Hillstead's favorite techniques, using normal conversation as a cover for the soul-revealing zingers he shoots at you, casual.

Like the little Scud missile he'd just popped in my direction: You have an incisive mind, Smoky, he'd said, but you don't apply it to solving yourself. Ouch. Truth hurts.

"But here I am, in spite of what anyone may think of me. One of the most trusted therapists when it comes to handling cases involving FBI agents. Why do you think that is?"

He is looking at me again, waiting. I know this is leading up to something. Dr. Hillstead never rambles. So I think about it.

"If I had to guess, I'd guess that it's because you're good. Good always counts more than looks good, in my line of work."

That slight smile again.

"That's right. I get results. That's not something I parade around, and I don't pat myself on the back about it before I go to bed every night. But it's true."

Said in the simple, nonarrogant tones of any accomplished professional. I understand this. It isn't about modesty. In a tactical situation, when you ask someone if they are good with a gun, you want them to be honest. If they suck, you want to know, and they want you to know, because a bullet will kill a liar as quick as an honest man. You have to know the truth about strengths and weaknesses when the rubber meets the road. I nod, and he continues.

"That's what matters in any military organization. Can you get results. Do you think it's odd that I think of the FBI as a military organization?"

"No. It's a war."

"Do you know what the primary problem of any military organization is, always?"

I'm getting bored, restless. "Nope."

He gives me a disapproving look. "Think about it before you answer, Smoky. Please don't blow me off."

Chastised, I comply. I speak slowly when I reply. "My guess would be ... personnel."

He points a finger at me. "Bingo. Now—why?"

The answer leaps into my mind, the way answers sometimes did when I was on a case, when I was really thinking. "Because of what we see."

"Uh-huh. That's part of it. I call it 'see, do, lose.' What you see, what you do, and what you lose. It's a triumvirate." He counts them off on his fingers. "In law enforcement you see the worst things a human being is capable of. You do things no human should have to do, from handling rotting corpses to, in some cases, killing another person. You lose things, whether it's something intangible, like innocence and optimism, or something real, such as a partner or ... family."

He gives me a look I can't read. "That's where I come in. I'm here because of this problem. And it's also this problem that prevents me from being able to do my job the way it should be done."

Now I am puzzled as well as interested. I look at him, a signal to continue, and he sighs. It's a sigh that seems to contain its own "see, do, lose," and I wonder about the other people who sit across from this desk, in this chair. The other miseries he listens to, takes home with him when he leaves.

I try to picture this, looking at him. Dr. Hillstead, sitting at home. I know the basics; I had checked him out in a cursory fashion. Never married, lives in a two-story, five-bedroom house in Pasadena. Drives an Audi sports sedan—the doc likes a little speed under him, a hint at some part of his personality. But these are all flat facts. Nothing to really tell you what happens when he walks in the front door of his home and closes it behind him. Is he a microwave dinner kind of bachelor? Or does he cook steak, sipping red wine alone at an immaculate dining table while Vivaldi plays in the background? Hey, maybe he comes home, slips on a pair of high heels and nothing else, and does the housework, hairy legs and all.

I warm to this thought, a little secret humor. I'll take my laughs where I can get them these days. I make myself focus again on what he's saying to me.

"In a normal world, someone who's gone through what you've gone through would never go back, Smoky. If you were the average person in the average profession, you'd stay away from guns, and killers, and dead people, forever. Instead, my job is to see if I can help you be ready to return to that. This is what is expected of me. To take wounded psyches and send them back into the war. Melodramatic, maybe, but true."

Now he leans forward, and I feel that we are getting to the end of it, to whatever point he's leading toward.

"Do you know why I'm willing to work toward that? When I know I may be sending someone back into the thing that harmed them in the first place?" He pauses. "Because that is what ninety-nine percent of my patients want."

He pinches the bridge of his nose again, shaking his head.

"The men and women I see, all mentally shot up, want to be fixed so they can go back to the battle. And the truth is, whatever it is that makes you people tick—most of the time, going back is exactly what you need. Do you know what happens to most of those who don't? Sometimes they turn out okay. A lot of the time they turn into drunks. And every now and then, they kill themselves."

He looks at me as he says this last part, and I'm momentarily paranoid, wondering if he can read my mind. I have no idea where this is going. It's making me feel off balance, a little bit wobbly, and a whole lot uncomfortable. All of which annoys me. My response to being uncomfortable is all Irish, from my mother's side—I get pissed off and blame the other person for it.

He reaches over to the left side of his desk, picks up a thick file folder I hadn't noticed before, puts it in front of him, and flips it open. I squint and am surprised to see that it is my name on the tab.

"This is your personnel file, Smoky. I've had it for some time, and I've read it through more than once." He flips over the pages, summarizing out loud. "Smoky Barrett, born 1968. Female. Degree in criminology. Accepted into the Bureau 1990. Graduated top of her class at Quantico. Assigned to assist in the Black Angel case in Virginia in 1991, administrative capacity." He looks up at me. "But you didn't remain on the sidelines of that one, did you?"

I shake my head, remembering. I sure hadn't. I was twenty-two years old, greener than green. Excited about being an agent, even more excited about being a part of a major case, even if it was pretty much just desk work. During one of the briefings, something about the case had stuck in my mind, something in a witness statement that didn't seem right. It was still turning in my head when I went to sleep, and I awoke with a 4:00 A.M. epiphany, something that was going to become familiar to me in later years. The thing was, it ended up being an insight that broke the case wide open. It had to do with what direction a window opened. A tiny, forgettable detail that became the pea under my mattress and ended up closing the door on a killer.

I called it luck at the time and downplayed myself. True luck was that the agent in charge of the task force, Special Agent Jones, was one of those rare bosses. One who doesn't hog the glory and instead gives credit where credit is due. Even to a green female agent. I was still new, so I got more desk work, but I was on the fast track from that point on. I was groomed for NCAVC—the National Center for the Analysis of Violent Crime, the part of the FBI that deals with the worst of the worst—under the watchful eye of SAC Jones.

"Assigned to NCAVC three years later. That's a pretty quick jump, isn't it?"

"The average agent assigned to NCAVC has ten years of prior Bureau experience." I'm not bragging. It's true. He continues reading.

"A few more cases solved, glowing performance reviews. And then you were made the NCAVC coordinator in Los Angeles in '96. Charged with creating an efficient local unit, and repairing relations with local law enforcement that your predecessor had damaged. Some might have thought this was a demotion, but the truth is, you were handpicked for a difficult task. It's where you really began to shine."

My mind wanders back to that time. *Shine* is the perfect word. 1996 was a year when nothing seemed to go wrong. I'd had my daughter in late 1995. I was appointed to the LA office, a huge feather in my professional cap. And Matt and I were going strong, strong as ever. It was one of those years when I woke up every morning excited, fresh.

Back when I could reach over and find him next to me, where he should be.

It was everything that the here and now is not, and I feel myself getting angry at Dr. Hillstead for reminding me of this. For making the present all the more bleak and empty by comparison.

"Is there a point here?"

He raises a hand. "Just a little bit more. The office in LA hadn't been doing well. You were given carte blanche in restaffing it, and you picked three agents from offices around the United States. They were thought, at the time, to be unusual choices. But they proved out in the end, didn't they?"

That, I think to myself, is an understatement. I just nod, still angry.

"In fact, your team is one of the best in Bureau history, isn't it?"

"The best." I can't help it. I'm proud of my team, and I'm incapable of being modest when it comes to them. Besides, it's the truth. NCAVC Los Angeles, known as "NCAVC Coord" or internally as "Death Central," did its job. Period and always.

"Right." He flips through a few more pages. "Lots of solved cases. More glowing reviews. Some notes that you were being considered to become the first female Acting Director ever. Historic."

All of this is true. All of it also continues to anger me, for reasons I can't quite understand. I just know that I am getting pissed off, coming to a boil, and if this continues, I am going to have an explosive meltdown.

"Something else in your file caught my eye. Notations about your marksmanship."

He looks up at me, and I feel blindsided, though I don't know why. Something stirs in me, and I recognize it as fear. I grip the arms of the chair as he continues.

"Your file states that you possibly rank within the top twentieth percentile, worldwide, with a handgun. Is that true, Smoky?"

I stare at my therapist, and I feel myself going numb. The anger is disappearing.

Me and guns. Everything he's saying is true. I can pick up a gun and shoot it like other people grab a glass of water, or ride a bike. It's instinctive, and always has been. There's no genius to it that you can put a finger on. I didn't have a father who wanted a son and so taught me how to use a gun. In fact, my dad disliked them. It was just something I could do.

I was eight years old, and my dad had a friend who had been in Vietnam as a Green Beret. Now *he* was a gun nut. He lived in a run-down condo in a run-down area of the San Fernando Valley—which fit him. He was a run-down man. Even so, to this day I remember his eyes: sharp and youthful. Sparkling.

His name was Dave, and he managed to drag my father out to a shooting range in a somewhat disreputable area of San Bernardino County, and my dad had brought me along, maybe in hopes of keeping the trip short. Dave got my dad to shoot a few clips, as I stood, watching, wearing protective earmuffs that were too big for my little-girl head. I watched them both as they held the weapons, and I was fascinated by it. Drawn to it.

"Can I try?" I piped up.

"I don't think that's a good idea, honey," Dad said.

"Aww, come on, Rick. I'll get her a little twenty-two pistol. Let her squeeze off a couple of shots."

"Please, Daddy?" I looked up at my father with my best pleading look, the one I knew, even at eight, could bend his will to mine. He looked down at me, the struggle apparent in his face, and then sighed.

"Okay. But just a few shots."

Dave went and got the twenty-two, a tiny little thing that fit my hand, and they dug up a stool for me to stand on. Dave loaded the weapon and placed it in my hands, standing behind me as my dad watched, apprehensive.

"See the target down there?" he asked. I nodded. "Decide where you want your shot to land. Take your time. When you pull the trigger, you want to do it slow. Don't jerk it, or that will throw off your aim. You ready?"

I believe I replied, but the truth was, I barely heard him. I had the gun in my hand, and something was clicking inside me. Something right. Something that fit. I looked down the range at the human-shaped target, and it didn't seem far away at all. It seemed close, reachable. I pointed the gun toward it, took a breath, and pulled.

I was startled and thrilled by the jerk of the little pistol in my small hands.

"Damn!" I heard Dave crow.

I squinted down toward the target again and saw that a little hole had appeared in the center of the head, right where I had wanted it to go.

"You just might be a natural, young lady," he said to me. "Try a few more."

The "couple of shots" turned into an hour and a half of shooting. I hit what I aimed for over ninety percent of the time, and by the end of it, I knew I'd be shooting guns for the rest of my life. And that I'd be good at it.

My dad supported this habit in the years to come, in spite of his distaste for guns. I guess he recognized that this was a part of me, something he wouldn't be able to keep me away from.

The truth? I'm scary-good. I keep this to myself, and I don't show off in public. But alone? I'm an Annie Oakley. I can shoot out candle flames and put holes in quarters that you toss in the air. One time, at an outdoor shooting range, I put a Ping-Pong ball on the back of my gun hand, the same one I use to draw my weapon. It sat on the back of my hand, and then that hand flew down to grab my gun. I came back up and blew the Ping-Pong ball away before it could fall to the ground. A silly trick, but I found it very satisfying.

All of this goes through my head while Dr. Hillstead watches me.

"It's true," I say.

He closes the file. Clasps his hands and looks at me. "You are an exceptional agent. Certainly one of the best female agents in the Bureau's history. You hunt the worst of the worst. Six months ago a man you were hunting, Joseph Sands, came after you and your family, killed your husband in front of you, raped and tortured you, and killed your daughter. Through an effort that could only be called superhuman, you turned the tables on him, taking his life."

I am fully clothed in the numbness now. I don't know what all of this is leading to, and I don't care.

"So here I am, in a profession where two plus two doesn't always equal four, and things don't always fall when you drop them, trying to help you go back to all of that."

The look he gives me is so filled with honest compassion that I have to look away from it; it burns me with its feeling.

"I've been doing this for a long time, Smoky. And you've been seeing me for quite a while. I develop feelings about things—you'd probably call them hunches in your line of work. Here's what my hunches have to say about where we're at. I think you're trying to choose between whether or not to go back to work or kill yourself."

My gaze snaps back up to his, an involuntary admission that's been shocked out of me. As the numbness rushes away from me in a scream, I realize that I've been played, played with great finesse. He's talked around, rambled, prodded, keeping me unaware and off balance, and then moved in for the kill. Right for the jugular, without hesitation. And it's worked.

"I can't help you unless you really lay it all on the table, Smoky."

That compassionate look again, too truthful and honest and good for me right now; his eyes are like two hands reaching out to grab my spiritual shoulders, shaking me hard. I feel tears prickling. But my look back is filled with anger. He wants to break me, the way I've broken plenty of criminals in plenty of interrogation offices. Well, fuck that.

Dr. Hillstead seems to sense this, and smiles a soft smile.

"Okay, Smoky, that's fine. Just one last thing."

He pulls open a desk drawer and lifts a plastic evidence bag out. At first I can't tell what it holds, but then I can, and it causes me to shiver and sweat at the same time.

It's my gun. The one I carried for years, and the one I shot Joseph Sands with.

I can't tear my eyes away from it. I know it like I know my own face. Glock, deadly, black. I know how much it weighs, what it feels like—I can even remember how it smells. It sits there in that bag, and the sight of it fills me with an overwhelming terror.

Dr. Hillstead opens the bag, removing the gun. He lays it down on the desk in front of us. Now he looks at me again, except this time, it's a hard look, not a compassionate one. He's done fucking around. I realize that what I thought was his best shot wasn't even close. For reasons I don't understand, and apparently he does, it is this that is going to break me wide open. My own weapon.

"How many times have you picked up that gun, Smoky? A thousand? Ten thousand?"

I lick my lips, which are as dry as dust. I don't reply. I can't stop looking at the Glock.

"Pick it up, right now, and I'll recommend you fit for active duty, if that's what you want."

I can't respond, and I can't tear my eyes away from it. Part of me knows I'm in Dr. Hillstead's office, and that he is sitting across from me, but things seem to have narrowed to one world: me and the gun. Sounds have filtered out, so that there is a strange, still silence in my head, except for the thudding of my heart. I can hear it, beating hard and fast.

I lick my dry lips again. Just reach over and take it, I tell myself. Like he said, you've done it ten thousand times. That gun is an extension of your hand; picking it up is an afterthought, like breathing, or blinking.

It just sits there, and my hands have stayed on the arms of the chair, stiff and clenching.

"Go ahead. Pick it up." His voice has gone hard. Not brutal, but unyielding.

I've managed to get one of my hands to come off the arm of the chair, and I move it forward with all the force of will I can muster. It doesn't want to respond, and part of me, the very small part that remains analytical and calm, cannot believe that this is happening. When did an action that, for me, is close to a reflex become the hardest thing I've ever done?

I'm aware that sweat is streaming down my forehead. My entire body is shaking, and my vision has started to get dark around the edges. I'm having trouble breathing, and I can feel panic building in me, a claustrophobic, hemmed-in, suffocating feeling. My arm is shaking like a tree in a hurricane. Muscles spasm up and down it like a bagful of snakes. My hand gets closer and closer to the gun, until it's hovering just above it, and now the shaking is huge, has moved to my entire body, and the sweat is everywhere.

I leap up from the chair, toppling it over backward, and scream.

I scream, and I beat my head with my hands, and I feel myself starting to sob, and I know he's done it. He's cracked me, split me open, torn my guts out. The fact that he's done it to help me isn't any comfort, none at all, because right now everything is pain, pain, pain.

I back away from his desk, to the left wall, sliding down it. I register that I am moaning as I do this, a kind of keening wail. It is a terrible sound. It hurts me to hear it, like it always has. It is a sound I've heard too many times before. The sound of a survivor who has realized that they're still alive, while everything they love is gone. I've heard it from mothers and husbands and friends, heard it as they identified bodies in the morgue or got the news of death from my own lips.

I wonder that I can't feel ashamed right now, but there's no room for shame here. Pain has filled me up.

Dr. Hillstead has moved near me. He won't hold me or touch me—that's not good form for a therapist. But I can feel him. He is a crouched blur in front of me, and my hatred of him, at this moment, is perfect.

"Talk to me, Smoky. Tell me what's happening."

It is a voice so filled with genuine kindness that it sparks a whole new wave of anguish. I manage to speak, broken, sobbing gasps.

"I can't live like this I can't live like this no Matt, no Alexa, no love no life all gone all gone and—"

My mouth forms an *O*. I can feel it. I look up at the ceiling, grab my hair, and manage to rip out two handfuls by the roots before I pass out.

3

IT SEEMS STRANGE that a demon would speak with a voice like that. He stands nearly ten feet tall, he has agate eyes and a head covered with gnashing, crying mouths. The scales that cover him are the black of something that's been burned. But the voice is twangy, almost Southern-sounding, when he speaks.

"I love to eat souls," he says in a conversational tone. "Nothing like devouring something that was destined for heaven."

I'm naked and tied to my bed, tied by silver chains, chains thin and yet unbreakable. I feel like Sleeping Beauty, written by accident into an H. P. Lovecraft story. Waking to a forked tongue against my lips rather than the soft kiss of a hero. I am voiceless, gagged with a scarf of silk.

The demon is standing at the foot of the bed, looking down at me as it speaks. It looks both at ease and possessive, staring at me with the look of pride a hunter gives a deer strapped to the hood of his car.

It waves the serrated combat knife it's holding. The knife seems so small in those huge, clawed hands.

"But I like my souls well done—and spicy! Yours is

missing something…maybe a dash of agony and a side of pain?"

Its eyes go empty, and black saliva that looks like pus dribbles from between its fangs, sliding along its chin and onto its huge and scaly chest. The demon's absolute unawareness of this is terrifying. Then it smiles a leering smile, showing all those pointy teeth, and shakes a claw at me, playful.

"I have someone else here too, my love. My sweet, sweet Smoky."

It steps aside to reveal my prince, the one whose kiss I should have awoken to. My Matt. The man I've known since I was seventeen years old. The man I know in every way a person can know another person. He is naked, and tied to a chair. He's been given a long, terrible beating. The kind of beating designed to harm without causing death. The kind of beating made to feel endless, to kill hope, while keeping the body alive. One eye is swollen shut, his nose is broken, and teeth are missing behind the shredded meat of his lips. His lower jaw is formless and shattered. Sands has used his knife on Matt. I see small, deep cuts all over that face I've loved and kissed and cradled. There are big slashes down his chest and around his belly button. And blood. So much blood everywhere. Blood that runs and drips and bubbles as Matt breathes. The demon has smeared the blood on Matt's stomach to play a game of tic-tac-toe. I notice that the Os won.

Matt's one open eye meets mine, and the perfection of the despair I see there fills my mind with a terrible howling. It's a howl from the gut, a soul-shattering sound, horror put to voice. A hurricane shriek strong enough to destroy the world. I am filled with a rage so complete, so intense, so overwhelming that it destroys conscious thought with the violence of a bomb blast. This is a rage of insanity, the total darkness of an underground cavern. An eclipse of the soul.

I screech like an animal through my gag, the kind of screech that should make your throat bleed and your eardrums explode, and I slam against my bonds so hard that the chains cut into my skin. My eyes bug out, trying to burst from their sockets. If I were a dog, I would be foaming at the mouth. I want only one thing: to snap these chains and kill the demon with my bare hands. I don't just want it to die—I want to eviscerate it. I want to tear it apart so that it is unrecognizable. I want to split the atoms that make up the demon and turn it into mist.

But the chains stay strong. They don't break. They don't even loosen. Through this, the demon watches me in bemused fascination, one hand resting on the top of Matt's head, a monstrous parody of a fatherly gesture.

The demon laughs and shakes its monstrous head, causing its multiple mouths to mew in protest. Speaks again with that voice that doesn't match its form.

"There we go! Cook and baste, bake and broil." It winks. "Nothing like a little despair to bring out the taste of a heroic soul. . . ." A pause, and then the voice goes serious for just a moment, fills with a kind of perverse regret: "Don't blame yourself for this, Smoky. Even a hero can't win all the time."

I look at Matt again, and the look in his eye is enough to make me want to die. It's not a look of fear, or pain, or horror. It's a look of love. He has managed, for just a moment, to push the demon out of the world of this bedroom, so that it's just he and I, looking at each other.

One of the gifts of a long marriage is the ability to communicate anything—from mild displeasure to the meaning of life—with a single glance. It's something you develop in the process of mixing your soul with your spouse's, if you're willing to mix your soul. Matt was giving me one of those looks and saying three things with that one, beautiful eye: I'm sorry, I love you, and ... good-bye.

It was like watching the end of the world. Not in flame and fire, but in cold, drenching shadows. Darkness that would go on forever.

The demon seems to sense it as well. It laughs again and does a little prancing dance, waving its tail and dripping pus from its pores.

"Ahh—*amore*. How sweet it is. That'll be the cherry on top of my Smoky sundae—the death of love."

The door to the room opens, closes. I don't see anyone enter ... but there is now a small, shadowy figure at the periphery of my vision. Something about it fills me with desperation.

Matt closes his eye, and I feel the rage again and tear at my bonds.

The knife goes down, I hear the wet, cutting, sawing sound, and Matt screams through his ruined lips as I scream through my gag, and Prince Charming is dying, Prince Charming is dying—

I wake up screaming.

I am lying on the couch in Dr. Hillstead's office. He is kneeling next to it, touching me with words, not hands.

"Shh. Smoky. It's okay, it was just a dream. You're here, you're safe."

I'm shaking hard, and I'm covered with sweat. I can feel tears drying on my face.

"Are you all right?" he asks me. "You back?"

I can't look at him. I bring myself to a sitting position.

"Why did you do that?" I whisper. I'm done with the pretense of being strong in front of my shrink. He's shattered me, and he holds my heart, still beating, in his hands.

He doesn't reply right away. He stands up, grabs a chair, and brings it close to the couch. He sits down, and though I still can't look at him, I can feel him looking at me, like a bird beating its wings against a window. Tentative, persistent.

"I did that...because I had to." He's silent for a moment. "Smoky, I've been working with FBI and other law-enforcement agents for a decade now. You people, you are made of such strong stuff. I've seen all the best parts of humanity in this office. Dedication. Bravery. Honor. Duty. Sure, I've seen a little evil, some corruption. But that's been the exception, not the rule. Mostly, I've seen strength. Unbelievable strength. Strength of character, of the soul." He pauses, shrugs. "We're not supposed to discuss the soul, in my profession. Not supposed to believe in it, really. Good and evil? They're just broad concepts, not things defined." He looks at me, grim. "But they aren't just concepts, are they?"

I continue to stare at my hands.

"You and your peers, you hoard your strength like a talisman. You act as if it has some finite source. Like Samson and his hair. You seem to think if you break down and really open up in here, you'll lose that strength and never get it back." He's quiet again, for a good long while. I feel empty and desolate. "I've been doing this for some time, Smoky, and you're one of the strongest people I've ever met. I can say with near certainty that none of the people I've treated in the past would be able to endure what you've suffered, are suffering. Not one of them."

I manage to make myself look at him. I wonder if he's making fun of me. Strong? I don't feel strong. I feel weak. I can't even hold my gun. I look at him, and he looks back at me, and it's an unflinching gaze that I recognize with a jolt. I've given blood-drenched crime scenes that gaze.

Dismembered corpses. I am able to look on those horrors, and not look away. Dr. Hillstead is giving me the same look, and I realize that this is his gift: He is able to give the horrors of the soul a steady, unwavering gaze. I'm his crime scene, and he'll never turn away in distaste or revulsion.

"But I know you are at your breaking point, Smoky. And that means I can do one of two things: Watch you break and die, or force you to open up and let me help you. I choose the second one."

I can feel the truth of his words, their sincerity. I've looked at a hundred lying criminals. I like to think I can smell a lie in my sleep. He's telling me the truth. He wants to help me.

"So now the ball's in your court. You can get up and leave, or we can move on from here." He smiles at me, a tired smile. "I can help you, Smoky. I really can. I can't make it not have happened. I can't promise that you won't hurt for the rest of your life. But I can help you. If you'll let me."

I stare at my shrink, and I can feel it all struggling inside me. He's right. I'm a female Samson, and he's a male Delilah, except that he's telling me it won't hurt me to cut my hair this time. He's asking me to trust him in a way I don't trust anyone. Except myself.

And . . . ? I hear the little voice inside ask. I close my eyes in response. Yeah. And Matt.

"Okay, Dr. Hillstead. You win. I'll give it a shot."

I know it's right the moment I say it, because I stop shaking.

I wonder if what he'd said was true. About my strength, I mean.

Do I have the strength to live?

4

I'M STANDING AT the front of the LA FBI offices on Wilshire. I look up at the building, trying to feel something about it.

Nothing.

This is not a place I belong to right now; instead, I feel it judging me. Frowning down at me with a face of concrete, glass, and steel. Is this how civilians see it, I wonder? As something imposing and perhaps a little hungry?

I catch my reflection in the glass of the front doors and cringe inside. I was going to wear a suit, but that felt like too much of a commitment to success. Sweats were too little. As a testimony to indecisiveness, I had opted for jeans and a button-down blouse, simple flats on my feet, light makeup. Now it all feels inadequate, and I want to run, run, run.

Emotions are rolling in like waves, cresting and crashing. Fear, anxiety, anger, hope.

Dr. Hillstead had ended the session with one dictate: Go and see your team.

"This wasn't just a job for you, Smoky. It was something that defined your life. Something that was a part of who you are. What you are. Would you agree?"

"Yeah. That's true."

"And the people you work with—some of them are friends?"

I shrugged. "Two of them are my best friends. They've tried to reach out to me, but . . ."

He raised his eyebrows at me, a query he already knew the answer to. "But you haven't seen them since you were in the hospital."

They'd come to visit me while I was wrapped in gauze like a mummy, while I wondered why I was still alive, and wished I wasn't. They'd tried to stay, but I'd asked them to leave. Lots of phone calls had followed, all of which I let go to voice mail and didn't return.

"I didn't want to see anybody then. And after . . ." I let the words trail off.

"After, what?" he prodded.

I sighed. I gestured toward my face. "I didn't want them to see me like this. I don't think I could stand it if I saw pity on their faces. It would hurt too much."

We'd talked about it a little further, and he'd told me that the first step toward being able to pick up my gun again was to go face my friends. So here I am.

I clench my teeth, call on that Irish stubbornness, and push through the doors.

They close in slow silence behind me, and I'm trapped for a minute between the marble floor and the high ceiling above. I feel exposed, a rabbit caught in an open field.

I move through the metal detectors of security and present my badge. The guard on duty is alert, with hard, roaming eyes. They flicker a little when he sees the scars.

"Going to say hi to the guys in Death Central and the Assistant Director," I tell him, feeling (for some reason) like I have to tell him something.

He gives me a polite smile that says he really doesn't

care. I feel even more foolish and exposed and head to the elevator lobby, cursing myself under my breath.

I end up in an elevator with someone I don't know, who manages to make me feel even more uncomfortable (if that were possible) by doing a bad job of hiding his sideways glances at my face. I do my best to ignore it, and when we get to my floor, I leave the elevator perhaps a little faster than normal. My heart is pounding.

"Get a grip on yourself, Barrett," I growl. "What do you expect, looking like the hunchback of Notre Dame? Get it together."

Talking to myself works most of the time, and this is no exception. I feel better. I head down the hallway and now I'm in front of the door to what used to be my office. Fear rises again, replacing the nonchalance I had mustered. There are parallels here, I think. I've gone through that door without thinking about it more times than I can count. More times than I've picked up my gun. But I feel a similar fear here, in a more minor key.

The life I have left, I realize, is beyond that door. The people who make up that life. Will they accept me? Or are they going to see a broken piece in a monster mask, glad-hand me, and send me on my way? Am I going to feel eyes full of pity burning holes in my back?

I can picture this scenario with a clarity that appalls me. I feel panicked. I shoot a nervous glance down the hall. The elevator door is still open. All I have to do is turn on my heel and run. Run and just keep running. Run and run and run and run and run. Fill those flats with sweat and buy a pack of Marlboros and go home and smoke and cackle in the dark. Weep for no reason, stare at my scars, and wonder about the kindness of strangers. This appeals to me with a strength that makes me shiver. I want a cigarette. I want the security of my loneliness and my pain. I want to be left alone so I can just keep losing my mind and—

—and then I hear Matt.

He's laughing.

It's that soft laugh I always loved, a cool breeze of kindness and clarity. *Riiiiiight, babe...hightailing it away from danger. That's so you.* This had been one of his gifts. The ability to chide without ridicule.

"Maybe it's me now," I murmur.

I'm trying to sound defiant, but the quivering chin and sweaty palms make it hard to pull off.

I can feel him smile, gentle and smug and not really there.

Damn it.

"Yeah, yeah, yeah..." I mutter to the ghost as I reach out and turn the knob.

I push him away in my mind, and I open the door.

5

I STARE INSIDE for a moment without entering. My terror is pure and clean and nausea-producing. It occurs to me that this is the core of what I hate the most about my life since the "big bad" happened. The constant uncertainty. One of the qualities I always liked about myself was my decisiveness. It was always simple—decide and do. Now it's: *what if what if what if, no yes no maybe, stop go, what if what if what if . . .* and, behind it all, *I'm afraid. . . .*

God, I am afraid. All the time. I wake up afraid, I walk around afraid, I go to sleep afraid. I am a victim. I hate it, I cannot escape it, and I miss the effortless certainty of invulnerability that used to be me. I also know, however much I heal, that that certainty will never return. Never.

"Get a grip, Barrett," I say.

This is the other thing I do now: I wander, without ever going anywhere.

"So change it," I murmur to myself.

Oh yeah—and I talk out loud all the time.

"You one cwazy wabbit, Barrett," I whisper.

One deep breath and I move through the door.

It's not a big office. Just the four of us, desks and computer stations, a small acting conference room, phones. Corkboards covered with photos of death. It looks no different now than when I was here six months ago. But the way I feel, I might as well be walking on the moon.

Then I see them. Callie and Alan, backs to me, talking to each other as they point at one of the corkboards. James is there, focused with his usual cold intensity on a file that lays open on the desk in front of him. It's Alan who turns and sees me first. He sees me, and his eyes open wide, his mouth drops, and I am bracing myself for a look of revulsion.

He laughs out loud.

"Smoky!"

It is a voice filled with joy, and in that moment, I am saved.

6

"**DAMN, HONEY-LOVE,** you won't have to dress up for Halloween anymore." This is Callie. What she says is shocking, crass, and unfeeling. It fills me with an easy joy. If she'd done anything else, I probably would have burst into tears.

Callie is a tall, skinny, leggy redhead. She looks like a supermodel. She's one of those beautiful people; staring at her too long is like looking into the sun. She's in her late thirties, has a master's in forensics with a minor in criminology, is brilliant, and lacks any social veneer at all. Most people find her intimidating. Many decide, on first blush, that she's uncaring, maybe even cruel. This couldn't be further from the truth. She is loyal to an extreme, and her integrity and character couldn't be tortured out of her. She is blunt, forever truthful, brutal in her observations, and refuses to play games, political, PR, or otherwise. She would also put herself in front of a bullet for anyone she calls a friend.

One of Callie's most admirable features is the one that's easiest to miss—her simplicity. The face she shows to the world is the only one she has. She doesn't believe in self-importance and has no patience with those who do. This is probably the crux of what confuses those who judge her harshly: If you can't take her poking fun at you, she's not going to lose any sleep over your discomfort. Lighten up or get left behind, because—as she likes to say—"If you can't laugh at yourself, you're of no use to me."

It was Callie who found me in the aftermath of Joseph Sands. I was naked and bleeding, screaming and covered with vomit. She was dressed to kill, as always, but she didn't hesitate to gather me in her arms and hold me while she waited for the ambulance. One of the last things I remember before I passed out was the sight of her beautiful tailored suit, ruined by my blood and tears.

"Callie…"

This reproval comes from Alan, quiet, serious, to the point. Alan's way. Alan is a huge, scary-looking African-American. He's not just big, he is gargantuan. He is a mountain with legs. His scowl has caused more than one suspect in an interrogation room to wet himself. The irony, of course, is that Alan is one of the kindest, gentlest people I have ever known. He has a tremendous patience I have always admired and aspire to, and he brings this to our cases. He never tires of going through the evidence, of examining the smallest thing. Nothing bores him when he is tracking a killer. And his eye for detail has broken more than one case. Alan is the oldest of us, in his mid-forties, and he brought ten years of experience as a Los Angeles homicide detective with him when he joined the FBI.

A new voice. "What are you doing here?" If displeasure was a musical instrument, this would be a symphony.

It's said without preamble or apology; blunt, like Callie, but without her humor. This comes from James. We call him Damien behind his back, after the character in *The Omen,* the son of Satan. He's the youngest of us all, only twenty-eight, and he's one of the most irritating, unlikable people I've ever known. He grates on you, sets your teeth on edge, and infuriates. If I ever want to piss someone off, James is the gas to throw on the fire.

James is also brilliant. That off-the-charts, white-hot nova kind of brilliant. He graduated from high school at fifteen, got perfect scores on the SATs, and was wooed by every college worth a damn in the nation. He picked the one with the best criminology curriculum and proceeded to burn his way through to a PhD in four years. Then he joined the FBI, which had been his goal all along.

When he was twelve, James lost his older sister to a serial killer with a thing for blowtorches and screaming young women. He decided he was going to work in this office the day they buried her.

James is a closed and faceless book. He seems to live for just one thing—what we do. He never jokes, never smiles, never does anything unnecessary to the job at hand. He doesn't share his private life or anything else that would give a clue to his passions, likes, dislikes, or tastes. I don't know what kind of music he enjoys, what movies he prefers to watch, or even if he does.

It would be too simple and neat to think of him as just efficient and logic-driven. No, there is a hostility to James that comes out in sharp bursts. His disapproval can be acrid, and his thoughtlessness is legendary. I can't say that he takes joy in the discomfort of others; I would say instead that he just doesn't care about it one way or the other. I think James is forever angry at a world where individuals like the one who killed his sister can exist. Even so, I long ago stopped forgiving him for himself. He's too much of an ass.

But he is brilliant, a brilliance forever blinding those around him, like a permanent camera flash. And he shares an ability with me that ties us together, a gift that creates an umbilicus between us, that gives me an evil twin. He can get inside the mind of a killer. He can slide into the nooks and dark places, consider the shadows, understand the evil. I can do it too. It's not uncommon for us to end up working together on certain parts of a case, in a very intimate sense. During those times, we get along like oil and ball bearings, smooth, flowing, unstoppable. All the rest of the time, being around him is about as pleasant as someone sanding me like a two-by-four.

"Nice to see you too," I reply.

"Hey, asshole," Alan purrs, a low chord of menace.

James folds his hands in front of him and gives Alan a cold, direct look. It's a trait James has that I have to admire: Even though he's only five foot seven and maybe 130 pounds soaking wet, he's almost impossible to intimidate. Nothing seems to scare him. "It was just a question," he replies.

"Well, how about you drink a nice big cup of shut the fuck up?"

I place a hand on Alan's shoulder. "It's okay."

They glare at each other for a moment longer. It's Alan who breaks away with a sigh. James gives me one long, appraising look, then turns back to the file he was reading.

Alan shakes his head at me. "Sorry."

I smile. How can I explain to him that even this, those Damien ways, is somehow a *right* thing right now? It is something that is still "the way things used to be." James still pisses me off, and this is a comfort.

I decide to change the subject. "So what's new around here?"

I walk all the way into the office, scanning the desks

and the corkboards. Callie has been running things while I've been gone, and she takes the lead in responding.

"It's been quiet for us, honey-love." Callie calls everyone honey-love. As legend goes, she has an actual written reprimand on file for calling the Director honey-love. It's a complete affectation, taken on to amuse herself. Callie isn't Southern in the slightest. It annoys some people to no end; to me it's just Callie. "Nothing serial, two abductions. We've been working on some of the older, colder cases." She smiles. "Guess all the bad guys went on vacation with you."

"How did the abductions turn out?" Child kidnappings are part of the butter on our bread, and are something dreaded by all decent men and women in law enforcement. They are rarely about money. They are about sex and pain and death.

"One recovered alive, one recovered dead."

I stare at the corkboards, not really seeing them. "At least both were recovered," I murmur. Far too often, this is not the case. Anyone who thinks no news is good news has never been the parent of a kidnapped child. In this case, no news is a cancer that does not kill but instead hollows out the soul. I have had parents coming to see me over the years, hopeful for news of their child, news I didn't have. I have watched them get thinner, more bitter. Seen hope die in their eyes, and gray hairs cover their heads. In those cases, finding the body of their child would be a blessing. It would at least let them grieve with certainty.

I turn to Callie. "So how do you like being the boss?"

She gives me a patented, pretend-haughty Callie smile. "You know me, honey-love. I was born to be royalty, and now I have the crown."

Alan snorts at this, followed by an actual guffaw.

"Don't listen to this peasant, dear," Callie says with disdain.

I laugh, and it's a good laugh. A real one that catches you by surprise the way a laugh ought to. But then it continues a little longer than it should, and I'm horrified to feel tears welling up in my eyes.

"Oh, shit," I mumble, wiping my face. "Sorry about that." I look up at them and give them both a weak smile. "It's just really good to see you guys. More than you know."

Alan, the man-mountain, moves to me, and without warning, wraps me in those tree-trunk arms. I resist for only a moment before hugging him back, my head against his chest.

"Oh, we know, Smoky," he says. "We know."

He lets me go, and Callie steps forward, pushing him aside.

"Enough touchy-feely," she snaps. She turns her head to me. "Let me take you to lunch. And don't bother trying to say no."

I feel tears coming again, and all I can manage is a nod. Callie grabs her purse, then grabs my arm, and hustles me toward the door. "Be back in an hour," she calls over her shoulder. She shoves me out the door, and once it closes, the tears begin to flow freely.

Callie gives me a little sideways hug.

"Knew you wouldn't want to start bawling in front of Damien, honey-love."

I laugh through my tears and just nod, taking the tissue she gives me, and letting her strength lead me in my moment of weakness.

7

WE'RE SITTING INSIDE a Subway sandwich store, and I'm watching in fascination as Callie fills her apparently hollow leg with a foot-long meatball sandwich. I've always wondered how she does it. She can pack away more food than a linebacker, and yet she never gains a pound. I smile, thinking maybe it's those five-mile jogs she does, every morning, seven days a week. She licks her fingers loudly, smacking her lips with such enthusiasm that two older ladies shoot us a look of disapproval. Satisfied, she sighs and settles back, sipping on her Mountain Dew through a straw. It strikes me that this, right here, is the essence of Callie. She does not just watch life go by, she devours it. She gulps it down without chewing, and always goes back for more. I smile to myself, and she frowns, shaking a finger at me.

"You know, I brought you to lunch because I wanted to tell you how pissed off I am at you, honey-love. No returning my calls, not even an e-mail. Not acceptable, Smoky. I don't care how fucked up you are."

"I know, Callie. And I'm sorry. I mean it—I'm really, truly sorry."

She stares at me for a moment, an intense stare. I've seen her give it to a criminal or two, and I feel I deserve it.

It passes and she smiles one of those radiant smiles, waving her hand. "Apology accepted. Now for the real question: How are you? I mean, really. And don't lie to me."

I stare off for a moment, stare at my sandwich. Look at her. "Until today? Bad. Real bad. I have nightmares, every night. I've been depressed, and it's only been getting worse, not better."

"Been thinking about killing yourself, haven't you?"

I feel the same jolt, at a lower frequency, that I felt in Dr. Hillstead's office. Here, I somehow feel more ashamed. Callie and I have always been close, and whether spoken or expressed, there is a love there. But it's been a love based on strength, not weeping on each other's shoulders. I am afraid that this love would lessen or disappear if Callie had to pity me. But I answer.

"I thought about it, yes."

She nods and then is silent, looking off to something or somewhere I can't see. I feel a prick of déjà vu; she looks as Dr. Hillstead looked, trying to decide which fork in the road to take. "Smoky, there's nothing weak about that, honey-love. Weakness would be actually pulling the trigger. Crying, having nightmares, being depressed, thinking about killing yourself, those things don't make you weak. They just mean you hurt. And anyone can hurt, even Superman."

I stare at her and am at a loss for words. One hundred percent lost, I can't think of a thing to say. This is just not what Callie does, and it has caught me by surprise. She gives me a soft smile.

"You know, you have to beat it, Smoky. Not just for you. For me." She sips her drink. "You and I, we're alike. We've always been golden. Things have always gone our way. We're good at what we do—hell, we've always been able to be good at anything we put our minds to, you know?"

I nod, still speechless.

"I'm going to tell you something, honey-love, something philosophical. Note it on your calendar, because I'm not one to get deep in public." She puts down her drink. "A lot of people paint that same, tired old picture: We start out innocent and bright-eyed, and then we become jaded. Nothing's ever quite as good again, blah, blah, blah. I've always thought that was a pile of poop. Not all lives start out innocent and Norman Rockwell, now, do they? Ask any child in Watts. I've always thought it's not so much that we learn that life is shit. It's that we learn that life can hurt. Does that make sense?"

"Yes." I'm mesmerized.

"Most people get hurt early. You and I—we've been lucky. Very, very lucky. We see the hurt, doing what we do, but it's never been us. Not really. Look at you—you found the love of your life, had a beautiful child, and you were an ass-kicking FBI agent, a woman no less, all on the rise like a bright, shooting star. And me? I haven't done so bad either." She shakes her head. "I've managed not to get too full of myself, but the truth is, I've always had my pick of the guys, and I was lucky enough to have a brain to go with the bod. And I'm good at what I do at the Bureau. Real good."

"You are," I agree.

"But, see, that's just it, honey-love. You and I have never really experienced tragedy. We're alike in that way. Then all of sudden, the bullets stopped bouncing off of you." She shakes her head. "The moment that happened, I couldn't be fearless, not anymore. I was afraid, really afraid, for the first time in my life. Ever. And I've been afraid ever since. Because you are better than me, Smoky.

You always have been. And if it can happen to you, it can damn sure happen to me." She sits back, puts her hands flat on the table. "End of speech."

I have known Callie for some time. I have always known that she has depths uncharted. The mystery of those depths, glimpsed but not revealed, has always been a part of her charm for me, her strength. Now the curtain has parted for a moment. It's like the first time someone lets you see them naked. It is the essence of trust, and I am touched in a way that makes me weak at the knees. I reach over and grab her hand.

"I'll do my best, Callie. That's all I can promise. But I do promise that."

She squeezes my hand back, and then pulls it away. The curtain has been closed. "Well, hurry it up, will you, please? I enjoy being arrogant and untouchable, and I blame you for the lack thereof."

I smile and look at my friend. Dr. Hillstead had told me earlier that I was strong. But for me, it is Callie who has always been my private hero when it comes to strength. My crass-talking patron saint of irreverence. I shake my head. "I'll be back in a minute," I say. "I have to use the restroom."

"Don't forget to put the lid down," she says.

I see it when I exit the bathroom, and what I see tells me to stop.

Callie isn't aware of me yet. Her attention is focused on something in her hand. I step to the side, so that the doorway blocks her view of me a little, and stare.

Callie looks sad. Not just sad—bereft.

I have seen Callie be scornful, gentle, angry, vengeful, witty—any number of things. I have never seen her sad.

Not like this. And I know, somehow, that it has nothing to do with me.

Whatever she holds in her hand is bringing my hero to something just short of grief, and I am shocked.

I am also certain that this is a private thing. Callie will not want to know that I have seen her this way. She may only have one face to show the world, but she chooses what parts of it to show. She hasn't chosen to show me this, whatever *this* is. I go back into the bathroom. To my surprise, one of the older women is there, washing her hands, and she glances at me in the mirror. I look back, biting a thumbnail as I think. Come to a decision.

"Ma'am," I say, "can you please do me a favor?"

"What's that, dear?" she asks, not missing a beat.

"I have a friend outside..."

"The rude one with the awful eating habits?"

Gulp.

"Yes, ma'am."

"What about her?"

I hesitate. "She...I think she's having a private moment right now. Because I'm in here, and she's alone....I—"

"You don't want to surprise her in that moment, is that it?"

Her instant and perfect understanding makes me pause. I stare at her. Stereotypes, I think again. So useless. I had seen an uptight, judgmental crone. Now I see kind eyes, wisdom, and a well-honed appreciation of the ridiculous. "Yes, ma'am," I say, quiet. "She—well...she'll always be crass, but she's got the biggest heart I know."

The woman's eyes soften and her smile is beautiful. "Many great people have eaten with their hands, dear. Leave it to me. Wait thirty seconds and then come out."

"Thank you." I mean it; she knows it.

She leaves the bathroom without another word. I wait for a little more than thirty seconds and follow. I peek around the corner and now my eyebrows raise. The woman is standing by our table, shaking a finger at Callie. I walk toward them.

"Some people like a quiet lunch," I hear the woman saying. Her tone is reprimand as a weapon, as an Olympic sport. The kind that has the ability to make you feel ashamed rather than angry. My mom was world-class at it.

Callie is scowling at the woman. I can see the storm clouds building, and I hurry over. The woman is doing me a favor; better not let it become fatal.

"Callie," I say, placing a warning hand on her shoulder. "We should get going."

She scowls harder at the woman, who looks about as intimidated as a dog sleeping on its back in a patch of sun.

"Callie," I say again, more insistent. She looks at me, nods, stands up, and puts on her sunglasses with a haughty flourish that fills me with admiration. 9–9–10, I think, a near-perfect score. The Olympics of the ice queens is a heated one this year, and the crowd is roaring....

"Can't get me out of here fast enough," she says with disdain. She grabs her purse and inclines her head to the woman. "Good day," she says. *Drop dead,* her voice implies.

I hurry us out. I shoot one last glance over my shoulder at the woman. She gives me another one of those beautiful smiles.

The kindness of strangers rears its bittersweet head once again.

The drive back is entertaining, with Callie at a slow

boil. I nod and murmur at the right places as she mutters about "old bats" and "wrinkly, raisined people" and "elit-ist mummies." My private thoughts are filled with that sad look, so alien to see on my friend's face.

We arrive back at the parking lot, near my car.

I've decided it's enough for today. I'll go and see the Assistant Director some other time.

"Thanks, Callie. Tell Alan I'll be by again sometime soon. Even if it's just to say hi."

She shakes her finger at me. "I'll tell him, honey-love. But don't you dare ignore any more phone calls. You didn't lose everyone who loves you that night, and you have friends beyond the job. Don't forget that."

She squeals off before I can reply, having gotten in the last word. This is Callie's hallmark, and it makes me feel nice inside to have been the victim of it.

I get into my car, and I realize that I had been right last night. Today had been the day. I wasn't going to go home and blow my brains out.

How could I? I couldn't even pick up my gun.

8

I HAVE A terrible night, a kind of Greatest Hits of bad dreams. Joseph Sands is there in his demon suit, while Matt smiles at me with a mouth full of blood. This morphs into Callie at the Subway shop, looking up from her sad piece of paper, pulling out her gun, and shooting the Subway lady through the head. She then goes back to slurping on her straw, but her lips are too red and too full, and she catches me watching and gives me a wink like a corpse closing one eye.

I wake up, shivering, and realize that my phone is ringing. I look at my clock. It's five in the morning. Who'd be calling now? I haven't gotten any early-morning calls since I went on leave.

I can still feel the dream bouncing around inside my head, but I push the images away and take a moment to stop shivering before I grab the phone.

"Hello?"

There's a silence at the other end. Then Callie's voice. "Hi, honey-love. Sorry to wake you, but...we have something that concerns you."

"What? What's happened?" She doesn't speak for a minute, and I'm getting pissed off. Little shivers still spasm through me as I hold the phone. "Dammit, Callie. Tell me."

She sighs. "Do you remember an Annie King?"

My voice is incredulous. "Remember her? Yeah, I remember her. She's one of my best friends. She moved to San Francisco about ten years ago. We still talk on the phone every six months or so. I'm her daughter's god-mother. So yeah, I remember her. Why?"

Callie is silent again. "Damn," I hear her whisper. She sounds like she was punched in the stomach. "I didn't know she was a friend. I thought she was just someone you used to know."

I feel dread filling me. Dread, and knowledge. I know what's happened, or at least I think I do. But I need to hear Callie say it before I will believe it. "Tell me."

A long sigh of surrender, then: "She's dead, Smoky. Murdered in her apartment. The daughter's alive, but she's catatonic."

My hand has gone nerveless with shock, and I'm in danger of dropping the phone. "Where are you now, Callie?" My voice sounds small to me.

"At the office. We're getting ready to go to the scene, going on a private jet in an hour and a half."

I sense something through my shock, a heaviness at Callie's end. I realize that there's something else she's not telling me.

"What is it, Callie? What are you holding back?"

A hesitation, and then she sighs again. "The killer left a message for you, honey-love."

I sit for a moment, silent. Letting these words sink in. "I'll meet you at the office," I say. I hang up before she can respond.

I sit on the edge of my bed for a moment. I put my

head into my hands and try to weep, but my eyes stay dry. Somehow, it hurts more that way.

It's only six o'clock by the time I arrive. Early morning is the best time to drive in LA, the only time the highways are uncrowded. Most of the people driving are up to no good, or on their way to no good. I know these early mornings well. I've driven through fog and the gray light of breaking dawns many times, toward scenes of bloody death. As I am now. All the way there, all I can think about is Annie.

Annie and I met in high school, when we were both fifteen. She was a soon to be ex-cheerleader, I was a reckless tomboy who smoked pot and enjoyed fast things. In the hierarchy of high school, our paths were not destined to cross. Fate intervened. At least I always thought of it as fate.

My time of the month arrived in the middle of math class, and I had put up my hand, grabbed my purse, and rushed out the door to the bathroom. I was blushing as I went down the hallway, and hoping that no one else was there. I had been getting my period for only eight months, and the whole thing was still an excruciating embarrassment to me.

I peeked in, saw with relief that the bathroom was deserted. I ducked into one of the stalls and was preparing to take care of my problem when a sniffling sound made me freeze, pad in hand. I held my breath, listening. The sniffling repeated itself, only this time, it broke into a quiet sob. Someone was crying, two stalls over from me.

I have always been a sucker for things in pain. When I was young, I even considered being a veterinarian. If I came upon a hurt bird, dog, cat, or any other walking, crawling, living thing, it would end up coming home with me. Most of the time, the things I brought home didn't make it. But sometimes they did, and the few victories in this regard were enough to keep my crusade alive. My parents thought it was cute at first, but it went from cute to annoying after the umpteenth trip to the emergency vet. Annoyed or not, they never discouraged me from these Mother Teresa–like efforts.

As I got older, I found that this concern extended to people as well. If someone got bullied, while I wouldn't step in and rescue them from the fight, I couldn't keep myself from going over afterward to see how they were. I kept a small first-aid kit in my backpack and handed out any number of bandages during the eighth and ninth grades. I was not self-conscious about this quirk in my character. It was a strange thing: I was mortified by having to leave in the middle of class to handle menstruation, but no amount of teasing, or being called "Nurse Smoky," ever bothered me. Not even a little. I know that this characteristic is what led me to the FBI. The decision to go after the source of pain, the criminals who enjoyed causing it. I also know that what I saw in the years that followed changed it in some way. I became more careful with my caring. I had to. My first-aid kit became me and my team, and the bandages became a pair of handcuffs and a jail cell.

This being the case, when I realized that someone was crying in the bathroom with me, I placed my pad as a hurried afterthought, all embarrassment forgotten, pulled up my jeans, and rushed out of the stall. I paused in front of the door the sobs were coming from.

"Uh—hello? Are you okay in there?"

The sobs stopped, though the sniffles were still audible.

"Go away. Leave me alone."

I stood there for a second, trying to decide what to do. "Are you hurt?"

"No! Just leave me alone."

I realized that there wasn't any pressing physical injury to attend to, and I was about to take the voice's advice when something stopped me. Fate. I leaned forward, tentative. "Um, listen...any way I can help?"

The voice was forlorn when it responded. "No one can help." There was a silence, followed by another one of those awful, poignant sobs. No one can cry like a fifteen-year-old young woman. No one. It is done with all of the heart, nothing held back, the end of existence.

"Come on. It can't be that bad."

I heard a scuffling sound, and then the door to the stall slammed open. Standing in front of me was a puffy-faced, very pretty blond girl. I recognized her right away and wished I'd listened when she first asked me to leave. Annie King. She was a cheerleader. One of those girls. You know, the snobby, perfect ones who use their beauty and flawless bodies to rule the kingdom of high school. I couldn't help it, that was what I thought at the time. I had her pigeonholed and judged, the same way I hated being judged myself. And she was mad.

"What do you know about it?" It was a voice filled with fury, and it was directed at me, full on. I stared at her, caught flat-footed and flabbergasted, too astonished to be angry back. Then her face crumpled, and the rage vanished faster than it had appeared. Tears ran down her face. "He showed everyone my panties. Why would he do something like that, after everything he said to me?"

"Huh? Who—what about your panties?"

Sometimes, even in high school, it's easiest to talk to a stranger. She talked to me then, while it was just the two of us in that bathroom. The quarterback of the football team, a David Rayborn, had been dating her for almost six months. He was handsome, smart, and seemed to really care about her. He'd been pushing her for a few months to go "all the way," and she'd been resisting his advances. But he'd been so sincere in his romance of her that a few days ago she'd finally given in. He'd been gentle, and caring, and when it was over he'd held her in his arms and asked her if he could keep her panties to remember the moment by. He said it would be a little secret between them, something they knew but no one else did. A little naughty, but also kind of nice. Somehow romantic. Looking back at it now, as an adult, it seems silly to think of it in that way. But when you are fifteen . . .

"So today I'm walking off the field after practice, and they're all there. The guys from the team. David is with them, and they're all pointing at me, and hooting and making these nasty faces. Then he did it." Her face crumpled again, and I winced, realizing what was coming. "He held them up. My panties. Like a trophy. And then he smiled at me, winked, and said it was the best addition to his collection yet."

And this cheerleader started crying again, except that now she gave herself over to it in the fullest sense of the word. Her knees gave, and she fell against me, and she was weeping like her heart was broken and would never be whole again. I hesitated for a moment (but only a moment), and then I wrapped my arms around her and held her as she cried. Right there on the tile, I hugged this stranger and whispered into her hair, told her it'd be okay.

After a few minutes, the sobs died down to sniffles, and then the sniffles stopped as well. She pushed off me and wiped her face. She couldn't look at me, and I realized she was a little embarrassed.

"Hey, I have an idea," I said. It was a from-the-hip decision, unexplainable, but somehow undeniably right. "Let's get out of here. Cut the rest of the day."

She looked at me, and squinted. "Play hooky?"

I nodded and smiled. "Yep. Just a day. I think you've earned it, don't you?"

I've always thought her decision in response was probably as sudden as mine had been in asking her. I mean, she didn't even know my name at that point. She smiled back at me, a slight smile.

"Okay."

That's how we met. She smoked her first joint that day (something I introduced her to), and about a week later she quit being a cheerleader. I'd like to say that we got revenge on David Rayborn, but we never did. Despite his reputation as an asshole, girls continued to fall for him, and he continued to take their panties as trophies. He went on to become a star quarterback, which continued through college and even a few seasons second-stringing for an NFL team. One could say this was proof of no justice in the world, but you could also say that he brought Annie and I together, something that was to have such beauty and value that I could almost forgive him for what he did.

We'd bonded at the molecular level, the way only combat soldiers and teenagers do. We spent all of our time out of school together. She encouraged me to quit smoking pot, advice I followed, since my grades had been dropping. I got her to start dating again. She was there for me when Buster, the dog I'd had since I was five years old, had to be put to sleep. I was there for her when her grandmother died. We learned to drive together and spent time getting into and out of scrapes, growing up, becoming women.

Annie and I shared one of the most intimate relationships a person can have: friendship while you go from child to adult. The types of experiences and memories you take with you through life, all the way to the grave.

What happened after was what happens all the time. We graduated from high school. I was with Matt by then. She'd met a guy and decided to ride around the country with him before going to college. I didn't wait and went straight to UCLA. We did what everyone does, swore to stay in touch twice a week and forever, and then did what everyone does, got caught up in our own lives and didn't speak for nearly a year.

One day I was walking out of class...and there she was. She looked wild, and beautiful, and I felt joy and pain and longing twang through me like a chord plucked from a Gibson guitar.

"How's things, college girl?" she asked, eyes twinkling.

I didn't respond, but I gave her one hell of a long hug.

We went out to lunch, and she told me all about her adventures. They'd traveled through fifty states on almost no money, seen and done a lot, had enough sex in enough different places to last a lifetime. She smiled a secret smile, and then placed her hand on the table.

"Check it out," she said.

I looked, saw the engagement ring, gasped like I was supposed to, and we giggled and talked about the future, about the plans for her wedding. It was like being back in high school.

I was her maid of honor, and she was mine. She moved up to San Francisco with Robert, while Matt and I stayed in LA. Things drifted, but we'd always manage to find time every six to eight months to place a call, and whenever we did, we were back there again, that first day we'd played hooky, free and young and happy.

Robert was a flake, who eventually left her. Some years later, I ran a background check on him, hoping to find that he was failing and miserable in his life. I found instead that he had died in a car accident. Why Annie had never shared this with me, I still don't know.

When I started working for the Bureau, and by that I mean really working, the time between calls drifted to a year. Then a year and a half. I agreed to be her daughter's godmother but am ashamed to say that I met her child only once, and she never met mine. What can I say? Life moved on, the one thing it always does.

Some might judge that. I don't care. All I know is that whether it was six months or two years, whenever we talked, it was like no time had passed at all.

About three years ago her father died. I went up there right away and stayed for over a week, helping. Or trying to. Annie was older and drained and full of pain. I remember being struck by a single irony: Her agony and her age had made her more beautiful than ever. The night after the funeral, after she'd put her daughter to bed, we sat on the floor of her bedroom, and she cried in my arms while I whispered into her hair.

I did not hear from her when Matt died, but I didn't wonder about this. Annie had this quirk: She abhorred the news, whether in print or on TV, and I never called to tell her what happened. I still don't know why.

I thought about Annie on my way to the Bureau offices. I thought and I wondered at my reaction to her death. I felt sad. Devastated even. But it didn't seem as monumental, emotionally, as it should be.

I've just arrived, and I just realized that I've lost all of my youth now. The love of my youth, the friend of my youth. It's all gone. Maybe losing Matt and Alexa was just too much. Maybe that's why I don't feel as much as I think I should about Annie.

Maybe I just don't have any more pain to give.

"What the hell are you doing here, Smoky?"

It's SAC Jones, my old sponsor. Except now he's Assistant Director Jones. I'm surprised to find him here. It's not that he's not dedicated or hesitates at stepping into the trenches; it's that he simply doesn't *need* to be here, and his dance card is never empty. What's so urgent about this case?

"Callie called me, sir. She told me about Annie King and mentioned that the killer left a message for me. I'm going with."

He shakes his head. "Oh no you're not. No fucking way. Aside from the fact that she's your friend, which means you can't touch this case with a ten-foot pole, you are not cleared to go back to work."

Callie is trying to eavesdrop, and Jones notices this. He gestures me toward his car, lighting a cigarette as we walk. Everyone's out in front of the Bureau offices, getting ready to head to the Van Nuys private airport. He takes a deep drag and I watch him, wistful. I forgot to bring my own.

"Can I have one of those, sir?"

His eyebrows arch in surprise. "I thought you quit."

"I took it up again."

He shrugs and gives me the pack. I pull out one of the cigarettes, and he lights it for me. I, too, take a nice, long puff. Yum.

"Listen, Smoky. You know how it goes. You've been around long enough. Your shrink keeps the content of what you guys talk about in complete confidence. But he does submit a report, once a month, giving an overview of where he thinks you're at."

I nod. I know this is true. I don't take it as any kind of violation. It's not about privacy or rights. It's about whether or not I can be trusted to represent the FBI. Or hold a gun.

"I got a report yesterday. He says you still have a ways to go and are not ready to go back to work. Period. Now you show up at six in the morning and want to go to the scene of a murdered friend?" He shakes his head, vehement. "Like I said: no fucking way."

I draw on the cigarette, weighing it in my fingers as I watch him, and try and figure out what to say. I realize that I know why he's here. Because of me. Because the killer wrote to me. Because he's worried.

"Look, sir. Annie King was my friend. Her daughter is still alive up there. She's got no other family, her dad's dead, and I'm her godmother. I'd be flying up there anyway. All I'm asking the Bureau for is the courtesy of a ride."

He draws smoke down the wrong pipe at this, and actually sputters. "Puh-leeeze! Nice try, but who the fuck do you think you're talking to, Agent Barrett?" He stabs a finger at me. "I know you better than that, Smoky. Don't bullshit me. Your friend is dead—and I'm sorry about that, by the way—and you want to go up and get yourself on the case. That's the truth. And I can't allow it. One, you're personally involved, and that excludes you from the get-go. That's straight from the manual. Two, you're probably suicidal, and I can't allow you to step in the middle of a crime scene in that condition."

My mouth hangs open. Then my words are filled with fury and shame. "Jesus Christ! Do I have a sign hanging from my neck that says *I've thought about killing myself*?"

His eyes soften at this. "Nah, no sign. It's just that we all know we'd think about it if any of us experienced even half of what you did." He tosses the cigarette to the pavement and doesn't look at me when he continues speaking. "I thought about smoking on my gun, once."

As with Callie at lunch yesterday, I am speechless. He catches this and nods. "It's true. I lost a partner, about twenty-five years ago, when I was on the LAPD. Lost him because I made a bad decision. I led us into a building without backup, and it was more than we could handle. He paid the price. Family man, beloved husband and father of three. It was my fault, and I thought about correcting that inequity for almost eight months." He looks at me, and there's no pity in his gaze. "It's not that you have a sign hanging from your neck, Smoky. It's that most of us think we would have blown our brains out by now if we were in your position."

This is the essence of AD Jones. No small talk, no dancing around things. It fits him well. You always know where you stand with him. Always.

I can't meet his eyes. I throw down my cigarette, half smoked, and grind it out with my foot. I'm doing some careful thinking about what to say next. "Sir. I appreciate what you're saying. And you're right, on just about every point, except one." I look back up at him. I know he'll want to see my eyes when I say what I say next, to gauge the truth of my words. "I have thought about it. A lot. But yesterday? Yesterday was the first day I knew for sure I wasn't going to do it. You know what changed?" I point at my team, standing and waiting on the steps. "I went and saw those guys, for the first time since it happened. I went and saw them, and they were still there, and they accepted me. Well, the jury's still out on James—but the point is, they didn't pity me or make me feel like a broken piece. I can tell you, flat out, that I'm no longer suicidal. And the reason is that I stepped foot back into the Bureau." He's listening. I can tell I haven't won him over, but I do have his attention. "Look, I'm not ready to take NCAVC Coord back over. I'm sure as hell not ready to be in any tactical situation of any kind. All I'm asking is that you let me dip my toe in the water. Let me go up, make sure Bonnie is taken care of, and let me just lend my mind to this thing, just a little. Callie will still run things. I won't be armed, and I promise, if I think it's too much, I'm out."

He puts his hands in his coat pockets and gives me a long, fierce look. He's studying me, hard. Weighing all the possibilities, every risk. When he looks away and sighs, I know I have convinced him.

"I just know I'm going to regret this, but fine. Here's the deal. You go, you get the kid, you look around. You can put in your two cents with the team. But you are not running the show. And the moment you feel even a little wobbly, you pull yourself the fuck out. I mean it, Smoky. I need you back, don't misunderstand me. But I need you back whole, and that means I don't necessarily need you back now. You understand?"

I bob my head like a child or a new army recruit, yes sir, yes sir, yes sir. I'm going, and I feel that this is an important thing. A victory. He raises a hand, waving Callie over. When she arrives, he tells her what he told me.

"You got it?" he asks, stern.

"Yes, sir. Understood."

He shoots me one last glance. "You guys have a plane to catch. Get out of here."

I walk away with Callie before he can change his mind.

"I'd love to know how you pulled that one off, honey-love," she murmurs to me. "Just know that as far as I'm concerned, it's your show until you tell me otherwise."

I don't reply. I'm too busy wondering if I've made a terrible mistake by getting back on the team.

9

SINCE WHEN DID we rate a private jet?" I ask.

"Remember I told you that we'd had two child abductions and recovered one alive?" Callie asks.

I nod.

"Don Plummer was the father of the little girl we got back alive. He owns a small flight company. They sell planes, have a flying school, things like that. He offered to give the Bureau a jet pro bono, which of course we had to turn down. But—with no prompting from us—he wrote the Director and worked out giving us access when needed for a low price." She shrugs and gestures at our surroundings. "So when we need to get somewhere fast..."

There's an addition to the team on this flight. Some young-looking kid who seems to barely fit into his FBI persona. He looks like he should have an earring in one ear and gum in his mouth. I squint and see a hole for a piercing in his left lobe. Jeez. Maybe he does wear one when he's not on duty. He'd been introduced to me as a loaner from Computer Crimes. He sits a little off from everyone else, looking rumpled and half awake. An outsider.

I look around. "Where's Alan?" I ask.

A response comes from the front of the plane. More of a growl. "I'm up here." And that's all he says.

I look at Callie, eyebrows raised. She shrugs.

"Something's bugging him. He looked pretty pissed when we got here." She gazes toward him for a moment, then shakes her head. "I'd leave it alone for now, honey-love."

I look toward the shadows that Alan is sitting in, wanting to do something. But Callie is right. And I need to be brought up to speed.

"Fill me in," I say, accepting this. "What do we have?"

I turn to James as I say this. He stares back at me, and I can see the hostility flaring up in his eyes. He radiates disapproval.

"You shouldn't be here," he says.

I fold my arms and look at him. "Yeah, well, I am."

"It violates procedure. You'll be a liability to this investigation." He shakes his head. "You probably don't even have psych clearance yet, do you?"

Callie remains silent, and I'm thankful. This is a key moment, something I need to resolve myself.

"AD Jones cleared me." I frown at him. "Jesus, James. Annie King was a friend of mine."

He stabs a finger toward me. "All the more reason you shouldn't be here. You're too close to the investigation, and you'll fuck it up."

Some part of me registers that an outsider, listening to this, would be aghast. They would not be able to believe that James is saying what he is saying. I'm inured to it—to some extent. This *is* James. This is how he is, and what he does. Besides, it's working for me. I'm feeling something stir inside. The old coldness, what I always used to use to handle James, to rein him in. I grip on to this and let it leak into my eyes.

"I'm here. I'm not going away. Deal with it, and give me all the details. Stop fucking with me."

He pauses for a moment, examines me. I see him settle back. He shakes his head once in disapproval, but I know that he's given in. "Fine. But I want it on record that I think this is a blatant violation of Bureau policy."

"Duly noted." My voice is a knife edge of sarcasm that dulls against his indifference.

"Good." Now I see his eyes unfocus a bit. He doesn't have a file in front of him, but that computer brain of his is putting all the facts at his fingertips. "Her body was found yesterday. They figure she was killed three days before that."

I start at this. "Three days?"

"Yes."

"So how was the body found? Where?"

"The SF cops got an e-mail. It included an attachment, some photos. Of her. They went over to check it out, and they found the body and the child."

My heart thuds in my chest, and I sense my stomach acids churning. I feel a sour burp just waiting to get out. "Are you telling me that her daughter was there for more than three days with her dead mother?" My voice comes out loud. Not a yell, but close. James looks at me, his face calm. Just relating the facts.

"Worse. The killer tied her to her mother's corpse. Face-to-face. She was tied like that for the whole time."

Blood rushes to my head, and I feel faint. The burp comes up, silent but awful. I can feel its taste in my mouth. I put a hand to my forehead.

"Where's Bonnie now?"

"She's at one of the local hospitals, under guard. She's catatonic. Hasn't said a word since they found her."

Silence at that. Callie breaks it.

"There's more, honey-love. Things we need you to hear before we land. Otherwise you are going to be caught flat-footed."

I dread what is coming. I dread it like I dread going to sleep at night. But I grab on to myself, hard, and shake. I hope no one notices. "Go ahead. Hit me with all of it."

"Three things, and I'll just lay them all out, one after the other. First, she left her daughter to you, Smoky. The killer found her will and left it next to the body for us to find. You're named as the guardian. Second, your friend was running a sex site on the Internet that she was personally starring in. Third, the killer's e-mail to the cops included a letter addressed to you."

My mouth hangs open. I feel like I have been beaten. As if, instead of speaking, Callie had grabbed a golf club and whacked me with it. My head is spinning. Through my shock, I register a very selfish emotion, one that shames me, but one I also grab on to with a death grip. It is fear of losing it in front of my team. Of how that will make me look, especially to James. Selfish, yes, but I recognize it for what it is, the tool I can use to get myself under control.

I grapple with the shock and sorrow that are struggling for dominance and manage to push them aside enough to speak. I'm surprised at the sound of my voice when it comes out: flat and steady.

"Let me take this point by point. On the first one, I'll deal with that myself. Let's address the second one. You're saying she was some kind of . . . Internet prostitute?"

A voice pipes up. "No, ma'am, that's not accurate at all."

It's the young kid from Computer Crimes. Mr. Earring. I look at him.

"What's your name?"

"Leo. Leo Carnes. I'm on loan here because of the e-mail, but also because of what your friend did for a living."

I give him a good once-over. He returns my gaze without flinching. He's a good-looking kid, probably twenty-four or twenty-five. Dark hair, calm eyes. "Which was what? You said I wasn't accurate. So explain it to us."

He moves up a few seats nearer to us; invited into the inner circle, he leaps at the opportunity. Everyone wants to belong. "It's kind of a long explanation."

"We have the time. Go ahead."

He nods, a gleam coming to his eye that I recognize as excitement. Computers are his thing, what he is passionate about. "To understand it, you have to understand that pornography on the Internet is an entirely different subculture from pornography in the 'real world.'" He's settling back, relaxing, getting ready to give a lecture on a subject he knows everything about. It's his moment in the spotlight, and I'm happy to let him have it. It gives me time to settle my thoughts and my stomach. And something to think about besides little Bonnie, staring at her dead mother's face for three days.

"Go on."

"Starting in around 1978, you had something called BBSs—Bulletin Board Systems. Actually the full name was Computerized Bulletin Board Systems. These were the first nongovernment, public-accessible networks. If you had a modem and a computer, you could post up messages, do file sharing, and so on. Of course, back then, almost all the users were scientists or supernerds. But the reason this is relevant is that BBSs became a place to post up porn pics. You could share them, trade them, whatever. And at this point, we're not just talking Wild

West, we are talking undiscovered country. No oversight, nada. Something important to porn users because—"

James chimes in: "It was free, and it was private."

Leo grins and bobs his head. "Exactly! You didn't have to sneak in the back of some porno shop and brown-bag it. You could lock your bedroom door and download your porno pics without fear of discovery. It was HUGE. So, BBSs were the only public game in town, and they were everywhere, and porn was already everywhere on them.

"BBSs pretty much drop away as the Internet evolves and Web sites start coming out, and browsers, and dot-com names, and all that stuff. BBSs were always basically for posting, with the viewing being done after download. Now you have Web sites, where you can see it as fast as you connect to it. So what happens with porn?" He smiles. "What actually happened is twofold: You had some smart businessmen—I'm talking guys who already had money—who started to develop adult Web sites on the Net. Some were from the audiotext industry—"

"Which is what?" I interrupt.

"Sorry. Phone sex. These guys who were already raking in the dough on phone sex saw the Web and realized its potential for porn. Private, pay-per-view, on-demand whack-off material for the everyday guy. They poured a bunch of money into buying existing pornography. Pics scanned in by the hundreds of thousands and posted up on Web sites. In order to view them, you had to whip out your credit card. And that is where things changed in porn."

Callie frowns. "What do you mean, changed?"

"I'm getting to that. See, up to that point, porn was pretty much a 'hands on' kind of thing. If you were sell-ing videos, for example, you were up to your neck in the industry. In other words, you'd been on movie sets, seen sex going on in front of you, knew the people, maybe even been in front of the camera yourself. It's always been a very tight, small group. But with Web sites, these early guys, they were a whole new breed. There was a layer between them and the actual creation of the stuff. They had money, and they paid the pornographers for their pics. They put them up on the Web and charged to view them. You see the difference? These guys weren't pornographers, not in the classical sense. They were businessmen. With marketing plans, offices, staff, the whole nine yards. They weren't coming across as some sleazy substrata of society anymore. And it paid off. Some of those first companies make eighty to a hundred million a year now."

"Wow," Callie says. Leo nods.

"Yeah, wow. It may not seem like a big deal to us, but if you really dig into the history of porn, it was a paradigm shift. To be honest? Most of the people making porn in the early eighties were from the seventies. We're talking a lot of drugs, promiscuous sex, all the clichés. But these new Internet guys? Most of them weren't involved in wife swapping or snorting coke while getting a blow job, any of that. Most of them had never been on a porn set in their life. They were guys in business suits, making millions off the newest thing. They started to make it, well, respectable. As much as porn can be."

"You said 'twofold.' What's the other part of it?"

"While these business guys were carving out their empires, you had another whole 'adult revolution' happening. This was at a more grassroots level. Rather than Web sites that were a collection of pics of professional porn stars, you had women or couples creating Web sites that were centered around themselves and their real-life sexual escapades. These weren't people trying to make a living off porn. These were people doing it for fun. Getting off on the exhibitionism of it. It was called 'amateur porn.'"

Callie rolls her eyes. "You're not talking to babes in the woods here, honey-love. I think most of us know what amateur porn is. The 'girl next door,' swingers, blah blah blah."

"Sure, sorry. I'm in lecture mode. The relevance is, the demand for that type of porn turned out to be just as big as the demand for 'pro porn.' So much so that most of these women or couples couldn't afford to keep it up for free, as a hobby. The costs of having their Web sites accessed by so many people became prohibitive. So they started charging as well. A few of those who started early on made millions. And—and this is the key thing you have to understand—these were not porn-industry people. They didn't know anyone in the adult-video industry. They weren't in magazines, or in videos in adult bookstores. These were people driven first not by money but by the enjoyment of what they were doing.

"Whether or not you or I think this is a healthy way to be, the truth is, it created an entirely new demographic within the porn industry. Moms and dads, members of the PTA. All the while having a secret life *and* raking in the dough showing themselves off to the world." He turns to me. "So, what I meant when I said you weren't accurate is just that. I saw your friend's Web site. She did soft-core stuff—as in no sex. She *did* masturbate and use sex toys and . . . stuff like that. She charged for viewing it, and I don't necessarily approve—but she wasn't a hooker." He fumbles with his words for a moment. "I mean, I don't know if that'll help you, when you think about it, but…"

I give him a tired smile. Close my eyes. "It's a lot to take in, Leo. I'm not sure how I feel about any of it. But, yeah. It helps."

My mind is spinning, spinning, spinning. I think about Annie, posing nude as a chosen profession. I wonder about the secrets people keep. She was always beautiful, always a little wild. I would not have been surprised by any number of sexual secrets. But this—this throws me for a loop. Partly because I am unsure of my own ambivalence about it.

A picture floats into my mind, sudden and unbidden. Matt and I were both twenty-six. The sex we were having that year could only be called spectacular. No area of our home was unchristened. No position had been left untried. My lingerie collection had grown by leaps and bounds. Best of all, none of this was happening because we were working at it. We weren't trying to "spice things up"—things were just spicy all by themselves. We were drunk on each other, cavorting with horny abandon.

I was always the more sexually adventurous of the two of us. Matt tended to be more conservative and quiet. But like they say: Still waters run deep. He could follow my lead into dark territories without hesitation. He'd howl full-throated at the moon right beside me. It's one of the things I loved about him. He was a wonderful, gentle man. But he could shift gears when I needed him to, could be rough and dark and a little dangerous. He was always my hero. But… when I needed a little bit of villain, Matt would provide.

We were a modern-day couple. We watched naughty movies together every now and then. I'm the one who would drag him into perusing some of the adult sites on occasion. Always on his screen name. Even though I *was* Big Brother, I was paranoid about Big Brother. I couldn't afford to tarnish the image of the FBI. So Matt's screen name was the one looking at all the dirty pictures. I'd tease him about this, calling him the pervert in the marriage.

We also had a digital camera. One night during this year, while he was at the store, the impulse struck me. I stripped off my clothes and took a few naked photos of myself from the neck down. Heart pounding, giggling like a maniac, I submitted the photos to a Web site that collected such things. I was fully dressed and demure by the time he got back.

A week went by and somehow I had forgotten about the incident. I was mired in a case. Anything else other than Matt and eating and sleeping and sex was not on my mental agenda. I came home late, exhausted, and dragged my way up to the bedroom. There I found Matt, lying on the bed. His hands were laced behind his head and he had the strangest look in his eyes.

"Something you want to tell me?" he asked.

I stopped, puzzled. Trying to think of anything. "Not that I know of. Why?"

"Follow me." He got out of bed and walked past me, heading toward our home office. I followed, mystified. He sat down at the desk where we had our computer. Jiggled the mouse to make the screen saver disappear.

What I saw made me blush so hard, I thought my face was going to catch on fire. It was a page on the Web, and there, for the world to see, were the photos I had taken. Matt swiveled around. He had a small smile on his face.

"They e-mailed back. Apparently they *loved* the pics you sent them."

I stammered. Blushed some more. Blushed harder as I realized that I was getting turned on.

"I don't think you should do that again, Smoky—neck down or not, it's probably not real smart. In fact, it's pretty stupid. If anyone found out, you'd be fired in a heartbeat."

I stared at him, my face still hot, nodded. "Yeah. I mean, you're right. I won't. But ..."

He arched his eyebrows in that way I'd always thought was sexy as hell. "But ...?"

"But for now—let's fuck."

And I was tearing off my clothes, and he was tearing off his, and we ended up howling at the moon. The last thing he said to me before we both fell asleep that night was so funny at the time, so Matt, that it stabs me in the heart to remember now. He'd grinned, eyes half lidded.

"What?" I asked.

"Not my daddy's FBI anymore, now, is it?"

I started giggling, and he started laughing, and we made love again and fell asleep spooned against each other.

I am not judgmental of the harmless excursions adults make, whatever the Bureau's public stance may be. I see the ending of life. It's hard to get excited about someone showing their boobs. But that's a far cry from running a Web site and charging people to watch me stuff things between my legs. I wonder if Annie got more from it than just money, or if it was only about the money. Remembering my friend, it was probably about more than just money. She was always a free-range runner, a female Icarus flying just a little too close to the sun.

I shake myself from this reverie. I wonder for a moment if I have lost time, if I'm going to become one of those shell-shocked people who stop talking mid-sentence to stare off into the distance. I see James studying me. For some reason, the image of him—of all people—finding out about those pictures that got posted flies into my mind, sparking an irrational bit of paranoia. God, I really would have to kill myself then.

"You sound like you know your stuff, Leo. We're going to need you on the computer angle, so I hope you are a supergeek."

"The superest." He grins.

"Let's hear about the note."

Callie reaches over to her satchel, opens it, pulls a printout from a folder. She hands it over to me.

"Did you read this?" I ask James.

"Yes." He hesitates. "It's ... interesting."

I nod, meeting his eyes, and I feel the connection. Oil and ball bearings. This is where we meet, and he wants to know what I think of it, whatever else he might feel or say.

I focus my attention on the words as I read them. I need to get into this killer's mind, and these are words he gave a lot of thought to. To us this document is priceless. It can tell us a lot about this monster, if we can unravel it.

> To Special Agent Smoky J. Barrett. I wish this was "eyes only," but I know how little your FBI respects privacy when it comes to a chase. Every door is thrown open, the shades are rolled up, the shadows chased away.
>
> I'd like to apologize first for the lapse between killing your friend and alerting the police to her death. It couldn't be helped. I needed time to get certain things into motion. I will strive to be honest with you, Agent Barrett, and I will be honest here. While the needed

time was the primary factor, I'll admit
that thinking about little Bonnie, face-
to-face with her mother's corpse for those
three days, staring into her dead eyes,
smelling the stink as it began, held a
curious thrill for me.

Do you think she'll ever recover from
that? Or do you think she'll be haunted by
it until the day she dies? Will that day
come sooner, perhaps by her own hand, as
she tries to chase away the nightmares with
a sharp razor or some sleeping pills? Only
time will tell, but thinking about it is
interesting.

Further honesty: I didn't touch the
child. I enjoy the pain of people, I am
that serial cliché. I am not morally
against the sexual rape of youth, but it
holds no particular allure for me. She
remains chaste, at least physically. Raping
her mind was far more fulfilling.

As you are one of those people who cannot
turn away from death, I'll tell you about
the death of your friend, Annie King. She
did not die quickly. She was in much pain.
She begged for her life. I found this both
amusing and arousing. What, I wonder, does
that make you tick off on your checklist
about me, Agent Barrett?

Let me help you along.

I was not the victim of sexual or
physical abuse as a child. I was not a
bedwetter, and I did not torture
small animals. I am something far purer.

I am a legacy. I do what I do because I come from a bloodline, from the FIRST.

It is truly what I was born to do. Are you ready for this next, Agent Barrett? You will scoff, but here it is: I am a direct descendant of Jack the Ripper.

There. It's said. You are, no doubt, shaking your head as you read this. You've consigned me to the status of another nut, an unfortunate soul who hears voices and gets his orders from God.

We'll clear up that misconception, and soon. For now, let's leave it at this: Your friend, Annie King, she was a whore. A modern-day whore of the information superhighway. She deserved to die screaming. Whores are a cancer on the face of this world; she was no exception.

She was the first. She will not be the last.

I am carrying on in the footsteps of my ancestor. Like him, I will not be caught, and like him, what I do will become history. Will you play the Inspector Abberline to my Jack?

I hope so, I truly do.

Let's begin the chase in such a way: Be at your office on the 20th. A package for you will be delivered, and it will authenticate my statements. Though I know you won't listen, I give you my word that the package I send will contain no traps or bombs.

Go and visit little Bonnie. Perhaps you

can wake each other up screaming at night,
now that you're her new mommy.

   And remember—there are no voices, no
commands from God. All I have to listen to,
to know who I am, is the beating of my own
heart.

   From Hell,
   Jack Jr.

I finish reading and am silent and still for a moment. "That's some letter," I say.

"Just another wacko," Callie says in a voice that's brimming with scorn.

I purse my lips. "I don't think so. I think this one's more than that." I shake my head to clear it, look at James. "We'll talk about this later. I need to think about it for a little while."

He nods. "Yes. I also want to see the scene before I draw any real conclusions."

That connection again. I feel the same way. We need to be there where it happened. To stand on the killing ground. We need to smell him.

"Speaking of that," I say, "who caught this at SFPD?"

"Your old friend Jennifer Chang," Alan rumbles from the front of the plane, surprising me. "I talked to her last night. She doesn't know you're coming up with us."

"Chang, that's good. She's one of the best." I met Detective Jennifer Chang on a case nearly six years ago. She was about my age, competent as hell, and had an acidic, biting sense of humor that I liked. "Where are they at on this thing? Have they started processing the scene?"

"Yep," Alan says, moving down the aisle, sitting closer to us. "Crime Scene Unit in SF was all over it, with Chang playing the little dictator. I talked to her again at midnight. She already had the body at the coroner's, all the photo work done, and CSU in and out. Fiber, trace, everything. That woman is a slave driver."

"That's how I remember her. What about the computer?"

"Other than dusting for prints, they haven't touched it." He jerks a thumb at Leo. "The Brain told them he'd take care of it."

I look at Leo, nodding my head. "What's your plan on that?"

"Pretty simple. I'll do a cursory examination of the PC, check for any booby traps that might have been set to wipe the hard drive, stuff like that. Look for anything immediate. Beyond that, I'll need to take it back to the office to really work on it."

"Good. I need you to scour her computer, Leo. I need any and all deleted files, including e-mail, pictures, anything—and I mean anything—that can help us on this. He found her through the Internet. That makes the computer his first weapon."

He rubs his hands. "Just lemme at it."

"Alan, you take your usual avenue. Gather up copies of everything SFPD has so far in terms of reports, canvassing, and then second-guess all of it."

"No problem."

I turn to Callie. "You take CSU. They're good up there, but you're better. Try and be nice about it, but if you have to push someone aside..." I shrug.

Callie smiles at me. "My specialty."

"James, I want you to take the coroner for now. Put on the pressure. We need the autopsy done today. After, you and I will go over and walk the scene."

The hostility percolates, but he doesn't say anything, just nods.

I stop for a second. I run through it all in my head, making sure I've covered all the bases. I have, I think.

"That it?" Alan asks.

I look up at him, surprised at the anger in his voice. Having no idea where it's coming from. "I think so."

He stands up. "Good." He walks away, back to the front of the plane, as all of us watch and wonder.

"Who put a big fat bug up his ass?" Callie asks.

"Yeah, what a grouch!" Leo chimes in.

Callie and I swivel our heads to stare at him. Hostile gazes all around.

Leo glances back and forth between us, nervous. "What?" he asks.

"It's like the saying goes, child," Callie says, poking a finger at his chest. "'Don't beat up my friend. Nobody gets to beat up my friend but me.' Do you follow?"

I watch as Leo's face closes down, becomes impassive. "Sure. You mean I'm not your friend, right, Red?"

Callie cocks her head at him, and I see some of the hostility leave her face. "No, honey-love—that's not what I'm saying. This isn't a clique, and we're not in high school. So drop the poor besieged nerd persona." She leans forward. "What I'm saying is that I love that man. He saved my life once. And you don't get to pick on him like I do. Yet. Do you follow, sweetie pie?"

Leo appears less hostile but not quite ready to back down. "Yeah, okay. I understand. But don't call me child."

Callie turns to me and grins. "He just might fit in after all, Smoky." She looks back at Leo. "If you value your life, don't ever call me Red again, earring boy."

"I'm going to talk to Alan," I say. I'm distracted, not as

amused by this banter as I would normally be. I move forward, leaving them to their good-natured bickering. Some small part of me that used to be a leader registers that what Callie is doing is, in fact, good for Leo and thus for the team. She's accepting him in her own way. I'm glad. Sometimes when teams work together for a long while, they become too insular. Almost xenophobic. It's not healthy, and I'm happy to see that they haven't gone down that path. Well, at least Callie hasn't. James stares out the window, closed and cold and not taking part. Quintessential James, nothing new.

I arrive at the row Alan is sitting in. He's staring at his feet, and the tension that pours off him is choking. "Mind if I sit down?" I ask.

He waves a hand, doesn't look at me. "Whatever."

I sit and regard him for a moment. He turns to stare out the window. I decide to try the direct approach. "What's up with you?"

He looks at me, and I almost recoil from the anger in his eyes.

"What's that supposed to be? Show you can talk to the 'brotha'? 'What up?'"

I'm speechless. Struck dumb. I wait, thinking this will pass, but Alan continues to glare at me, and his rage only seems to be building.

"Well?" he asks.

"You know that's not what I meant, Alan." My voice is quiet. Even calm. "It's obvious to everyone that you're upset about something. I'm just—asking."

He continues to glare for another moment, but this time the fire does burn down. A little. He looks down at his hands. "Elaina is sick."

My mouth falls open. I'm flooded with shock and concern, instant and visceral. Elaina is Alan's wife, and I have known her for as long as I have known him. She is a beautiful Latin woman, beautiful in both form and heart. She came to see me in the hospital, the only visitor I had. The truth is, she gave me no choice. She barged in, brushing the nurses aside, walked up to my bed, sat on the edge, and fought my hands aside to draw me into her arms, all without speaking a single word. I melted against her and wept until I was dry. My strongest memory of her will always be that moment. The world a blur behind my tears, Elaina, comfortable and warm and strong, stroking my hair and crooning comfort to me in a mix of English and Spanish. She is a *friend*, the rare, forever kind.

"What? What do you mean?"

Perhaps it's the real fear he hears in my voice, but now the rage disappears. No more fire in those eyes. Just pain. "Stage-two colon cancer. They removed the tumor, but it had ruptured. Some of the cancer spilled into her system before the surgery happened."

"And what does that mean?"

"That's the fucked-up part. It might mean nothing. Maybe the cancer cells that came out when it ruptured are nothing to worry about. Or maybe they're there, floating around, ready to spread through her system. They can't give us any for-sures." The pain is building in his eyes. "We found out because she was having really bad pains. We thought it might be appendicitis. They took her right into surgery and found the tumor, took it out. Afterward, do you know what the doc told me? He told me she was stage four. That she was probably going to die."

I look at his hands. They are shaking.

"I couldn't tell her. She was recovering, you know? I didn't want her to worry, just wanted her to concentrate on getting better from the operation. For a whole week, I thought she was going to die, and every time I looked at her, that's what I thought about. She didn't have a clue." He laughs, mirthless. "So we go back in for her checkup, and the doctor has good news for us. Stage two, not stage four. Seventy to eighty percent survival rate over five years. He's all grins, and she starts crying. She found out that her cancer wasn't as bad as we thought, and she didn't know till just then that this was good news."

"Oh, Alan..."

"So she's going to be getting chemo. Maybe some radiation; we're still gathering all the information. Making our choices." He stares at those big hands again. "I thought I was going to lose her, Smoky. Even now, even when the facts say she's going to be fine, I don't know. What I do know is what it would feel like. I had a whole week to feel that. I can't stop feeling it." He looks at me, and the anger is back. "I felt the possibility of losing her. And what am I doing? Flying toward our next skell. She's at home, sleeping." He looks out the window. "Maybe up by now. But I ain't with her."

I stare at him, aghast. "Jesus, Alan! Why don't you take a leave? Be with Elaina, not here. We can handle this without you."

He turns to look at me, and the pain I see in those eyes takes my breath away and almost stops my heart.

"Don't you get it? I'm not mad because I'm here. I'm mad because there's no reason for me not to be here. Either everything is going to be fine, or it's not. And it doesn't make a damn bit of difference what I do." He holds up his hands, splays them. Two huge catcher's mitts. "I can kill with these hands. I can shoot with them. I can make love to my wife and thread a needle with them. They're strong. Lot of dexterity too. But I can't reach in and take out that cancer. I can't help her. I can't fucking stand it."

The hands go back down into his lap, and those helpless eyes go back to watching them. I look at them too, try to find words for my friend. I feel his fear, and mine. I think of Matt.

"Helplessness is something I understand, Alan."

He looks at me, emotions warring in his eyes. "I know, Smoky. But—don't take this the wrong way—all things considered, that's not confidence-inspiring." He grimaces. "Ah, shit. Sorry. That sounds all wrong."

I shake my head. "Don't worry about that. This isn't about what happened to me. It's about what's happening with you and Elaina. You can't tell me what you're feeling and walk on eggshells at the same time."

"I guess not." He blows air out through his lips. "Fuck, Smoky. What am I going to do?"

"I . . ." I sit back for a moment, thinking. What is he going to do? I catch his eyes again. "You're going to love her and do everything you can. You're going to let your friends help you if you need it. And here's the most important thing, Alan. You're going to remember that it just might turn out okay. That the deck isn't stacked against you."

He gives me a crooked grin. "Cup half full kind of thing, huh?"

My response is fierce. "Damn right. This is Elaina. Cup half full is the only acceptable way to look at it."

He looks out the window, down at his hands, and now at me. The gentleness I have always cherished in my friend is back in his eyes. "Thanks, Smoky. I mean it."

"So far from not a problem it's not even funny."

"Let's keep it between us for now, though, all right?"

"Deal. Are you okay?"

He purses his lips, nods his head. "Yeah. Yeah, I'm fine." He looks at me, squints. "What about you? You okay? We haven't really talked ... since." He shrugs.

"It's not like you didn't try. And yeah, for now, I'm doing fine."

"Good."

We gaze at each other for a moment, not speaking, just understanding. I stand up and give his shoulder a last squeeze before I walk away.

First Callie, now Alan. Problems and heartache and mysteries. I feel a twinge of guilt. I've been so caught up in my own agony these last six months, I realize I hadn't even considered that the lives of my friends might be something less than perfect, that they might have their own fears and pain and miseries. It shames me.

"Everything copacetic, honey-love?" Callie asks me as I sit down.

"Everything's fine."

She looks at me for a moment with that patented Callie intensity. I don't think she's really buying it, but she lets it go. "So, honey-love, while we're all running around on our assigned tasks, what are you going to be doing?"

The question brings me back to the purpose of this flight, makes me shiver. "First I'm going to talk to Jenny. I'll take her out to a coffee shop or something." I look at James. "She's good, and she saw the scene fresh. I want to get her firsthand impressions of it." He nods. "And then I'm going to see the best possible lead we have."

No one asks who I mean, and I know all of them are glad to let me do it. Because I'm talking about Bonnie.

10

WE WALK INTO SFPD, ask for Jennifer Chang, and are directed toward her office. She sees us coming. I am gratified as her eyes light up when she spots me. She moves toward us, towing along a male partner I don't recognize.

"Smoky! They didn't tell me you were coming."

"It was kind of a last-minute thing."

Jennifer stops close to me and gives me a once-over, head to toe. Unlike other people, she doesn't bother to cover her interest in my scars. She gives them a frank look.

"Not so bad," she remarks. "Healed up good. How about on the inside?"

"A little raw, but healing too."

"Good. So—is this a takeover, or what?" Jenny is right to business. I have to handle this part well; it is a takeover, but I don't want Jenny or other members of SFPD to get disgruntled about it.

"Yeah. But only because of the message to me. You know the rules, the e-mail constitutes a threat to a federal agent." I shrug. "That makes it a federal matter. But this has nothing to do with anyone here thinking SFPD can't do the job."

She mulls this over for a second. "Yeah, well. You guys have always dealt straight with me."

We follow her into her office, which is a small room with two desks. Nonetheless, I'm surprised. "Your own office, Jenny. Pretty impressive."

"Best solve rate three years in a row. The Captain asked me what I wanted, and I said this. He gave it to me." She grins. "Kicked out two old-timers to do it too. Didn't make me very popular. Like I care." She points to her partner. "Sorry. Should have introduced you earlier. This is Charlie De Biasse, my partner. Charlie, the feds."

He inclines his head. De Biasse is obviously an Italian name, and Charlie looks it, though perhaps not pure-blooded. He has a calm, easygoing face. His eyes don't match. They look sharp. Sharp and watchful. "Pleased to meet you."

"Likewise."

"So," Jenny says, "what's the game plan?"

Callie gives her a rundown of the various assignments we have laid out. Jenny gives a nod of approval when she's done. "Sounds good. I'll get copies of everything we have so far put together for you. Charlie, can you call CSU and give them a heads-up?"

"Yep."

"Who has the keys to her apartment?" I ask.

Jenny picks up an envelope on the side of her desk and hands it to Leo. "They're in there. Don't worry about con-taminating the scene. Evidence collection is done. The address is the one on the front of the envelope. See Sergeant Bixby at the desk. He can get you a ride."

Leo looks at me, eyebrows raised, and I nod, sending him on his way.

I catch Jenny's eye. "Can we go somewhere? I'd like to talk to you about your impressions of the scene."

"Sure. You and I can go and get a cup of coffee. Charlie can set everyone up here, right, Charlie?"

"Yep."

"That would be great."

"Is your medical examiner any good?" James asks. Of course, since it's James, it doesn't come out as a harmless question but a challenge. Jenny frowns at him.

"According to Quantico she is. Why—have you heard differently?"

He waves his hand at her, a gesture of dismissal. "Just tell me how I can hook up with her, Detective. Save the sarcasm."

Jenny's eyebrows shoot up, and I see her eyes cloud over. She glances at me, and perhaps it's the look of anger she sees on my face, directed at James, that pacifies her. "Talk to Charlie." Her voice is tight and terse. It has no effect on James. He turns away from her without a glance back.

I touch her elbow. "Let's get out of here."

She shoots one last brooding look at James before nodding. We head toward the precinct door.

"Is he always such a dick?" she asks as we're walking down the front steps.

"Oh yeah. The word was invented for him."

We only have to walk a block to reach the coffee shop, something San Francisco seems to have as many of as Seattle. It's a mom-and-pop place, not a franchise, with a relaxed, earthy feel to it. I order a café mocha. Jenny gets some hot tea. We settle down at a table next to the window and enjoy not talking for a moment. Sipping at our respective cups. The mocha is exquisite. Exquisite enough,

I realize, for me to enjoy it, even with all the death around me.

I look outside at the city passing by. San Francisco has always intrigued me. It's the New York of the West Coast. Cosmopolitan, with European influences, it has its own charm and character. I can usually tell if someone is from San Francisco by their clothing. It's one of the few places on the West Coast where you see wool trench coats and hats, berets and leather gloves. Stylish. The day outside is nice; San Francisco can tend to run chilly, but today the sun is out, and the weather hovers in the low seventies. A scorcher by this city's standards.

Jenny puts down her tea and runs a finger around the rim of the cup. She seems thoughtful. "I was surprised to see you here. Even more surprised to find out you're not heading up your team."

I look over my cup at her. "That was the deal. Annie King was a friend of mine, Jenny. I have to stay on the periphery of this. At least officially. Besides, I'm not ready to run NCAVC Coord again, not yet."

Her gaze at me reveals nothing, but neither does it judge. "Not ready as in you say you're not ready, or the Bureau says it?"

"It's me saying it."

"So ... don't be offended, Smoky, but if that's true, how did you even get authorization to come up here? I don't think my Captain would have let me, in a similar situation."

I explain to her about the changes that I had felt in myself by virtue of connecting back up with my team. "It seems to be good therapy for me right now. I guess the Assistant Director saw it that way too."

Jenny is silent for a moment before speaking. "Smoky, you and I are friends. We don't trade Christmas cards or come over for Thanksgiving. We're not that kind of friends. But still friends, right?"

"Sure. Of course."

"Then as a friend, I have to ask: Are you going to be able to deal with this case? All the way? This is bad stuff. Real bad. You know me, and you know I've seen a lot. But that thing with her daughter..." She shudders, an involuntary spasm. "I'm gonna have nightmares about it. On top of that, what was done to your friend wasn't pretty either. Oh yeah, and she was your friend. I can understand what you're saying about it being healthy for you to test the waters again, but do you really think this is the case to do it with?"

I am honest in my reply. "I don't know. That's the truth. I'm messed up, Jenny, make no mistake about that. I guess it doesn't make a lot of visible sense for me to get involved, but..." I think for a minute. "It's like this. Do you know what I've been doing since Matt and Alexa died? Nothing. I don't mean nothing as in taking it easy. I mean nothing. As in sitting in a single place all day long, staring at a blank wall. I go to sleep and have nightmares, wake up, and stare at things till I go back to sleep. Oh, or sometimes, I look at myself in the mirror for hours and trace over these scars with my fingers." Tears prick my eyes. I'm gratified to find that they are tears of anger and not weakness. "All I can tell you is that that—living like that—is even more terrible than what I'll see being involved with Annie's death. I think. I know that sounds selfish, but it's the truth." I run out of words like a clock that needs to be wound. Jenny sips from her tea. The city continues to churn around us, unaware.

"Makes sense to me. So, you want my impressions of the scene?" This is all she says. She is not brushing me off.

She is acknowledging me in her way. Telling me she understands, so let's get down to business. I am grateful.

"Please."

"I got the call yesterday."

I interrupt. "As in you, personally?"

"Yep. Asked for me by name. Voice was disguised, and told me to check my e-mail. I might have ignored it, but he mentioned you."

"Disguised how?"

"It was muffled. Like he'd put a cloth over the mouthpiece of his phone."

"Any notable inflections? Unusual use of slang? Hint of an accent of any kind?"

Jenny looks at me, a bemused smile on her face. "You going to work me like a witness, Smoky?"

"You are a witness. For me, at least. You're the only person who actually talked to him, and you saw the scene fresh. So, yeah."

"Fair enough." I see her thinking about my question for a moment. "I'd have to say no. In fact, I would say just the opposite. There was an absence of inflection. His voice was very flat."

"Can you remember what he said, exactly?" I know the answer to this question is yes. Jennifer has an unusual memory. It's as scary in its own way as my skill with a handgun, and is feared by defense attorneys.

"Yeah. He said: 'Is this Detective Chang?' I said it was. 'You've got mail,' he said, but then he didn't laugh. That was one of things that got my attention, first. He didn't push the melodrama of it. Just said it as a flat fact. I asked who this was, and he said, 'Someone's dead. Smoky Barrett knows them. You've got mail.' And then he hung up."

"Nothing else?"

"That was it."

"Hm. Do we know where the call originated?"

"From a pay phone in LA."

My ears perk up at this. "Los Angeles?" I think about it. "Maybe that's why he needed three days. So either he's a traveler, or he's actually from LA."

"Or he's just messing with us. If he is from LA, then my guess would be that he came up here for Annie." Her face looks strained and uncomfortable as she says this. I know why.

"Which would mean I was the person whose attention he wanted to get." I have already accepted this possibility—no, make that probability—although I have not confronted it emotionally. The fact that Annie may be dead not only because of what she did but because she was my friend.

"Right. But that's all conjecture. Anyway, so I go and check my e-mail—"

I interrupt her. "Where did he send the e-mail from?"

She looks at me, hesitant. "He sent it from your friend's computer, Smoky. It was her e-mail address."

This sparks a sudden, unexpected wave of anger in me. I know he did this not just to cover his tracks, but to show that what was Annie's was now his. I push it aside. "Go on."

"It gave Annie King's name and address, nothing else, and there were four attachments. Three were photos of your friend. The fourth was the letter to you. At this point, we are taking it seriously. You can fake anything when it comes to photos these days, but it's like a bomb threat—you evacuate just in case. So my partner and I gathered up some uniforms and went over to the address." She sips her tea. "The door wasn't locked, and after some knocking without any answer, we pulled our weapons and entered. Your friend and her daughter were in the bedroom, on the bed. She had her computer set up in there." She shakes her head, remembering. "It was a bad scene, Smoky. You've seen more of that than I have, that kind of methodical, intentional killing, but I don't think you'd have seen it differently. He cut her open, removed her insides, and bagged them. Slit her throat. But the worst of it was the daughter."

"Bonnie."

"Right. She was tied face-to-face with her mother. Nothing fancy. He just put them stomach to stomach, and wrapped rope around them both until she couldn't move. She was there like that for three days, Smoky. Tied to her own dead mother. You know what happens to a body in three days. The air-conditioning wasn't on. And the fucker had left a window cracked. There were blow-flies."

I do know. What she's describing is unimaginable.

"The kid is ten years old, and the smell is already bad, and she's there with flies all over. She'd turned her head so her cheek was resting on her mom's face." Jenny grimaces, and I get a hint of the horror she felt at that moment. I'm thankful, so thankful, I wasn't there for that. "She was quiet. Didn't say a word when we got into the room. Not while we were untying her. She was just limp, and stared. Unresponsive to questions. She was dehydrated. We got EMS over right away, and I sent her off with an officer. She's fine physically, and I have a guard posted at the door of her room just in case. I got her a private room, by the way."

"Thanks. I appreciate that. A lot."

Jenny waves it off, sips her tea. I'm surprised to see the smallest of trembles as she does this. She is truly, deeply affected by the memory, as tough as she is. "She hasn't said a word since. Do you think she'll ever get over it? Could anyone?"

"I don't know. I'm always surprised at what people can live through. But I don't know."

She gives me a speculative look. "I guess so." She is silent for a moment before continuing. "Once we had her off in the ambulance, I shut the place down. I called CSU in, and I kicked their ass, hard. Maybe a little harder than I needed to, but I was just so … pissed. That's not even a good word for how I felt."

"I understand."

"While all that was happening, I called and talked to Alan, and here we are. I don't have much more than that. We're at the dead beginning of it, Smoky. Evidence collection only. I haven't had time to slow down and really look at anything."

"Let's step back a little. Let me walk you through it like a witness."

"Sure."

"We'll do it as a CI."

"Okay."

By CI I mean "cognitive interview." Witness recollections and accounts are one of our bugbears. People see too little, or don't remember what they've seen, due to trauma and emotion. They can remember things that didn't really happen. Cognitive-interview technique has been in use for a long time, and while it has a specific methodology, its application is more of an art form. I'm very good at it. Callie is better. Alan is a master.

The basic concept behind the cognitive interview is that simply walking a witness through from the start of the event to the end, over and over, does not, as a rule, lead to more recollection. Instead, three techniques are used. The first is context. Rather than starting from the beginning of the event, you take them prior to it. What their day was like, how it was going, what life worries/happinesses/banalities were running through their head. Get them to recall the normal flow of their life prior to the abnormal event you want them to remember. The theory is that this serves to put the event you want them to recall into context. By grounding them in memories prior to the event, they are more able to move forward through the event and will remember in greater detail. The second technique is to change the sequence of recall. Rather than starting them from the beginning, start them from the end, and go backward. Or begin in the middle. It makes the witness start and stop and reexamine. The last part of a good CI is changing perspective. "Wow," you might say, "I wonder what that looked like to the person standing by the door?" This shifts their inspection of the event and can jar more facts loose.

With someone like Jenny, who is a trained investigator with excellent memory, cognitive interviewing can be very, very effective.

"It's late afternoon," I say, starting. "You're in your office, doing...?"

She looks up toward the ceiling, remembering. "I'm talking to Charlie. We're going over a case we've been working on. Sixteen-year-old prostitute, beaten to death and left in an alley in the Tenderloin."

"Uh-huh. What are you saying about it?"

Her eyes get sad. "It's what he's saying. About how no one gives a shit about a dead whore, even if she's just sixteen years old. He's mad and sad, and venting. Charlie doesn't do well with dead kids."

"How did you feel at the time, listening to that?"

She shrugs, sighs. "About the same. Mad. Sad. Not venting about it the way he was, but understanding. I remember looking down at my desk while he was ranting away, and noticing that the side of one of the photos from her file was sticking out. It was a picture from the scene, where we found her. I could see part of her leg from the knee down. It looked dead. I felt tired."

"Go on."

"Charlie wound down. He finished spewing, and then he just sat there for a second. He finally looked over and gave me that silly, lopsided smile of his, and said he was sorry. I told him it was no big deal." She shrugs. "He's listened to my ranting in the past. It's one of the things partners do."

"How did you feel about him, at that moment?"

"Close." She waves a hand. "Not lovey or sexual, or anything like that. That's never come up between us. Just close. I knew he'd always be there for me and vice versa. I was happy to have a good partner. I was about to tell him that, when the call came in."

"From the perp?"

"Yeah. I remember feeling kind of . . . disoriented when the perp started talking."

"Disoriented how?"

"Well, life was—normal. I was sitting there with Charlie, and someone says 'you got a phone call' and I say 'thanks' and pick it up—circumstances and motions I've experienced and done a thousand times. Normal. Suddenly, it wasn't. I went from the usual to talking to something evil"—she snaps her fingers—"just like that. It was jarring." Her eyes are troubled as she says this.

This is the other reason I decided to use CI technique with Jenny. The biggest problem with witness memory is the trauma of the event. Strong feelings cloud recall. People outside law enforcement don't understand that we experience our own trauma. Strangled children, chopped-up mothers, raped young boys. Talking to murderers on the phone. These experiences are shocking. They are filled with emotion, however well suppressed. They are traumatic.

"I understand. I think we have context here, Jenny." My voice is smooth and quiet. She's letting me put her in the "then," and I want to keep her close to it. "Let's move forward. Take it from when you are walking up to the door of Annie's apartment."

She squints at nothing I can see. "It's a white door. I remember thinking it was the whitest door I'd ever seen. Something about that made me feel hollow. Cynical."

"How so?"

She looks at me and her eyes seem ancient. "Because I knew it was a lie. All that white. Total bullshit. I felt it in my gut. Whatever was behind that door wasn't white, not at all. It was going to be dark and rotten and ugly."

Something cold twinges inside of me. A kind of vicarious déjà vu. I have felt what she is describing.

"Go on."

"We knock, and we call her name. Nothing. It's quiet." She frowns. "You know what else was strange?"

"What?"

"No one peeked out their door to see what was going on. I mean, we were 'cop knocking.' Loud and pounding. But no one looked. I don't think she really knew her neighbors. Or maybe they just weren't close."

She sighs.

"Anyway. Charlie looks over at me, and I look back at him, and we both look at the uniforms, and we all unholster our weapons." She bites her lip. "That bad feeling was really strong. It was an anxiety ball bouncing around in my stomach. I could feel it in the others too. Smell it. Sweat and adrenaline trembles. Shallow breathing."

"Were you scared?" I ask her.

She doesn't answer for a moment. "Yeah. I was scared. Of what we were going to find." She grimaces at me. "Want to know something weird? I'm always scared just before I get to a scene. I've been on homicide for over ten years, and I've seen everything, but it still scares me, every time."

"Go on."

"I tried the doorknob, and it turned, no problem. I looked at everyone again and opened the door, wide. We all had our weapons up and ready."

I switch perspectives on her. "What do you think the first thing Charlie noticed was?"

"The smell. It had to be. There was the smell, and the dark. All the lights were off, except for the one in her bedroom." She shivers, and I realize that she's unaware of it. "You could see the doorway to her bedroom from where we were standing. It was down a hallway almost directly in line with the front door. The apartment was close to being pitch-black, but the bedroom doorway was kind of . . . outlined by light." She runs a hand through her hair. "It reminded me of that whole 'monster in the closet' thing I had sometimes as a kid. Something scratching on the other side of that door, wanting out. Something awful."

"Tell me about the smell."

She grimaces. "Perfume and blood. That's what it smelled like. The smell of perfume was stronger, but you could smell the blood underneath it. Thick and coppery. Subtle, but kind of . . . aggravating. Disturbing. Like something you could see out of the corner of your eye."

I file this away. "What then?"

"We did the usual. Called out to the occupants, cleared the living room and the kitchen. We used flashlights, because I didn't want anyone touching anything."

"That's good." I nod, encouraging.

"After that, we did what made sense—we went toward the bedroom door." She stops and looks at me. "I told Charlie to put on gloves before we even entered, Smoky."

She is telling me she knew, felt, that murder was on the other side of that door. That she was going to be dealing with evidence, not survivors. "I remember looking at the doorknob. Not wanting to turn it. I didn't want to look inside. To let it out."

"Go on."

"Charlie turned the knob. It wasn't locked. We had a little trouble opening it because there was a towel stuffed along the bottom of the door."

"A towel?"

"Soaked in perfume. He'd put it there so the smell of your friend's corpse wouldn't come wafting out. He didn't want anyone finding her until he was ready."

And just like that, part of me wants to stop this. Wants to get up, walk out the door of this coffee shop, hop in the jet, and go home. It is a feeling that surges over me, almost overpowering. I fight it back.

"And then?" I prompt her.

She is quiet, staring off. Seeing too much. When she begins to speak again, her voice is flat and empty. "It hit us all at once. I think that's what he wanted. The bed had been moved so that it was in line with the door. So that when we opened it, we could see it all, smell it all, in an instant." She shakes her head. "I remember thinking of that white, white front door. It made me feel so fucking *bitter*. It was just too much to process. I think we stood there for at least a minute. Just looking. It was Charlie that realized it first—that Bonnie was alive." She stops talking, staring into that moment. I wait her out. "She blinked, that's what I remember. Her cheek was lying against her dead mother's face, and she looked dead herself. We thought she was. And then she blinked. Charlie started cursing, and"—she bites her lip—"crying a little. But that's between us and the uniforms we had there, okay?"

"Don't worry."

"That was the first and—I hope—only fuckup. Charlie just ran into the room and untied Bonnie. Trampled all over the scene." Her voice sounds both hollow and bemused. "He wouldn't stop cursing. He was cursing in Italian. It sounds very pretty. Strange, huh?"

"Yeah." I'm gentle in my reply. Jenny is there, completely in the moment, and I don't want to jar her out of it.

"Bonnie was limp and nonresponsive. Boneless. Charlie untied her and whisked her right out of that apartment. Right out, before I could even think to say or do anything. He was desperate. I understood." Her face twists. "I sent the uniforms out to call EMS and CSU and the ME, blah, blah, blah. That left me there with your friend. In that room, smelling like death and perfume and blood. Feeling so angry and sad I could have puked. Staring down at Annie." She shivers again. Her fist clenches and unclenches. "You ever notice that about the dead, Smoky? How still and quiet they are? Nothing alive could ever fake that kind of stillness. Still and silent and nobody home. I shut off at that point." She looks at me and shrugs. "You know how it works."

I nod. I do. You get over the initial shock, and then you shut down the part of you that feels so that you can do your job without weeping or puking or losing your mind on the spot. You have to be able to give horror a clinical eye. It's unnatural.

"It's funny to look back at it, in a way. It's like I can hear my own voice in my head, some kind of robotic monotone." She mimics this as she speaks. *"White female, approximately thirty-five years of age, tied to her bed in the nude. Evidence of cuts from neck to knees, probably made by a knife. Many cuts look long and shallow, showing probable torture. Torso"*—her voice wavers for a second—*"torso cavity open and seems to be empty of organs. Victim's face is twisted, as though she was screaming when she died. Bones in her arms and legs appear to be broken. Killing looks purposeful. Appears to have been slow. Posing of the body suggests prior thought and planning. Not a crime of passion."*

"Tell me about that," I say. "What's the sense you got of him from the scene, at that exact moment?"

She is silent for a long time. I wait, watching as she looks out the window. She turns her eyes to me.

"Her agony made him come, Smoky. It was the best sex he ever had."

These sentences stop me. They are dark, cold, and horrible.

But they are some of what I was looking for. And they ring true. Even as they empty me out, leave me hollow, I begin to smell him. He smells like perfume and blood, like doorways in shadow, outlined by light. He smells like laughter mixed with screams. He smells like lies disguised as truth, and decay seen out of the corner of your eye.

He is precise. And he savors the act.

"Thanks, Jenny." I feel empty and dirty and filled with shadows. But I also feel something beginning to stir inside. A dragon. Something I was afraid was dead and gone, amputated from me by Joseph Sands. It's not awake, not yet. But I can feel it again, for the first time in months.

Jenny shakes herself a little. "Pretty good. You really put me in it."

"It didn't take much skill on my part. You're a dream witness." My response sounds listless to me. I feel so tired right now.

We sit for a moment, quiet. Contemplative and disturbed.

My mocha no longer tastes exquisite, and Jenny seems to have lost interest in her tea. Death and horror do that. They can suck the joy from any moment. It's the one thing that you have to struggle with, always, in law enforcement. Survivor's guilt. It seems almost sacrilegious to savor a moment in life while talking about the screaming end of someone else's.

I sigh. "Can you take me to see Bonnie?"

We pay the check and leave. The whole way over, I'm dreading the thought of seeing those staring eyes. I smell blood and perfume, perfume and blood. It smells like despair.

11

I HATE HOSPITALS. I'm glad they are there when they're needed, but I have only one good memory of being at one: the birth of my daughter. Otherwise, a visit to the hospital has always been because I am hurt, or someone I care for is hurt, or someone is dead. This is no exception. We have entered a hospital because we need to see a young girl who was bound to her dead mother for three days.

My own time in the hospital is a surreal memory. It was a time of intense physical pain and an unending wish to die. A time of not sleeping for days, until I'd pass out from exhaustion. Of staring at a ceiling in the dark, while monitors hummed and the soft sound of nurses' shoes shuffled down the hallways, overloud in the cotton-stuffed quiet. Of listening to my soul, which had the empty rushing sound you hear when you put your ear to a seashell.

I smell its smell, and shiver inside.

"Here we are," Jenny says.

The cop in front is alert. He asks to see my identification, even though I'm with Jenny. I approve.

"Any other visitors?" Jenny asks.

He shakes his head. "Nope. It's been quiet."

"Don't let anyone in while we're inside, Jim. I don't care who it is, got it?"

"Whatever you say, Detective."

He sits back in his chair and unfurls a newspaper, and we enter.

I feel dizzy the moment the door closes and I see Bonnie's still form. She's not asleep, her eyes are open. But they don't even move in response to the sound of our entrance. She is small, tiny, made more so as she is dwarfed not just by the hospital bed, but by her circumstances. I am amazed how much she looks like Annie. The same blond hair and upturned nose, those cobalt-blue eyes. In a few more years she will be almost a twin of the girl I held on a bathroom floor in high school so many years ago. I realize I've been holding my breath. I exhale, walking over to her.

She's on the barest of monitoring. Jenny had explained on the way over that a thorough exam showed no rape and no physical injury. There is a part of me that is thankful for that, but I know her wounds run much deeper. They are gaping and bloody and no doctor can stitch them, these wounds of the mind.

"Bonnie?" I speak in a soft, measured voice. I remember reading somewhere about talking to people in a coma, how they can hear you and it helps. This is close enough to that. "I'm Smoky. Your mother and I were best friends, for a long time. I'm your godmother."

No response. Just those eyes, staring at the ceiling. Seeing something else. Maybe seeing nothing. I move to the side of the bed. I hesitate before taking her small hand in mine. A wave of dizziness crashes over me at the feel of her soft skin. This is the hand of a child, not fully grown, a symbol of that which we protect and love and cherish. I held my daughter's hand like this many times, and an emptiness opens up as Bonnie's hand fills that space. I start to speak to her, not sure of the words until they tumble from my lips. Jenny stands off, silent. I'm barely aware of her. My words sound low and earnest to me, the sound of someone praying.

"Honey, I want you to know that I'm here to find the man who did this to you and your mother. That's my job. I want you to know that I know how bad this is. How much you are hurting inside. Maybe how you want to die." A tear rolls down my cheek. "I lost my husband and my daughter to a bad man, six months ago. He hurt me. And for a long time, I wanted to do exactly what you're doing now. I wanted to just crawl inside myself and disappear." I stop for a moment, draw a ragged breath, squeeze her hand. "I just wanted you to know I understand. And you stay in there, as long as you need. But when you're ready to come out, you won't be alone. I'll be here for you. I'll take care of you." I'm weeping openly now, and I don't care. "I loved your mother, sweetheart. I loved her so much. I wish she and I had spent more time together. Wish I'd seen more of you." I smile a crooked smile through my tears. "I wish you and Alexa had known each other. I think you would have liked her."

I am growing dizzier, and the tears just seem to keep on coming. Grief is like that sometimes. Like water, it finds any opening, forces itself through any crack until it explodes, inexorable. Images flash through my mind of Alexa and Annie, turning the inside of my head into some insane, strobe-lit disco. I have only a moment to realize what's happening. I'm passing out.

Then things go dark.

* * *

This is the second dream, and it is beautiful.

I'm in the hospital, in the throes of labor. I'm giving serious thought to killing Matt for his part in putting me here. I am being cleaved in two, I'm covered in sweat, grunting like a pig, all in between screams of pain.

There is a human being moving through me, trying to come out. It does not feel poetic, it feels like I'm shitting a bowling ball. I've forgotten about the supposed beauty of having a child, I want this thing out of me, I love it I hate it I love it, and all of this is reflected in my screams and curses.

My doctor's voice is calm, and I wish I could smack his stupid silly bald head. "Okay, Smoky, the baby's crowning! Just a few more pushes and she'll be out. Come on, hang in there."

"Fuck you!" I yell, and then push. Dr. Chalmers doesn't even look up at me at this. He's been delivering children for a good long time.

"You're doing great, honey," Matt says. He's got his hand in mine, and a part of me registers a perverse hope that I'm grinding his bones into powder.

"How would you know?" I snarl. My head snaps back at the force of the contraction, and I am cursing like I have never cursed before, blasphemous, horrible words to make a biker blush. There is the smell of blood and of the farts that have been escaping as I've been pushing. I think, there is no beauty here, and I want to kill all of you. Then the pain and pressure increases, something I would not have thought possible. I feel like my head should be rotating around, I am cursing with such terrible abandon.

"One more time, Smoky," Dr. Chalmers says from between my legs, still calm in this maelstrom.

There is a gushing, sucking sound, and pain, and pressure, and then—she is out. My daughter has emerged into the world; the first sounds she hears are words of profanity. There is a silence, some snipping sounds, and then something that pushes all the pain and anger and blood away. That stops time. I hear my daughter crying. She sounds as pissed off as I had been moments ago, and it is the most wonderful thing I have ever heard, the most beautiful music, a miracle beyond my capacity to imagine. I am overwhelmed, I feel like my heart should stop beating. I hear that sound, and look at my husband, and I begin to bawl.

"Healthy baby girl," Dr. Chalmers says, leaning back as the nurses clean Alexa and wrap her up. He looks sweaty, and tired, and happy. I love this man that I wanted to swat just seconds ago. He has been a part of this, and I am thankful, though I can't stop crying or find the words.

Alexa was born just after midnight amid the blood and pain and profanity, and that was something you get only a few times in life—a moment of perfection.

She died after midnight as well, taken back into a womb of darkness from which she would never be reborn.

I come to, gasping, shaking, and weeping. I am still in the hospital room. Jenny is standing over me. She looks stricken.

"Smoky! Are you okay?"

My mouth feels gummy. My cheeks are cracking with the salt of my tears. I am mortified. I shoot a look toward the hospital door. Jenny shakes her head.

"No one else has been in here. Though I would have called someone if you hadn't woken up soon."

I gulp in air. They are the deep, gulping breaths of post-panic attack. "Thank you." I sit up, there on the floor, put my head in my hands. "I'm sorry, Jenny. I didn't know that was going to happen."

She is silent. Her tough exterior has faded for a moment, and she looks sad without pity. "Don't worry about it."

These are the only words she says. I sit there gulping air, my breathing getting calmer. And then I notice something. Just as in the dream, the pain of the moment is rushed away.

Bonnie has turned her head, and she is looking at me. A single tear rolls down her cheek. I stand up, move to her bed, take her hand in mine.

"Hi, honey," I whisper.

She doesn't speak, and I say nothing more. We just stare at each other, letting the tears roll down our cheeks. That's what tears are for, after all. A way for the soul to bleed.

12

SAN FRANCISCANS DRIVE a lot like New Yorkers: They take no prisoners. Traffic is medium-heavy at the moment, and Jenny is intent on ferocious negotiations with the other vehicles as we drive back toward SFPD. A symphony of honks and curses fills the air. I have a finger stuck in one ear so I can hear Callie as I talk to her on the cell phone.

"How's it going at CSU?"

"They're good, honey-love. Very good. I'm going over everything with a fine-tooth comb, but I think they covered every base, from a forensic standpoint."

"And I take it that they didn't find anything."

"He was careful."

"Yeah." I feel depression knocking, push it away. "Have you checked in with the others? Any word from Damien?"

"I haven't had time yet."

"We're almost back at the station anyway. Keep doing what you're doing. I'll check in with everyone else."

She is silent for a moment. "How's the child, Smoky?"

How is the child? I wish I had an answer to that. I don't, and I don't want to talk about it right now. "She's in bad shape."

I click off the phone before she can reply, and stare out the window as we travel through the city. San Francisco is a maze of steep hills and one-way streets, aggressive drivers, and trolley cars. It has a certain foggy beauty I've always admired, a singularity all its own. It is a mix of the cultured and the decadent, moving fast toward either death or success. At this moment, it doesn't seem so unique to me. Just another place where murder happens. That's the thing about murder. It can happen at the North Pole or on the equator. It can be committed by men or women, youths or adults. Its victims can be sinners or saints. Murder is everywhere, and its children are legion. I am filled with darkness right now. No whites or grays, just solid coal pitch-blacks.

We arrive at the station, and Jenny moves us out of the still-busy river of the street into the more peaceful parking lot belonging to SFPD. Parking is hard to come by in San Francisco—God help anyone stupid enough to try and pirate these spaces.

We head in through a side door and make our way down a hallway. Alan is in Jenny's office with Charlie. Both are engrossed in the file in front of them.

"Hey," Alan says. I can feel his eyes examining me, taking stock. I don't acknowledge it.

"Any word from the others yet?"

"No one's talked to me."

"You come up with anything?"

He shakes his head. "Not so far. I wish I could say that the cops here are fuckups, but they aren't. Detective Chang runs a tight ship." He snaps his fingers, smiles at Charlie. "Oh yeah—sorry. And her faithful sidekick too, of course."

"Blow me," Charlie replies without looking up from the file.

"Keep at it. I'm going to call James and Leo."

He gives me a thumbs-up, goes back to reading.

My cell phone rings. "Barrett."

I hear James's sour voice. "Where the hell is Detective Chang?" he snarls.

"What's up, James?"

"The ME won't start cutting until your little friend shows up. She needs to get her ass over here now."

He hangs up on me before I can reply. Asshole.

"James needs you at the morgue," I tell Jenny. "They won't start without you."

She smiles a little smile. "I take it the dick is pissed off?"

"Very."

She grins. "Good. I'll head over there right now."

She leaves. Time to call Leo, our rookie. A disconnected musing as I dial: What kind of jewelry does he wear in his ear when he's not on the job? It rings five or six times before he answers, and when he does, the sound of his voice puts me on alert. It is hollow and terrified. His teeth are chattering.

"C-C-C-Carnes..."

"It's Smoky, Leo."

"V-v-v-video..."

"Slow down, Leo. Catch your breath and tell me what's happening."

When he speaks next, his voice comes out as a whisper. What he says fills my head with white noise.

"V-v-video of the m-m-m-m-murder. Terrible..."

Alan is looking at me, concern in his eyes. He can tell that something's happened.

I manage to find my voice. "Stay there, Leo. Don't go anywhere. We'll be there as fast as we can."

13

I REMEMBER THIS area from when I came to visit Annie after her father died. She lived in a towering apartment building—again, à la New York state of mind, where the apartments are more like condos, replete with dining rooms and sunken baths. We pull up to the front of the building.

"Nice place, nice area," Alan remarks, looking up at it through the windshield.

"Her dad did okay," I say. "He left her everything in his will."

I look around at this clean, safe area. While no area of San Francisco can *truly* be called suburban, it definitely has its "nice neighborhoods." They take you away from the noise of the city, the good ones taking you up high so that you can look out across the bay. There are the old neighborhoods, with their Victorian-style homes, and then there are the areas of new development. Like this one.

It strikes me now as it did before: No place is safe from the possibility of murder. No place. The fact that it is less expected here than in a slum will make you no less dead in the end.

Alan calls Leo as we climb out of the car. "We're in front, son, hang on. We'll be up in a sec."

We head through the front doors and into the lobby. The man at reception watches us as we pour into the elevator, but says nothing. We ride in silence to the fourth floor.

Alan and I were quiet on the way over, and we are quiet still. This is the worst part of the job for anyone who does it. Seeing the actuality of the act. It is one thing to process evidence in a lab, to peer into a killer's mind as an exercise. It is another to see a dead body. To smell the blood in a room. As Alan once said, "It's the difference between thinking about shit and eating it."

Charlie is silent and grim-looking. Perhaps remembering last night, turning that knob and seeing Bonnie.

We arrive at the floor and exit, walk down the hallway and turn. Leo is outside. He's sitting down, back against the wall, his head in his hands.

"Let me handle this," Alan murmurs.

I nod and we watch as he moves to Leo. He kneels down in front of him and places a huge hand on the young man's shoulder. I know from experience that as big as that hand is, the touch is gentle.

"How're you doing, kid?"

Leo looks up at him. His face is white and pale. It shines with a greasy sweat. He doesn't even try to smile. "I'm sorry, Alan. I lost it. I saw it, and then I puked, and I couldn't stay in there..." His words taper off, listless.

"Listen up, son." The big man's voice is quiet, but it demands attention. Charlie and I wait. As much as we want to get inside and move forward in our jobs, we both have compassion for what Leo is going through. This is a crucial moment for those in our profession. It is the blooding. The point where you peer into the abyss for the first time, where you find out that the boogeyman really does exist and really has been hiding under the bed all those years. Where you come face-to-face with real evil. We know this is where Leo will either recover or find a new line of work. "You think there's something wrong with you because you got freaked out by what you saw?"

Leo nods and looks ashamed.

"Well, you're mistaken. See, the problem is, you've seen too many movies, read too many books. They give you this crazy-ass idea about what being tough means. How a cop is supposed to act when he sees dead bodies or violence, stuff like that. You think you're supposed to have some smart one-liners on the tip of your tongue, a ham sandwich in your hand, and be all unmoved and shit. Right?"

"I guess."

"And if you don't, then you must be a pansy, and you have to be embarrassed in front of the old-timers. Shit, maybe you're thinking because you puked you're not cut out for this line of work." Alan swivels, looking back at us. "How many scenes did you see before you stopped barfing, Charlie?"

"Three. No, four."

Leo's head pops up at this.

"How about you, Smoky?"

"More than one, that's for sure."

Alan turns back to Leo.

"Me, it was about four. Even Callie's puked, though she won't admit it, since she's the queen and all." He squints at Leo. "Son, there's nothing in life that prepares you for seeing that kind of thing for the first time. Not a damn thing. Doesn't matter how many pictures you've looked at, or case files you've examined. Real dead is a whole different game."

Leo looks at Alan, and I recognize the look. It's the

look of respect, bordering on worship, that a student gives a mentor. "Thanks."

"No problem." They both stand up.

"You ready to brief me, Agent Carnes?" I make my voice a little stern. He needs it.

"Yes, ma'am."

He has some color in his cheeks again and looks a little more determined. To me, he just looks young. Leo Carnes is a baby, introduced to murder, now destined to get old before he should. Welcome to the club.

"Well, go ahead, then."

His voice is calm as he talks. "I came over and ran through the initial checks, verifying that there were no booby traps or viruses present. I then did the first thing you always do—I checked to see what file was last modified. It turned out to be a text file named *readmefeds*."

"Really?"

"Yes. I opened it up. It contained a single sentence: *Check the pocket of the blue jacket.* There was no blue jacket I could see, but then I looked in the closet. Inside the left pocket of a woman's blue jacket, I found a CD."

"So you decided to take a look. It's okay. I would have done the same thing."

He continues, encouraged. "When you make a CD, you can give it a title. When I saw the title of this one, I got very interested." He swallows. "It was named *The Death of Annie.*"

Charlie grimaces. "Son of a bitch. Jenny's going to be pissed that we missed this."

"Go on," I say to Leo.

"I looked to see what files were on the CD. There was just one. It's a high-quality, high-resolution video file. It essentially fills the entire CD." He swallows again. Some of the paleness is coming back. "I clicked on the file, which launched a player, which then played the video. It was..." He shakes his head, tries to get a grip on himself. "Sorry. The killer encoded and created this video. It's not a complete start-to-finish timeline—that would probably be too big for a CD, in terms of the size of the video—it's more of a... montage."

"Of Annie's murder." I say it for him; I know he doesn't want to have to say it himself.

"Yeah. It's—*indescribable*. I didn't want to keep watching, but I couldn't help myself. Then I started puking, and then you called. I left the apartment and I waited outside until you came."

"You didn't puke in the bedroom, did you?" Charlie asks.

"I made it to the bathroom."

Alan claps him on the back with one of those catcher's-mitt-size hands. If Leo had dentures, they would have gone flying out of his mouth. "See? You do have the stuff, Leo—you kept your head about losing your stomach. That's good."

Leo gives him a sheepish half smile.

"Let's go see this," I say. "Leo, you don't need to be there if you don't want to be. I mean it."

He gives me a very direct look. It is a surprising mixture of maturity and contemplation. I realize in a flash of insight that I know what he is thinking. He is thinking that Annie was my friend. That if I'm going to go and watch her die, anybody should be able to. I can almost hear his thoughts. His eyes confirm it; they get hard and he gives a determined shake of his head. "No, ma'am. The computer end of things is my job. I'll do my job."

I acknowledge his strength the way we acknowledge things like that—by making nothing of it. "Fair enough. Take us inside."

Leo opens up the door to the apartment and we enter. It hasn't changed much from how I remember it. It's a three-bedroom layout, with two bathrooms, a large living room, and a great kitchen. Most striking is the fact that Annie is everywhere. She lives through the decor, the essence of the place. Blue was her favorite color, and I see blue in the drapes, a blue vase, a photograph containing a broad blue sky. The place is classy, it has a kind of effortless quality, without gilt edges or gold leaf. Everything matches, but not in that irritating obsessive-compulsive way, that "keep up with the Joneses" way. It is a study in muted beauty. It is serene.

Annie always had that gift. The ability to accessorize without having to think about it. Everything, from the clothes she wore to the watch on her wrist, was always stylish, without being arrogant or frumpy. Elegant without being ostentatious. It was instinctive for her, and I always viewed it as evidence of her inner beauty. She did not choose things because of how others would see them on her. She chose them because they called to her. Because they were right. Because they fit. The apartment is a reflection of this. It is covered in the ghostly dust of Annie's soul.

But there is another presence here as well.

"You smell that?" Alan asks. "What is it?"

"Perfume and blood," I murmur.

"The computer is this way," Leo says. He leads us into the bedroom.

Harmony dies in here. This is where *he* did his work. It is a conscious opposite of Annie's unconscious beauty. Here someone strove for dissonance. To break the serenity. To destroy something exquisite.

The carpet is stained with blood, and my nose picks up the strong, rotten odor of decay, mixed with the smell of Annie's perfume. They are two opposites: one the smell of life, the other the stench of death. An end table is overturned, a lamp smashed. The walls have been scratched, and the whole room feels jagged and wrong. The killer raped this room with his presence.

Leo sits down at the computer. I think of Annie.

"Go ahead," I tell him.

Leo pales. Then he moves the mouse and positions the arrow over a file, double-clicking it. A video player fills the screen, and the video begins. My heart almost stops as I see Annie.

She's nude from head to toe and handcuffed to the bed. Bile rises in my throat as I think of myself with Joseph Sands. I force it back.

The killer is dressed in black. He has a hood over his face.

"Is that a fucking ninja outfit?" Alan rumbles. He shakes his head in disgust. "Christ. It's all a fucking joke to him."

My gift as a hunter kicks in on automatic. The killer looks to be about six feet tall. He's in shape—somewhere in between muscular and wiry. I can tell from the skin exposed around his eyes that he is white.

I'm waiting to hear him speak. Voice-recognition technology has come very far, and this could be a crucial break. But then he disappears from the camera view for a moment. I can hear small sounds of him fumbling with something. When he comes back into the camera's view he looks right into the lens, and I get the sense from the crinkles around his eyes that he is smiling behind that mask. He lifts up a hand and gives a count with his fingers. *1, 2, 1–2–3–4 . . .*

Music fills the room in the video. It drowns out all

other noises. It takes me only a moment to place it. When I do, I am almost sick. Almost.

"Jesus Christ," Charlie whispers, "is that the Rolling Stones?"

"Yep. 'Gimme Shelter,' " Alan says. His voice is flat with rage. "Just a barrel of laughs for this sick fuck. Giving himself a little *mood* music."

The volume is up and the song is loud. As it picks up speed, the killer starts to dance. He has a knife in one hand, and he dances for Annie and for the camera. It's frenetic, crazy, but he does move with the beat. Insanity with a rhythm.

"Ra-a-ape, murder…"

This is why he picked this song. That's his message. It echoes my sentiments earlier in the day. What he can do, it's always just a step away. I close my eyes for a moment as I see that Annie, too, realized this. It is something I can see in her eyes. Terror mixed with a loss of hope.

The killer has stopped dancing, though he still twitches to the beat. His movements seem almost unconscious. Like someone tapping their foot to a song without realizing they're doing it. He is standing by the bed, his eyes fixed on Annie. He seems mesmerized. Annie is struggling. I can't hear it over the music, but I can tell she is screaming through her gag. He looks at the camera once more. Then he bends forward with the knife.

The rest of it is as Leo had said. A montage. Flashes of Annie's torture, rape, horror. The knife is what he uses on her, and he takes his time with it. He likes to cut slowly, and he likes to cut long. He touches her everywhere with its blade. I physically jolt as each new image flashes. Full body spasms that make me feel like I'm being shocked by a car battery. Flash, shock, jolt, Annie getting tortured. Flash, shock, jolt, Annie getting raped. Flash, shock, jolt, he cuts, he cuts, he cuts, dear God, he won't stop cutting. Her eyes fill with agony, her eyes fill with terror, and eventually they empty and fill with an endless gaze at nothing. Still alive, but no longer there. The killer is joyous, exultant. He is doing a rain dance, and the rain is blood. I watch as my friend dies. It is slow and awful and without dignity. By the time he is done, she is long since gone, a gutted fish. Watching her die, this woman I held as a child, this woman I grew up with and loved, it's like being back in that bed, watching Matt scream.

I have not truly wept for Annie since she died. I find that I am weeping now, that I have been throughout.

They are silent tears, rivers running down my cheeks. They mourn the death of the only other person besides Matt who knew all of me. I am alone in this world. I have no roots, and it is unbearable.

Annie, I think—you so didn't deserve this.

I don't wipe them away. I'm not ashamed of these tears. They make sense.

The video finishes playing, and everyone is silent.

"Play it again," I say.

Play it again, because there is a dragon inside me, and she is awakening.

I need her to wake up angry.

14

So, LET ME get this straight," Alan says. "He not only shot this video, he sat down and edited it?"

Leo bobs his head up and down. "Yep. But not on this computer. Hard drive isn't big enough, and there's no editing software on it. He probably brought a high-powered laptop with him."

Alan whistles. "He's a cold one, Smoky. That means he sat and edited the video while your friend was lying there dead, and Bonnie was watching. Or worse."

No one has said anything about my tears. I feel empty, but I am no longer numb. I respond.

"Cold, organized, competent, technically proficient—and he's definitely the real thing."

"What do you mean?" Leo asks.

I look at him. "He's crossed a line, as a person, and he'll never come back from that. He loved what he was doing. It really made him come alive. You're not going to do something you love that much just one time."

He looks at me, taken aback by this concept. "So now what?"

"Now you all get out, and we get James over here."

I hear my own voice as I say this, note its coldness. Well, well, I think. It's started. It's still there. How about that?

Charlie and Leo look confused. Alan understands. He smiles, not really a happy smile. "She and James need some space, is all. We have plenty to do in the meantime. You want me to take over for James at the ME's?" he asks me.

"Uh-huh..." My reply is distracted and distant. I barely register it when they leave. My mind is a huge, open space. My gaze is fixed on the faraway.

Because the dark train is coming.

I can hear it in the distance, *chug-a-chug-a-chug-a-chug-a*, belching smoke, made up of teeth and heat and shadows.

I met the dark train (as I call it) during my very first case. It is a thing hard to describe. The train of life runs on the tracks of normality and reality. It is the train most of humanity rides, from birth to death. It is filled with laughter and tears, hardships and triumphs. Its passengers are not perfect, but they do their best.

The dark train is different.

The dark train runs on tracks made of crunching, squishy things. It's the train that people like Jack Jr. ride. It's a train fueled by murder and sex and screams. It's a big, black, blood-drinking snake with wheels. If you hop off the train of life and run through the woods, you can find the dark train. You can walk next to its tracks, run alongside as it passes, get a glimpse of the weeping contents of its boxcars. Jump aboard, move through its corpse cars, through the whispers and bones, and you will reach the train's conductor. The conductor is the monster you are chasing, and he has many guises. He can be short and bald and forty. He can be tall and young and blond. Sometimes, rarely, he can be a she. On the dark train, you see the conductor as he really is, underneath the fake smiles and three-piece suits. You stare into darkness, and at that moment, if you look without flinching, you will understand.

These killers I hunt are not quiet and smiling inside. Every cell in their body is an unending, eternal scream. They are gibbering and wide-eyed and evil and blood-covered. They are things that masturbate as they gobble human flesh, that groan in ecstasy as they rub themselves with brains and feces. Their souls don't walk: They slither, they spasm, they crawl.

The dark train, simply, is where I remove the killer's mask in my mind. Where I look and don't turn away. It is the place where I don't back off, or excuse or look for reasons, but instead accept. Yes, his eyes are filled with maggots. Yes, he drinks the tears of murdered children. Yes, there is only murder here.

"Interesting," Dr. Hillstead had remarked during one of our sessions, after I had explained the dark train to him. "I guess my question—and my concern—Smoky, would be: Once you get on, what keeps you from never getting off the train? What keeps you from becoming the conductor?"

I had to smile. "If you see it—really see it—then there's no danger of that. You can see that you aren't like that. Not even close." I turned my head to stare at him. "If you really unmask the conductor, you realize that he's alien. He's an aberration, a different species."

He'd acknowledged me, smiled back. His eyes didn't seem convinced.

What I didn't tell him was that the problem wasn't becoming the conductor. The problem was to stop *seeing* him, how he looked in his unmasked state. That could take months sometimes, months of waking nightmares and cold sweats at dawn. The thing that was always hardest on Matt was that it was made up of silences. Closed rooms he couldn't join me in.

That's the price you pay for riding the dark train. A

part of you becomes a solitude that normal people will never have and no one else can ever enter. A little sliver of you becomes alone, forever.

Standing here, in Annie's death place, I can feel it rushing toward me. When it's coming, whether I'm just watching it pass or moving through its cars, I can't have others around me. I get distant and cold and . . . not nice. The exception is a fellow hobo. Someone else who understands the train.

James does. Whatever other faults he has, however much of an asshole he can be, James has the same gift. He can see the conductor, ride the rails.

Removing all the metaphors, the dark train is a place of heightened observation, created by a temporary empathy with evil.

And it's unpleasant.

I look around the room, letting it seep into me. I can feel him, smell him. I need to be able to taste him, hear him. Rather than pushing him away, I need to pull him close. Like a lover.

That is the thing I never told Dr. Hillstead. I don't think I ever will. That this, that intimacy, is not only disturbing— it is addictive. It is exciting. He hunts everything. I only hunt him. But I suspect my taste for blood is just as rich and strong.

He was here, so this is where I need to be. I need to find him, and snuggle close to his shadows and maggots and screams.

The first thing I sense is always the same, and this time is no different. His excitement at the invasion of another's boundaries. Human beings divide themselves, create spaces to call their own. They agree between them to respect that ownership. This is very basic, almost primal. Your home is your home. Once the door is closed, you have privacy, relief from keeping up the face you show the world. Other human beings come in only if invited. They respect this because it's what they want as well.

The first thing the monsters do, the first thing that excites them, is to cross that line. They peek into your windows. They follow you throughout your day, watching. Maybe they enter your home while you are away and walk into your private spaces, rub up against your private things. They invade.

And destruction of others is their aphrodisiac.

I remember an interview with one of the monsters I caught. His victims were young girls. Some were five, some were six, none were older. I saw the pictures of them before—bows in their hair and radiant smiles. I saw the pictures of them after—raped, tortured, murdered. Tiny corpses screaming forever. I was wrapping up, about to head out the door of the interrogation room, when the question occurred to me. I turned to him.

"Why them?" I asked. "Why the young girls?"

He smiled at me. A big, wide, Halloween smile. His eyes were two twinkling, empty wells. "Because it was the worst thing I could think of, darlin'. The badder it is"— and he'd licked his lips at this—"the better it is." He'd closed those nothing eyes and had shaken his head back and forth in a kind of reverie. "The young ones... GOD...the badness of that was just so damn *sweet*!"

It's rage that fuels this need. Not pinprick annoyance, but full-blown, world-on-fire rage. A constant, roaring blaze that never dies. I feel it here. As deliberate as he might want to be, in the end he destroyed in a frenzy. He was out of control.

This rage usually comes from extreme sadism visited upon them when they were children. Beatings, torture, sodomy, rape. Most of these monsters are made by Frankenstein parents. Twisted ones create children in their own image. They beat their souls to death and send them out in the world to do unto others.

None of that makes any pragmatic difference. Not in terms of what I do. The monsters are, without exception, irredeemable. It doesn't matter why the dog bites, in the end. That he bites and that his teeth are sharp are what determines his fate.

I live with all of this knowledge. This understanding. It is an unwanted companion that never leaves my side. The monsters become my shadow, and sometimes I feel like I can hear them chuckling behind me.

"How does that affect you, long term?" Dr. Hillstead had asked me. "Is there any constant emotional consequence?"

"Well—sure. Of course." I had struggled to find the words. "It's not depression, or cynicism. It's not that you can't be happy. It's . . ." I'd snapped my fingers, looking at him. "It's a change in the climate of the soul." I'd grimaced as soon as the words left my mouth. "That's some silly poetic bullshit."

"Stop that," he'd admonished me. "There's nothing silly about finding the right words for something. It's called clarity. Finish the thought."

"Well . . . you know how land masses that are near the ocean have their climates determined by it? By that proximity? There may be some freak twists in the weather, but pretty much it's a constant, because the ocean is so big and it doesn't really change." I'd looked at him; he'd nodded. "It's like that. You have this constant proximity to something huge and dark and awful. It never leaves, it's always there. Every minute of every day." I shrugged. "The climate of your soul is affected by it. Forever."

His eyes had been sad. "What is that climate like?"

"Someplace where there's a lot of rain. It can still be beautiful—you do have your sunny days—but it's dominated by grays and clouds. And it's always ready to rain. That proximity is always there."

I look around Annie's bedroom, hear her screams in my head. It's raining right now, I think. Annie was the sun, and he is the clouds. So what does that make me? More poetic bullshit. "The moon," I whisper to myself. Light against the black.

"Hi."

James's voice startles me out of my reverie. He's standing at the door, looking in. I see his eyes roaming over the room, taking in the bloodstains, the bed, the overturned night table. His nostrils flare.

"What is that?" he murmurs.

"Perfume. He coated a towel with perfume and stuffed it under the door so the smell of Annie's body wouldn't get out right away."

"He was buying himself time."

"Yeah."

He holds up a file folder. "I got this from Alan. Crime-scene reports and photos."

"Good. You need to see the video."

When it starts, this is how it goes. We talk in short bursts, automatic gunfire. We become relay racers, passing the baton back and forth, back and forth.

"Show me."

So we sit down, and I watch it again. Watch as Jack Jr. capers around, watch as Annie screams and dies a slow death. I don't feel it this time. I'm untouched—almost. I'm detached and distant, examining the train with narrowed eyes. I get an image in my head of Annie, lying dead in a grassy field, while rain fills her open mouth and dribbles down her dead gray cheeks.

James is quiet. "Why did he leave this for us?"

I shrug. "I'm not there yet. Let's take it from the beginning."

He flips open the file folder. "They discovered the body at approximately seven P.M. last night. Time of death is rough, but based on the decomposition, ambient temperatures, et cetera, the ME estimates she died three days before, at around nine or ten P.M."

I think it through. "Figure he took a few hours raping and torturing her. That means he'd have gotten here at around seven o'clock. So he doesn't come in while they're asleep. How does he get inside?"

James consults the file. "No sign of forced entry. Either she let him in, or he let himself in." He frowns. "He's a cocky fucker. Doing it early evening, when everyone is still up and about. Confident."

"But how does he get in?" We look at each other, wondering.

Rain, rain, go away . . .

"Let's start in the living room," James says.

Automatic gunfire, *bang-a-bang-a-bang.*

We walk out of the bedroom and down the hall until we're standing in the entryway. James looks around. I see his eyes stop roaming and freeze. "Hang on." He goes to Annie's bedroom and comes back holding the file. He hands me a photo.

"That's how."

It's a shot of the entryway, just inside the door. I see what he wants me to see: three envelopes lying on the carpet. I nod. "He kept it simple—he just knocked. She opens the door, he slams through it, she drops the mail she's holding. It was sudden. Fast."

"It was early evening, though. How did he keep her from screaming and alerting the neighbors?"

I grab the folder from him and scan through photos. I point to one of the dining table. "Here." It shows an opened grade-school math book. We glance over at the table. "It's less than ten feet away. Bonnie was right here when Annie answered the door."

He nods in understanding. "He controlled the kid, so he controlled the mother." He whistles. "Wow. That means he came right in. No hesitation."

"It was a blitz. He didn't give her any time at all. Pushed his way in, slammed the door, moved right to Bonnie, probably put a weapon to her throat—"

"—and told the mother if she screamed, the kid would die."

"Yeah."

"Very decisive."

Rain, rain, go away . . .

James purses his lips, thoughtful.

"So the next question is: How soon before he got down to business?"

Here is where it really begins, I think. Where we don't just consider the dark train, we climb aboard. "It's a series of questions." I count them off on my fingers. "How soon before he started on her? Did he tell her what he was going to do? And what did he do with Bonnie in the meantime? Did he tie her up or make her watch?"

We both look at the front door, considering. I can see it in my head. I can feel him. I know James is doing the same.

It's quiet in the hallway, and he's excited. His heart is pounding in his chest as he waits for Annie to open the door. One hand is poised to knock again, the other holds . . . what? A knife?

Yeah.

*He has a story to give her, and he's rehearsed it many times.
Something simple, like…he's a neighbor from the floor below
with a question. Something that feels like it belongs.*

*She opens the door, and not just a crack. It's early evening; the
city is awake. Annie is at home, inside a security-gated apartment
building. All of her lights are on. She has no reason to be afraid.*

*He comes through the door before she can react, an unstop-
pable force. He pushes inside, knocking Annie down, closing the
door behind him. He rushes to Bonnie. He pulls her close and puts
the knife to her throat.*

"Make a sound and your daughter dies."

*Annie forces back the instinctive scream that had been build-
ing in her throat. Her shock is total. Everything has happened too
fast for her to process. She's still looking for some kind of rational
explanation. Maybe she's on a hidden-camera show, maybe a
friend is pulling a prank on her, maybe…crazy ideas, but crazy
would be better than the truth.*

Bonnie is gazing up at her, eyes full of fear.

Annie would have accepted then that this was no
prank. A stranger had a knife to her daughter's throat.
This was REAL.

*"What do you want?" was her first question. She was hoping
that she could bargain with this stranger. That he wanted something less than murder. Perhaps he was a burglar, or a rapist.
Please, oh please, she's thinking, don't let him be a pedophile.*

I remember something. "She had a small cut on her
throat," I say.

"What?"

"Bonnie. She had a small cut in the hollow of her
throat." I touch my own. "Here. I noticed it at the hospital."

I see James think about this. His face goes grim. "He
made it with the knife."

We can't be sure, of course. But it feels right.

The stranger takes the point of his knife and pricks the hollow of Bonnie's throat. Nothing major, just enough to draw a single bead of blood, a single gasp. Enough to show that he means business, to make Annie's heart jump and thud and quiver.

"Do what I say," he says, "or your daughter dies slow."

And right then, it was over. Bonnie was his leverage, and Annie belonged to him.

"I'll do whatever you want. Just don't hurt her."

He smells Annie's fear, and it excites him. An erection stirs in his trousers.

"I think Bonnie was there while he raped and tortured Annie. I think he made her watch it all," I say.

James cocks his head. "Why?"

"A few reasons. The main one is that he kept Bonnie alive. Why? It gave him an extra person he had to control. It would have been easier if he'd just killed her. But Annie was the prey. He's into torture, he likes fear. Anguish. Having Bonnie there, having Annie know she was there and seeing what was happening...it would have driven her insane. He would have liked that."

James mulls this over. "I agree. For another reason too."

"What?"

He looks me in the eye. "You. He's hunting you too, Smoky. And hurting Bonnie makes the cut that much deeper."

I stare at him in surprise.

He's right.

Chug-a-chug-a-chug-a-chug-a, the dark train is picking up speed...

"Do what I tell you, or I'll hurt your mommy," he says to Bonnie. He uses their love of each other like a cattle prod, driving them toward the bedroom.

"He moves them into the bedroom." I walk down the hall. James follows. We step inside. "He closes it." I reach over and shut the door. I imagine Annie, watching it close and not realizing that she would never see it open again.

James stares at the bed, thinking. Envisioning. "He still has two of them to control," he says. "He wouldn't have been afraid of Bonnie, but he can't relax yet, not until Annie's secured."

"Annie was handcuffed in the video."

"Right. So he made her handcuff herself. Just one wrist is all he'd need."

"Take these," he'd said to Annie, removing a pair of handcuffs from a bag, tossing them at her—

No, that wasn't right. Rewind.

He has the knife to Bonnie's throat. He looks at Annie. Looks her up and down, owning her with his eyes. Making sure she understands this.

"Strip," he says. "Strip for me."

She hesitates, and he wiggles the blade against Bonnie's throat. "Strip."

Annie does, weeping, as Bonnie watches. She leaves her bra and panties on, one last resistance.

"All of it!" he growls at her. Wiggles the knife.

Annie complies, weeping harder now—

No. Rewind.

Annie complies and forces herself not to weep. To be strong for her daughter. She removes her bra and panties and holds Bonnie's eyes with her own. Look at my face, she's thinking, willing. Look at my face. Not this. Not him.

Now he removes the handcuffs from the bag he'd brought in.

"Handcuff your wrist to the bed," he tells Annie. "Do it now."

She does. Once he hears the click of the ratchet, he reaches into the bag and pulls out two other pairs of handcuffs. These go around Bonnie's tiny wrists and ankles. She is trembling. He ignores her sobs as he gags her. Bonnie looks at her mother, a pleading look. A look that says: "Make it stop!" This makes Annie cry harder.

He's still cautious, careful. He's not letting himself relax yet. He moves over to Annie and handcuffs her other wrist to the bed. Followed by her ankles. Then he gags her.

Now. Now he can relax. His prey is secure. She can't escape, won't escape.

Didn't escape, I think.

Now he can savor the moment.

He takes his time setting up the room. Positioning the bed, getting the video camera just right. There is a way that things are done, a symmetry that is important, vital. You don't rush this. To miss a step is to take away from the beauty of the act, and the act is everything. It's his air and his water.

"The bed," James says.

"What?" I look at it, puzzled.

He stands up and walks over to the baseboard. Annie's bed is queen-size, formed of smooth, rounded wooden pieces. Sturdy.

"How did he move it?" He walks to the headboard and looks down at the carpet. "Drag marks. So he pulled it toward him." He moves back to the base of the bed. "He would have gripped it somewhere here and pulled it by walking backward. He'd need leverage..." James kneels down. "He'd have grabbed it at the bottom and lifted it." He stands up, walks to the side of the bed, drops onto his back, and squirms under the bed up to his shoulders. I see the light of his flashlight go on, then back off. When he comes back out, he is smiling. "No print powder there."

We look at each other. I can almost feel each of us crossing our fingers.

People make the mistake of thinking that latex gloves prevent the transfer of fingerprints. In most cases, this is true. But not always. These types of gloves were originally developed for surgeons so they could maintain a sterile buffer during operations. The flip side of this is that the gloves have to fit like a second skin for the surgeons to use their instruments with no loss of precision or sensitivity. This tightness and thinness can cause the gloves to form-fit into the ridges and bifurcations of the prints on the hand and fingertips. If—and this is a big if, but still possible—someone wearing the gloves then touches a surface that can take an impression, they can leave a usable print. Annie's bed is made of wood. It's possible that cleaning solutions used on it could have left a residue that would retain a fingerprint impression, even through the killer's gloves.

A long shot. But possible.

"Good one," I say.

"Thanks."

Oil and ball bearings, I think. On the killing ground, this is the only place that James plays nice.

The stage is set. He's moved the bed . . . just so. The camera is positioned . . . just so. He does one last check to make sure that everything is perfect. It is. Now he gives Annie his full attention, gazing down at her.

This is the first time she truly sees. He's been distracted, setting up his theater. She still had hope. Now his gaze is fixed on her, and she understands. She sees eyes that have no horizon. They are bottomless, black, and filled with an unending hunger.

He knows when she knows. When she understands. It enflames him, like it always does. He has extinguished hope in another human being.

It makes him feel like a god.

James and I have arrived at the same place on thi

timeline. We are there. We see him, we see Annie, and out of the corner of our eyes, we see Bonnie. We smell the despair. The dark train is picking up speed, and we are along for the ride, tickets punched.

"Now let's watch the video again," he says.

I double-click the file, and we watch as the montage rolls by. He dances, he slices, he rapes.

The sheer violence of what he is doing sprays blood everywhere, and he can smell it, taste it, feel the slick of it through his clothes. At one point, he turns to look at the child. Her face is white, and her body shakes as though she's having a seizure. This creates an almost unbearable, near-orgasmic symphony of delicious extremes for him. He shivers, every muscle shaking with emotion and sensation. He isn't just being bad. He is raping good. Fucking it to death. Music and blood and guts and screams and terror. The world is shaking, and he is its epicenter. He is climbing toward the pinnacle, and he lets it come to him—that point where all of it explodes in a searing, blinding light, where all reason and anything human disappears.

It is a brief moment, and it is the only time that the hunger and need fade to nothing. A tiny instant of fulfillment and relief.

The knife comes down and there is blood and blood and wet and blood and he is climbing, climbing, climbing, standing on tiptoes at the peak of a mountain, stretching his body as far as it will go, reaching a finger out, not to touch the face of God, not to become something MORE, but to become nothing, nothing at all, and he throws his head back as his body shakes with an orgasm more powerful than he can stand.

Then it's over, and the anger that is always there returns.

Something jitters in my mind. "Hold it," I say. I use the controls of the player to rewind the video. I let it play. That jitter again. I frown, frustrated. "Something's not [can]'t put my finger on it."

[frame] by frame on this?" James asks.

We play around with it a bit until we find a setting that, though not frame by frame, at least takes us through it in slow motion.

"Somewhere in here," I murmur.

We both lean forward, watching. It is toward the end of the tape. He is standing next to Annie's bed. I see a flicker, and he is still standing next to Annie's bed, but something is different.

James sees it first. "Where's the picture?"

We roll it back again. He is standing next to the bed, and on the wall behind him is a picture of a vase of sunflowers. The flicker again, he is still standing next to the bed—but the picture is gone.

"What the hell?" I look over at the place on the wall where the picture would have hung. I see it, leaning up against the overturned end table.

"Why did he remove it from the wall?" James asks. He's asking himself, not me.

We run through it again. Standing, picture, flicker, standing—no picture. Over and over. Standing, flicker, picture, no picture, picture no picture...

Understanding doesn't just rush over me. It roars. My mouth falls open, and I get light-headed. "Jesus Christ!" I yell, startling James.

"What?"

I rewind the video. "Watch it again. This time, note where the top of the picture frame is, and track that point on the wall once it's gone."

The video moves through, we pass the flicker. James frowns. "I don't—" He stops and his eyes widen. "Is that right?" He sounds incredulous. I run through it again.

There's no doubt. We both stare at each other. Everything has changed.

We know now why the picture had been removed. It

had been removed because it was a frame of reference. For height.

The man standing over Annie while the picture was still on the wall was a good two inches taller than the man standing over her after it was removed.

We'd reached the engine room on the dark train and had been thrown out of it by the shock of what we saw.

Not one conductor.

Two.

15

"YOU'RE RIGHT," LEO says. He looks up at James and me in amazement.

He has just finished examining the video. "That flicker is a bad splice."

Callie, Jenny, and Charlie are there, crowded around the monitor. We had filled them in on the sequence of events as we saw them, ending with this bombshell.

Jenny looks at me. "Wow."

"You run across anything like this before?" Charlie asks. "Two of them working together?"

I nod. "Once. It was different, though. A male-female team, and the male was dominant. Two males working together, that's very unusual. What they do, it's personal to them. Intimate. Most don't like to share the moment."

Everyone is quiet, mulling this over. Callie breaks the silence. "I should check for those prints, honey-love."

"I should have thought of that," Jenny says.

"Yes, you should have," James bites. He's back to his old self.

Jenny glares at him. He ignores her, turning to watch Callie.

Callie is unpacking a UV scope and its accoutrements. The scope uses intensified ultraviolet reflectance to detect fingerprints. It emits intense light in the UV spectrum. This light reflects uniformly off flat surfaces. When it hits imperfections—such as the ridges and whorls of finger-prints—it reflects these as well, making them stand out against the uniformity of the surface they are on. You can take crystal-clear photographs of these imperfections with a UV camera, usable in fingerprint matching and identification.

The imager boasts a head-mounted display that pro-tects the eyes from the UV rays, a UV emitter, and a hand-carried, high-resolution UV camera. The scope doesn't always work, but the advantage of trying it first is that it does nothing to the surface you're examining. Powders, superglue...once these substances are applied, you can't take them back. Light leaves it the way you found it.

"All ready," Callie says. She looks like something from a science-fiction movie. "Turn out the lights."

Charlie hits the switch, and we watch as Callie gets onto her back and squirms under the bed. We can see the glow of the UV emitter as she passes it across the surface of the baseboard. A pause, some fumbling, and we hear a few clicks. A few more clicks. The emitter light goes out and Callie squirms back out, stands up. Charlie turns the lights on.

Callie is grinning. "Three good prints from the left hand, two from the right. Nice and clear, honey-love."

For the first time since Callie called me to tell me about Annie's death, I feel something besides anger, grief, and coldness. I feel excited.

"Gotcha," I say, grinning back at her.

Jenny shakes her head at me. "You guys are truly, truly spooky, Smoky."

Just riding the dark train, Jenny, I think to myself. Let-ting it lead us to their mistakes.

"Question," Alan says. "How come no one complained about the music? They had the volume up pretty high."

"I can answer that one, honey-love," Callie says. "Just be quiet and listen."

We do, and I hear it right away. The thumps of loud bass, mixed with muffled treble, coming from various places in floors above and below.

Callie shrugs. "Young people and couples live here, and some like to play their music loud."

Alan nods. "I'll buy that. Second point." He gestures around at the room. "They were messy. Real messy. There's no way they just walked out of here covered in blood. They had to clean up first. The bathroom looks pristine, so I'm thinking that they washed up in there and scrubbed it down after." He turns to Jenny. "Did the Crime Scene Unit check the drains?"

"I'll find out." Her cell phone rings, and she answers it. "Chang." She looks at me. "Really? Right. I'll tell her."

"What now?" I ask.

"That was my guy at the hospital. He said Bonnie spoke. Just a sentence, but he thought you'd want to know."

"What?"

"She said, 'I want Smoky.' "

16

JENNY GOT ME to the hospital fast; she pulled out the stops, used her siren to run red lights. Neither of us spoke on the way over.

I'm standing by Bonnie's bed now, looking down at her as she gazes up at me. I am again struck by how much she looks like her mother. It's disorienting; I just came from watching her mother die, and yet here Annie looks up at me, alive through her daughter.

I smile down at her. "They said you asked for me, honey."

She nods, but doesn't speak. I realize there won't be any more words coming from Bonnie right now. The glazed look of shock is gone from her eyes, but something else has settled in and put down roots. Something distant and hopeless and heavy.

"I need to ask you two questions first, honey. Is that okay?"

She looks at me, speculative. Apprehensive. But she nods.

"There were two bad men, weren't there?"

Fear. Her lip trembles. But she nods.

Yes.

"Good, honey. Just one more, and then we won't talk

about it anymore right now. Did you see either of their faces?"

She closes her eyes. Swallows. Opens them. Shakes her head.

No.

Inside, I sigh. I am not surprised, but it's still frustrating. Time for that later. I take Bonnie's hand.

"I'm sorry, honey. You asked to see me. You don't have to tell me what you want if you still can't talk. But can you show me?"

She continues to look up at me. She seems to be looking for something in my eyes, some reassurance. I can't tell from her expression whether she is finding it or not. But she nods.

Then she reaches over and takes my hand. I wait, but that's all she does. And then I understand.

"You want to come with me?"

She nods again.

A million thoughts shoot through my head at this. About how I'm unfit to care for myself, much less her. How I'm on a case, and so who's going to watch her? I think these things, but none of it really matters. All I do is smile down at her and squeeze her hand. "I have some things to do, but when I'm ready to leave San Francisco, I'll come get you."

She continues to gaze into my eyes. Seems to find that thing she'd been looking for. She gives my hand a squeeze, and then she lets go, turns her head into her pillow, and closes her eyes. I stand there for a moment, looking down at her.

I walk out of that room knowing something's changed in my life. I wonder whether it's good or bad, and realize that just now, that doesn't really matter. This isn't about good or bad or indifferent. It's about survival.

That's the level we're operating at right now, Bonnie and me.

We're headed back to SFPD. The car is filled with silence.

"So, you're going to take her?" Jenny asks, breaking it.

"I'm all she's got. Maybe she's all I have too."

Jenny chews on this. A small smile appears on her face. "That's good, Smoky. Real good. You don't want a kid her age in the system. She's too old. No one would adopt her."

I turn to her. I sense something hidden here. Some undercurrent accompanying her words. I frown. She shoots me a tense look. Then relaxes with a sigh.

"I was an orphan. My parents died when I was four, and I grew up in the system. No one seemed interested in adopting a Chinese kid at the time."

I'm shocked and surprised. "I had no idea."

She shrugs. "It's not something you share a lot. You know, 'Hi, I'm Jenny Chang, and I was an orphan.' I don't like to talk about it much." She looks at me, emphasizing that this moment is no exception. "But I will say this: You did a good thing there. Something pure."

I think about this and know what she says is true. "It does feel right. Annie left her to me—or so I hear. I haven't seen her will yet. Is it true he left it next to Annie's body?"

"Yeah. It's in the file."

"Did you look at it?"

"Yep." She pauses again. Another one of those thoughtful, weighty pauses. "She left everything in your hands, Smoky. The daughter is the true beneficiary, but she named you as executor and trustee. She must have been some friend."

I ache at this sentiment. "She was my best friend. Since high school."

Jenny is quiet for a few moments after this. When she speaks, it's a single word, but it's filled with everything she wants me to know. "Fuck."

Fuck that, and fuck the world, and injustice, and what happened to you, and your daughter dying, and kids getting killed in general, and fuck it all till it's dead and buried and turned to dust and the dust is gone forever. That's what she's saying.

I reply in kind.

"Thanks."

17

DO YOU WANT the full version, or the condensed version?"

Alan opens the folder containing the autopsy report as he says this.

"The condensed version. Please."

"Here are the basics. The killer or killers raped her, both pre- and postmortem. He or they cut her with a sharp blade before she died, with most of the damage inflicted being nonlethal."

Torture. I nod for him to go on.

"Cause of death is exsanguination. She bled out, due to the severing of the jugular." He glances at a page in the folder. "Once she was dead, and they were done having their fun with her body, they cut her open. They removed the internal organs and placed them in Baggies, which were left by the body." He looks up at me. "All the organs are accounted for except the liver."

"They probably took it with them," James says into the silence that follows. "Or ate it." I hide a shiver at these words. I'm sure he's right.

"Examination of the wounds shows that they're consistent with those caused by a scalpel, which fits. Because the ME says that the removal of the organs was skillful.

Not just the surgery, but knowing where the organs were and how to remove them intact. They not only separated the large and small intestines, they divided them into their component parts. Three for the small intestine, four for the large."

I think about this for a moment. "Did he—sorry, *they*—dissect any other organ in the same way?"

He consults the file, then shakes his head. "No." He looks up at me. "They were showing off."

"That's good," I say, grim.

Leo's look at me is incredulous. "How is that good?"

Alan turns to him, answering the question for me. "It's good because the way we catch these guys is that they make mistakes. If they're showing off, that means the act itself isn't enough for them. They also want our attention. That means they're not going to be as careful as they could be. Or should be. So they're more likely to make mistakes."

"In simpler terms, child," Callie says, "it means they're even more Looney Tunes than usual. That increases the chances of them slipping up."

"I get it." Leo says this but looks a little bit disturbed as he thinks it over. I understand. Looking at the dissection of human organs by two psychopaths as a bright spot is hard to get your mind around. He's probably wondering if he wants to get his mind around it.

Alan continues. "Once they'd removed the organs, they left the body cavity open and tied Bonnie to her body." He closes the folder. "No seminal fluids found, and there was some evidence of latex in the vagina."

They'd used rubbers to prevent leaving their DNA.

"Nothing else. No hairs or fingerprints found on or in the body. That's it."

"So what does that leave?"

James shrugs. "Look at the rest of the picture. There weren't any hesitation wounds. They were operating at a high level of certainty in what they were doing when it came to cutting her open. One of them may have had formal medical training. I think it's probable."

"Or they've just had a lot of practice," Callie murmurs.

"What else do we know?" I look around at each of them. Alan pulls out a legal pad and a pen at my words. This is a part of our routine. He's ready to jot down any relevant thoughts and musings.

"We know they're both white, both males," Callie says. "One is close to six feet tall, the other is approximately five ten. Both are in shape."

Alan speaks next. "They're careful. They understand the basics of transference and take precautions to avoid it. No hair, no epithelials, and no semen."

"But they're not as smart as they think they are," I note. "We have the fingerprints on the bed. And we figured out that there are two of them."

"Well, that's the problem, isn't it?" Alan says in a wry voice. "If they really understood transference, they'd understand it always happens, somehow."

Alan is referring to "Locard's Principle." Locard is considered the father of modern forensics, and we all know the principle by heart: *When two objects come into contact, there is always transfer of material from one to the other, and such material may be small or large, may be difficult to detect; nevertheless it occurs, and it is the responsibility of the investigating team to gather all such material however small they may be and prove the transference.*

Our killers were careful. The absence of semen is telling. It shows control. With the advent of crime books, television shows, and HIV, rapists using rubbers is on the rise. But it's still unusual. Rape is about sexual power and violation. Rapists get high on the intensity of sensation this gives them. Condoms get in the way of both the violation and the sensation. Jack Jr. and friend used them, making Alan's point for him.

"We know they're not perfect," James says. "They have an immediate weakness—showing off and wanting to taunt us. That's higher risk and creates the possibility of them screwing up at some point."

"Right. What else?"

"At least one of them is technically proficient." This is from Leo. "I mean, it's not rocket science these days, editing video. But there is a learning curve, the way they did it. Not something your average computer user is going to know right off the bat."

"We think they're based in LA, right?" Callie says.

I shrug. "We're going on that premise. But it's something we suspect, not something we know. We do know their victim type. They told us—they're planning to go after other women like Annie." I turn to Leo. "What did they call her in the letter?"

"A modern-day whore of the information superhighway."

"What about that? What kind of numbers are we talking about?"

Leo grimaces at the question. "Thousands, if you take the U.S. as a whole. Maybe close to a thousand even if you narrow it to just California. But that's not the only problem. Think of it this way: Every girl with a site is potentially an independent contractor. While some are sponsored under the umbrella of a single company, a *lot* of them are like your friend. They design, maintain, and operate their own Web sites. It's a business of one, with a single employee. And there's no chamber of commerce for this type of business. There are lists of these types of sites in various places, but there isn't any one single consortium."

I think on this bit of bad news. Something occurs to me. "Fair enough, but what if we take it from this view: Instead of looking at everyone in that industry, let's look for the places where the killers could have found Annie. You say there are lists of these types of sites, right?"

He nods.

"It's unlikely that she's on every one of those. We look for the ones she does appear on, then we narrow the field to just the other women on those particular lists."

Now he is shaking his head again, but not in agreement. "It's not that simple. What if they found her by using a search engine? And if they did, what word or phrase did they use? Also, most site operators like her put up their own 'feeder sites.' Small, free sites with sample photos and a link to their primary site. Kind of a 'sample the goods and if you like it, come into the store.' They could also have found one of those sites."

"Not to mention the fact that they could have found her through you, Smoky." Callie sounds reluctant as she says this. I give her a look of agreement. Followed by a sigh of discouragement.

"So the Web end of it leads us nowhere?"

"Not nowhere," Leo says. "The one place to look is her subscriber list. The people who paid to see her 'members only' area."

My ears perk up at this. Alan is nodding. "Right, right," he says. "That's how they got all those perps in the kiddie-porn sting, yeah?"

Leo smiles at him. "Yep. There are a lot of laws and oversight when it comes to credit-card processing. Fairly precise records are kept. Best of all, most processors have a built-in address check. Where the address given at sign-up has to match the address of the cardholder they have on record."

"Do we know how many subscribers she had?"

"Not yet. It won't be hard to find out. We'll need to get a warrant, but most of those companies are easy to work with. I wouldn't expect any trouble."

"I want you to work on that when we get back," I tell him. "Alan can walk you through the warrant end of things. Get the list and start combing through it. I also want her computer scrutinized. Look for anything—*anything*—that might be a clue. Maybe she noticed something off, made a note to herself..."

"Right. I'll also get her e-mail. Depending on who her provider is, they should still have copies of anything recent that's not already sitting on her computer."

"Good."

"There's something else," Jenny says. "They went to a lot of trouble to make us think there was only one of them."

"Maybe they were hoping to confuse us with it later, somehow," I say. "I don't know. I haven't worked that one out yet." I shake my head. "Bottom line is, we have something to run with. The prints." I turn to Callie. "Where do we stand on that?"

"I'm going to enter the prints into AFIS when we're done here and get the guys back in LA to run it. It can scan through a million prints in a minute or two, so just a few hours."

This, more than anything, excites everyone. It could be that simple. The Automated Fingerprint Identification System is a formidable tool. If we're lucky, we'll find our guy, quick.

"Let's get onto that right away."

"What did you and James figure out about them, Smoky?" Callie asks.

"Yeah, let's hear it," Alan rumbles. Both of them stare at me, waiting.

I knew they'd ask; they always do. I rode the dark choo-choo train, I saw the monsters, at least one of them. Callie and Alan want to know: What did you see?

"This is all just based on feelings and surmise," I say.

Alan waves his hand at me, a dismissive gesture. "Yeah, yeah, yeah. You always give us that same, lame disclaimer. Just tell us."

I smile at him and lean back, looking up at the ceiling. I close my eyes and gather it all in. Snuggle up against it, catch the scent.

"They're a little bit of an amalgam. I don't have them separated out yet. They are . . . smart. Very smart. Not just faking smart. I'm thinking at least one of them has a higher education." I glance at James. "Possibly medical school." He nods in agreement. "They're deliberate. Planners. Precise. They spent hours studying up on forensics so they could make sure to leave nothing behind. This is a very, very important part of it for them. Jack the Ripper was one of the most famous serial killers of all time. Why? For one thing, he *never got caught*. They're following in his footsteps, in this and other ways, mimicking him. He taunted the cops, so they're taunting us. His victims were prostitutes, so they're going after what is—to them—a modern-day equivalent. There will be other parallels."

"Narcissism is a problem for them," James interjects.

I nod. "Yeah."

Charlie frowns. "What do you mean?"

"Think of it this way: When you drive a car, do you have to think about it?" I ask.

"No. I just drive."

"Right. But for Jack Jr. and friend, driving isn't

enough. They need to admire how *good* their driving is. How perfect and artful it is. That type of narcissism, where they admire what they do as they're doing it…" I shrug. "If you take the time to watch yourself drive, you don't have both eyes on the road."

"Hence the fingerprints on the bed," James says. "That's not a small fuckup. We're not talking hair or fibers. We're talking about five prints. Too busy watching themselves be clever."

"Gotcha," Charlie replies.

"You know, when I said they were an amalgam, that's not entirely true." I purse my lips, considering. "There is a Jack Jr. I think that's a single identity. It's just too important to share." I look at James. "You agree?"

"Yeah."

"So what does that make the other guy?" Alan asks.

"I'm not sure. Maybe a student?" I shake my head. "I can't see it clearly. Not yet. I do think that Jack Jr., whichever one he is, is dominant."

"That's consistent with past 'double teams,'" Callie says.

"Yep. So, they are smart, precise, and narcissistic. But one of the things that makes them so dangerous is their willingness to commit. They don't have a problem with decisive action. That's bad for us, because it means they don't make things *too* complicated. They keep it clean and simple. Knock on the door, bust in, close the door, take control. A, B, C, D. That isn't a natural ability as a general rule. It's possible one or both of them has a background in the military or law enforcement. Something that would train them in the unhesitating subduing of another human being."

"The taste for rape and murder is real," James says.

"Isn't that a given?" Jenny asks.

I shake my head. "No. Sometimes someone tries to hide a regular murder in the guise of a serial killing. But what they did to Annie, how they did it...that was real. They're genuine."

"They have a dual victimology," James says.

Callie frowns. Sighs. "You mean they target us as well as the women they go after."

James nods. "That's right. The victim selection, in this instance, was specific and reasoned. Annie King fit two profiles for them. She ran an adult Web site, and she was the friend of someone on this team. They went to a lot of effort to get your attention, Smoky."

"Well, they got it." I sit back for a moment, running through it all in my head. "I guess that covers everything. Let's not forget the most important thing right now that we know about these guys."

"What's that?" Leo asks.

"That they're going to do it again. And keep doing it until we catch them."

18

I **HAD ASKED** Jenny to give me a ride to the hospital so that I could check in on Bonnie while everyone else worked on their appointed tasks.

When we arrive at the door to her room, the cop guarding it holds up a legal-size manila envelope. "This came for you, Agent Barrett."

Right away, I know something is wrong. There's no reason for anyone to be dropping anything off for me here. I snatch it out of his hands and look at it. Block letters on the front in black ink give it a simple address: ATTN.: SPECIAL AGENT BARRETT.

Jenny glares at him. "Jesus Christ, Jim! Use your head!" She's gotten it. Jim is a little slower on the uptake. I know when it hits him because his face turns ashen.

"Oh . . . shit."

I will give him this: His first action is to spin up and out of his chair and open the door to Bonnie's room, hand on his weapon. I'm right behind him, and I feel a relief that almost overwhelms me when I see her there asleep and safe. I motion for the cop to come back out. Once we're all outside, he puts it into words.

"This is probably from the killer, isn't it?"

"Yeah, Jim," I say, "it probably is." I don't have the

energy to make my voice sound biting. It comes out sounding tired. Jenny has no such problem. She stabs a finger into his chest with enough force to make him wince.

"You fucked up! Which pisses me off, because I know you're a good cop. You know how I know you're a good cop? Because I specifically requested you for this duty and knew you'd be more than just a warm body." She's fuming, far beyond being pissed off. For his part, Jim takes it all without a trace of resentment or justification.

"You're right, Detective Chang. I don't have a defense. The nurse at the station in reception brought it by. I saw Agent Barrett's name, but I didn't make the connection. I went back to reading my paper." He looks so hangdog at this point that I almost feel sorry for him. Almost. "Damn! I let myself get lulled into a routine! A rookie mistake! Damn, damn, damn!"

Jenny seems to feel for the cop a little too, now that he's so busy beating himself up. Her next words are more conciliatory. "You're a good cop, Jim. I know you. You'll remember this screwup till the day you die—which you should—but you probably won't ever let it happen again." She sighs. "Besides, you have done your primary duty here. You kept the kid safe."

"Thanks, Lieutenant, but that doesn't make me feel any better."

"How long ago did this get delivered to you?"

He thinks about it for a second. "I'd say...about an hour and a half. Yeah. The nurse at the station brought it to me and said that some guy delivered it. She figured I could get it to you."

"Go get all the details. How it was delivered, who, everything."

"Yes, ma'am."

I look at the envelope as Jim runs off. "Let's take a peek inside."

I open it. Inside is a sheaf of papers clipped together. I see at the top, *Greetings, Agent Barrett!* Which is enough for now. I look up at Jenny. "It's from him. Them."

"Damn it!"

My palms are a little sweaty. I know I need to read what's inside, but I dread this killer's next revelations. I sigh, fishing the ever-present pair of latex gloves I keep with me during investigations out of my jacket pocket. I slip them on, open it up, and pull out the clipped sheaf of papers. The letter is on top.

Greetings, Agent Barrett!

> *By now I imagine you are into the thick of it, you and your team. Did you enjoy the video I left for you? I thought the music I selected was particularly apropos.*
>
> *How is little Bonnie? Does she scream and weep, or is she simply silent? I wonder about this from time to time. Please, tell her I said hello.*
>
> *Most of my thoughts are, of course, devoted to you. How is the healing going, Agent Barrett? Still sleeping in the nude these days? With that pack of cigarettes on the nightstand to the left of your bed? I have been there, and I must say, you talk quite loudly in your sleep.*

"Holy shit," Jenny whispers.

I hand her the papers. "Hold on to these for a second."

She takes them. I run to the nearest trash can, where I proceed to vomit up everything inside my stomach. They'd been inside my house! Had watched me sleep! A thrill of terror spikes through me, followed by a nauseating sense of violation. Then anger. Beneath it all, terror remains as the backdrop. One thought shouts inside my head: It could happen again! My entire body is trembling, and I slam a fist against the rim of the trash can. I wipe my mouth with the back of my hand and walk back over to Jenny.

"You okay?"

"No. But let's finish it." She hands me back the papers. They shake in my hands as we continue.

> *Matthew and Alexa, such a shame. You, alone in that ghost ship of a home, staring at your disfigurement in the mirror. So sad.*
>
> *I think you are more beautiful scarred, though I know you believe that to be untrue. I'll say something helpful to you, Agent Barrett, just this once. Scars are not marks of shame. They are the brands of the survivor.*
>
> *You might wonder why I'd offer a helping hand. It springs from a sense of fairness. A need to make the game exciting. There are many in this world who could hunt me well, but you . . . I think you can hunt me best.*
>
> *I've gone to great effort to ensure that you are back in the game, and just one more thing is left, one last wound to stitch up.*
>
> *A hunter needs a weapon, Agent Barrett, and you cannot touch yours. We need to correct this, to bring balance to the game. Please find attached some information that I believe to be at the heart of this difficulty you are having. It may leave a scar of its own when you read it, but don't forget: A scar is always better than an unhealed, open wound.*
>
> *From Hell,*
> *Jack Jr.*

I flip over the page. It takes only a few moments for me to understand what it says. Everything around me goes silent and slow. I can see that Jenny is speaking to me, but I cannot hear her words.

I am cold, and getting colder. My teeth chatter, I start shivering, and the world begins tilting away from me. My heart pounds, faster, faster, and then sound returns in a chaotic flash, like a thunderclap. But I am still so cold.

"Smoky! Jesus—Doctor!"

I hear her, but I cannot speak. I can't stop my teeth from chattering. I see a doctor come over to me. He feels my head, looks into my eyes. "She's going into full-blown shock here," he says. "Lay her down flat. Put her feet up. Nurse!"

Jenny leans over me. "Smoky! Say something."

I wish I could, Jenny. But I am frozen, and the world is frozen, and the sun is frozen too. Everything and everyone is death, dead, or dying.

Because he was right. I read the paper and, just like that, I remembered.

It's a ballistics report. The part he'd circled for me said this: *Ballistics tests prove conclusively that the bullet removed from Alexa Barrett came from Agent Barrett's weapon....*

I was the one who shot my daughter.

I hear the sound and marvel at it, before I realize that it is coming from me. It is a shriek, beginning low in the throat and then climbing, octave after octave, until it seems high enough to break glass. There it hangs, like an opera singer's vibrato. It seems to go on forever.

Everything is going black now. Thank God.

19

I WAKE UP in a hospital bed to Callie hovering above me. There is no one else here. When I look at Callie's face, I know why.

"You knew, didn't you?"

"Yes, love," she says. "I knew."

I turn my face away from her. I have not felt so listless, so drained of life, since I woke in the hospital after that night with Sands. "Why didn't you tell me?" I don't know if there's any anger in my voice. Don't care.

"Dr. Hillstead asked me not to. He didn't think you were ready. And I agreed. Still do."

"Really? You think you know so goddamn much about me?" My voice sounds raw to me. The anger is there now, hot and poisonous.

Callie doesn't even flinch. "I know this: You're still alive. You didn't put a gun in your mouth and pull the trigger. I have no regrets, honey-love." She says the next in a whisper. "That doesn't mean it didn't hurt, Smoky. I loved Alexa, you know I did."

I snap around at this, look at her, and the anger drains away. Just like that. "I don't blame you. Or him. And maybe he was right, after all."

"Why do you say that, love?"

I shrug. I'm tired, so tired. "Because I remember every-thing now. But I still don't want to die." I hunch into my-self for a moment as pain shoots through me. "Which feels like such a betrayal, Callie. I feel like, if I want to live, then I didn't love them enough."

I look over at her, and I see that she is stricken by my words. My Callie, my happy-go-lucky Queen-Hell-on-Wheels, looks like I just punched her in the face. Or maybe the heart.

"Well," she says after a long moment, "that's not true. Going on after they're dead, Smoky—that doesn't mean you didn't love them. All it means is that they died and you didn't."

I file this profundity away for future thought; I can feel its merit. "Funny, isn't it? I've always been able to hit what I want with a gun. It's always come naturally to me. I remember aiming at his head, and then he was so damn fast. I've never seen anyone move that fast. He yanked Alexa off the bed and made her take the bullet for him. She was looking right into my eyes when it happened." My face twists. "You know, he almost looked surprised. With everything he'd done, he still had this look on his face, like for just a moment he thought he'd gone too far. And then I shot him."

"Do you remember that part, Smoky?"

I frown. "What do you mean?"

Callie smiles. It's a sad smile. "You didn't just shoot him, honey-love. You filled him up with bullets. You emp-tied four clips into him, and you were about to reload when I stopped you."

And just like that, I am there and I do remember.

He'd raped me, cut on me. Matt was dead. I was coast-ing on waves of pain, surfing in and out of consciousness. Everything was slightly surreal. Like being a little bit drugged. Or the hungover feeling you can get when you take an afternoon nap that's just a half hour too long.

There was a sense of urgency, I could feel it. But it was far away. I was feeling it through soft gauze. I'd have to wade through syrup to get to it.

Sands leaned forward, putting his face close to mine. I could feel his breath on my cheek. It was unnaturally hot. A flash of something sticky—I realized it was his spit, drying on my chest. I shivered once, a full-body shiver. A long, rolling shake.

"I'm going to undo your hands and feet now, sweet Smoky," he whispered in my ear. "I want you to touch my face before you die."

My eyes roll toward him, and then roll up into my head. I lose time. I coast back into awareness and feel him at my hands, loosening them. Coast back out, into the black. Surf in again, he's at my feet. Cowabunga. Light to shadow, shadow to light.

I come to again, and he's next to me, spooned into my side. He's naked, and I can feel that he's hard. His left hand is fisted into my hair, bending my head back. The right is draped over my stomach, and I can feel the knife in it. That breath again, sour and hot.

"Time to go, sweet Smoky," Sands whispers. "I know you're tired. You just have one more thing to do before you sleep." His breathing quickens. His erection stirs at my side, poking into my hip. "Touch my face."

And he's right. I am tired. So damn tired. I just want to coast into the black, have it all be done and gone and over. I feel my hand coming up, to do this last thing he wants—and then it happens.

"MOMMY!" I hear Alexa scream. It is a scream of full-throated terror.

It's a backhanded, bone-rattling slap across my face.

"He told us Alexa was dead, Callie," I whisper in the hospital room. "Said he killed her first. I heard her scream, and I realized that he'd lied to me, and I knew—I KNEW—he was going to see her next!" I clench my fist as I remember, and feel my body trembling in anger and terror, all over again.

It was as though someone had detonated a bomb inside me. I did not just come awake, I exploded. The dragon crawled up from inside my belly, and she roared, and roared, and roared.

I smashed Sands's face, felt his nose crunch under the heel of my hand. He grunted, and I was off the bed and heading for the nightstand where I kept my gun, but he was like an animal. Feral and oh-so-fast. No hesitation. He rolled onto the floor and was sprinting out the bedroom door. I heard his feet pounding on the hardwood floors of the hallway, heading toward Alexa.

And I began to scream. I felt like I was on fire. Everything was turning white hot, adrenaline was burning me up, and the intensity of it was excruciating. Time had changed. It hadn't slowed down, just the opposite. It sped up. Faster than thought.

I had my gun and was not so much *running* down the hallway as *teleporting* down it, moving toward Alexa's room in flashes rather than steps. And I was fast, damn fast, because he was only just turning into her doorway, and then I was there too, and I saw her. On the bed, the gag he had placed around her mouth now loosened. Good girl, I remember thinking.

"MOMMY!" she screamed again, eyes wide, cheeks flushed, rivers of tears. And now I was the animal, no hesitation, raising my gun, aiming for his head...

Then horror. Horror, horror, horror, going on forever, never ending, hell on earth.

Then me, screaming. Screaming, screaming, screaming, going on forever, never ending, hell on earth. Me, shooting Sands, over and over and over, determined to shoot him till I was out of ammo, and then—"Oh Jesus, Callie." Tears fill my eyes. "Jesus, Jesus, Jesus, I'm so sorry."

She takes my hand, shakes her head once. "Don't worry about it, Smoky." She squeezes my hand, a fierce squeeze. It almost hurts. "I mean it. You weren't in your right mind."

Because I remember hearing Callie bust in through my front door, seeing her appear, weapon drawn. I remember her moving toward me with exaggerated caution, telling me to put down my gun. Me screaming at her. Her moving toward me. I knew she wanted to take it away from me, and I knew I just couldn't let her do that. I still needed to put it to my head, to shoot myself, to die. I deserved to die for killing my child. So I did the only thing that seemed to make sense to me. I pointed the gun at Callie, and I fired.

It's pure luck that the chamber was empty. Thinking of it now, I remember that she didn't even slow down, just kept moving toward me until she got close enough to take away the gun, which she tossed to one side. After that I don't remember very much at all.

"I could've killed you," I whisper.

"Naw." She smiles again. It's still a little bit sad, but some of the mischievous Callie shines through. "You were aiming at my leg."

"Callie." I say it as a reprimand, albeit a gentle one. "I remember." I hadn't been aiming at her leg. I'd been aiming at her heart.

She leans forward and looks me right in the eyes. "Smoky, I trust you more than I trust anybody in this world. And that hasn't changed. I don't know what else to tell you. Except that I'll never talk about it with you again."

I close my eyes. "Who else knows?"

Silence. "Me. The team. AD Jones. Dr. Hillstead. That's it. Jones clamped down on it pretty hard."

Except that's not it, I think. *They* know.

I can tell she has something else to say.

"What?"

"Well...you should know: Dr. Hillstead is the only person who knows about your reaction to finding out today. Aside from Jenny and the rest of the team."

"You didn't tell AD Jones?"

She shakes her head. "No."

"Why not?"

Callie lets go of my hand. She looks uneasy, a rare thing for her. She stands up and paces a little. "I'm afraid—we're afraid—if we do, then that's it. He'll decide you can never go back to work. Ever. We know you may decide that, anyway. But we wanted to leave the options open."

"Everyone agreed to this?"

She's hesitant. "Everyone but James. He says he wants to speak to you first."

I close my eyes. Right now, James is the last person I want to talk to. The very last.

I sigh. "Fine. Send him in. I don't know what I'm going to decide just yet, Callie. I do know this—I want to go home. I want to get Bonnie and go home, and try to figure this out. I need to get my head straight, once and for all, or I'm done. You guys can follow up on AFIS and the rest of it. I need to go home."

She looks down at the floor, then back up at me. "I understand. I'll get it all into motion."

She walks toward the door. Stops and turns back to me as she gets to it. "One thing you should think about, honey-love. You know guns better than anyone I've ever met. Maybe when you pointed your gun at me, you pulled the trigger because you knew it was empty." She winks, opens the door, and walks out.

"Maybe," I whisper to myself.

But I don't think so.

I think I pulled the trigger because, at that moment, I wanted the whole world to die.

20

JAMES WALKS IN and closes the door behind him. He takes a seat in the chair next to my bed. He's silent, and I can't read him. Not that I ever could.

"Callie said you needed to talk to me before deciding whether or not you were going to rat me out to AD Jones."

He doesn't reply right away. He sits there, looking at me. It's exasperating.

"Well?"

He purses his lips. "Contrary to what you probably think, I don't have a problem with you coming back to full and active duty, Smoky. I don't. You're good at what we do, and competence is all I ask for."

"So?"

"What I do have a problem with is you being only halfway." He gestures at me lying on the hospital bed. "Like this. It makes you dangerous, because you're unreliable."

"Oh, please eat shit and die."

He ignores me. "It's true. Think about it. When you and I were in Annie King's apartment, I saw the old you. The competent one. So did everyone else. Callie and Alan started to defer to you again, to rely on you. Together we found evidence that would have been missed. But then all it took was a letter and you collapsed."

"Little more complicated than that, James."

He shrugs. "Not in the way that matters it's not. Either you are back all the way, or not at all. Because if you come back like this, you're a liability to us. And that leads to what I *am* willing to agree to."

"What?"

"That you either come back fixed, or you stay the fuck away. If you try to come back still screwed up, I'm going straight to AD Jones, and I'll just keep climbing until someone listens to me and puts you out to pasture."

The fury in me is white hot. "You are some arrogant prick."

He's unmoved. "This is the way it is, Smoky. I trust you. If you give me your word, then I know you'll keep it. That's what I want. Come back fixed, or don't come back at all. It's nonnegotiable."

I stare at him. I don't see judgment or pity.

He's really not asking much, I realize. What he's saying is reasonable.

I hate him anyway.

"I give you my word. Now get the fuck out of here."

He gets up and leaves without looking back.

21

WE LEFT IN the early morning, and the flight back was a silent one. Bonnie sat next to me, holding my hand and staring off into the distance. Callie spoke once to let me know that two agents would be posted at my home until I said otherwise. I didn't think he would be back now that he'd tipped his hand, but I was more than happy to have the protection. She also told me that AFIS had come up empty. Oh, happy day.

I am boiling over inside, a big mess of harm and confusion lit by little starbursts of panic. It is not the emotion overwhelming me, it is the reality. The reality of Bonnie. I glance at her. She unsettles me even more, responds by turning her head to give me a full, frank look. She regards me for a moment, and then goes back to her stillness and that thousand-yard stare.

I clench a fist and close my eyes. Those little panic starbursts glitter and burst and crack.

Motherhood terrifies me. Because that's what we're talking about here, plain and simple. I am all she has, and there are many, many miles to go. Miles filled with school days, Christmas mornings, booster shots, eat your vegetables, learn to drive, home by ten, on and on and on. All the banalities, big and small and wonderful, that go into being responsible for another life.

I used to have a system for this. The thing was, it wasn't just called motherhood. It was called parenthood. I had Matt. We bounced things off each other, argued about what was best for Alexa, loved her together. A large part of being a parent is a constant near certainty that you are screwing it up, and it is comforting to be able to spread the blame around.

Bonnie has me. Just me. Screwup me, towing a freight train of baggage while she tows a freight train of horror and a future of . . . what? Will she ever speak again? Will she have friends? Boyfriends? Will she be happy?

I realize as my panic builds that I know nothing about this little girl. I don't know if she's good in school. I don't know what TV shows she likes to watch, or what she expects to eat for breakfast in the morning. I know nothing.

The terror of it grows and grows, and I am babbling to myself inside and I just want to open the hatch on the side of the plane and jump out screaming into the open air, cackling and weeping and—

And there's Matt's voice again, inside my head. Soft and low and soothing.

Shhhh, babe. Relax. First things first, and you have the most important one out of the way already.

What's that? I whimper back to him in my mind.

I feel his smile. *You've taken her on. She's yours. Whatever else happens, however hard it is, you've taken her on, and you'll never take that back. That's the First Rule of Mom, and you did it. The rest will fall into place.*

My heart clenches at this, and I want to gasp.

The First Rule of Mom . . .

Alexa had her problems; she wasn't a perfect child. She needed a lot of reassurance, sometimes, that she was loved. In those times, I would always tell her the same thing. I would cuddle her in my arms, and put my lips in her hair and whisper to her.

"You know what the First Rule of Mom is, honey?" I would say.

She did, but she always answered the same way:

"What, Mommy? What's the First Rule of Mom?"

"That you're mine, and I'll never take that back. No matter what, no matter how hard things are, no matter if—"

"—the wind stops blowing and the sun stops shining, and the stars stop burning," she'd say, completing the ritual.

It was all I had to do, and she'd relax and be certain.

My heart unclenches.

The First Rule of Mom.

I could start with that.

The starbursts stop glittering inside me.

For now.

We all get off the plane. I walk away without saying anything, Bonnie in tow.

The agents in question accompany us home, driving behind us the whole way. The air outside is chilly, just a little foggy. The freeway has only started getting busy, not quite up to speed yet, like a hill of sluggish ants waiting for the sun to warm them up.

The inside of the car is quiet the whole way home. Bonnie isn't talking, and I am too busy thinking, feeling, fretting.

Thinking a lot about Alexa. It had not occurred to me until yesterday how little I have thought about her since her death. She's been...*vague*. A blurred face in the distance. I realize now that she was the shadowy figure in my dream about Sands. The letter from Jack Jr., and remembering, has brought her crashing into focus.

Now she is a vivid, blinding, painful beauty. Memories of her are a symphony turned up too loud. My ears hurt, but I can't stop listening.

The symphony of motherhood, it's about loving with absolute abandon, loving without regard for self, loving with a near totality of being. It's about a passion that could outburn the sun with its brightness. About a depthless hope and a fierce, rending joy.

God, I loved her. So much. More than I loved myself, more than I loved Matt.

I know why her face has been so blurred for me. Because a world without her, it is—*unbearable*.

But here I am, bearing it. That breaks something inside me, something that will never heal.

I'm glad.

Because I want this to hurt, forever.

When we get to the house twenty minutes later, the agents don't speak, just give me a nod. Letting me know they're on the job.

"Wait here a sec, honey," I tell Bonnie.

I walk over to the car. The window on the driver's side rolls down, and I smile as I recognize one of the agents. Dick Keenan. He had been a trainer at Quantico while I was going through the academy. Heading into his fifties, he decided he wanted to finish out on the "streets." He's a solid man, very old-school FBI, crew cut and all. He is also a practical joker and a marksman.

"How'd you get this detail, Dick?" I ask him.

He smiles. "AD Jones."

I nod. Of course. "Who's that with you?"

The other agent is younger, younger than me. Brand-new and still excited about being an FBI agent. Looking forward to the prospect of sitting in a car doing nothing for days at a time.

"Hannibal Shantz," he says, sticking his hand out the window for me to shake.

"Hannibal, huh?" I grin.

He shrugs. He's one of those good-natured guys, I can tell. It's impossible to get under his skin, impossible not to like him.

"You up to speed on everything, Dick?"

His nod is terse. "You. The little girl. And, yeah, I know how she came to be with you."

"Good. Let me be clear on something: She's your principal. Understand? If it comes down to a choice between shadowing her or me, I want you to keep an eye on her."

"You got it."

"Thanks. Good to meet you, Hannibal."

I walk away, reassured. I see Bonnie waiting for me, with my house as a backdrop.

I had time in the car to wonder about why I stayed in that house. It had been an act of stubbornness. Now it might also be an act of stupidity. I realized that it's something basic to my nature. It is my home. If I were to relent, to give that up, then some part of me knew that I'd never be whole again.

Here there be tygers, true. But I still wasn't leaving.

We're in the kitchen, and my next move comes to me without asking.

"You hungry, honey?" I ask Bonnie.

She looks up at me, nods.

I nod back, satisfied. The First Rule of Mom: Love. The Second Rule of Mom: Feed your offspring. "Let me see what we have."

She follows me as I open the refrigerator, peering in. Teach them to hunt, I think, and then I have to fight back a little hysterical bubble of laughter. Things don't look good in the fridge. There's a near-empty peanut butter jar and some milk that is putrefying past its expiration date.

"Sorry, babe. Looks like we'll have to do some shopping." I rub my eyes and sigh inside. God, I'm tired. But that's one of the truths of parenthood. Not a rule, really. More of a given natural law. They are yours, you are responsible for them. So too bad if you're tired, because, well—they can't drive and they don't have any money.

To heck with it. I look down at Bonnie and give her a smile. "Let's go stock this place up."

She gives me another one of those frank looks, followed by a smile. And a nod.

"Right." I grab my purse and keys. "Saddle up."

I had told Keenan and Shantz to stay on my house. I could take care of myself, and it was more important to me to know that no one would be waiting for us when we came back.

We're moving through the aisles of Ralph's supermarket. Modern-day foraging.

"Lead the way, honey," I tell her. "I don't know what you like, so you'll have to show me."

I push the cart and follow Bonnie as she glides across the floor, silent and watchful. Each time she points something out, I grab it and look at it for a moment, letting it set into my subconscious. I hear a loud, bass voice inside my head: *MACARONI AND CHEESE,* the voice booms. *SPAGHETTI WITH MEAT SAUCE—NO MUSHROOMS, EVER, UNDER PAIN OF DEATH. CHEETOS—THE HOT AND SPICY KIND.* The Food Commandments. Clues to Bonnie, important.

I feel like something rusty and dusty inside me is starting to get into motion, one screechy gear at a time. Love, shelter, macaroni and cheese. These things feel natural and right.

Like riding a bike, babe, I hear Matt whisper.

"Maybe," I murmur back.

I'm so busy talking to myself that I miss that Bonnie has stopped, and I almost run her over with my cart. I give her a weak smile. "Sorry, honey. We got everything?"

She smiles and nods. All done.

"Then let's get home and get eating."

It's not riding the bike that's the problem, I realize. It's the road the bike is traveling that's changed. Love, shelter, macaroni and cheese, sure. There's also a mute child and there's a new mom who's scarred, talks to herself, and is a little bit crazy.

I am on the phone with Alan's wife, and as I talk, I watch Bonnie wolf down her macaroni and cheese with dedication and intensity. Children have a real pragmatism when it comes to food, I muse. *I know the sky is falling, but, hey— you gotta eat, right?*

"I really appreciate it, Elaina. Alan told me what's going on, and I wouldn't ask, but—"

She cuts me off. "Please stop, Smoky." Her voice chides, gentle. It makes me think of Matt. "You need time to work things out, and that little girl needs a place to be when you're not there. Until you get things settled."

I don't respond, a lump in my throat. She seems to sense this, which is very Elaina. "You *will* get things settled, Smoky. You'll do the right things for her." She pauses. "You were a great mother to Alexa. You'll do just fine with Bonnie."

A mixture of grief, gratitude, and darkness comes over me when she says this. I manage to clear my throat, and get out a husky "Thanks."

"No problem. Call me when you need me to help."

She doesn't demand more response from me and hangs up. Elaina has always been long on empathy. She'd agreed to look after Bonnie if there were times I needed a sitter. No hesitation, no questions asked.

You're not alone, babe, Matt whispers.

"Maybe," I murmur back. "Maybe not."

My phone rings, startling me out of my conversation with a ghost. I answer it.

"Hi, honey-love," Callie says. "Little development I wanted to apprise you of."

My heart clenches. What now?

"Tell me," I say.

"Dr. Hillstead's office was bugged."

I frown. "Huh?"

"The things Jack Jr. said in that letter, honey-love: Didn't you wonder how he knew them?"

Silence. I'm startled and dumbfounded. No, I realize. I hadn't wondered. "Good grief, Callie. It never occurred to me. Jesus." I am reeling. "How is that possible?"

"Don't feel bad. With everything else that happened, it didn't occur to me, either. You can thank James for thinking of it." She pauses. "Dear God, did I really just say 'thank' and 'James' in the same sentence?" I can hear her mock-shudder through the phone.

"Details, Callie," I say. The words come out tight and

impatient. I'm not interested in humor right now and I'm too tired to apologize for it.

"He had two audio bugs planted in Dr. Hillstead's office—functional but not high end." She's letting me know that they aren't distinctive as gadgets go and probably not traceable. "Both were remote activated. They transmitted wirelessly to a miniature recorder placed in a maintenance closet. All he'd have to know is when your appointments with Dr. Hillstead were, honey-love. He could activate the bugs and pick up the recordings later."

A sense of violation surges through me, a powerful jolt of electricity. He'd been listening? Listening to me talk about Matt and Alexa? Listening to me be *weak*? My rage is so overwhelming I feel like I want to swoon, or vomit.

Then, as fast as it came, it goes. No more violation, no more rage, just exhausted desolation. My tide has gone out, my beach is dry and lonely.

"I gotta go, Callie," I mumble.

"Are you all right, honey-love?"

"Thanks for telling me, Callie. Now I have to go."

I hang up and marvel at my own emptiness. It is exquisite, in its way. Perfect.

"At least we'll always have Paris," I murmur, and feel a cackle building.

I realize that Bonnie has finished eating and that she is looking at me. Watching me. It startles me, shakes me down to my bones.

Jesus, I think. And it comes to me that this is the first thing I need to realize, once and for all. I am not alone. She is here, and she sees me.

My days of sitting in the dark, staring off at nothing and talking to myself—those days have to end.

No one needs a crazy mommy.

* * *

We're in my bedroom, on my bed, looking at each other.

"How's this, honey? Will it do?"

She gazes around, runs her hand over the bedspread, and then smiles, nodding her head. I smile back.

"Good. Now, I thought you would probably want to sleep in here with me—but if you don't, I'll understand."

She grabs my hand and shakes her head like a bobble-head doll. A definite yes.

"Cool. I do need to talk to you about some things, Bonnie. Is that okay with you?"

A nod.

Some people might disapprove of this approach. Getting down to business so soon with her. I don't agree. I'm going by feel here, and something tells me to be honest with this child, nothing less.

"First thing is, sometimes when I sleep—well, most of the time—I have nightmares. Sometimes they really scare me, and I wake up screaming. I hope that doesn't happen with you sleeping in here, but it's not really under my control. I don't want you to be scared if it does."

She studies my face. I watch as her eyes slide over to the picture on my nightstand. It's a framed photo of me, Matt, and Alexa, all smiles and with no idea that death was in the future. She gazes at it for a moment, then looks back at me, raising her eyebrows.

It takes me a moment to understand. "Yes. The nightmares I have are about what happened to them."

She closes her eyes. She lifts her hand up and pats her chest. Then opens her eyes and looks at me.

"You too, huh? Okay, honey. How about we make a deal—neither one of us gets scared if the other one wakes up screaming."

She smiles at this. It strikes me, for just a moment,

how surreal this is. I am not talking to a ten-year-old about clothing or music or a day at the park. I'm making a pact with her about screaming in the night.

"The next thing... it's a little harder for me. I'm deciding whether or not I'm going to keep doing my job. My job is to catch bad people, people who do things like what was done to your mom. And I might just be too sad to keep doing that. You understand?"

Her nod is somber. Oh yeah, she understands.

"I haven't decided yet. If I don't, then you and I can decide what to do next. If I do . . . well, I won't be able to keep you with me all the time. I'll have to have someone watch you when I'm working. I can promise you this: If I do that, I'll make sure you like whoever you're with. Does that sound all right?"

A careful nod. I'm getting the hang of this. *Yes*, that nod says—*but with reservation.*

"This is the last thing, babe. I think it's the most important, so listen to me carefully, okay?" I take her hand and make certain that I am looking right at her when I say what I say next. "If you want to stay with me, then you will. I won't leave you. Not ever. That's a promise."

Her face shows the first real emotion I've seen since I found her in that bed at the hospital. It crumples, overtaken by grief. Tears spill out onto her cheeks. I grab her and hug her to me, rocking her, as she weeps in silence. I hold her and whisper into her hair, and think of Annie and Alexa and the First Rule of Mom.

It takes a while, but she stops crying. She continues to hold on to me, her head against my chest. The sniffles die away and she pulls back, wiping her face with her hands. She cocks her head and looks at me. Really looks. I see her eyes roam over my scars. I start as her hand comes up to my face. With tremendous tenderness, she traces the scars with a finger. Starting with the ones on my fore-head, running feather touches over my cheekbone. Her eyes tear up, and she rests a palm against my cheek. Then she is back in my arms. This time, she is the one hugging me.

Strangely, I don't feel like weeping as she does this. I have a brief glimpse of peace. A place of comfort. Some warmth enters into that part of me that froze at the hospital today.

I pull back and grin at her. "We're some pair, huh?"

Her smile in return is genuine. I know it's only momentary. I know that her true grief, when it hits her, is going to be a tidal wave. It's still nice to see her smile.

"Listen, part of what I told you? About deciding whether or not I'm going to keep doing my job? There's something I need to do tonight. Do you want to come with me?"

She nods. Oh yeah. I give her another smile, a chuck on the chin. "Well, let's go, then."

I drive to a gun range in the San Fernando Valley. I give it a once-over before getting out of the car, trying to work up my nerve. The building is all function, with peeling paint on the exterior walls and windows that have probably never been washed. Like a gun, I think. A gun can be scratched and battered, have lost its shine. All that matters, though, is the basic truth: Will it still fire a bullet? This worn-out building is no different. Some very *serious* gun owners come here. By serious, I don't mean enthusiasts. I mean men (and women) who have spent their lives using guns to kill people or keep the peace.

People like me. I look over at Bonnie, give her a lopsided smile.

"Ready?" I ask.

She nods.

"Let's go, then."

I know the owner. He's an ex–Marine sniper, with eyes that are warm up front but cold in the back. He sees me and his voice booms out:

"Smoky! Haven't seen you in a while!"

I smile at him, gesture at the scars. "Had some bad luck, Jazz."

He notices Bonnie and smiles at her. She doesn't smile back. "And who's this?"

"That's Bonnie."

Jazz has always been a good reader of people. He knows Bonnie is not all right and doesn't bother with any "hey, honey, how are you" stuff. Just nods at her and looks at me, hands flat on the counter.

"What do you need tonight?"

"That Glock." I point at it. "And just a single clip. And ear protection for both of us."

"You bet, you bet." He removes the gun from the case and lays a full clip beside it. He grabs some ear protectors off the wall.

My hands are sweating. "I, uh, need a favor, Jazz. I need you to take it into the range for me and load in the clip."

He raises his eyebrows at me. I feel myself blushing with shame. My voice, when it comes out, is quiet. "Please, Jazz. This is a test. If I go in there and can't pick up that gun, then I'll probably never shoot again. I don't want to touch it before then."

I see those eyes, examining me, warm and cold at the

same time. Warm wins out. "No problem at all, Smoky. Just give me a second."

"Thanks. Thanks a lot." I grab the ear protectors and kneel down in front of Bonnie. "We have to wear these inside the firing range, honey. It's superloud when you fire a gun, and it'll hurt your ears if you don't."

She nods, holding out her hand. I give her the ear protectors. She puts them on and I do the same.

"Follow me," Jazz indicates with a gesture.

We go through the door into the range. Right away I smell that smell. The smell of smoke and metal. There's nothing quite like it. I'm relieved to see that the range is empty right now.

I make it clear to Bonnie that she has to stay back against the wall. Jazz looks at me and slides the clip home. He lays the gun down on the small wooden counter that faces the range. The cold eyes this time, but then he smiles at me and turns and heads back into the main part of the shop. He knows I want to be alone.

I look back at Bonnie, give her a smile. She doesn't return it. Instead, she looks at me, an intent look. She understands that I am doing something here, something important. She's giving it the seriousness it deserves.

I pick up the human-shaped target and attach it to the clip that holds it. I hit the button, watching it sail away from me, down the range, farther, farther, farther. Until it seems the size of a playing card.

My heart thuds in my chest. I am shivering and sweating at the same time.

I look down at the Glock.

Sleek, black instrument of death. Some protest its existence, some think it's a thing of beauty. For me, it's always been an extension of myself. Until it betrayed me.

This is a Glock model 34. It has a 5.32-inch barrel and

weighs just under thirty-three ounces with a fully loaded magazine. It fires nine-millimeter bullets and has a magazine capacity of seventeen. The trigger pull, unmodified, is a smooth 4.5 pounds. I know all of these mechanical things. I know them like I know my own height and weight. The question now is whether or not we can reconcile, this blackbird and I.

I move my hand toward it. I am sweating more profusely now. I feel light-headed. I grit my teeth, force myself to keep reaching. I see Alexa's eyes, the O of her mouth as my bullet, from my gun, entered her chest and silenced her forever. This plays over and over again in my head, like film that has been looped. Bang and death, bang and death, bang and the end of the world.

"GODDAMN YOU GODDAMN YOU GODDAMN YOU!" I don't know if I am screaming at God, Joseph Sands, myself, or the gun.

I snatch up the Glock in a single fluid motion, and I am firing it; the black steel jerks in my hand, *pow-pow-pow-pow-pow!*

Then I hear the click of an empty chamber, a spent magazine. I am shaking, crying. But the Glock, it's still there. And I have not passed out.

Welcome back, I think I can hear it whisper.

With a shaking hand, I push the button that will bring the target back to me. It arrives, and what I see fills me with a kind of exultation, tinged with sadness. Ten head shots, seven in the heart. I had hit everything I wanted to, where I wanted to. Just like always.

I look at the target, then at the Glock, and I feel that joy and sadness all over again. I know now that shooting will never be the simple joy it used to be. There's been too much death behind it for me. Too much grief I can never forget.

That's okay. I know now what I needed to know. I can hold a gun again. Loving it is unimportant.

I pop out the magazine, grab my target, and turn to Bonnie. She is goggling at the target, and at me. Then she smiles. I ruffle her hair and we head out of the range, back into the shop. Jazz is sitting on a stool with his arms crossed. He has a faint smile on his face. His eyes now are all warm, no cold in sight.

"I knew it, Smoky. It's in your blood, darlin'. In your blood."

I look at him for a moment, and I nod. He's right.

My hand and a gun. We're married again. While it may be a rocky relationship, I realize that I missed it. It's a part of me. Of course, the gun's not youthful anymore either. It's aged now, and scarred.

That's what it gets for picking me as its bride.

2

DREAMS AND CONSEQUENCES

22

BONNIE WAKES UP in the middle of the night, screaming.

This is not a child's scream. It is the howl of someone locked in a room in hell. I hurry to snap on the light next to the bed. I see with a shock that her eyes are still closed. Me, I always wake when I start screaming. Bonnie is doing her screaming in her sleep. She is trapped in her dreams, able to put a voice to her fears but unable to wake from them.

I grab her and shake her hard. The screaming dies, her eyes open, she is silent again. I can still hear that sound in my head and she is shivering. I pull her close to me, not saying anything, stroking her hair. She clutches on to me. Soon, her shivering stops. Soon after that, she sleeps.

I disengage from her, as gently as I can. She looks peaceful now. I fall asleep watching her. And for the first time in the last six months, I dream of Alexa.

"Hi, Mommy," she says to me, smiling.

"What's up, chicken-butt?" I say. The first time I ever said this to her she had giggled so hard she got a headache, which made her cry. I'd been saying it ever since.

She gives me her serious look. The one that both did and didn't fit her. It didn't fit her because she was too young for it. It did fit her because it was Alexa to the core. Her father's soft brown eyes look out at me from a face stamped by both our genes, turned pixielike by dimples that were hers alone. Matt used to joke about how the mailman had dimples, and maybe he'd given me a *special delivery,* ha ha ha.

"I'm worried about you, Mommy."

"Why, baby-love?"

Those eyes go sad. Too sad for her age, too sad for those dimples.

"Because you miss me so much."

I glance at Bonnie, look back at Alexa. "What about her, babe? Are you okay with that?"

I wake up before she can reply. My eyes are dry, but my heart twists in my chest, making it hard to breathe. After a few moments, this subsides. I turn my head. Bonnie's eyes are closed, her face untroubled.

I fall asleep watching her again, but this time, I do not dream.

It's morning. I look at myself in the mirror while Bonnie looks on. I've put on my best black business suit. Matt used to call it my "killer's suit." It still looks good.

I have been ignoring my hair for months. When I paid any attention to it at all, it was to move it so that it hung over my scars. I used to wear it free and flowing. Now I have drawn it back tightly against my head. Bonnie helped me with the ponytail. Instead of hiding my scars from the world, I am accentuating them.

It's funny, I think to myself as I look into my own eyes. Doesn't really look that bad. Oh, it's a disfigurement.

And it's shocking. But...taken as a whole, I don't look like I belong in a freak show. I wonder why I never noticed that before, why it's seemed so much uglier until now. I guess it was because I was holding so much ugliness inside.

I like the way I look. I look tough. I look hard. I look formidable. All of this fits with my current view of life. I turn away from the mirror. "What do you think? Good?"

Nod, smile.

"Let's get going, then, honey. We're going to make a few trips today."

She takes my hand and we head out the door.

First stop is Dr. Hillstead's office. I'd called ahead and he is waiting for me. When we arrive at the office, I convince Bonnie to stay with Imelda, Dr. Hillstead's receptionist. She's a Latin woman with a no-nonsense way of caring for people, and Bonnie seems to respond to this mix of warmth and brusqueness. I understand. We walking wounded hate pity. We just want to be treated normally.

I enter and Dr. Hillstead comes to greet me. He looks devastated. "Smoky. I want you to know how sorry I am about what happened. I never meant for you to find out that way."

I shrug. "Yeah, well. He's been inside my home. Watched me sleep. I guess he's keeping pretty good tabs on me. Not something you could have planned for."

He looks shocked. "He's been inside...your house?"

"Yep." I don't correct his or my use of the word *he*. The fact that *he* is actually *they* remains confined to the team, our ace in the hole.

Dr. Hillstead runs a hand through his hair. He looks shaken. "This is really disconcerting, Smoky. I deal with secondhand accounts of these kinds of things, but this is the first time it's entered my life in reality."

"This is how it goes sometimes."

Perhaps it's the calmness of my voice that gets his attention. For the first time since I entered his office, he really looks at me. He sees the change, and it seems to bring back the healer in him.

"Why don't you sit down?"

I sit in one of the leather chairs facing his desk.

He looks at me, musing. "Are you upset with me for withholding the ballistics report?"

I shake my head. "No. I mean—I was. But I understand what you were trying to do, and I think you were right to do it."

"I didn't want to tell you until I thought you were ready to deal with it."

I give him a faint smile. "I don't know if I was ready to deal with it or not. But I rose to the occasion."

He nods. "Yes, I see a change in you. Tell me about it."

"Not much to tell," I say with a shrug. "It hit me hard. For a moment, I didn't believe it. But then I remembered everything. Shooting Alexa. Trying to shoot Callie. It was like all the pain I've been feeling over the last six months hit me at once. I passed out."

"Callie told me."

"The thing is, when I woke up, I didn't want to die. That made me feel bad in a way. Guilty. But it was still true. I don't want to die."

"That's good, Smoky," he says in a quiet voice.

"And it's not just that. You were right about my team. They are like my family. And they're fucked up. Alan's wife has cancer. Callie has something going on she won't talk to anyone about. And I realize that I can't just let that pass. I love them. I have to be there for them if they need me. Do you understand?"

He nods. "I do. And I'll admit that I was hoping for that. Not that your team members would be in distress. But you've been living in a vacuum. I was hoping that getting back in touch with them would remind you of the one thing I know would give you a reason to go on living."

"What's that?"

"Duty. It's a driving force for you. You have a duty to them. And to the victims."

This idea catches me by surprise. Because I realize that it's dead-on. I may never be fully healed. I might wake up screaming in the night till the day I die. But as long as my friends need me, as long as the monsters kill, I have to stick around. No choice about it. "It worked," I say.

He smiles a gentle smile. "I'm glad."

"Yeah, well." I sigh. "On the way home from San Francisco I had a lot of time to think. I knew there was one thing I had to try. If I couldn't do it, then I was done. I would have gotten up today and handed in my resignation."

"What was that?" he asks. I think he knows. He just wants me to say it.

"I went to a shooting range. Got a Glock and decided to see if I could still shoot. If I could even pick it up without passing out."

"And?"

"It was all there. Like it had never been gone."

He steeples his fingers, looks at me. "There's more, isn't there? Your entire appearance has changed."

I look into his eyes, this man who has tried to help me through these months. I realize that his skill in helping people like me is an amazing dance, a mix of chaos and precision. Knowing when to back away, when to feint, when to attack. Putting a mind back together. I'd rather hunt serial killers. "I'm not a victim anymore, Dr. Hillstead. I can't put it any more simply. It's not something that needs a lot of words around it. It's just true. The way it is." I lean back. "You had a lot to do with that, and I want to thank you. I might be dead otherwise."

Now he smiles. He shakes his head. "No, Smoky. I don't think you'd be dead. I'm glad that you feel I've helped you, but you're a born survivor. I don't think you would have killed yourself, if it came to that."

Maybe, maybe not, I think.

"So what now? Are you telling me you don't need to see me anymore?" It's a genuine question. I don't get the sense that he has already decided what the correct answer would be.

"No, I'm not saying that." I smile. "It's funny, if you had asked me a year ago about seeing a shrink, I would have made some snide comment and felt superior to the people who think they need one." I shake my head. "Not anymore. I still have things to work through. My friend dying…" I look at him. "You know I have her daughter with me?"

He nods, somber. "Callie filled me in on what happened to her. I'm glad you took her with you. She probably feels very alone right now."

"She doesn't talk. Just nods. Last night she screamed in her sleep."

He winces. No one sane enjoys the pain of a child. "I would guess that she's going to take a long time to heal, Smoky. She may not talk for years. The best thing to do for now is what you're already doing—just be there for her. Don't try to approach what happened. She's not ready for that. I doubt she'll be ready for months."

"Really?" My voice sounds bleak. His eyes are kind.

"Yes. Look, what she needs right now is to know that she's safe and that you are there. That life is going to go on. Her trust in basic things for a child—her parents being there, the safety of a home—her trust in those fundamentals has been shattered. In a very personal, horrible way. It will take some time to rebuild that trust." He gives me a measured look. "You should know that."

I swallow once, nod.

"I would say, give it some time. Watch her, be there for her. I think you'll know when it might be right for her to start talking about it. When that time comes..." He seems to hesitate, but only for a moment. "When that time comes, let me know. I'd be happy to recommend a therapist for her."

"Thanks." Another thought occurs to me. "What about school?"

"You should wait. Her mental health is the primary issue." He grimaces. "It's hard to say what will happen on that front. You've heard the cliché—and it's true: Children are very resilient. She could bounce back and be ready for the complexity of social interaction that school provides, or"—he shrugs—"she might require home-schooling till she graduates. But I would say, at least for now, that that's the least of your worries. The simple truth is, get her better. If I can help, I will."

A certain relief comes over me. I have a path, and I didn't have to make the decision on my own. "Thanks. Really."

"What about you? How is taking her on affecting your state of mind?"

"Guilty. Happy. Guilty that I'm happy. Happy that I'm guilty."

"Why so much conflict?" His voice is quiet.

He's not saying that my being conflicted is wrong. He is saying, *Tell me why*.

I run a hand across my forehead. "I think 'why not' is probably a better question, Doc. I'm scared. I miss Alexa. I worry about fucking it up. Take your pick."

He leans forward, intent. He's got ahold of something, and he won't let it go. "Distill it down, Smoky. I understand there are many factors. Lots of reason for emotion. But break it down to something you can work with."

And just like that, it comes to me. "It's because she both *is* Alexa and *isn't* Alexa," I say.

And that *is* it, that simplicity. Bonnie is a second chance at Alexa, at having a daughter. But then, she isn't Alexa, because Alexa is dead.

Not all truths are good, on the surface. Some truths bring pain. Some are just the starting point for an uphill climb, for a lot of tortured work. This truth makes me feel empty. A bell being rung in a windless field.

If I can work through this truth, I know things will change. But the work is huge and ugly and it's going to hurt me.

"Yeah," I manage to say. My voice sounds ragged. I sit up, push away the pain. "Okay. I don't have time for this right now." It comes out sounding harsh. Too bad. I need my anger these days. The hard parts of me.

Dr. Hillstead isn't offended. "I understand. Just make sure that you make time for it at some point."

I nod.

He smiles. "So, back to my original question: What are you going to do now?"

"Now," I say, and just like that, my voice has turned cold, my heart along with it, "I'm going back to work. And I'm going to find the man who killed Annie."

Dr. Hillstead looks at me for a long, long time. It's a gaze like a laser. He's gauging me, deciding if he agrees with my decision. What he decides is evident when he reaches over to his desk drawer and pulls out my Glock. It's still encased in the plastic evidence bag. "I thought you might be telling me something like that, so I had this ready for you." He cocks his head. "That's why you really came to see me, isn't it?"

"No," I say, smiling, "but it was a part of it." I grab the gun and put it into my purse. I stand up and shake Dr. Hillstead's hand. "I also wanted you to see me looking better."

He holds my hand a little longer than is needed. I feel the gentle spirit of this man; it comes out through his eyes. "I'll be here if you need to talk again. Anytime."

And, surprise—tears. I thought I was done with them. Maybe it's a good thing. I don't ever want to be unaffected by kindness, whether from strangers or from friends.

23

"THIS IS THE building where I work, honey."

Bonnie has my hand, and she looks up at me, inquisitive.

"Yes, I'm going back to work. I have to tell my boss first."

She gives my hand a squeeze. She seems to approve.

We ride first up to the NCAVC Coord offices. When we enter, only Callie and James are there.

"Hi." Callie's voice is tentative. James looks on without speaking.

"Callie, I need to go up and see AD Jones. Can you watch Bonnie for me? I won't be gone long."

Callie studies me for a moment. She looks down at Bonnie, smiling. "How about it, honey-love? You okay to stay with me?"

Bonnie studies her, and Callie bears this with tender patience. Bonnie nods, letting go of my hand and going over to take Callie's.

"I'll be back in a little bit." I leave, knowing that I have left James and Callie wondering. That's okay. They'll know soon enough.

I make my way up to AD Jones's office, which is on the

top floor. Shirley, his receptionist, greets me with a professional smile. "Hi, Smoky."

"Hey, Shirley. Is he in?"

"Let me check." She picks up the phone and presses the intercom button. She knows he's in. What she meant was she would find out if he wanted to see me. I don't take it personally. I think Shirley would keep the President of the United States cooling his heels. "Sir? Agent Barrett is here. Uh-huh. Yes." She hangs up. "Go right in."

She snags my sleeve as I move toward the door. There's a slight smile on her face, and it's playful now. "Welcome back. Oh, don't look so surprised. Anyone with half a brain can tell that that's what's going on. You look good, Smoky. Real good."

"You should come work for me, Shirley, a sharp mind like that."

She laughs. "Oh, no thank you. Too tame for me. This job is a lot more dangerous."

I grin back, and open the door. I close it behind me. AD Jones is sitting at his desk, and he's giving me a keen-eyed once-over. He seems to see something he approves of, and nods to himself.

"Take a seat." Once I am sitting, he leans back. "I got a call from Dr. Hillstead about ten minutes ago. He gave you a pass to return to full, active duty. That what you're here to see me about?"

"Yes. I'm ready to come back to work. But I have a proviso: I want to run Annie's case."

He's shaking his head. "I don't know, Smoky. I don't think that's a good idea."

I give him a shrug. "Then I quit. I'll go private and keep looking for them that way."

AD Jones looks like he is trying to keep his jaw from

falling open. He also looks pissed. Volcano, H-bomb pissed. "You're giving me an ultimatum?"

"Yes, sir."

He continues to glare at me, shock and anger battling for dominance. Both disappear in a sudden flash. He shakes his head. A hint of a smile tugs at one corner of his mouth. "Pretty good hardball there, Agent Barrett. And okay. You're back, it's your case. Keep me in the loop."

That's it. He's dismissing me, telling me to get back to work. I stand up to leave.

"Smoky."

I turn to him.

"Get these motherfuckers."

Back at Death Central, Callie and James are waiting. They know something is up. I realize that this is a critical moment for them, for all of my team. A place where life might change forever. I should have told them when I came in, but I wasn't sure, not a hundred percent, that AD Jones was going to let me run Annie's case. I'd been serious about quitting if he hadn't.

"I'm going to drop Bonnie off with Elaina, Callie." She raises her eyebrows. James looks at me, questioning. "I've kept my word. I'm back."

He nods once, no other questions asked. Callie's face is filled with relief and happiness. I'm glad to see it, but I'm also a little bit sad. I wonder if she thinks things are going to go back to the way they were. I hope not. Things will be good again, yes. Working with my team will be rewarding, as always.

But we are older now. Harder. Like the undefeated team who loses their first game, we have learned that we are not invulnerable, that we can be hurt. Even die.

I am changed too. Will they notice that? If they do, will it make them happy, or sad? What I said to Dr. Hillstead is true. I'm done being a victim, but that does not mean that I'm the same Smoky Barrett I used to be.

It was an epiphany that came to me at the shooting range. Like a voice from the God I don't believe in. I realized that I will never love again. Matt was the love of my life, and he is gone. No one will ever replace him. This is not fatalism or depression. It is a certainty, and it brought me a kind of peace. I will love Bonnie. I will love my team.

Other than that, I will have only one love now, and it will define the rest of my life: the hunt.

I held the Glock in my hands, and I realized it right there, right at that very moment. I am not a victim, not anymore. Instead, I have become the gun.

For better or worse, till death do us part.

24

I LOOK AT Bonnie before we get out of the car. "You doing okay, honey?"

She gazes back at me with those too-old eyes. Nods.

"Good." I ruffle her hair. "Elaina is a very, very good friend of mine. She's Alan's wife. You remember Alan? You met him on the plane."

Nod.

"I think you'll like her a lot. But if you don't want to be here, you just let me know, and we'll figure something else out."

She cocks her head at me. Seems to be weighing the truth of my words. She smiles and nods. I grin back at her. "Great."

I look in the rearview mirror. Keenan and Shantz are parked in front of the house, ever-present. They know that I'm leaving Bonnie here and that they'll be staying. This almost makes me feel safe about leaving her. Almost.

"Let's go, babe."

We get out of the car and go up to the house, ring the doorbell. After a moment, Alan answers. He looks better than he did on the plane, but still tired. "Hey, Smoky. Hey, Bonnie."

Bonnie looks up at him, examining him by staring

straight into his eyes. He bears this with the gentle-giant patience that he personifies, until she gives him a smile that is her equivalent of a thumbs-up.

He smiles back. "Come on in. Elaina's in the kitchen."

We enter, and Elaina's head pokes around a corner. Her eyes light up at the sight of me, and it squeezes my heart. This is Elaina. She glows with kindness.

"Smoky!" she cries, rushing toward me. I let myself be embraced by her, return the hug.

She steps back, holding me at arm's length, and we examine each other. Elaina is not as short as I am, but at five foot two she's a dwarf in comparison to Alan. She is incredibly beautiful. Not in a way that stuns you, like Callie; her beauty is a combination of the physical mixed with pure personality. She is one of those women whose depth and goodness texture her entire presence, making you yearn to be near her. Alan summed it up once in a single simple sentence: "She is Mom."

"Hey, Elaina," I say, smiling. "How are you?"

A brief twinge of something appears deep in her eyes, disappears. She kisses me on the cheek. "Much better now, Smoky. We've missed you."

"Me too," I say. "I mean, I've missed you guys."

She looks at me for one meaningful moment, nods. "Much better," she says. I know she means me. She turns to look at Bonnie and hunches down so they are face-to-face. "You must be Bonnie," she says.

Bonnie looks at Elaina, and it is a moment suspended in time. Elaina just sits there, exuding love in her wordless, unconscious way. It's a force of nature all its own, a power people like Elaina have. Something made to beat down the barriers that pain can erect around the heart. Bonnie freezes. Her body shudders, and something undefined goes shivering across her face. It takes me a moment to place that something, and when I do, pain jolts through me like a lightning strike. It's suffering and yearning, deep and dark and soulful. Elaina's love is powerful. It is raw and elemental. It is not something to fuck with; it takes no prisoners. And it has cut into Bonnie like a knife made of sunlight, cut deep and exposed her hidden pain. All in an instant. Just like that. I watch Bonnie lose an internal battle, watch as her face crumples against her will, and watch as silent tears begin to pour down her cheeks.

Elaina holds out her arms, and Bonnie rushes into them. Elaina gathers her up, hugs her close, strokes her hair, croons in that mixture of English and Spanish I remember so well.

I am dumbstruck. A lump fills my throat, demanding tears. I fight it back. I glance at Alan. He's fighting too. The reasons are the same for both of us. It's not just Bonnie's pain. It's Elaina's kindness, and Bonnie's instant understanding that Elaina's arms are a safe place to be if something hurts.

This is who she is. She is Mom.

The moment seems to hang forever.

Bonnie pulls away, wiping her face with her hands.

"Better now?" Elaina asks.

Bonnie looks at her and gives a tired smile in answer. It's not only her smile that's tired. She just wept out some part of her soul, and it exhausted her.

Elaina strokes her cheek with one hand. "You sleepy, baby?"

Bonnie nods, her eyes blinking. I realize she is falling asleep on her feet. Elaina gathers her up in her arms without another word. Bonnie's head falls against her shoulder and, just like that, she's out.

It was something magic. Elaina had sucked the pain

out of her, and now she could sleep. I'd slept that night at
the hospital too, after her visit. The first sleep I'd had in
days.

It blindsides me as I see Bonnie there, asleep in her
arms, trusting. I hate myself for the selfishness of it, but I
can't help the fear. What if Bonnie got close to this wonderful woman and lost her too? I find that the thought of
this possibility terrifies me, in the most Mom of ways.

Elaina squints her eyes at me, smiles. "I'm not going
anywhere, Smoky." Long on empathy as always. I feel
ashamed. But she smiles again and sweeps my shame
away. "I think we'll be fine here. You two can get to work."

"Thanks," I mumble, still fighting that lump in my
throat.

"You want to thank me, you come for dinner tonight,
Smoky." She comes over and touches my face, the side
with scars. "Better," she says. Then, more firmly, "Definitely better."

She gives Alan a single kiss and walks off, trailing that
elemental love and goodness behind her. Changing everything she touches just by being who she is.

Alan and I walk outside, stopping on his front porch
for a moment. Moved and dazed and jittery.

Alan breaks the silence with actions, not words. Those
catcher's-mitt hands fly up to his face in a single, sudden,
desperate motion. His tears are as silent as Bonnie's were,
and just as agonizing to watch. The gentle giant shakes. I
know they are tears of fear, more than anything else. I understand. Being married to Elaina, it must be like being
married to the sun. He's afraid of losing her. Of being in
darkness forever. I could tell him that life goes on, blah,
blah, blah.

But I know better.

So instead I put a hand on his shoulder and let him

cry. I'm not Elaina. But I know he'll never let her see his worry and pain about her like this. I do my best. I know from experience that while it's not enough, it's far far better than nothing at all.

As quick as it came, the storm passes.

His eyes are already dry, which doesn't really surprise me. This is who we are, I think, sad.

As much as we might like to break, we're really only made to bend.

25

EVERYONE LOOKS WORN down, with that rushed-to-get-ready look. Hair combed, but imperfectly. Shaves not as close as they could be. Everyone but Callie, of course. She's beautiful and impeccable.

"How's Bonnie?" she asks.

I shrug. "Hard to say. She seems okay for now. But..." I shrug again.

No one says anything to this. She might be fine, she might never be fine...However you slice it, it comes up sucky.

A loud *ding-dong* fills the air.

"What the hell is that?" I ask, startled.

"That means I have mail, honey-love. I have a program that checks it automatically every half hour and alerts me if something's there."

I look at Callie, perplexed. "Really?" This seems bizarre to me. I see tolerant looks on everyone's faces. I have a feeling that I am showing myself as being behind the times.

Callie walks over to the laptop on her desk, taps at the keyboard. She frowns, looks up at me. "I have psycho mail," she says.

The feeling of lethargy that had been blanketing the

room vanishes in a single electric jolt. We all crowd around her desk. The in-box listing of her e-mail is displayed, with the newest message on top. The subject is: *A Message from Hell*, the sender: *You Know Who*. Callie double-clicks to open the message full screen.

> Greetings, Agent Thorne! And Agent Barrett as well—I'm sure you are reading this together.
>
> You are back at the nest now, I feel sure, plotting the pursuit. I must admit, I am becoming excited at the prospects of the days to come. The hunt is on, and I could not have asked for a better cast of foes.
>
> I have specific business with you here, Agent Thorne, but before we get to that, I must digress. You'll forgive me, I hope.
>
> I am sure you have all wondered: Why am I challenging you so directly? Perhaps you already have a team of profilers, picking apart my motivations, trying to pluck the meanings from my actions.

"You wish," Callie murmurs.

This isn't an idle comment on her part. "They" are showing us something important here, part of what makes them tick. The thought of us investing time and resources to figure them out is an ego trip for them. It's part of their turn-on.

> The answer, however, is not complex. Just as I am not complex. My motivations are not arcane, Agent Thorne and Co. They are not hidden in murky waters. They

gleam with the cool simplicity of the
scalpel. Sterile and brightly lit.

I challenge you because you deserve me.
You hunt the hunters, and, I feel certain,
you have spent many years patting each
other on the back. Filling the air with
your mutual congratulations, your skill at
putting those who kill into the cages you
feel they deserve.

And so you deserve me. Because if these
others you have hunted are shadows, I am
darkness itself. They are the jackals to my
lion. You feel you are skilled? Then hunt
me, Agents. Hunt me.

I desire opponents worthy of me, Agent
Barrett. Read my letters with care. Smell
my scent. Catch a whiff of something
deadly. You will need this, in the days to
come.

Learn to live with the assumption of
being under siege. You don't know what I
mean, just now, but you will. Learn it,
take it into your blood. And then use it to
drive you in your hunt for me. Because I
promise you, so long as you leave me free
to cut and tear, you will live a life of
peril.

This sends a shiver through me, against my will.

Now, back to you, Agent Thorne. Let's
make this personal, shall we? While it is
Agent Barrett I challenge face-to-face, I
realize that any gauntlet I throw her way

```
is thrown at all of you. And since we have
a day before my package arrives into your
eager hands, let's use that time wisely.
    Agent Barrett lost her best friend. Let's
see if we can use this time making sure
each of you lose something equally
important.
```

Alarm bells go off in my head at this last sentence. I don't know my prey yet, in the way I come to know all the killers we go after. I haven't soaked them into my bones. But I have absorbed one certainty that makes that sentence a chiller: I know they do not bluff.

```
    Here is a link to a Web site for you,
Agent Thorne. Visit it, and all will become
clear if you look hard enough. I think you
will enjoy the irony.
    From Hell,
    Jack Jr.
```

There is a hyperlink embedded in the e-mail message, a line that says, *Click Here.*

"Well?" Callie asks.

I nod. "Go ahead."

She clicks on the link, and a browser window flies open. We wait as the Web site is contacted and begins to fill the screen. The background is white. A red logo appears. *RED ROSE,* it says, then, below it, in smaller letters, *A TRUE REDHEAD AMATEUR.*

The rest of the graphics fill in, and what I see makes me blink.

Alan frowns. "What the hell? . . . Is that . . . ?"

The picture on the screen shows a tall, beautiful red-headed woman in her early twenties, dressed in red thong panties and nothing else. She's staring directly at the camera, smiling a seductive smile, so we have a very good shot of her face. I turn to Callie. She is bone white. Blood-drained. Her eyes are filled with unending fear.

"Callie—what does this mean?"

We are all looking at her. Because the young woman who calls herself Red Rose looks enough like Callie to be her sister.

"Callie?" Alan's voice is filled with alarm, and he moves toward her as she backs away from the screen, slamming into the wall behind her. She brings a fist up to her mouth. Her eyes go wide. Her entire body is shaking. Alan reaches out a hand to her.

And then she explodes. It's like watching a hurricane appear, full force, in the middle of a clear day. The fear vanishes from her eyes, replaced by a rage so intense that I flinch. She turns to Leo with a snarl, and he jolts backward. When she speaks, it comes out as a roar.

"Find her fucking address now! Now Now Now Now Now!"

Leo stares at Callie for only a split second and gets into motion, sitting down at the nearest computer terminal. Callie leans forward over the desk, grips it hard enough to whiten her knuckles. The air around her is charged. It feels like it should be crackling.

James is the one who braves her rage. "Callie," he says, voice quiet. "Who is she?"

She looks at him. Her eyes are lightning-filled.

"She's my daughter."

Then she screams and upends her desk, sending it and the laptop flying.

We stand back, open-mouthed, in shock. Not at the destruction, but at the revelation.

"Dead, dead, dead, he's fucking dead!" She whirls at me. *"Do you hear me, Smoky?"* It is a howl of agony.

And I see myself, pointing a gun at Callie those months ago, firing on an empty chamber. Yeah, I hear her.

"Get that address, Leo," I say, not taking my eyes from Callie. "Get it fast."

26

I AM IN the passenger seat of Callie's car, praying we'll survive getting to our destination in Ventura County. Callie is driving down the 101 freeway like a madwoman, breaking the sound barrier. I can only hope that the others are behind us. Leo had found the address belonging to the registered owner of the Red Rose Internet domain, and Callie had raced out the door before any of us could react. All I could do was run after her.

I look at her. She's terror and danger, all rolled up together.

"Talk to me, Callie," I say as I grip the armrest on the door.

"Look in my wallet," she growls. "It's in my purse."

I grab the wallet and open it. I know what she wants me to find the moment I see it. It's a small picture. A black-and-white, the kind of baby photo they take at the hospital. It shows a newborn, eyes squinched shut, head still a little bit cone-shaped from having fought through the birth canal.

"I was fifteen," Callie says as she makes a hairpin turn, tires squealing. Her voice is tight. "Fifteen and silly and stupid. I slept with Billy Hamilton because he managed to charm the skirt off me and he smelled so good. Isn't that funny, honey-love?" she says, bitter. "That's what I remember about Billy. He smelled good. Like sun and rain, mixed up together."

I don't reply. None is needed.

"Billy knocked me up, and it was a scandal like no other in the history of the Thorne household. Or the Hamilton household, for that matter. My dad almost disowned me. My mom went to church and stayed there for days. An abortion was out of the question—we were a good Catholic family, you know." The words are biting, full of sarcasm and pain. "The dads got together and worked it all out. That's how things went then in upscale Connecticut. Billy had a future, I might have one—though of course I was tainted now." She grips the steering wheel. "They decided I'd finish out that year being homeschooled, have the baby quietly, and it would be put up for adoption. The homeschooling would be explained with a cover story—I was going through treatment for severe allergies, which required a few months of isolation. That's what they decided, and that's exactly what happened. The timing was perfect. I had her over the summer, and I was ready to go back to school the next year like nothing had happened. Which is almost how it was. Like it hadn't happened." Another hairpin turn, more squealing tires. "I wasn't allowed to go out, and Billy was warned to keep his mouth shut under pain of death." She shrugs. "He wasn't a bad one. He did keep his mouth shut, and he never treated me badly after that. The whole thing just sort of . . . went away." She nods at the picture in my hand. "But even though I was stupid and silly, I knew it wasn't right to pretend it was just a dream. One of the nurses took that picture for me. I forced myself to look at it at least once a month. And I made some decisions." Her voice is low, earnest. I can imagine her, sitting alone in her room, taking a silent oath. "I was never going to be stupid and silly again. I was done being Catholic. And that was the last time that life-changing decisions were going to be made on my behalf by anyone."

"Jesus, Callie." I don't know what else to say.

She shakes her head, once. "I never tried to find her, Smoky. I didn't feel it would be right to. I mean, I knew she had been adopted. I did know that much. Beyond that, I decided that she needed to be allowed to live her own life." She laughs, a painful laugh, like a knife cutting metal. "But I guess what they say is true, honey-love. You never get to stop being a parent, not even if you've given up your child. She runs a porn site, and she's probably dead because I'm her mommy. Isn't life a hoot?"

Her hands are shaking on the wheel. I look down at the photo again. This is what she'd been looking at when I came out of that bathroom. Callie, crass and irreverent and quick-tongued, so full of unbreakable confidence. How many times a year did she pull out this picture, look at it, and feel the sadness I'd seen on her face?

I look out the window. The rolling hills whip past us, along with the occasional exit sign. The day is engorged with sunlight gold, the sky perfect and cloudless. This is the kind of brightness people think of when they hear the word *California*.

Fuck perfect skies and sunlight. Some part of me wants to scream right now. Because reality keeps knocking down those pins, boy: Matt, Alexa, Annie, Elaina… now Callie. Instead, I try to put the force of what I'm feeling into my words.

"Listen to me, Callie. She might not be dead. They might just be screwing with you."

She doesn't respond. Looks at me for a moment. Her eyes are filled with despair. She drives faster.

* * *

We arrive in Moorpark about thirty minutes after we'd pulled away from the office, thanks to Callie's race-car driving. It's a small but growing city near Simi Valley and Thousand Oaks, a mix of middle and upper-middle class, and we are in the center of the suburbs. We pull up to the house. It's a two-story, painted white with blue trim. Everything is quiet. A neighbor across the way is mowing his lawn. The banality is surreal.

Callie jumps out of her car, gun at the ready. A red-headed death machine driven by fear.

"Fuck," I mutter, getting out to follow her. This is all wrong.

I look down the street, hoping to see Alan or James barreling after us, but the surburban quiet prevails. I follow Callie to the door. The neighbor who'd been mowing his lawn has turned off the mower and is backing away, eyes agoggle.

Callie pounds on the front door without hesitation. "FBI!" she yells. "Open up!"

There is silence. Then we hear footsteps coming to the door. I look at Callie. Her eyes are wide, nostrils flaring. I see her hands grip her weapon tighter.

A voice comes through the door. Female. "Who is this?"

"FBI, ma'am," Callie says, finger poised outside her trigger guard. "Please open the door."

I imagine the hesitation on the other side, can feel it. Then the knob turns, the door opens, and—

I am looking at Callie's daughter, alive, eyes wide and frightened at the sight of the guns in our hands.

She's holding a baby in her arms.

27

WE'RE INSIDE, **CALLIE** seated in the living room, head in her hands. I'm in the kitchen on my cell phone, talking to Alan.

"Nothing here," I say. "He was messing with Callie."

"James and I are about ten minutes out. You want us to keep coming?"

I look into the living room, at Callie and her daughter. The air is tense, filled with fear and the exhaustion of post-adrenaline rush.

"Nooo . . . I think the fewer people here, the better. Get back to the office. I'll call you."

"Got it."

He hangs up. I take a deep breath and walk into the emotional cyclone. Callie's daughter, whose name is Marilyn Gale, is frenetic and pacing, patting the baby on the back as she stops and starts, stops and starts. Patting more for her comfort than the baby's, I think.

God, she looks like Callie. Something she doesn't seem to have noticed herself yet. A tad shorter, a touch heavier, her features a little softer. But the red hair is distinctive. And the face and figure have the same model-quality beauty to them. The eyes are different. Billy Hamilton's ghost, I muse. It's Marilyn's anger that reminds me most of Callie right now. She's pissed, the over-the-top pissed that sudden fear can create.

"Do you want to tell me what's going on here?" she shrills. "Why two FBI agents show up at my door with their guns out?"

Callie doesn't respond. Her head is still in her hands. She looks drained.

I'm going to have to do the talking for now. "Do you want to sit down, Mrs. Gale? I'll explain everything, but I think step one is to try and relax."

She stops pacing and glares at me. It's almost enough to make me think genetics does play some part in personality. I see Callie's steel shining out from those angry eyes. "I'll sit down. But don't ask me to relax."

I give her a weak smile. She sits. Callie still hasn't lifted her head from her hands.

"I'm Special Agent Smoky Barrett, Mrs. Gale, and—"

She interrupts. "It's Ms., not Mrs." She pauses. "Barrett? You're the agent who was attacked by that man six months ago? The one who lost her family?"

I flinch inside. But nod. "Yes, ma'am."

This, more than anything, seems to drive the fear from her. She's still not happy, but her anger is tinged with compassion. The cyclone subsides. Just little flashes of lightning on the fringes now. "I'm sorry," she says. She seems to notice my scars for the first time. Her gaze on them is measured and careful, but not repulsed. She looks right into my eyes, and I see something there that surprises me. Not pity. Respect.

"Thank you," I say. I take a deep breath. "I'm in charge of the section of the LA branch of the FBI that deals with violent crimes. Serial murders. We're after a man who has already killed one woman that we know of. He sent an e-mail to Agent Thorne that indicated you were a target."

She goes pale at this, clutches her baby to her chest. "What? Me? Why?"

Callie looks up now. I hardly recognize her. Her face is haggard, drawn. "He goes after women who run personal pornography sites on the Internet. He sent us a link to your Web site."

Puzzlement replaces fear on Marilyn's face. Not just puzzlement. Out-and-out shock. "Huh? But...I don't *have* a Web site. I certainly don't have a porn site, for God's sake! I'm going to college—well, I'm on maternity leave right now. This is my parents' second home; they're letting me stay here for now."

Silence. Callie stares at her, taking in her confusion. Realizing, as I did, that it's the kind of bewilderment that can't be faked. Marilyn is telling the truth.

Callie closes her eyes. Some form of relief floods her face, mixed with just a trace of sadness. I understand. She's relieved that her daughter doesn't do porn. But now she knows there's only one reason that Marilyn has gotten Jack Jr.'s attention. Limp-kneed relief combined with soul-racking guilt, my favorite.

"Are you sure it was me this—man was talking about?"

"We're sure," Callie says, quiet.

"But I don't run a porn site."

"He has other reasons." Callie looks at her. "Were you adopted, Ms. Gale?"

Marilyn frowns. "Yes, I was. Why do you..."

Her voice trails off as she looks at Callie, really looks at her for the first time. Her eyes widen and her mouth falls open. I can see her examining Callie's face, can almost hear her doing the comparisons in her head. See in her eyes when the revelation hits.

"You...You're..."

Callie smiles, a bitter smile. "Yes."

Marilyn sits there, stock-still, stunned. Emotions fly across her face. Shock, wonder, grief, anger—none of them able to find a home. "I—I don't know what to . . ." In a single quick motion, she stands, clutching her baby. "I'm going to go lay him down. I'll be right back." She whirls away, moving up the stairs to the second floor of the house.

Callie leans back, closes her eyes. She looks like she could sleep for about a zillion years. "That went well, honey-love."

I turn to her. Her face is weary and haunted. Depleted. What can I say to her? "She's alive, Callie."

This simple truth seems to hit home. A profundity similar to the one she'd given me in the hospital. Callie's eyes open and she looks at me. "How very sunny optimist of you," she says with a smile. I hear nervousness in her voice, but I'm encouraged.

We hear footsteps coming back down the stairs. Marilyn comes into the living room. She seems to have taken the time upstairs to compose herself. She looks cautious now, thoughtful. Maybe even a little intrigued.

I marvel at the speed of her recovery for a moment, then remember who her mother is.

"Can I get you something? Water or coffee?"

"Coffee would be good," I say.

"Water for me," Callie says. "I don't need any more stimulants in my system right now."

This draws just a hint of a smile from Marilyn. "Coming right up."

She goes into the kitchen and comes back with a serving tray. Hands me my coffee and indicates the creamer and sugar. Hands Callie her water and takes a cup of coffee for herself. She sits back, tucking her legs under, holding the cup in two hands as she regards Callie.

Now that the initial shock is gone, I can see her intelligence. It's in the eyes. And her strength. It's not the same strength that Callie has, not quite as hard. Almost a mix of Elaina and Callie. Mom and steel.

"So you're my mom," she says, getting right to the point. Very Callie.

"No."

Marilyn frowns. "But ... I thought you said—"

Callie holds up a hand. "Your mom is the one who raised you. I'm the one who gave you up."

I grimace at the pain I hear in her voice. The hint of self-loathing. Marilyn's frown smooths out.

"Fine. You're my birth mother."

"Guilty as charged."

"How old are you?"

"Thirty-eight."

Marilyn nods to herself, looking off, adding it up. "So you were fifteen when you had me." Takes a sip of coffee. "That's young."

Callie says nothing. Marilyn looks at her. I don't see any anger there, just curiosity. I wish that Callie would notice it.

"So tell me all about it."

Callie looks off. Sips her water. Looks back at Marilyn. I try to be still and unnoticeable. It's funny, I think. We show up, guns drawn, with a story about a serial killer. But what Marilyn wants to know about first is her mother. I wonder at this, wonder whether it says something good or ridiculous about us as human beings.

Callie starts speaking, slow at first, then picking up speed, telling the story of the charming Billy Hamilton and the overbearing Thornes. Marilyn listens, not prompting, sipping her coffee. When Callie finishes, Marilyn is quiet for a long time.

She whistles. "Wow. That sucks."

I grin. Definitely very Callie. Mistress of the understatement.

Callie remains silent. She's the picture of someone waiting for judgment to be passed.

Marilyn waves a hand, a gesture of dismissal. "It wasn't your fault, though." She shrugs. "I mean, it sucked. But you were fifteen. I don't blame you." It comes out as an abrupt statement. Callie looks down at the coffee table.

Marilyn catches her eye. "No, really. I don't. Look, I did get adopted, by great people. They love me, I love them. I've had a good life. I guess it should all be more momentous somehow—and it is, don't get me wrong—but I haven't spent twenty-three years feeling betrayed or hating you." She shrugs. "I don't know. Life isn't all straight lines and square pegs. From what I can see, it's been harder for you than it has been for me." She's quiet for a moment. When she starts speaking again, her voice is tentative. "I did wonder about you sometimes. And I have to admit, the truth is better than what I imagined. Almost a relief, really."

"What do you mean?" Callie asks.

Marilyn grins. "You could have been a crack whore. You could have given me up because you hated me. You could be dead. Trust me, this explanation is a lot easier to take."

These words seem to have an almost magical effect on Callie. I watch as color flows back into her skin, life back into her eyes. She sits up straighter. "Thanks for saying that." She pauses. Her eyes go back down to her lap. "I am sorry." God, she sounds woebegone. I just want to hug her.

Marilyn's eyes twinkle. Her voice chides. "Stop beating yourself up. Kind of makes sense, though."

Callie frowns. "How's that?"

"Well, look at me. Did you notice the baby? And the Ms., not Mrs., Gale?"

Callie's eyebrows lift. "You mean..."

Marilyn nods. "Yep. I had my own Billy Hamilton." Another shrug. "But that's okay. He's gone, and I have Steven. It's more than a fair trade. My parents are supporting us and are going to make sure I get back and finish college." She smiles. "I like my life. It's turned out fine." She leans forward, making sure Callie is looking at her. "You need to know that what you did, it didn't ruin me, okay?"

Callie sighs. Taps her fingers. Looks around the room, sips her water. Thinks about this. "Well, hell." She smiles. "It feels strange to be let off the hook so easily." She hesitates and reaches into her purse. "Want to see something?" she asks Marilyn. She pulls out the baby photo I had seen and hands it over.

Marilyn examines it. "That's me?"

"The day you were born."

"Wow, I sure was ugly." She looks up from the photo at Callie. "You've carried this around with you since then?"

"Always."

Marilyn hands the photo back to Callie. Her eyes are gentle. What she says next is Callie, all the way.

"Gee, this is a real Lifetime made-for-TV moment, huh?"

Shocked silence, then we all burst into laughter.

It's going to be okay.

28

WE ARE UPSTAIRS, on Marilyn's computer, looking at the Red Rose site.

"I wish that was me," she says. "But trust me, it isn't."
She smiles at Callie. "My boobs aren't that big. And I have
stretch marks on my tummy."

"Simple cut and paste," Callie says. "Your face on the
body of Ms. Topless." She runs a hand through her hair.
"He did it just to mess with me. He even registered the domain to you. That's how we got this address—he led me
here."

Marilyn turns away from the computer. "Am I in danger? Are we—Steven and I—in danger?"

Callie doesn't reply right away. Weighing her words.
"It's possible. I can't be sure. You don't fit his profile,
but..."

"Serial killers are unpredictable."

"Yes."

Marilyn nods, thinking. I am surprised that she is not
more fearful. "This is almost enough to make me rethink
my major."

Callie frowns. "What's your major?"

"Criminology."

Callie's mouth falls open. So does mine. "You're kidding."

"Nope. Weird, huh?" A lopsided grin. "Coincidence?" she says, sotto voce. "I think not!"

A smile ghosts across Callie's face. "Strange days, indeed."

"Most peculiar, Momma," Marilyn quips back, not missing the opening or the reference to the John Lennon song. They both laugh.

"I don't want to take any chances," Callie says, serious again. "I'm going to arrange for police protection until this is over."

Marilyn nods, accepting this. She's a mother; she's not going to turn the offer down. "You think it's going to be over at some point?"

Callie gives her a grim smile. It's filled with all kinds of promises for Jack Jr. "We're good, Marilyn." Callie points at me. "And she's the best. Bar none."

Marilyn looks me over. Examines my scars. "Is that true, Agent Barrett?"

"We'll get him," I say. I decide to leave it at that. Confident, without my own self-doubts. "We usually do. These guys almost always screw up. He will, and that will lead us to him."

Marilyn looks back and forth between us. Seems to accept this. "What now?" she asks.

"Now," I say, "Agent Thorne is going to call the local police and set up a twenty-four-hour watch on your home. I'm going to call the team and let them know what's happening. They're probably all jumping out of their skins."

We make our calls. Alan's relief sounds visceral. Callie meets no resistance from the locals.

"They're on their way," she says.

I don't want to say it, but I have to. "We need to do the same once they arrive. We have to get back."

She hesitates, then nods. "I know." She turns to Marilyn, biting her lower lip. "Marilyn...can I..." She laughs, shaking her head. "This is all so surreal and bizarre, honey-love. But...can we get together again?"

Marilyn's smile is immediate. "Of course we can. On one condition."

"What's that?" Callie asks.

"You tell me your name. I can't call you 'Agent Thorne' forever."

We are sitting in the car. Callie hasn't started it yet. She is gazing at her daughter's house. I can't decipher her expression or guess at her thoughts.

So I ask the obvious question. "How are you?"

She continues to look off before turning to me. Her face is tired, but thoughtful.

"I'm...fine, honey-love. I'm not just saying it to reassure you. That went better than I had ever imagined. Or hoped. But it makes me wonder."

"About?"

"What they thought I was going to lose. They said they were going to make us each lose something. But I came out ahead. Do you think that's how they meant for it to go?"

I think about this. "No," I say. "I don't. I think they were convinced that she wouldn't accept you. I also think they were convinced that it would knock you off your game fatally."

She purses her lips. "I don't know about that. I agree with the first. But I don't think they were hoping I was going to be useless as a result of this. I think they were hoping just the opposite, in fact. I'm getting a feel for this one, honey-love. They don't want to be caught. But they do want to be hunted. And they want us at our best." She looks at me, a fierce look. "And do you know what? It worked. I won't quit now until we get them. That was the whole point of this for them, you understand? To let me know that she'll never be safe until we catch them."

Her words feel right to me. Callie has insight, gets the same little epiphanies that I do. It's part of what makes her good. I say the only thing that it makes sense to say.

"Then let's catch them."

29

IT TAKES FOREVER to get back. It was early afternoon by the time we left, and rush hour starts early in southern California. When we arrive in the office, everyone stands up, faces filled with expectancy.

"Don't ask, honey-loves," she says, putting up a hand. "Nothing to say right now." Her cell phone rings and she turns away to answer it.

That Callie curtain has been closed again. I'm relieved, and I can tell the others are as well. It means that she's going to be fine. Everyone would be there for her in an instant, but seeing Callie vulnerable is unsettling. I wonder if this is part of the reason that she closed herself off again. Not so much for herself as for us.

Alan fills the silence. "I'm going through the case file on Annie again," Alan says. "Something's bothering me. Not sure what yet."

I nod, but I'm distracted. Or perhaps just tired. I look at my watch, and I'm shocked to see that it's near the end of the day.

Not that the limits of our schedule are anything but theoretical. The stakes are too high, doing what we do. I always thought this must be what it's like to be in combat. When the bullets are flying, you shoot back, whatever time it is. And if you have an opportunity to advance on the enemy, you take it, whether it's four in the morning or four in the afternoon. The other parallel is that you take advantage of times of silence, the opportunities to rest, because you don't know when they'll come again.

This seems to be one of those times, so I make the decision any good general should.

"I want everyone to head home," I say. "Things may start getting crazy tomorrow. Crazier, I should say. Rest up."

James comes up to me. "I won't be in till lunch," he says, quiet. "Tomorrow's that day for me."

It takes me a moment to place what he's talking about. "Oh!" I grimace. "I'm sorry, James. I'd forgotten. Please give my best to your mom."

He turns and leaves without reply.

"I'd forgotten as well, honey-love," Callie murmurs. "Probably because it gives Damien a human side."

"Forgot what?" Leo asks.

"Tomorrow is the anniversary of the death of James's sister," I say. "She was murdered. They go to her grave every year to pay their respects."

"Oh." His face twists into a sour grimace. "Fuck, man!"

It comes out with a passionate vehemence that startles me.

He waves it off. "Sorry. I just…this shit is getting to me."

"Welcome to the club, honey-love." Callie's voice is not unkind.

"Yeah. I guess." He takes in a deep breath, lets it out. Runs a hand through his hair. "I'll see you guys tomorrow."

He leaves with a last, halfhearted wave. Callie looks

after him, thoughtful. "First case is always hard. And this one is especially bad."

"Yeah. He'll be okay, though."

"I think so too, honey-love. I wasn't sure of him at the beginning of this, but little Leo is coming along." She turns to me. "So, what are you going to be doing tonight?"

"She's coming over for dinner, that's what," Alan rumbles. He looks at me. "Elaina insists."

"I don't know..."

"You should go, Smoky. It would do you good," Callie says. She gives me a meaningful look. "And it might be good for Bonnie as well." She walks over to her desk, grabs her purse. "Besides, that's what I'm going to be doing."

"You're eating dinner at Alan's?"

"No, silly. That was my daughter on the phone." She pauses. "That sounds strange, doesn't it? Anyhoo...I'll be eating over there tonight with her and my—shudder at the thought—grandson."

"That's great, Callie!" I grin at her. "Or should I say—Granny?"

"Not if you want to remain a friend, honey-love," she says, airy. She heads to the door of the office, stops and looks back at me. "Go to dinner. Do something normal, with other people."

"Well?" Alan asks. "You gonna come over or get me in trouble with Elaina?"

"Oh for God's sake. Fine."

He grins at me. "Cool. I'll meet you over there."

And he and Callie are gone, and I am alone in our offices. I do plan to follow Callie's advice. The kicker for me had been the comment about Bonnie. It would be good for her. Certainly better than going straight home to my—what had *he* called it?—*ghost ship of a home*.

But I want to sit here for a moment. Things have been

moving at such a breakneck speed, physically, mentally, spiritually. I am both energized and exhausted. I sum up the past days to myself. I have gone from suicidal to wanting to live. I have lost my best friend in the world. I have reacquainted myself with an even older friend, my gun. I have acquired a mute daughter, who might never recover. I have remembered killing my own daughter. I have found out that Callie has not just a daughter, but a grandson. I've discovered that a woman I love, Elaina, has cancer and might or might not be fine. I have become more familiar with the business of pornography than I ever wanted to be.

Yes, the bullets have, indeed, been flying.

Right now, though, the chatter of gunfire is absent, and silence rules. Time to use that silence, like a good soldier. I get up and leave the office myself, locking the door behind me, heading down the elevator.

On the way down, I realize that my silence is different from the silence of the average, everyday person. It's an opportunity to rest, true. But it's a silence filled with tension and waiting. Because you never know when the gunfire will start up again.

Are Jack Jr. and friend doing the same thing right now? Resting up before their next murder?

When Alan answers the door, I go on alert. He looks upset, enraged, fighting tears and the desire to murder at the same time.

"That *motherfucker*," he hisses.

"What?!?" I ask, alarmed, brushing into the house past him. "Is Elaina all right? Bonnie?"

"No one's hurt, but that fucker..." He stands there for a moment, clenching his fists. If he was not my friend, I'd be terrified. He rushes over to an end table, picks up a legal-size manila envelope, hands it to me.

I look at the front. It's addressed, *To Elaina Washington: R.I.P.* I go cold.

"Look inside," Alan growls.

I open it up. There's a typed note, clipped to a series of pages. When I look at the pages, I understand.

"Shit, Alan..."

"Her fucking medical history," he says, and begins pacing back and forth. "All about the tumor, the doctor's notes." He grabs the packet from me, flips a few pages. "Look at this part that he highlighted for her!"

I take it back from him and read what he'd indicated.

Mrs. Washington is stage two, bordering on a stage three. Outlook good, but must ensure the patient understands that full stage three still possible, though unlikely.

"Read his fucking note!"

I look at it, see the familiar salutation.

Greetings, Mrs. Washington!

I wouldn't call myself a friend of your husband. More of a... business acquaintance. I thought you'd appreciate knowing the truth about your current situation.

Do you know what the survival rates are for stage three, dearie? I quote: "Stage III: Metastasis to lymph nodes around the colon, a 35–60 percent chance for five-year survival."

Goodness! If I was a betting man, I'm afraid I'd have to bet against you!

Best of luck—I'll be keeping an eye on your progress!

From Hell,
Jack Jr.

"Is this true, Alan?"

"Not the way he put it, no," he snarls. "I called the doctor. He said that if he was *really* concerned about it, he would have said so. He wasn't withholding anything. Shit, the note was written to remind himself what to tell us during her next visit."

"But Elaina saw it as written, with no explanation."

I get the answer from the misery in his eyes.

I turn away from him for a moment, putting a hand to my forehead. An almost blinding rage has flared up inside me. Of all the people he could hurt, other than Bonnie, Elaina is perhaps the most undeserving. I remember this morning, the way her presence alone broke through Bonnie's barriers. I remember her with me, in the hospital. I want to kill Jack Jr.

He continues to gain access to our lives, to the personal parts of us. Bugs in Hillstead's office to get to me. Now what? Breaking into a hospital to get Elaina's medical records?

What else does he know?

I turn to Alan. "How is she?"

He takes a sudden seat in an easy chair. Looks lost. "First she was scared. Then she started crying."

"Where is she?"

"Up in the bedroom, with Bonnie." He gives me a tired look. "Bonnie won't leave her side." He puts his head in his hands. "Goddammit, Smoky...why her?"

I sigh, and move to him, putting a hand on his shoulder. "Because they knew it would hurt you like this, Alan."

His head snaps up, eyes filled with fire. "I want these fuckers so bad."

"I know." Boy, do I. "Listen, Alan. I know it probably won't help...but I don't think Elaina's in any physical danger from Jack Jr. and company, at least not right now. I don't think that's the purpose of this."

"What makes you say that?"

I shake my head, thinking about what Callie had said earlier today. "This is a part of their game. They *want* us to hunt them. And they wants us at our best. To give us a personal stake in this."

His face grows grim. "It's working."

I nod. "No shit."

He leans back, sighs. The sigh is belly-deep and full of sadness. He looks up at me, eyes pleading. "Can you go up and see her?"

I touch his shoulder. "Of course I can."

I dread it, but of course I can.

I knock on the bedroom door, open it, and peek my head in. Elaina is lying on her side, back to me. Bonnie is sitting next to her, stroking her hair. Bonnie looks at me as I enter, and I stop. Her eyes are full of fury. We stare at each other for a moment, and I nod in understanding. They'd hurt her Elaina. She was mad.

I move around the bed, sitting down on its edge. The memory of the hospital flies into my mind. Elaina's eyes are open, staring off at nothing. Her face is puffy from tears. "Hey," I say.

She glances up at me. Goes back to looking at nothing. Bonnie keeps stroking her hair.

"Do you know what upsets me the most, Smoky?" she says, breaking the silence.

"No. Tell me."

"That Alan and I never had children. We tried and tried and tried, but it just never happened. Now I'm too old, and I have to deal with cancer." She closes her eyes, opens them. "And this man gets to invade our lives. Gets to laugh at us. At me. Make me afraid."

"That's what he's trying to do."

"Yes. And it worked." Silence. "I would have made a good mom, don't you think, Smoky?"

My face twists. I'm horrified by the depth of Elaina's pain. It's Bonnie who answers her question. She taps on Elaina's shoulder, and Elaina turns her head to look at her. Bonnie makes sure she's watching, and then she nods.

Yes, she's saying. You would have made a wonderful mom.

Elaina's eyes go soft. She reaches out to touch Bonnie's face. "Thank you, sweetheart." Silence. She looks at me. "Why is he doing this, Smoky?"

Why did he do it, why is he doing it, why did this happen? Why my daughter, my son, my husband, my wife? This is the unending question from victims. "The short answer is that he likes hurting you, Elaina. That's the simple motivation. The other side of it is that he knows it'll make Alan afraid. That makes him feel powerful. And he likes that very much."

Of course, I know there isn't really a good answer to that unending question. Why me? I'm a good mother/father/brother/daughter/son. I keep my head down, do my best. Sure, I lie a little, but I tell the truth more than I lie, and I love the people in my life the best I can. I try to do more right than wrong, and I'm happier when there are more smiles than pain. I'm no hero; I'm not going to end up in any history books. But I'm here, and I matter. So why me?

I can't tell them what I really think. Why? Because you breathe and walk, and because evil does exist. Because the cosmic dice were rolled and you came up short. God either forgot about you that day, or it's a part of His master plan, pick your belief. The truth is, bad things are going to happen somewhere, every single day, and today was just your turn.

Some people might call that a bleak or cynical outlook. To me, it's what keeps me sane. Otherwise you start thinking that maybe it's the bad guys who have the edge. I prefer to think, *Nope. No edge. The simple fact is that evil preys on good, and today, good had a bad day.* Which brings with it an acceptance of the other side of that argument, that tomorrow might be evil's turn for some rain. And that's called hope.

None of this is helpful when they ask why, so I tell them some lesser truth like the one that I just gave Elaina. Sometimes it eases their pain, sometimes it doesn't. Usually it doesn't, because the fact is, if you have to ask the question, then you don't really care about the answer.

She mulls this over. When she looks back at me, I see an unfamiliar emotion on her face. Anger. "Get this man, Smoky. Do you hear me?"

I swallow. "Yeah."

"Good. I know you will." She sits up. "Now, can you do me a favor?"

"Anything." I mean it. If she asked me to pull a star down from the sky right now, I'd do my best.

"Tell Alan to come up here when you go down. I know him. He's sitting there blaming himself. Tell him to knock it off. I need him."

Shaken but back as strong as ever. I realize afresh something I've known for a long time: I love this woman. "I will." I turn to Bonnie. "Let's go, sweetheart."

She shakes her head. No. Pats a hand on Elaina's

shoulder, then grips it, possessive. I frown. "Honey, I think we need to leave Elaina and Alan alone tonight."

She shakes her head again, fierce now. No way, José.

"It would be fine with me for her to stay, if you don't mind. Bonnie's lovely."

I look at Elaina, dumbfounded. "Are you sure?"

She reaches over, strokes Bonnie's hair. "I'm sure."

"Well…okay." Besides, I think to myself, it would take a miracle to pry her away from Elaina right now. "Then I'll go. Bonnie, I'll come see you in the morning, honey."

She nods. I head out the door, turn as I hear small footsteps behind me. Bonnie has gotten off the bed and is looking up at me. She snags my arm, pulls me down to her level. Her face is filled with concern.

"What, honey?"

She pats herself, reaches over and pats me. Does this again, insistent. And again, the concern growing on her face. Then I get it. It makes my face flush, my eyes prick with tears. I'm with *you*, she's saying. I'm only staying here to help Elaina. But I'm with *you*. She wants to make sure I understand. Yes, Elaina is Mom. But I'm with you.

I don't speak. Instead, I nod in reply and hug her to me before leaving the room.

Downstairs, Alan is standing and staring out the window at the coming dusk.

"She's going to be okay, Alan. She wanted me to tell you to stop blaming yourself and that she needs you. Oh, and you have Bonnie for tonight. She refused to leave Elaina."

This seems to perk him up. "Really?"

"Uh-huh. She's being very protective." I poke him in

the chest. "You know I sympathize, Alan. You know I do. But you need to get your ass up there and hug your wife." I smile. "Bonnie's got your back."

"Yeah," he says, after a space of time. "You're right. Thanks."

"No problem. And, Alan? If you need time off tomorrow, take it."

His face is somber. "No fucking way, Smoky. They got what they wanted. I'm after those motherfuckers till they're caught or dead." He smiles, and this time, it's a scary smile. "I think they're going to get more than they bargained for."

"Damn right," I reply.

30

THE DRIVE BACK feels lonely. Keenan and Shantz are where they should be, with Bonnie, so I really am alone. It's dark out, and highways at night have a distinct, isolated feel to them. At times in my life this has been a welcome feeling. This isolation is filled with angry thoughts, sadness, and me gripping the steering wheel, imagining it's Jack Jr.'s neck. The moon shines strong. Somewhere in me, I know it's a beautiful light. Tonight, it reminds me of the times I've seen blood pooled in the moonlight. Black and reflective and final.

I ride through the moonlight that reminds me of blood all the way home. I'm pulling into the driveway when my cell phone rings.

"It's James."

I sit straight up. There is something in his voice I've never heard before. "James? What is it?"

His voice is trembling. "Those—those *motherfuckers*!"

Jack Jr.

"Tell me what happened, James."

I can hear his breathing over the phone. "I got to my mom's house about twenty minutes ago. I was going up to knock on the door when I noticed an envelope was taped to it. It had my name on it. So I opened it up." He takes a deep breath. "It had a note in it, and—and..."

"What?"

"A ring. Rosa's ring."

Rosa was James's sister, the one who had died. The one whose grave he was going to visit tomorrow with his mother. A dark understanding is starting to flutter in the back of my mind. "What did the note say, James?"

"Just one line. *Rosa, no longer R.I.P.*"

I feel a plummeting sensation in my stomach.

James's voice is desperate. "The ring in that envelope, Smoky? We buried her with it. Do you understand?"

The fluttering is becoming noisier, like bats' wings. I don't respond.

"So I called the cemetery. Got hold of security. And they went out and verified it."

"Verified what, James?" I think I know, but I ask because I hope I'm wrong. The bats' wings are in full roar now.

He takes a deep breath. When he speaks, his voice is breaking. "She's gone, Smoky. Rosa. Those fuckers dug up her grave."

I lay my forehead against the steering wheel. The fluttering is silent now. "Oh, James..."

"Do you know how old she was when that scumbag murdered her, Smoky? Twenty. Twenty and she was smart and kind and beautiful and it took him three days to kill her. That's what they told me. Three days. You know how long it took my mother to stop crying about it?" Now he screams. *"Never!"*

I sit up. My eyes are still closed. I know what it is that I hear in James's voice that is so foreign. Grief. Grief and vulnerability. "I don't know what to say. Are you...do you want me to come over? What do you want to do?" My words echo how I feel inside. Helpless.

There's a long silence, followed by a ragged sigh. "No. My mother's upstairs, curled up and sobbing and pulling at her hair. I need to go to her, I need to . . ." He trails off. "They're doing what they said they were going to do."

I feel empty. "Yeah." I tell him about Elaina.

"*Son* of a bitch!" he shouts. I can almost feel him struggling to get himself under control. "Motherfucker." More silence. "I'll handle it. Don't come over. I have a feeling you'll be getting another phone call tonight."

My stomach flutters. He said he was going to make each of us lose something. He still has Leo to go.

"I want this scumbag, Smoky. I want him bad."

I've heard these words, in different ways, two other times today. The thought of hearing them again fills me with both anger and despair. I manage to keep my voice even. "Me too, James. Go help your mom. Call me if you need me."

"I won't need you."

So much for grief and vulnerability.

He hangs up and I sit in my car in my driveway, looking up at the moon. For a minute, just a minute, I'm consumed by one of those selfish, self-absorbed moments only life-or-death leadership positions can bring. These people are my responsibility. I feel that I am failing them, but in this selfish moment, I don't worry about their well-being—I only wish that it wasn't my responsibility.

I grip the steering wheel, and I twist it hard.

"It *is* your responsibility," I whisper, and the selfishness goes away, replaced by white-hot hate.

So I do something I've done before: I scream inside my car, pounding the steering wheel, under the fucking moon.

Smoky therapy.

31

WHEN I GET inside, I dial Leo's cell number. It rings and rings. "Goddammit, Leo, pick up!" I snarl.

Then he does. His voice sounds tired and dead, and my heart sinks. "Hello?"

"Leo! Where are you?"

"I'm at the vet with my dog, Smoky."

The normality of this lifts my hopes, for just a moment.

"Someone cut off all his legs. I have to put him down." I stand, gaping. Poleaxed. Then his voice breaks. The clean, poignant break of a china plate hitting brick. "Who would do something like that, Smoky? I got home and he was there in the living room, trying to ... trying to ..." His grief makes him sound like he is gagging, as he finds the words. "Trying to crawl to me. There was blood everywhere, and he was making these awful sounds, like ... like a baby. Looking at me with those eyes, it was like ... he looked like he thought he'd done something *wrong*. Like he was asking me, 'What, what did I do wrong? I'll fix it, just tell me. See? I'm a good dog.'"

Tears track down my cheeks.

"Who would do something like that?"

If he really thought about it, he'd know who. What

he's really saying is that no one should exist who could do this. "Jack Jr. and friend, Leo. That's who."

I hear him gasp, and it is filled with agony. *"What?"*

"They either did it or had someone do it. But it was them."

I sense him putting it all together. "What they said in that e-mail..."

"Yeah." Yes, Leo, I think. They do exist, and what they did to your dog, that was *nothing* to them.

A long, hard silence. I can imagine his thoughts. My dog was tortured because of who I am. Guilt coming home to roost, debilitating and awful. He clears his throat, a miserable sound. "Who else, Smoky?"

So I take a breath and I tell him. About Elaina and James. Omitting the specifics of Elaina's illness. He's quiet when I'm done. I wait him out.

"I'll be fine." It's a short statement, and full of lies. But he's letting me know he understands.

I say the phrase again, the one I'm growing to hate. "Call me if you need me."

"Yeah."

I hang up and stand there for a moment in my kitchen, forehead in one hand. I can't get that picture out of my mind. Those pleading eyes. *What did I do wrong...?* And the answer is a terrible one, all the more terrible because the dog will die never knowing the truth.

Nothing. You did nothing wrong.

"They're really turning up the volume," Callie says.

"Yeah. I wanted you to know. Be careful."

"Both ways on that, honey-love."

"Don't worry."

After hanging up, I go to the kitchen table, sit down,

put my head in my hands. This has been the worst day in a long time. I feel beaten up and I feel sad and I feel empty. I also feel alone.

Callie had her daughter, Alan had Elaina. Who did I have?

So I cry. It makes me feel silly and weak, but I do it because I can't help it. It goes on long enough that it makes me feel angry, and I wipe my face with my hands, willing the weakness away. "Stop with the pity party already," I growl to myself. "Fact is, this is your own fault. You wouldn't let them come and be with you when you were hurting, so if you want to blame anyone, blame yourself."

I feel anger building, and I go with it. It dries my eyes. Jack Jr. and his buddy were messing with my family. They were reaching into their lives and harming the most intimate parts of them.

"They're dead meat," I say to the empty house. Which makes me smile. Still loony after all these months, giving pep talks to the air.

This is it, I realize. The new me. The way it's going to stay. I still have the dragon waking up inside me, and I can still see the dark train and fire my gun. But I'm not built from straight lines and certainty anymore. I bounce and jostle, and parts of me get knocked out of place. I have a new feature: fragility. It is alien, I don't really like it—but it's the truth.

I move up the stairs toward my bedroom, feeling like I'm dragging chains behind me, I'm so tired. So much emotion.

I pass the little home office Matt had set up for us, and something makes me stop and peer in. I see my computer, dust-covered and unused for so many months. And I wonder.

I sit down in front of it, wait as it powers up. Do I still

have an Internet connection? I can't remember how it's billed. But I open up a browser and see that I do. I lean back for a moment, looking at the icon on my desktop that leads to my e-mail program. Thinking.

I double-click it and it opens up. I hesitate for a moment, then click the *check mail* button. All kinds of things begin to download. Months of messages and spam ignored. What I thought I might see is there as well. The most recent message, sent just an hour ago. The subject is *How Much Is That Doggy in the Window?*

I feel energized by my hatred of him at this moment. I open it up, and read.

> Dearest Smoky,
>
> By now I'm sure that you've found I am a man of my word. Callie Thorne has had to face her daughter, Alan Washington's wife has to wonder if she's going to die. Poor Leo, he's grappling with the untimely demise of man's best friend. As for young James—well...I'm looking at Rosa as I write this. She's a bit worse for wear, but you would be amazed at the efficacy of the preserving fluids they use on the dead. Her eyes are gone, but her hair still looks lovely. Be sure to pass that along to James for me, will you?
>
> I think vengeance is the most effective way to sharpen a sword, don't you? Well, think about it. If you didn't think so before, I'm sure that you do now. How you all must want my blood! Perhaps some of you will even dream about it. Me, begging for

mercy and receiving none. You, giving me a
bullet in the head instead of a jail cell.

But there are two sides to this coin, and
I wish to up the ante. To make something
clear, if it is not already so: Nothing you
hold dear is safe.

Hunt me well, because as long as I am out
here, free to slink through the woods at
the edges of civilization, I will take and
take and take from you. These things I have
now touched and taken will seem like
nothing.

Every week that you fail to catch me,
I will take something from each of you. I
will take Callie Thorne's long-lost
daughter and grandchild. I will take Alan's
wife. I will kill James's mother. On and on
and on until everyone lives the life you
do, Smoky. Until everything they love is
gone, until their houses are empty and they
are left with only one thing: the terrible
knowledge that all of it happened because
of who they are and what they do.

I hope you know by now that I mean what I
say. And I hope this ever-present gun to
the head provides the final impetus needed
to bring you all to a state of focused
readiness. I need you, all of you, honed.
I need you to have killer's eyes.

Now run along and do your best. You have
one week. During that time, the things you
love are safe. After that, I begin to eat
your worlds, and your souls begin to die.

Can you feel the excitement? I know that I can. Best of luck.

From Hell,

Jack Jr.

P.S. Agent Thorne, perhaps you are wondering—did I really take something from you? Perhaps, in truth, you feel I have done you a service by mistake. In some ways, this may be possible. But think upon it more. Perhaps I simply reminded you of what you have lost forever. Have you figured it out yet? What have you lost?

I look at these words for a long, long time, sitting here in my empty home. I'm not sorrowful, or even angry. Instead, I am filled with what they wanted all along.

Certainty.

I will die before anyone else in my small family ends up as I have: talking to themselves as they weep alone.

32

IT IS MORNING, and I have given the team an edited version of Jack Jr.'s e-mail. I look at them, take stock of my troops.

They all look like hell. But they all look angry. No one is interested in talking about what happened. They want to hunt. And they look to me for guidance, waiting.

It's funny, I think. Responsibility is such an easy coat to put on, such a hard one to take off. Just a week ago, I was thinking about blowing my brains out. Now they want me to tell them what to do.

"Well," I say, "we've established one thing firmly."

"What's that?" Alan says.

"Jack Jr. and his buddy? They're real assholes."

There is a brief silence, and then everyone is laughing. Everyone except for James. Some of the tension leaves the room.

Some of it.

"Listen up," I say. "Round one goes to them, hands down. No question. But they've made a big mistake. They wanted us to want to get them, and they've gotten their wish. They have no idea what that means." I pause, gauging their reaction. "They think they're ahead of us. What else is new? They always think that. But we have fingerprints on one of them, and we know that there are two of them. We're closing the gap. Okay?" Nods. "Good. So let's get down to business. Tell me again what Dr. Child said about the profile on our killers, Callie, I wasn't paying attention."

Dr. Kenneth Child is one of the few profilers whose opinion I respect. I had asked Callie to get him a copy of all the information on Jack Jr. and to ask him for a consultation, soonest.

"He said to tell you that he read the letter and has some opinions, but he wants to wait until after he sees whatever is in the package. The one that's supposed to arrive on the twentieth." She shrugs. "He was pretty firm about it."

I let it go. Dr. Child has never brushed me off. I'll have to trust his instincts on this. I turn to Alan and Leo. "What's the status on the warrant for Annie's subscriber list?"

"We should have it in an hour," Leo says.

"Good. Stay on that." I snap my fingers. "Do we have someone from the LAPD bomb squad lined up?"

Alan nods. "Yep. They're bringing a bomb sniffer with them."

"Bomb sniffer" is the name given to a machine utilizing ion mobile spectrometry. In short, it can detect traces of ionized molecules that are specific to explosive materials.

Much debate had gone on about how to set things up for the twentieth. AD Jones wanted a SWAT team there, in case Jack Jr. or friend decided to make this delivery personally. I had nixed this idea.

"That's not how they've operated so far," I had said. "And that's not how they're going to operate now. I expect it to be simple. Regular delivery."

He'd agreed after some protest. And after I'd made the point that bringing in SWAT would likely bring the media with it. He and I had seen eye-to-eye on having a bomb tech there, however. Not taking that precaution would be foolhardy.

"Something's still bothering me about Annie's file," Alan says. He glances at James. "Be nice to get another point of view on it."

"Help him out, James."

James nods. He hasn't said a single word this morning.

"There is another question that begs an answer, honey-love," Callie murmurs. "How are they getting all their information? I mean—we found the bugs in Dr. Hillstead's office, but medical records, my daughter?"

"It's not that hard," Leo pipes up. We look at him. "Information just isn't as secure as people think it is. Elaina's medical records?" He shrugs. "A white coat and attitude, and you can walk just about anywhere in a hospital. Combine that with computer know-how, and you've hacked into the hospital servers. You can buy information, steal information, hack information." He shrugs. "You'd be shocked at how easy it can be. I've seen it, working in Computer Crimes. Good hackers, or identity thieves, can get their hands on all kinds of personal data. Things that would surprise you." He looks at Callie. "Give me a week, and I could find out everything about you. From your credit rating to what medications you take." He looks around at all of us. "The stuff he's come up with so far? Disturbing, I know. But not rocket science to acquire."

I stare at him for a moment, letting this sink in. We all do. Finally, I nod. "Thanks, Leo. So—does everyone know what they're working on?" I look around. "Good."

The door to the office opens, breaking the moment. I glance to see who's coming in, and concern floods me.

Marilyn Gale is standing in the doorway, looking worried. A uniformed policeman is standing next to her, holding a package in his arms.

33

IT CAME AN hour ago," she says. "Addressed to you, Agent Barrett, care of me. I figured..." she trails off, but we all understand. Who else would be sending something for me to Marilyn's address?

We're back in the office. Everyone is crowded around the desk, looking at the package while sneaking curious glances at Marilyn. Callie notices the latter, and her exasperation at this seems to overtake her concern about the package.

"Oh, for heaven's sake," she says. "This is my daughter, Marilyn Gale. Marilyn, meet James, Alan, and Leo, lower functionaries."

Marilyn grins at this. "Hi," she says.

"Did you intercept it?" I ask the policeman, a Sergeant Oldfield.

"No, ma'am." He's a solid-state-looking guy. Been around, very comfortable being the police, and not cowed by myself or the FBI in general. "Our assignment was to watch the residence. And Ms. Gale when she goes out, of course." He jerks a thumb at Marilyn. "She came to us with the package, explained her concerns, and asked us to transport her and the package here."

I turn to Marilyn. "You didn't open it, did you?"

Her face grows serious again. "No. I didn't think I should. I mean, I've only done my first year in criminology"—I see Alan and Leo exchange glances at this—"but even if I hadn't, all you have to do is watch some TV to know you don't mess with possible evidence."

"That's good, Marilyn," I say. I choose my next words with care. I don't want to frighten her too much, but they have to be said. "That's not the only reason, though. What if he decided to do something crazy? Like send a letter bomb."

Her eyes go wide. She gets a little pale. "Oh—I . . . Jesus. I mean, it never occurred to me . . ." She gets paler. Thinking of her baby, I bet.

Callie puts a hand on her shoulder. I see anger and concern in Callie's eyes. "Nothing to worry about now, honey-love. It was x-rayed by security before you came up, right?"

"Yes."

"That's exactly the kind of thing they look for."

Marilyn's color is coming back. She recovers fast.

So then what we have here, I think, is something new and exciting. And maybe not pretty to look at.

"Callie, why don't you take Marilyn to lunch?"

She gets the message. I'm going to open this up; there could be something in here that Marilyn doesn't need to see.

"Good idea. Come on, honey-love." She grabs Marilyn by the arm, moving her toward the door. "Where's little Steven, by the way?"

"My mom's watching him. Are you sure you can leave right now?"

"It's fine," I say to her, smiling though I don't feel it inside. "And thanks for bringing this by. If this happens again, call us. Don't touch the package."

Her eyes widen again, and she nods. Callie hustles her out.

"Mind if I hang around, ma'am?" Sergeant Oldfield asks. He shrugs. "I'd like to see what's in the package. Get a feel for the perp."

"Sure. As long as you add intercepting packages to your list of duties in the future." I look at him. "Not a rebuke, just a request."

He nods. "Already done, ma'am."

I open a drawer, reach in, and extract some latex gloves, slip them on. Now I focus on the package. It's another legal-size manila envelope. The familiar block printing in black ink is on the front: ATTN.: AGENT SMOKY BARRETT. The package is about a half to three quarters of an inch thick.

I turn it over, check the flap. Not sealed. Just the brad holding it closed. I look up. Everyone is silent, waiting. Might as well open it.

The letter is on top. I rifle through the other contents, a brief look. My eyes narrow at the sight of a few pages of printed photos. Each picture shows a woman, naked from the waist up, wearing panties, some tied to chairs, some tied to beds. In every case, a hood is over the woman's head. Something else is in the envelope, and my heart sinks. A CD.

I turn my attention to the letter. What now? I think, bleak.

Greetings, Agent Barrett!

I realize this was circuitous, being sent care of Ms. Gale. But that served just one purpose: to continue to push my prior point home. That no one you love is safe, should I decide to reach out and . . . touch them.

*No, this is all for you, Agent Barrett. Please bear
with me as I walk you through it. There is a
philosophical basis behind it, some history you need to
understand, if you are to grasp these contents in their
entirety.*

*Do you know what the most searched-for word on the
Internet is? Sex. Keeping that in mind, do you know what
one of the other most sought-after words is? Rape.*

*With the millions who access the Web, with all that
exists upon it, two of the things most looked for, most
desired, are sex and rape.*

*What does this mean? One could argue, with the
demographics of the Net, that it means there are a million
men sitting in their homes right now, thinking about the
subject of rape. All sweaty palms and tents in their
trousers. This is something, is it not?*

*Now let me take you down another, related path. A
new type of Web site has begun to proliferate on the
Internet. Sites devoted to men sharing their hatred of
women with each other. Let us take the site aptly named
"revengeonthebitch.com." On this Web site, jilted men
post compromising photos of their former girlfriends or
wives. Nude photos. Sexual photos. All with one end in
mind: degradation and embarrassment. Below each
photo, others are invited to post their opinions. I've
enclosed a sample of this, the first attachment. Give it a
once-over.*

I find the attachment he's referring to. At the top is a
picture of a smiling, brown-haired woman. She's twenty
or twenty-five. She's naked, legs spread for the camera.
The caption says: *My stupid, cheating girlfriend. One skanky
fucking slut.* Below it is a listing of responses. I read through
them.

CALIFORNIADUDE: WHAT A FUCKING SKANK! BE
GLAD SOMEONE ELSE IS HITTING THAT NASTY
PUSSY!

JAKE 28: SHOULD HAVE SLIPPED THAT BITCH
SOME ROOFIES AND PASSED HER OFF TO ME AND
MY CREW TO BUTT-RAPE HER! SLUT!

RIZZO: ROOFIES RULE!

DANNYBOY: I'D HIT IT!

TNINCH: NICE COOZE. TOO BAD SHE'S SUCH A
CUNT.

HUNGNHARD: DO WHAT I DO! SHOVE YOUR
COCK IN HER MOUTH AND TELL HER TO SHUT THE
FUCK UP!

I put it aside. I've read enough. The careless hatred is
nauseating.

"Wow," Leo whistles. "That is incredibly fucking disturbing."

I continue reading.

> Revelatory, isn't it? So, what do we have in our
> cauldron, then? Let's take stock: sex and rape, hatred of
> women as a pastime. Mix them together, and what do
> we get?
>
> An environment perfectly conducive to a meeting of
> the minds. Minds like mine, Agent Barrett.
>
> True, most of these minds are puerile, unworthy. But
> if you are willing to search, as I am, to poke, coddle,
> cajole . . . you can find a few who are poised to take that
> leap to the other side. All they are lacking, in most
> instances, is little bit of encouragement. A mentor, if
> you will.

I feel my stomach beginning to churn. Some part of
me thinks I know where this is going.

*I believe I've laid the groundwork for your full
understanding. Now let's jump to the photos, shall we?
You've probably already glanced at them. Give them a
good once-over.*

I do. There are five women in total. I take a closer look.
"What do you think?" I ask Alan. "Do the bed and chair
look the same in each picture?"

Alan takes the pages, scans them. "Yeah." He squints,
then puts the pages down on my desk, next to each other.
He points to the carpet in one. "Look at that."

I do. I see a stain.

"Then here," he says, pointing to another one of the
pictures.

Same stain.

"Shit," Leo says. "Different women, same guy."

"But it's not Jack, is it?" James says, breaking his silence. "Jack's not the guy. Maybe Jack's current companion."

Silence at this. I go back to the letter.

*You are a sharp one, Agent Barrett. I'm sure you've
realized by now, after poring over these photos, that these
young lasses all appear in the same location. The reason is
simple: All five were killed by the same man!*

I curse. Part of me knew it, but he had confirmed it.
These women were already dead.

*Perhaps you, or one of your compatriots, have already
deduced the rest as well. That the man who killed these
women is not me. If so, then let me be the first to give
applause.*

I found the talented young man who took these

*pictures in that vast, dark environment, those wild plains
that make up the World Wide Web. I recognized his
hungers and his hatreds, and it did not take long at all for
him to take his leap. To relinquish his last, silly hold on the
light and embrace the dark.*

*Of course, this could be a hoax on my part, yes? Take a
look at the CD I have enclosed, and when you are done,
feel free to call Agent Jenkins in the New York office of
your FBI. Ask him about Ronnie Barnes.*

*Oh, and if some hope is leaping in your breast that
Barnes will provide you with that lead you yearn for, I'm
sorry to be the one to tell you, but Mr. Barnes isn't with us
anymore. Watch the CD. You'll understand.*

*Down to the point of it all, as I end this for now. The
point remains the same: Hunt me. Hunt me well, and
remember this: Ronnie Barnes was just one of so many
with those special hungers. And I am always looking for
those meetings of the minds.*

*From Hell,
Jack Jr.*

"Jesus Christ," Alan says in disgust.

"Interesting," James muses. "He's like a living computer virus. That's what he's showing us. That he can
replicate in others."

"Yeah," Leo replies. "And he's still upping the ante.
Letting us know he ain't gonna stop escalating until we
get him."

I'm too tired and disturbed to reply. I hand Leo the
CD. "Put it in."

We move over to stand behind him as he places the
CD in the tray and opens it up. We see what is now becoming all too familiar—a video file. Leo looks up at me.

"Go ahead."

He double-clicks it. Video and sound start. We see a woman bound to a chair. This time, she's fully nude, and her face isn't hooded. She's a brunette, I note. A pretty girl in her early twenties. And she's terrified to the point of insanity.

A man steps in next to her. He's grinning, naked. I swallow in disgust as I notice he's also fully erect. Turned on by the terror. I assume this is Ronnie Barnes.

"Geeky-looking guy," Oldfield notes.

Unkind, but he's right. Ronnie Barnes is a pimply-faced, only-just-postadolescent, with a scrawny chest and thick-lensed glasses. The kind who draws jeers from shallow women. He'll masturbate thinking about them even though he hates them for the things they say. He'll despise them even more for being desirable, despise himself for desiring them. I know all of this not because he's scrawny and pimply, but because he holds a knife in his hands, and it's giving him a hard-on.

He looks toward something we can't see, off camera. "You want me to do it now?" he asks. I don't hear a response, but he nods and licks his lower lip, excited. "Cool."

"Who is he talking to?" Alan wonders.

"Two guesses," I say.

Barnes bends over, seems to gather himself. What he proceeds to do next is so decisive, so brutal, that we all recoil in shock.

"*Fucking cunt!*" he screams. He raises the hunting knife and brings it down point-first, with all the brutality he can muster. It almost seems to disappear into her. He doesn't just pull the knife out, he *yanks* it, savage and furious. He raises it high above his head, again, and brings it down, again.

He is putting his entire body into it, all his muscles; his neck is corded with the effort.

Again.

This is not the methodical method of Jack Jr. This is the out-of-control mindlessness of a madman.

Again.

"*Cunt!*" Barnes screams. Then he just keeps screaming.

"Mother*fucker*!" Leo says. He jumps and runs for a trash can, vomiting into it.

None of us begrudges him this.

As soon as it has started, it's over. The woman has ended up on her back. She's barely recognizable as human. Barnes is on his knees, leaning backward, arms out, eyes closed, covered in blood and sweat. Hyperventilating in his bliss. His erection is gone.

He looks off again. His expression is worshipful. "Can I say it now?" He turns to face the camera, looking right into it. He smiles, nothing human or sane evident. "This one's for you, Smoky."

"Oh, man..." Leo moans.

I say nothing. Some part of me has shut down. I keep watching.

Barnes looks off again. "Did I do good? The way you wanted?" I see his expression change. First puzzlement. Then fear. "What are you doing?"

When the gunshot comes, blowing his brains out, I jump up without meaning to, my chair falling behind me.

"*Fuck!*" Alan yells, just as startled.

I lean forward, gripping the sides of the desk, arms trembling. I know what's coming. It has to be. He wouldn't miss the opportunity. He doesn't disappoint. That hooded face is in front of the camera, eyes crinkling because of the grin we can't see. He gives us a big thumbs-up.

The video ends.

Everyone is shocked and silent. Leo wipes his mouth. Sergeant Oldfield's hand has strayed to his weapon, an unconscious reflex.

My mind feels like an empty, hollow place. Tumbleweeds blowing through it, pushed by the wind.

Getting a grip on myself is almost a literal thing.

My voice is full of heat when I speak. Tight and smoking. "Back to work," I say.

They all look at me like I'm nuts.

"Come on!" I snap. "Pull it together, guys. This is just one more fucking distraction. He's messing with us. Get a grip, and get back to work. I'm going to call this Agent Jenkins." My voice sounds firm, but I'm still trembling.

It takes them a minute, then my words get through. They start moving. I pick up the phone, call the switchboard, and get them to dial me into the New York FBI headquarters, all on automatic. My head is spinning. When reception answers, I ask for Agent Jenkins. Surprise, surprise, he's in NCAVC Coord too.

The phone rings, is picked up. "Special Agent Bob Jenkins."

"Hi, Bob. This is Smoky Barrett, from NCAVC Coord Los Angeles." The normal tone of my voice surprises me. *Hi, how are you, just watched a woman get eviscerated, what's new with you?*

"Hi, Agent Barrett. I know who you are." His voice is curious. I would be too, if our roles were reversed. "What's up?"

I sit down. Take a breath. My heartbeat feels like it's coming back down to normal. "What can you tell me about Ronnie Barnes?"

"Barnes?" He sounds surprised. "Wow, that's an old one. About six months or so. Killed and mutilated five women. And I mean *mutilated*. To be honest, it was a grounder for us. Someone noticed a smell and reported it. Cops went into his apartment, found one of the dead women, and him with a self-inflicted hole in the head. Case closed."

"I have news for you, Bob. It wasn't self-inflicted."

A long pause. "Do tell."

I give him a synopsis of Jack Jr. and the package he'd just sent us. The video. When I'm done, he's quiet for a while.

"I think I've been doing this for about as long as you have, Smoky. You ever run across anything like this before?"

"Nope."

"Me neither." He sighs. It's a sigh I find I recognize. An acknowledgment that the monsters just continue to mutate, and seem to get worse every time. "Anything I can do?" he asks.

"Can you send me a copy of the case file on Barnes? I doubt anything's there. My guy is very, very careful. But..."

"Sure. Anything else?"

"Just one more thing. Out of curiosity. When did Barnes die?"

"Hold on." I hear him tapping on a keyboard. "Let's see...body was found November twenty-first....Based on decomp and other factors, the ME estimates he died on the nineteenth."

I feel like the air has been sucked from my lungs. My hand on the phone is nerveless.

"Agent Barrett? You there?"

"Yes. Thanks for the help, Bob. I'll look for that file."

My voice sounds far away to me, and mechanical. He doesn't seem to notice.

"I'll courier it out tomorrow."

We hang up, and I stare at the phone.

November 19.

I can't believe it.

While Ronnie Barnes was destroying that girl, Joseph Sands was destroying my life. That very night. Not just the same date a year or a decade later, but that very same *day*.

Was it a coincidence? Or was there some other meaning there, something I couldn't see?

34

THE REST OF the day passes like a dream. Callie has come back; Marilyn is fine. Sergeant Oldfield lets me know before leaving that there is no way he'll let Jack Jr. do to Marilyn what we saw Barnes do on that video. Everything is set up for the delivery of Jack Jr.'s package tomorrow. We continue to do what we do.

But I am wobbly as I drive toward Alan and Elaina's. I keep coming back to the coincidence of those dates. I feel like I've been put into a time warp. Knowing that as Ronnie Barnes was smiling at the camera, I was screaming, and Matt was dying. That as he put a knife to that poor woman's body, Joseph Sands was putting a knife to my face.

As it was happening, Jack Jr. was already hard at work. And he already knew about *me*.

This is perhaps the thing that rattles me the most. How long have I been on his mind? Is he going to be another Joseph Sands?

I'm afraid. I admit this to myself. I'm terrified.

"God damn you!" I scream, and pound a hand on the steering wheel, hard enough to numb my palm. My whole body is trembling.

"That's better," I growl, even as I tremble. "Hold on to that, Smoky."

So I keep feeding that rage, making myself more and more angry at him for making me feel that fear.

It doesn't dispel the fear completely.

But it'll see me through the moment.

35

I HAD TAKEN Alan and Elaina up on yesterday's offer of dinner. I needed some normality, and Elaina did not disappoint. She was looking better, closer to her old self. She got me to laugh more than once, and, most important, she drew multiple smiles from Bonnie. I could tell Bonnie was falling in love with her. I knew just how she felt.

Elaina is getting Bonnie ready to go home with me, and Alan and I are sitting together in the living room, waiting. It's a companionable silence.

"She seems to be doing good," I say.

He nods. "She's doing better. Bonnie's helped."

"I'm glad."

Bonnie bounds into the living room, ending the moment, with Elaina behind her. "You ready to go, honey?" I ask her.

She gives a smile and a nod. I stand up, hug Alan, hug Elaina, give Elaina a kiss on the cheek.

"Alan told you we're starting early tomorrow?"

"He told me."

"It's going to be okay if I bring Bonnie by at seven?"

She smiles, reaches down, and ruffles Bonnie's hair.

Bonnie looks back up at her, eyes adoring. "Of course it's okay." She kneels down. "Give me a hug, honeybunch."

They exchange hugs and smiles and we head out the door.

"Go up to bed, honey," I tell Bonnie. "I'll be up in just a minute."

She nods her head and patters up the stairs. My phone rings.

"It's Leo."

"What's up?"

"Alan and I got the warrant for Annie King's subscriber list," he says. "Didn't have a chance to tell you that before you left. I got in touch with the company. They were cooperative."

"So you have it?"

"I've been going over it for the last four hours. Just came up with something too."

"Tell me," I reply, hopeful.

"It turns out that your friend had a fairly extensive list of members. Nearly a thousand. I thought it would be worth a try to set the search parameters for names that relate to the whole Jack the Ripper scenario. You know, London, hell, that kind of thing."

"And?"

"I found it right away. Frederick Abberline. The name of the inspector who's most famous for hunting our old buddy Jack back then."

"Why didn't you call me?"

"Because I'm not done yet. Think about it. It's too obvious. They wouldn't give up a real address that easily. I checked it anyway. It's a post-office box."

"Damn," I say.

"But it's still a lead," he says. "I'm also following up on it from another angle. Whenever someone signs up using a credit card, their IP number is logged."

"Which is . . . what?"

"Everything that exists on the Web, whether it's a dot-com or your dial-up connection, has a number behind it. That's an IP, or Internet Protocol number. Anytime you are surfing on the Web, you have an identity—you are your IP number."

"So when you sign up for something using a credit card, that number gets logged."

"Yes."

"Where is that likely to lead us?"

"That's the problematic part. There are two ways that IP numbers can be related to your Internet connection. One is good for us, one is not so good. The IP numbers are owned by the company providing your access to the Internet. In most cases, each time you dial up or connect, you are assigned a different IP number. No continuity."

"That's the one that's not so good for us," I say.

"Right. The other kind is an 'always on' connection. Your IP is actually assigned to you by the service provider and always remains the same. That's good for us, if that's what he used. Because that number is specifically trace-able to an individual."

"Hmmm . . ." I muse. "I could be wrong, but I think our guy is smarter than that."

"Probably," Leo replies. "But maybe not. Even so, it'll be helpful. The Internet service provider he used will have logs showing when the IP numbers were used, and you can get a general location from that. Maybe even an exact location."

"That's good, Leo. Good work. I want you to follow up on this aggressively."

"I will."

I believe him. I hear the excitement in his voice, and I doubt he'll be getting any sleep tonight. He smells blood, the hunter's intoxicant, irresistible.

I head to bed, Bonnie, sleep.

I have a dream. It's a strange one, disconnected from the others. This one is a true memory.

"Soul like a diamond . . ."

This is something Matt said to me once, in a fit of anger. I had been involved with a case that had stolen all of my time for a period of three to four months. I almost never saw Matt or Alexa. He bore this for the first three months, being supportive, not saying anything. One night I got home to find him sitting in the dark.

"This can't go on," he'd said. I could hear the poison in his voice.

I was dumbstruck. I had thought that things were fine. But that had always been Matt's way. He'd be stoic about something that bothered him until it boiled over and exploded. It was always unfortunate when it happened, because it was always like it was at that moment: from no hint of a storm to a full-blown hurricane.

"What are you talking about?"

His voice had been taut, trembling with anger. "What am I talking about? Jesus, Smoky! I'm talking about you not being here. One month, okay. Two months, not good, but okay. Three months—no fucking way. I've had it! You're never here, and when you are, you don't interact with me or Alexa, you're snappish and irritated—that's what I'm talking about."

I've never dealt with direct attacks well. In lazy moments I ascribe this to the Irish side of me, but in truth,

my mother was a testament to patience. No, this personality trait is all mine. Back me into a corner, and concepts
of right or wrong go out the window. All I care about is
getting out of that corner, and I'll fight as dirty as I have
to to make it happen. Matt had his fault: letting his anger
simmer. It didn't go well with my fault: attacking without hesitation or thought of consequences if you put my
back against a wall. This mismatch never resolved; it was
one of the imperfections of our relationship. I still
miss it.

Matt had shoved me into that no-escape dead end,
and I responded as I always did when left without an exit:
I delivered a sucker punch, well below the belt.

"I guess I should tell the parents of those little girls
that I don't have time to catch the guy who did it, huh?
I'll tell you what, Matt, I'll get onto a nine-to-five schedule. But the next little girl who gets killed, you get to look
at the photos, and you get to talk to the parents, and you
get to try and balance that with doing right by our
family."

The words were cold, cruel, and horribly unfair. But
that is the cruelty of what I do, I had thought in my rage,
and at that moment I hated him for not understanding
it. If I sit at home with my family, I leave a killer free to
roam. If I devote myself to the pursuit of the killer, I leave
my family angry and alone. It is a constant balancing act,
forever draining.

Matt's face got red, and he muttered, "Fuck you,
Smoky." He shook his head. "Soul like a diamond, that's
what you have."

"What the hell is that supposed to mean?" I asked, ex-
asperated.

He'd scowled at me. "It means you have a beautiful

soul, Smoky. Beautiful like a diamond. But it can also be hard and cold like one."

These words were so hurtful and vicious that my anger rushed away from me. It was not like Matt to play the card of cruelty. That was always my specialty, and I found it devastating to receive. I also felt something deep inside me: fear that maybe, just maybe, he was right. I remember staring at him in open-mouthed shock. He had looked back at me, the smallest hint of shame beginning to dance across his face.

"Fuck this," he'd said, stomping off upstairs, leaving me in the dark of our living room, heart aching.

We made up, of course. We got through it. That's what love is about. I came to understand this in the deepest recesses of self. Love is not about romance or passion. Love is about a state of grace. You experience it when you accept the absolute truth of the other person, both the cruel and the divine, and they accept these things in you, and you find that you still long to share a life with them. To know the worst in another and still want them with all your soul. To know that they feel the same.

It is a sense of security and power. And once you have arrived at this, the richness of romance and passion that appears is not blinding. Instead, it is invulnerable and forever.

Forever, that is, unless they die.

I don't awake from the dream screaming. I just wake up. I feel the tears on my cheeks. I let them dry where they fell, and listen to my own breathing until sleep claims me again.

36

EVERYONE LOOKS LIKE I feel. Leo looks even worse.

"Didn't go home, did you?" I ask him.

He gives me a bleary-eyed look, and mumbles.

"Your own fault. So listen," I address them all. "Callie and Alan, you'll be with me in the parking lot. Leo and James, I want you to continue with what you're working on."

They nod in reply.

"Let's go."

The bomb tech holds up his badge. "Reggie Gantz." He appears to be in his late twenties. He has a bored look and steady eyes.

"Special Agent Barrett. Show me what you got."

He walks me over to the back of the bomb-squad van and opens it up. He grabs a laptop and what looks like a large movie camera. "First thing is this. It's a portable digital x-ray machine. Displays the contents of the package on the laptop screen. Since you said the box is being delivered by a third party, we don't have to worry about it being motion-activated. He wouldn't want it to go off on the way here."

"Makes sense."

"This'll take an x-ray. Then I'll use the Sniffer. I'll rub the package with some cotton swipes. They'll go into the Sniffer and it'll use spectrometry to detect trace elements, if they exist. Between the two, we should be pretty sure about it being a bomb or not."

I nod in approval. "We don't know when it's coming, so you'll need to settle in for a wait."

He tips his fingers in a salute and walks back to his van without another word, Mr. Laconic.

I run through things in my head. The driver would arrive to deliver the package and would be detained while we printed him. The package would be examined by Reggie, and once he gave it an all-clear, Alan and Callie and I would rush the package into the crime lab. They would search for prints on everything and use a vacuum to collect any and all trace evidence. Photographs would be taken. Only then would the contents be turned over to us.

This insistence on process is one of our advantages and one of our disadvantages. Something it takes a perpetrator only minutes or hours to do can take us days to process. We are always slower. But we also find everything that the perpetrator leaves behind, down to a microscopic level. Our ability, in this day and age, to interpret even the smallest piece of evidence is truly frightening. Criminals would need to wear a spacesuit to ensure they left nothing behind for us to find. Even then, we might well figure out that they wore a spacesuit.

Even the absence of evidence tells a tale. It tells us the perp has at least a passing knowledge of police and forensic procedure. It gives us insight into the methodology and psychology of the killer. Is he or she intelligent, composed, and patient, or frenzied, passionate, and insane? Evidence or its absence tells this tale.

"Hey," Alan says, pointing. "I think that's it."

I see a package delivery van moving toward us. The van pulls up in front of the building and stops. I can see the driver, a young man with blond hair and a peach-fuzz beard, looking at all of us with more than just a little bit of worry. I don't blame him. He's probably not used to seeing a contingent of serious-faced, somewhat scary-looking people waiting for him to arrive. I walk over to his side of the van, motioning for him to roll down his window.

"FBI," I say, holding up my Bureau ID. "You have a package for this address?"

"Uh, yeah. It's in the back. What's this about?"

"The package is evidence, sir. Mister . . . ?"

"Huh? Oh, Jed. Jedediah Patterson."

"I need you to step out of the van, Mr. Patterson. That package was sent by a criminal we're pursuing."

His mouth drops open. "Really?"

"Yes. We need to fingerprint you, sir. Can you please step out of the van?"

"Fingerprint me? Why?"

I force myself to remain patient. "We're going to be looking for prints on the package. We need to know which ones are yours and not the criminal's."

Light dawns. "Oh . . . yeah, I get it."

"Can you please step out of the van?" My patience is waning. Rapidly. Perhaps he senses this, as now he opens the door and gets out.

"Thank you, Mr. Patterson. Please see Agent Washington; he'll print you."

I point to Alan as I say this and watch as Jed Patterson

gives him a wary look. "Don't worry," I say, amused. "I know he's big, but he's only dangerous to the bad guys."

He licks his lips, still looking at the man-mountain. "If you say so." He walks over to Alan, who takes him inside for fingerprinting.

Now I can focus on the package. Reggie Gantz is already standing near the delivery van, carrying his equipment. He still looks bored.

"Ready to roll?" he asks.

"Go ahead," I tell him.

He moves toward the back of the van, opening the doors. We're in luck; there are only three packages back there. He finds the one we want immediately. It's addressed to me.

I watch as he starts up his laptop and powers up the mobile x-ray device. Moments later, we are looking at the contents of the package on his laptop screen.

"Looks like a bottle of something...and maybe a letter...and something else, flat and round. Could be a CD. And that's it. I need to fire up the Sniffer. Make sure that liquid isn't anything dangerous."

"Is that likely?"

"Nah. Just about all liquid explosives are unstable. The package would probably have blown up on its way here." He shrugs. "But we don't assume anything in bomb tech."

I'm glad Reggie is here, but I think he's crazy to do the job he does. "Do it," I tell him.

He pulls out a swatch of cotton cloth and proceeds to swipe the package with it. I watch as he feeds it into the Sniffer. Once inside, the spectrometry goes to work. Within minutes, he looks up at me. "Looks all clear to me. I'd say it's safe to open."

"Thanks, Reggie."

"No problem." He yawns. I shake my head as I watch him wander back to his van with his equipment. It takes all kinds.

Now I'm alone with the package. I look at it. It's not that big. Just big enough for what it holds: something the size of a jelly jar, a letter, and a CD. Probably a CD. I want to look inside. Burn to.

I walk back around the front of the van. Alan is returning with Jed Patterson, whose fingertips are now black with ink. I motion to Alan.

"The package is clear," I tell him. "Let's get it to the lab."

"No shit," Callie agrees.

Everyone's chafing at the bit on this one.

Gene Sykes runs the crime lab, and when he sees us walk through the door a look of resignation settles onto his face.

"Hey, Smoky. So how long do I have for this one?"

I grin at him. "Come on, Gene. It hasn't been that long."

"Uh-huh. So we're talking yesterday, then?"

"Yep."

He sighs. "Tell me about it."

"Package delivered through a parcel service, definitely from our guy. We had a bomb tech check it out, which means that the outer part of the box got wiped. We also got prints from the delivery driver for elimination."

"Do you know what's in it?"

"The tech did an on-the-spot x-ray. Looks like the box contains a jar of some kind, a letter, and maybe a CD. Not a hundred percent sure of anything since we haven't opened the box up."

"How do you know it's from your unsub?"

"Because he told us he'd be sending it."

"That was considerate of him." He ruminates on all of this information for a moment. "You've already run one crime scene related to this unsub?"

"Yeah."

"Anything show up?"

I tell him about the prints we'd found on Annie's bed.

Gene is scratching his head, thinking. Beginning to lose himself in the problem.

"I need this one really scrutinized, Gene. But I need it as fast as you can do it."

"Sure. I'm going to take it layer by layer. I'll remove the box, the contents, and address each separately. You say he's careful, so I doubt we'll get any plastic or visible prints. But sometimes they surprise us."

There are three types of prints at a crime scene: plastic prints, visible prints, and latent prints. Plastic and visible prints are our favorites. Plastic prints are created when the perpetrator leaves a print in a soft surface, like wax, putty, or soap. Visible prints are created when the perp has touched something—such as blood—and then touched another surface. Leaving, literally, a print you can see with the naked eye. The most common are latent, or invisible, prints. These are the ones you really have to look for, and the technology of getting them can be an art form at times.

Gene is an artiste. If something's there, he'll get it.

"It goes without saying, Gene, if it is a CD in there, I need the contents of it before you do anything that would damage it." Getting latent prints can involve the use of chemicals and heat. Either of these could damage the CD, making it unreadable.

He shoots me a look of injured scorn. "Please, Smoky. Who do you think you're dealing with here?"

I grin. "Sorry." I hand over two other plastic evidence bags, each containing the recent deliveries and correspondence from Jack Jr. "Check these out after. They're from the same unsub."

He scowls. "Anything else?" Sarcastic.

"You'll be getting the benefit of my assistance and expertise, honey-love," Callie says. Gene gives her a sour look.

"We're on a timetable here, Gene. He's let us know that he's going to kill again."

His face grows sober. "You got it."

I walk into the office and find Alan on the phone. He's talking fast. Something has him excited. He's holding Annie's case file in one hand. "I need to confirm it, Jenny. I want to be a hundred percent sure. Right." He taps his foot impatiently, waiting. "Really? Okay, thanks." He hangs up the phone, jumps out of the chair, and comes over to me. "Remember when I told you something was bothering me?"

"Yeah."

"It was in the inventory of things taken from her apartment." He opens the file, finds a page, and points to it. "A receipt for an exterminator service inspection of her apartment five days before she was killed."

"So?"

"So—most places like the one where she was living handle extermination for the building as a whole."

"That's not exactly conclusive. But keep going."

"Yeah, I might have dismissed it too. But I saw the actual receipt while we were there, and something about it has been nagging me ever since."

"Come on, Alan."

"Sorry—it was a notation on the receipt." He grabs a notepad from his desk and reads from it. "*Did Shoe Write-up*. I mean—what the fuck is that? And then the guy signed it *Armouried Murrey*."

"Strange name."

"They're anagrams, aren't they?" James says.

Alan turns to look at him, surprised. "That's right. How did you—never mind." He turns back to me, shows me the pad. "See—*Did Shoe Write-up*. Change the letters around and you get: *Die, Stupid Whore*."

My stomach lurches.

"Then *Armouried Murrey*—mix the letters up and you get—" He shows the notepad to me again.

I am your murderer.

"The final insult," James murmurs. "He tells her that she's going to die and that he's going to do it, right to her face. And she never has a clue."

I realize I expect to feel rage at this, but it is absent. I'm becoming hardened to their games. I glance at Alan. "That's pretty impressive work."

He shrugs. "Just always had a thing for anagrams. And niggling details."

"Yeah, yeah, yeah, you're amazing," James says. "The question is, what does it mean and how can we use it?"

"Why don't you tell me, asshole," Alan says.

The insult misses James by a wide mark. He is nodding, thinking. "I don't think he came to gloat. I think he came to scout. To make sure he knew the full layout of the place."

"Or to verify prior data," I say. "He might have been there before, and wanted to verify that nothing had changed."

"Casing the place," Alan says. "That makes sense, with these guys. They're smart, careful. Planners."

"Maybe it's their MO," I say. I feel an excitement building in me. "If we could get some kind of a jump on their next victim—anything—we might be able to catch whichever one does the recon." I turn to Leo. "Where do we stand on your end of things?"

Leo grimaces. "No good news, I'm afraid. The IP number was not a static IP. We were able to track where the usage originated, but it was a dead end."

"How's that?"

"He used a cybercafé. Think of a coffeehouse where you can get on the Internet. Completely anonymous."

"Damn. Anything else? At all?"

"No."

"Well, everyone put your thinking caps on. Hard."

The phone rings. Alan answers it, speaks, and hangs up. "They're ready for you down in the lab," he says to me.

I take the elevator down four floors, and when I get to the lab, I find Gene chattering away at a bemused Callie.

"Careful," I say to her, "he'll talk your ear off."

Gene turns to me. "I was telling Agent Thorne about the latest advances coming out in the identification of mitochondrial DNA."

"Heady stuff," Callie says in her driest voice.

Gene scowls. "Oh, knock it off," he says. "I know you better than that, Callie. You were one of my best interns."

She grins, winks at me.

I raise my coffee in a toast. "I've always sung your praises, Gene. In that vein—what do you have for me?"

He gives Callie a last frown. She sticks her tongue out at him. He turns to me with a sigh. "No immediate physical evidence. By that, I mean no fingerprints, fibers, hair, epithelials, anything. But what is there is very, very interesting. It tells us something about the unsub that even he is unaware of."

This perks me up. "How's that?"

"In good time, Smoky. To understand it, you have to read the letter first." He passes it to me. "Go ahead."

I don't like people being cryptic. But Gene is one of the best forensic scientists in the country. Maybe in the world. And Callie is nodding at me.

"It's worth the wait, honey-love."

I turn my attention to the letter.

Greetings, Agent Barrett!

So, I'm dying to know: How did you enjoy the tale of Ronnie Barnes? Not the brightest boy, I'm afraid, but perfect to demonstrate a point. You are wondering, I know. How many other Ronnies are out there? I'm afraid I find it far more satisfying to let you continue to wonder.

I saw you walk into that shooting range when you returned from San Francisco, by the by. I have to say, I was EXCITED! It's always rewarding when a gambit comes to such perfect fruition. Now my opponent is fully armed and operational. Something that gets my blood singing through my veins! Do you feel the same? The pounding of the heart? That sharpening of the senses?

"He's following you, honey-love."

"Yeah. We're going to have to address that."

You look different now, Agent Barrett. More dangerous. No longer hiding those scars you were so ashamed of.

Good for you. And for me. Because now we can dispense with the kid gloves. Now we can begin to make this game truly interesting!

I've enclosed two things for you. One of them, the contents of the jar, requires some explanation for full understanding.

Let us talk about Annie Chapman. Also known as Dark Annie. Does that name ring a bell for you, Agent Barrett? It should. She was my ancestor's second victim.

Poor, poor Annie Chapman. She wasn't always a dirty whore, you know. She waited until her husband died to start spreading her slut legs for money. Most offensive. When my ancestor killed her he was lancing a boil on the skin of society.

She was the second killed, but she was the first one dear Jack took keepsakes from. He excised her uterus, the upper portion of the vagina, and the posterior two-thirds of the bladder.

Of course, many different theories have been put forth about this. And of course, all of them have been wrong. No one had the vision to understand my ancestor's plan. I am sharing it with you now, so listen closely:

Jack knew that his bloodline, both past and future, was of an exceptional nature. Descended from the ancient predators. The original hunters. Above the cattle of humanity. He knew that it was his duty to pass on his knowledge and his power to future generations, to explain our holy mission.

And so he took many keepsakes. He took these pieces of whores and sealed them up, preserving them. He decreed that they be passed down, from generation to generation, as a reminder of what he had begun.

I told you I would provide proof of my claims, Agent Barrett. I am a man of my word. I am passing on to you

*one of the sacred keepsakes. The preserved uterus of
Annie Chapman.*

*Awe-inspiring, is it not? Run your tests. When you do,
I think you will find it harder to sleep at night. For you
will know that a descendant of the Shadow Man is out
and about.*

"Is what he's saying true, Gene? Is that a human
uterus in that jar?"

He smiles. Another cryptic smile. "We'll address that.
Finish reading the letter."

*The Shadow Man. While there is only one original,
you have known many pretenders, haven't you, Special
Agent Barrett? Those who live in the shadows, kill in
them. My ancestor was born in the shadows. His was a
heritage of darkness.*

*He loved the shadows, and the shadows . . . well, they
loved him back. He was their purest child.*

But I digress.

*I have included another CD for you. I have been
continuing the mission of my ancestor. I've cleansed the
earth of another whore, lanced another boil.*

"Damn," I say.

Enjoy it. I am quite proud of my work.

*That is all for now, Agent Barrett. Rest assured, I will
be in touch. Perhaps in a more personal fashion. One
week. Tick tock, tick tock.*

*From Hell,
Jack Jr.*

I put the letter down, and look at Gene. "Spill it."

He rubs his hands together. "After reading that, the jar was the first addressed, of course. I ran some basic tests, and that's how I found it."

"What?"

He pauses for effect. "There's no human tissue in that jar, Smoky. If I had to guess, I would say that it's bovine."

Shock strikes me speechless for a moment, and then: "Holy shit!"

He grins. "Yes. Our boy thinks he has something passed on by Jack the Ripper. But he doesn't. He has a piece of preserved cow flesh. He has an entire belief system built up that he doesn't know is a lie."

My mind is reeling. "It's all bullshit. Bullshit somebody spoon-fed him. He's no descendant of the Ripper. He's—"

"Just another killer," Callie says, completing the thought. She wiggles her eyebrows. "Not bad, huh? No physical evidence to identify our boys. But it's certainly a defining characteristic."

"Great, great work. Can you tag all of this and put together a report?"

"Certainly. I'll have it done this evening."

"Great. Wow." I turn to Callie. "We need to go share this with the rest of the team." We begin to head out the door.

"Ah—Agent Barrett?"

I turn around and see Gene holding it in a gloved hand.

Oh shit.

In the excitement, I'd forgotten about it for a moment. The CD. My elation fades.

It was time to go watch another murder.

37

WE'RE BACK IN the office.

"I have good news and bad news," I say.

"What's the good news?" Alan asks.

I relate the substance of the letter, ending with what Gene had found in the jar. Leo's and Alan's eyes widen. James gets an unfocused look. I can almost hear the thoughts spinning in his head.

"So," he says, "someone has indoctrinated him in this. Either they think it's true, or they wanted him to think it's true."

"Maybe he created the fantasy," Leo says. "Why does it have to involve another person?"

"Because the level of delusion he'd have to operate at for that to be the case would preclude his level of organization and competence. Think about it."

Callie nods. "I agree, honey-love. To create that belief system and then forget he created it . . . I don't think he'd be very functional. He'd be far too delusional."

I chew on this. "It's a big break," I say. "Another link. Now we aren't just looking for him, we're also looking for who worked to build this belief in him." I turn to Alan. "Call Dr. Child now. Get this over to him. Call him at home if he's not in. Tell him I need to see him tomorrow morning. This is one time a profile could really be helpful."

"Got it."

"He's starting to screw up," I say. "There's this, and him letting it slip that he's following me."

Alan looks up, alarmed. "What?"

"It's in the letter. I went to a shooting range when we got back from San Francisco. He told me that he saw me go there. Which is a bad move on his part."

"You need to be very, very careful, honey-love."

I smile. "Don't worry, Callie. I'm going to be calling an old friend on this one. Ex–Secret Service. I'm going to have him follow me."

She nods. "He'll shadow you, and by doing that, he'll be able to spot anyone else following you."

"Yep. My friend is very good. He'll also be able to find any tracking devices or bugs on my car. I'll have him sweep the house as well. I'll keep them there if he finds any. We'll know where the bugs are—but he won't know we know."

"Have you noticed that you are using 'he,' and not 'they'?" James asks me.

I look at him, surprised. I hadn't noticed. "I guess it's because, more and more, I'm convinced that there is a primary 'he.' There is a Jack Jr. The other is incidental. I can feel it. Look at Ronnie Barnes. Jack used him up and threw him away. He said it in his letter—he's looking for other killers to foster."

"That begs the question about perp number two from Annie's apartment," James says. "Is he still alive? Or dead like Barnes?"

"No way to be sure . . . but I think he's still alive."

"I agree," Alan says. "Think about it. He started something with Annie, something he's been planning for a while. He's not going to want to have to shift gears in the middle of it to train another killing buddy."

I look at all of them. "We're catching up."

James is staring at me. "Enough back-patting," he says. "What's the bad news?"

I hold up the CD. "He sent us this as well. He killed someone else."

The office goes quiet. Leo stands up, holding out his hand for the CD. "Let's get it over with."

I give it to him. "Go ahead."

His laptop is already on. He puts the CD in. Moments later, the video starts.

It begins with a title screen, white letters on a black background: *This death sponsored by http://www.darkhaired slut.com.*

"Note that down," I say to Leo.

A bound and struggling woman appears. She's naked and tied to a bed, just as Annie was. I estimate her age to be just under twenty-five. She's very natural-looking. By that I mean she doesn't have any breast enhancements—unless she had them enlarged to a B cup, which is doubtful. She still has the flawless body of the young, not yet marred by the rigors of carrying a child. Her hair is long, thick, and dark. Another brunette; he prefers them. Her eyes express everything she is feeling. Panic, terror, despair, all cranked up to an unbearable level.

Jack Jr. appears in camera view, dressed in the same costume he wore when he killed Annie. He waves to the camera, and again, I get the sense that he is smiling. The smile is all for us; he loves that he is committing this crime on tape, essentially in front of us, without giving away a clue to his identity. He steps outside the lens. A moment later the music begins. Loud, almost deafening.

I wish they all could be California giiirls...

He moves over to the woman, cocking his head this way and that as he stares down at her. Then he holds up his weapon. Not a knife this time. A bat. He begins to dance and caper, waving the bat, putting his evil to the rhythm of the song. He makes a few false swings, just to terrify her further. Her eyes are bulging out, her face is turning red as she tries to scream through her gag.

And now, like it did in the video of Annie, the montage begins. All of it is done with an unhesitating brutality. There's nothing clinical or workmanlike about it—when he prepares to swing the bat, he raises it back and above his head, and when he brings it down, he puts his entire body into it. He's not just breaking bones; I can imagine them shattering into powder. Each time she passes out, he stops and slaps her face until she wakes up. He wants her to be there with him, to be aware of what is happening to her. To feel every minute.

He puts the bat down and climbs astride her. The rape begins. It's brutal, designed for maximum motion. He wants to grind those broken bones, wants his fucking her to be the worst pain she's ever felt. Again, each time she passes out, he wakes her up. It must have been like waking up to a nightmare, over and over again, I think.

The rape finishes, and out comes the scalpel. He shows it to her. Grips her chin and makes her look at it, understand it. Her eyes follow the blade, fix on it as it moves down to her belly. I watch her start to go mad as he begins to dissect her, still alive. I look over at Leo. He is green, his face filled with horror. But he holds it together. He's toughened up now, become someone he can't unbecome.

When the woman is dead and eviscerated, Jack Jr. stands up. He stares down at her for a long, long time.

She looks like someone made her swallow a bomb and then blew her up from the inside out. He looks at the camera, giving us a thumbs-up. At that, the video ends.

"You think you're so funny," I murmur to myself, enraged. "Keep smiling, fucker."

It feels as impotent as it sounds.

Of course, part of me knows he never *really* smiles. There aren't any smiles in him.

Everyone else is silent, trying to process the images we just saw. Compartmentalizing.

Dealing with it.

"Check out that Web site address, Leo. Let's find out who this woman was."

"I'm on it," he says, quiet. He pauses. "How...how could anyone do that?" It's a real question. His eyes bore into me, and they plead for an answer. I think for a moment before responding, choosing my words.

"They can do it because they love it. It's their sex act, and their need for it is greater, more demanding, than any junkie's need could ever be. There are all kinds of reasons they become that way. But the bottom line is that they love what they do. Passionately." I look at James. "What's that phrase you came up with for them?"

"Sexual carnivores."

"Right."

Leo shivers. "It's not what I imagined. All of this."

"I know, believe me. This idea is perpetrated that it's exciting hunting serial killers or baby rapers or other monsters. It's not exciting. It's consuming. You don't wake up and go, 'Boy oh boy, I can't wait to catch that guy.' You wake up and look in the mirror and try not to feel guilty because you haven't caught him yet. Try not to think about the fact that he could be killing someone else because you haven't caught him yet." I lean back, shaking my head. "It's not about excitement. It's about feeling responsible when people die."

He looks at me for a moment longer, then does what he's learned to do in the face of horror: He turns to his computer and goes to work. A minute later, he has what I need. "I have an address for the owner of *darkhairedslut. com*. It's an apartment in Woodland Hills."

"Do you have a name?"

"No, sorry. It's registered to a business. Probably a sole proprietorship."

"Alan. Call LAPD for that area. Tell them to check it out. If it turns out that she's there, I want them to close off the scene and let us know. No one in or out."

"Got it."

"It wasn't obvious on this video," James says. "At least not to me."

I frown at him. "What wasn't obvious?"

"That it was two killers, and not just one."

I look at him in surprise and then nod. He's right. The fact that I had to ask him what he meant was proof that his observation was sound. If Jack Jr. had company, this time it wasn't visible to the naked eye.

"But they were both there," James says. "I can feel it."

I look at him again, nod again. The dark train rolls on, *chug-chug* and *choo-choo*, and James and I remain firmly aboard.

I turn to Leo. "I want to take a quick look at her Web site."

Callie looks bemused, or tries to. "I never thought I'd be ordered to surf porn, Smoky. This will make the second time."

"Something you usually do only at home?"

"Very funny."

It's a game attempt at gallows humor, but it falls flat. The images are still too vivid.

"Here it is," Leo says.

We move our chairs so we can see the site he's called up on the screen. The color scheme is a soft brown. I see a picture of the woman we watched Jack Jr. destroy, dressed in panties and nothing else. Her butt is facing us, cocked in an age-old saucy pose. She peers over her shoulder, smiling a coy smile, while one finger is cocked in a "come hither" way. She looks like someone doing porn. But she also looks pretty and alive and human. Unworthy of what we'd just seen.

I'M A DARK-HAIRED SLUT, a logo states across the top of the screen. To the right of her picture are additional, smaller photos. While the truly explicit is only hinted at, the message is clear. This is not about erotic posing or cheesecake shots. There are strategically censored photos of oral sex, anal sex, sex with other women, sex in groups. Smaller type confirms this: *I love to suck cock and swallow cum, I live for gang bangs and getting fucked up the ass, and I absolutely LOVE to eat PUSSY!*

"Versatile young woman," Callie remarks.

I shake my head. "I'll say."

Further graphics let us know that she does *live cam shows* and that she throws *sex parties for her fans*. Members only, of course.

Leo takes us through another two pages of this, leading toward the final destination of the sign-up page.

"Now what?" I ask. "I'm not using my credit card for this."

"I don't think we'll need to," Leo says. "I have a hunch."

He clicks on the link for *members entry*. A box appears on the screen, asking for a user name and password.

"I bet that he picked the same user name and password for this site that he did for your friend's. The user name was *jackis* and the password was *fromhell*." He types these in as he says them and hits the *OK* button. A page appears that says *Welcome to my hot members-only area!*

"Voilà," Leo says.

"Good thinking."

He scrolls down the page, which is essentially a menu of the features offered within this part of the site. Things like *personal photos, my video clips, my live cam, my amateur friends.* The one that catches my eye is *photos from the member sex parties.*

"I wonder..." I muse.

"What, honey-love?" Callie asks.

"The member sex parties...I'm thinking that he might not have been able to resist that opportunity. Having sex with her, knowing that he'd be killing her soon—it's something I can see him doing."

"It would heighten the anticipation. The sense of power he felt."

This is a common thread for serial killers. The tracking, the watching, the planning; these things can be almost as intoxicating for them as the finale.

"I think there's a high probability that that's true," James says. "We could download all the photos. Extract the faces of all the men and run them through some facial-recognition databases." He shrugs. "It's not all that thorough yet, but it's worth a try."

Anyone who thinks law enforcement is all excitement doesn't understand this part of what we do. We'd like to move at a dead run, but we are forced to be methodical. We cast out nets and lines, like fishermen. Not one, but many, over and over and over. Look for prints, one net. Warrant for a subscriber list, another. Facial recognition, yet another. Again and again, casting and pulling in, usually coming up empty. Not caring what we catch. A shark or a minnow, whatever, anything that will take us toward the killer. It's a race of turtles, measured in inches, not yards.

"Do it. You and Leo."

I walk over to Alan. "You reach LAPD?"

"I did, and I'm going to meet them there."

"What about Dr. Child? Did you reach him?"

"Yeah. He was pretty grumpy at first, but all I had to do was give him a quick rundown of what we found today. He got interested fast. Wants a copy of the report couriered over to him tonight, and he said he'll be ready to see you on it in the morning."

"Good. Callie, get that report from Gene and make sure it gets to Dr. Child."

Callie heads for a phone as Alan heads out the door. I go to my desk, rummaging through it until I find my address book. I look through it, finding the phone number I want.

Tommy Aguilera. A former Secret Service agent, now working as a private security consultant. We'd met during a case involving a senator's son who had developed a taste for rape and murder. Tommy ended up having to shoot him, and in the political firestorm that followed, my testimony was the only thing that kept him from losing his job. Tommy had said to let him know if I ever needed anything, with emphasis on "anything" and "ever."

I dial the number, thinking about him. Very, very serious guy. A constant poker face. Speaks in a soft voice, but it's not the softness of someone who is shy. More the softness of a snake confident in its ability to strike.

He answers after four rings. "This is Tommy." The voice is exactly as I remembered it.

"Hi, Tommy. It's Smoky Barrett."

A pause. "Hey, Smoky. How are you?"

I know Tommy is being polite. It's not that he doesn't care how I am. It's just that he's not a small talk kind of guy.

"I need your help on something, Tommy."

"Tell me what you need."

I explain it to him, telling him about Jack Jr., how he'd been in my house and appeared to be following me.

"There's a strong possibility he's tracking you electronically."

"That's one part of it. If he is, I want to know. But I don't want to let on that I know."

Silence for a moment. "I understand," he says. "You want me to tail you."

"Right."

"When?"

"First I want you to check my vehicle and my home for bugs or tracking devices. Then I want you to shadow me. This could be an opportunity to catch him. Maybe the one place he's being foolish." I hesitate for a moment. "To hell with it. You should know. There are two of them."

"Working together?"

"Yeah."

"When do you want me to start?" No hesitation.

"I should be home tonight around eleven. Do you mind meeting me then?"

"No. I'll see you there. Don't worry if you run a little late. I'll wait."

"Thank you, Tommy. I really appreciate it."

"I owe you, Smoky. I'll see you later tonight."

I hang up, musing. Tommy is definitely a no-nonsense guy.

I watch Callie finish her phone call.

"So?" I ask.

"I reached Gene, honey-love. He's getting a copy of the report couriered to Dr. Child."

"How long would it take you to put a scene kit together, Callie?"

She raises her eyebrows, surprised. "It depends on whether or not Gene has one already—a half hour?"

"Go see him and get things ready. If it turns out that there is a crime scene, I want you and Gene to do the initial processing personally, before we let LAPD forensics in there. This is our first opportunity to see things fresh."

"You got it, honey-love," she replies, and whirls out the door.

And then it hits me. One of my epiphanies. I shouldn't be surprised. I am in the groove, all forward motion and senses turned up to maximum.

"Listen up, James, Leo," I say, excited. "Tell me what you think about this." I sit up and they give me their full attention. "Both times they've killed, they've signed up for access to the members' areas of the Web sites concerned, right?"

"Yep."

"And both times, they chose the same user name and password combination. So . . ."

I see Leo's eyes widen. "Right! So there's a chance that they already picked their next victim and signed up there as well—maybe with the same user name and password. Or, if not the same, along the same lines. The Ripper theme."

I grin. "Exactly. I can't imagine that there are that

many companies that will process charges for adult sites."

"No, there aren't. Less than a dozen."

"We need to contact every one of them, James. You and Leo. We want them to search through their systems, looking for that user name and password combination, as well as variants. And then we need it matched up to a Web site. I'm talking about waking people up out of bed."

James gives me a look of grudging admiration. "Competent. Very competent."

"That's why I'm the boss and get paid the big money."

His lack of retort is like a compliment from someone else.

I'm talking to Alan on my cell phone. "We got a scene, Smoky," he says.

"Who's the primary from LAPD?"

"Barry Franklin. He wants to talk to you."

"Go ahead and put him on."

There's a pause, and Barry's voice comes through. He's not pleased. "Smoky. What's with denying us access to our crime scene?"

"It's not like that, Barry. At all. This is just our first chance to see a scene from this unsub fresh. You know how that is."

A pause, followed by a sigh. "Sure. Can I go in, at least? You know I won't fuck things up."

"Of course you can. Can you put Alan back on?"

"Sure thing."

"So he's cool to let us on the scene?" Alan asks me.

"Yep. And I'm leaving with Callie and Gene in about five minutes. We'll see you there."

"Got a name on her, Smoky. Charlotte Ross."

"Thanks." I hang up.

Charlotte Ross. Promiscuous, yes. Of dubious moral character, maybe.

None of these traits merits a penalty of torture, rape, and death.

38

RUSH HOUR ENDED at 8:00 P.M., so it doesn't take us long to get to the address in Woodland Hills. It is a small, single-level condo, not dripping with prestige, but nice. It fits the neighborhood.

I park and we all get out of the car, heading to the front door, where Alan waits.

"Where's Barry?" I ask.

He jerks a thumb toward the door. "Still inside."

"Have you taken a look?" I ask.

"No. I knew you'd want to see it first."

He knows. Years of working together creates this kind of symbiosis.

I poke my head in and call for Barry. He appears from inside another room, and he walks toward me, moving out of the house onto the porch.

"Thank God," he says, reaching into his coat. "I needed an excuse to come out and have a cigarette." He pulls out a pack and lights up, inhaling and then exhaling with a blissful expression on his face. "You want one?"

"No, thanks." I'm surprised to find that I mean it. The desire to smoke evaporated somewhere between finding out about Alexa and picking up my gun again.

I feel gratified and lucky that Barry is the primary on

this case from the LAPD. I've known him for almost a decade. He's short, pudgy, and balding. Wears glasses and has one of the more homely faces I've ever seen. Somehow, despite these shortcomings, Barry is always dating pretty, younger women. There's something about him; you get the sense that he is larger than the body he wears, and he has a supreme confidence without being arrogant. A lot of women find that combination of self-assurance and a good heart to be irresistible. He's also a brilliant homicide detective. Very, very talented. If he were in the Bureau, he'd be on my team.

"You itching to see the scene?" he asks.

"Tell me the basics first. Before I go inside."

He nods and begins to recount. He doesn't refer to any notes. He doesn't need to—Barry has a photographic memory. "Victim is Charlotte Ross, twenty-four years old. Found tied to her bed, already deceased. She was cut from sternum to pelvis. Internal organs appear to have been removed, bagged, and placed by the body. Tremendous bruising to arms at the elbows, legs at the knees. They look broken. Contusions look like he beat her with something."

"He did. With a bat."

He raises his eyebrows. "How do you know that?"

"He sent me a video of it. This is the second woman—that we know of—that he's done this to."

"There's no official time of death, but I'd guess it has to be at least three days. She's pretty ripe."

"That fits with the general timeline."

He draws in another lungful. Gives me a look of thoughtful regard. "So what's this about, Smoky?"

"What's it always about, Barry? A psycho who thrives on pain and terror." I rub my eyes. I'm tired. "This unsub targets women who run personal adult sites on the Internet. He..." I hesitate. "This all has to stay between us for now, Barry. I'm not ready to release anything to the press."

"No problem."

"First of all, 'he' is a 'they.' There's two of them. We think one is primary, dominant. And they're obsessing on me and my team. The first victim was a friend of mine from high school. My best friend. Something they knew."

Barry's face falls in dismay. "Ah, shit, Smoky."

"What you've described looks to be their MO. They killed my friend by cutting her throat—that's different from here—but the removal of the organs, that's their signature. The one we think is dominant says he's a descendant of Jack the Ripper."

A look of distaste flicks across Barry's face. "Bullshit."

I nod. "It is. We even have proof of it."

"So how do you want to work this?"

"I want to see the scene alone. And then I want Gene and Callie to give it an initial forensic once-over. Then your crime lab can process it in depth. I just need it done fast, and I need a copy of the results."

"Got it." He walks the cigarette out to the street to put out. So as not to contaminate the crime scene. He walks back up to me and indicates the doorway. "You want to see her now?"

"Yeah." I look at Alan, Callie, and Gene. "Alan, go home to your wife. There's no reason for you to be here right now."

He seems to hesitate, but ends up nodding. "Thanks." He turns and leaves.

"Callie, I'll probably be twenty, thirty minutes. After I'm done, you guys can go inside."

"No problem here, honey-love. Do your thing."

I move to the doorway and stand there for a moment, listening with my mind's ear. After a second, I hear it: *chug-a-chug-a-chug-a-chug-a*. I feel the coldness moving over me and the distance around me widen to a windless, open field. I can hear the dark train, and I'm ready to see it. Now I just need to find it again. Trace how it rode through this place.

I step inside. The condo isn't elegant, but it is simple and clean. It has the feel of someone who used to try too hard but had decided to drop the pretense. A faint, sad feeling. Disappointment wasn't a way of life yet, but that day was coming.

That day had arrived, I think.

The smell of death permeates the place. It is a veneer of decay that's settled like neglect on the condo. No perfume here. The odor of murder, raw and real. If souls had a scent, this is how Jack Jr.'s would smell.

I look to the right of the living room and see the kitchen. A sliding glass door leads out onto the backyard patio and a cool night. I walk over and examine the latch. It's standard, cheap. But unbroken.

"You just knocked again, didn't you?" I murmur to myself. "You and your buddy. Did he hide to one side while you stood in front? Ready to rush her when she least expected it?"

It occurs to me that their choice of timing with Annie, 7:00 P.M., might have been based on more than just bravado. It is a time when people are either coming home or have just arrived home, or are settling in from having arrived not long before. When they are in flux and don't want to know about the world outside.

"Is that what you did here too? Did you just stroll up in the early evening, all smiles, and knock on the door?

Did one of you have your hands in your pockets, not a care in the world?"

Because this is something I sense about them. It's a strong feeling. *Chug-a-chug-a-chug-a-chug-a.*

Their arrogance.

It's early evening, and they park right in front of the whore's house. Why not? Nothing strange about parking at the curb, after all. They get out of the car, look around. Things are quiet without being silent, empty without being still. It's dusk in the suburbs, and you can feel life and motion, hidden behind the walls of the other homes. Ants in their hills.

They walk up to her door. They know she's home. They know everything about her. One glance around to ensure no one is outside and watching, and he knocks. A moment passes, and she opens the door . . .

Then what? I look around in the entryway. I see no dropped mail here, no signs of a struggle. But I can feel it again, that arrogance.

They did the simplest thing they could do—they walked inside, pushing her backward, and closed the door. They knew she wouldn't stop them. It isn't in most of us to push back as a first response. Instead, we look for reasons, try to understand why something is happening. And in that moment of hesitation and wonder, the hunter seizes the initiative.

Perhaps she was fast, though. Perhaps she opened her mouth to scream even as the door closed. But they would have been prepared for that. With what? A knife. No. No child to hold hostage this time. They'd need a more imminent threat. A gun? Yes. Nothing like the dark tunnel of a gun barrel to keep you quiet.

"Shut up or you die," one of them had said. *His voice would have been calm, factual. This would have made it even scarier. More believable. She'd have sensed that here was someone who could shoot you and yawn about it.*

I move toward the bedroom. The stench is stronger

here. I recognize this place from the video. The motif is pink and soft and tasteful. It speaks of youth. Careless happiness.

In the middle of this softness, the hardest thing there is.

Her. Dead and already decaying, still tied to her bed.

She died with her eyes open. Her legs are spread. They left her that way on purpose, I know. To brag to us; *I had her,* they are saying, *and she's no one. A worthless whore. She was OURS.*

I see the bags arrayed next to the bed. While her body is a scene of violence, chaos, and depravity, the bags are a diametric contrast. They appear to have been placed next to each other in a nearly exact straight line. Neat and tidy. They are bragging to us here too. *See how neat and skillful we are,* it seems to say. Or perhaps they are speaking a language only they understand, writing in bloody pictographs we can't decipher.

It screams of careful ritual. This is what Jack the Ripper would have done, they think, and so this is what they do. I'm intrigued as well by the intensity of focus here. They were interested in her, and only her. Nothing else in the room has been touched or damaged. Their need to own did not extend to her environment. She was enough.

I move into the room and look around. Lots of books. They are dog-eared and haphazard in arrangement. Not just filling space—she was a reader. I lean forward to glance at the titles and am hit with a mixed pang of sorrow, irony, and bitter humor. True-crime novels, many focusing on serial killers.

"Helter Skelter," I murmur.

I turn to the bed. My eyes narrow as I notice her clothing in a pile on the floor. I walk over and bend down, examining without touching. Her bra strap is torn, as are her panties. She had not taken these off herself. They had been removed by force.

I stand up and look down at her dead face, caught in an eternal scream. "Did you fight them, Charlotte?" I ask her. "When they told you to take off your bra and panties, did you tell them to get stuffed?"

She is standing next to her bed, wearing only her underthings, shivering with the adrenaline of fear.

One of them points the gun. "All of it," he says. "Take it all off, now."

She looks at him, and the other one. Unlike Annie, she understands before they have tied her down.

Those empty eyes.

She knows.

"FUCK YOU!" she screams, and runs toward him, flailing and kicking. "HELP! HELP!"

I look down at her body again. I see bruising on her face, around her eyes. Caused after she was tied to the bed, or before? I'll never know for sure. I decide it was before. It doesn't really matter if it's true or not. But it makes me feel better to look at it that way.

He's enraged that this sow has put her whore hands on him. And he is afraid, for just a moment. The screaming has to stop. He punches her in the stomach, driving her breath out of her lungs and making her bend over.

"Hold her arms behind her back," he says to the other one, voice taut with rage.

She is gagging and gasping as the other grabs her arms by the elbows, pinning them back.

"You need to learn to obey, whore," the one with the gun says. His hand loops up, open palmed, cracking into the side of her face. Once. Twice. Again. Snapping her head back and forth. He reaches over and tears the bra from her with the kind of brutal strength only the insane have. Follows this by ripping her panties

from her thighs. She tries to scream again, but he punches her so-
lar plexus and follows it up with a few more devastating back-
hands to her face. She is naked, dazed, her eyes tearing and her
ears ringing, and her head in a red haze. Her knees buckle as she
tries to stay balanced.

Easy to control again.

This calms him.

He would have gagged her at that point. I look at her
hands and feet, note the handcuffs. Her left hand catches
my eye. I move to the head of the bed and lean forward.
Charlotte had fake nails. But the nail on her right index
finger is gone. I take a quick look at her other fingers. All
the other nails are there. I bite my lip, thinking.

Something occurs to me, and I go back out to the
front porch. "Do you have a flashlight?" I ask Barry.

"Sure," he says, handing me a small Maglite.

I grab it and go back into Charlotte's bedroom. I kneel
next to the bed, shining my light underneath.

I see it.

The lone nail, lying on the carpet near the head of the
bed. I squint and see what looks like blood on its tip.

I stand back up, looking down at Charlotte, feeling
sorrowful. It has crept up on me, a strong wave of hurting. All because of that lone nail. A last defiance, a fuck-
you from the grave.

Others could argue that it was an accident, but I
choose not to see it that way. I think of the books on serial killers she loved to read, the fascination with mystery
and forensics and murder. And I see a young girl who was
a fighter and knew she was going to die.

"Handcuff the whore to the bed," the one with the gun says.

The other manhandles her down in her dazed state, grabbing
her wrists and—

"Ow! Fucking CUNT!" he yells. "Cow scratched me!"

"Then cuff her, for fuck's sake!"

He smashes her stomach again and forces one wrist to the bed, cuffing it. Then the next.

Perhaps she did it while he cuffed her legs. Perhaps it took her longer, something she concentrated on through her terror and torture and rape. I can see it.

Everything is pain and fear and a red haze. They're going to kill her. She knows it. She's read about it. But because she's read, she knows about DNA. Knows what she has under her fingernail.

She pushes against the nail with her thumb, pushes, hard, hard, harder, praying they won't notice, until—

Snap. It breaks off, painless. She can't hear it fall to the rug. But some part of her mourns as it leaves her. It will live on after this, in a way. She won't.

She turns her gaze to the one with the gun, and he smiles.

She closes her eyes, and begins to weep, and thinks about the fingernail.

She knows she'll never see it again.

I stand up, feeling like a cold wind just blew through me. I look down at Charlotte.

"I found it," I whisper to her. "Right where you left it for me."

"Some sorry, sick stuff," Barry mutters. "I never seem to get used to it."

I glance at him. "That's probably a good thing, Barry."

He starts, looks at me. Then smiles a faint smile. "Yeah."

Callie and Gene are getting ready to go inside. I had told everyone about the fingernail.

"They won't take long, so go ahead and get your CSU guys over here, Barry. Kick their ass, and get me that report. Please. I'll make sure there's a quid pro quo. I'm pretty sure these guys are local. If it's at all possible, I'll have you there when we take them down."

He shakes his head. "Appreciate the thought, Smoky, but don't worry about it. This is one of those kinds of cases. Where you don't care who catches them, as long as they get caught."

"How about we just agree to keep each other in the loop and leave it at that?"

"That works for me."

"So what exactly do you want us to do here?"

Gene has a mixed look of exasperation on his face as he asks this—excitement and annoyance. He's excited to be out in the field for the first time in a long while, but he is annoyed that it is not "his scene" in its entirety. He cannot own it.

"I want anything immediate that will give me an edge on catching this guy. LAPD CSU is competent. They'll do the heavy lifting. I want you guys to skim the surface and see if there's anything here that will help us now."

"You want us to collect the fingernail?" Callie asks.

I balk at this. "Will we get faster DNA results?"

"Yes."

"Then take it. But you'll have to stay here until CSU arrives and log it in. Let's not screw up a conviction later because we messed up the chain of evidence."

Gene looks over at Callie. "You want the camera or the UV light?"

"I'll take the camera."

Callie will be photographing the scene—in particular, anything they touch or remove, before they do so. Gene is going to be using a small, handheld UV emitter. It is a smaller version of the UV scope that Callie used in

Annie's apartment, and it will help show evidence of blood, semen, hair, and other fluids.

"Let's go."

They walk in and I follow. It's my turn to be ignored, as they move in a dance that reminds me of James and me.

Callie sniffs the air. "What do you think, honey-love? Three days dead?"

"That would be my approximation."

Callie snaps some wide shots of the body, including the bagged organs.

Gene moves toward the Baggies and waves the UV wand over and around them. "No signs of prints." He glances at me. "Though that's cursory, not conclusive."

They turn toward the body. Callie takes more photos. Gene leans over to inspect Charlotte's right hand. "See the missing-nail area?" he says to Callie.

She responds by shooting a series of photos.

"The nail is on the carpet, between the bed and the wall," I say.

Callie squats down and takes some photos of the nail. "It looks like there may be some blood and tissue on it, Gene." She takes a few more photos.

He kneels and passes the wand under the bed. "There is a lot of particulate under here," he says. "I don't really want to disturb anything other than the nail…" He hands Callie the wand and reaches into a pocket, pulling out a pair of tweezers and a small evidence Baggie. I watch as he stretches, trying to contact as little of the carpet as possible while retrieving the nail. After a moment, he straightens back up, holding the evidence Baggie. "There could be DNA here."

"How long?" I ask.

Gene shrugs. "Twenty-four hours." I start to protest,

and he waves me off. "That's superrush, Smoky. Twenty-four hours, period."

I sigh. "Fine."

He takes the wand back from Callie and passes it over Charlotte, starting at her head, moving down to her neck, the open chest cavity, her legs. He stands up. "I don't see immediate evidence of seminal fluid on the body. Blood is everywhere, of course. No way to draw any conclusions on that with the naked eye."

Callie takes some more photos.

"I think your best, most immediate lead is going to be any DNA on the fingernail," he says to me. "And as there appears to have been a struggle, I'll tell LAPD CSU to take extra care on collecting trace, especially with the bra and panties."

"That's it?"

"For now, honey-love," Callie answers. "But the nail has potential, don't you think?"

"Yeah. Yeah, I do." I look at my watch. It's almost 11:00 P.M. "I have to go and meet that security specialist at my house, Callie. You guys stay here and wait for CSU. Gene—*please*—get right onto the DNA."

"As fast as I can."

He looks down at Charlotte. She is still screaming.

39

"**H**OW IS SHE?" I ask. I sound tired, even to myself.

"She's fine. Woke up in the afternoon, and we watched a little bit of TV. She helped me make dinner. Normal stuff. She's asleep now."

"Elaina..." I hesitate.

"She can stay here tonight, Smoky. I was going to recommend it. Besides, you sound exhausted, and there's no reason to wake her up."

Good ol' empathy. I feel guilty, but not enough to turn her offer down.

"Thanks. I am tired. But I won't make a habit of it, I promise. And I'll call her in the morning."

"Get some sleep, Smoky."

Would I have left Alexa with Elaina under the same circumstances, I wonder as I drive? I shove this thought aside. Push it into a closet, lock the door, sell the house the closet's in.

I arrive home just after eleven. God, it has been a marathon day.

Tommy is already here. His timeliness doesn't surprise me. Punctuality isn't a learned trait for him, it's a part of his core personality.

He gets out of his car as I pull up, walks over to me. Indicating that I need to roll down my window, which I do.

"Pull into the garage," he says. "They could be watching. When you're in the garage, don't say anything until I sweep it for bugs."

"Got it."

I hit the door opener and pull the car in. He follows me after a moment, carrying a backpack. I turn off the car and get out.

I watch in silence as he does an electronic sweep for bugs, using a high-dollar device that can sweep all frequencies up to four gigahertz. He takes his time, slow, methodical, and entirely focused. This takes almost ten minutes. Once he's completed this, he starts a physical inspection. It's not enough to sweep for bugs. You have to look for them as well.

I lean back and watch him work, give him the once-over. I have not seen Tommy in years. He looks amazing, as always. Tommy's heritage is Latin, and he is handsome in a very Latin way. Black, wavy hair. Deep, dark eyes. He has a slight imperfection, a small scar at his left temple, which somehow makes him more attractive. He's not rugged and he's not pretty. He's somewhere in between, and it looks good on him. He is to men what Callie is to women. He doesn't have the same gusto she has; he is defined more by his comfort with stillness and silence. When he sits, listening to you, he never fidgets, twiddles his thumbs, or taps his feet. It's not that he's stiff. On the contrary, he appears to be relaxed, at ease. It's more that he doesn't feel a need to move. All the motion is in his eyes. Always intent, interested, alert. I assume that this comes from his history as a Secret Service agent. Stillness and watching go hand in hand in that profession.

Tommy is not forthcoming. I know he's never been

married. I don't know if he's had many girlfriends, or just a few. I have no idea why he left the Service. As far as I know, they left him. Nothing came up on his background check, and I didn't feel right prying. I know the things I need to know: He's good at what he does; he has a sister he loves, a mother he supports. These are basic things, revelatory things. Things that tell you a lot about a person's character. I do wonder about those parts not seen, though. I can't help it.

His voice pulls me from my reverie. "No bugs I can find. Not likely they'd be out here, anyway. They wouldn't think of this as a place you'd spend a lot of time."

"They'd be right."

"This is the car you've been driving?"

"Yes."

He moves over behind my car and gets down on his back. I watch as he moves farther and farther under it.

"Found it. Very high-end, very pro, real-time GPS tracker." He crawls back out from under my car. "With that and the right software, they can track you on a laptop. I assume you want to leave it on for now."

"I don't want them to know that I know it's there. When you're following me, maybe you'll spot one of them."

"Right. You told me they'd been in your home?"

"Yes. I had the locks changed."

"But that means they could have planted bugs anytime before that. You want me to look for those? It could take a few hours."

"If they're there, I want to know where. But I want to leave them in place."

He picks up his bag. "Take me inside and I'll get to work."

* * *

Tommy cleared my cell phone first. While he continues on the bug hunt, I make a round of calls to my team.

"What's happening with tracking the user–pass combos, James?"

"It's going to take us through the night. We're tracking down the owners of the various companies."

"Stay on it."

He hangs up without replying. Still a prick.

Callie is at the lab with Gene, who, true to his word, is putting the heat on the DNA.

"He's calling in some favors, Smoky. Some people are getting up out of bed. Our Gene is very focused."

"Can you blame him?"

"No. I don't care what she did for a living, honey-love. She was young. She could have changed over time, picked a different profession. He took that opportunity away from her."

"I know, Callie. That's why we have to get him. Keep on it, and get some sleep if you can."

"You too, Smoky."

I reach Alan last. I fill him in on Bonnie staying with them tonight.

"Sure, that's no problem." He pauses. "Elaina starts chemo next week."

The lump, quickly becoming a familiar friend, is in my throat again. "It's going to turn out fine, Alan."

"Cup half full, right?"

"That's right."

"G'night." He hangs up, leaving me looking at the phone.

I can still hear Tommy moving through my house. It is quiet, and empty. I already miss Bonnie. The circumstances of her being here were terrible, and if I could change them, I would. But the truth remains. I miss her. Her absence echoes inside me.

I realize that I burn to clear this case for more than the usual reasons. Not just to get Jack Jr. and his insanity off the streets. But also to be able to start giving Bonnie a home. I am thinking of the future, and desiring it. Something I have not done since the day I killed Joseph Sands.

Tommy is still clomping around. I turn on the TV in the living room and settle back to watch as I wait.

I'm twelve years old, and it is summer. A beautiful summer. My father is still alive, and I have no idea that he will be dead before I turn twenty-one. We are at Zuma Beach, sitting on the hot sand. I can feel drops of the cold ocean water evaporating off my skin, can taste the salt on my lips. I am young, at the beach, and my father loves me.

It is a perfect moment.

My father is watching the sky. I look over and see him smile, shaking his head.

"What, Daddy?"

"Just thinking about all the different kinds of sun, sweetheart. Every place has its own kind of sun, did you know that?"

"Really?"

"Uh-huh. There's Kansas wheat-field sun. There's Bangor, Maine, sun, all peeking through gray clouds, lighting up gray sky. There's Florida sun, kind of like sticky gold." He turns to me. "My all-time favorite is California sun. That dry, hot, no-clouds, all-blue-sky sun. Like today. It says everything is starting, something exciting is going to happen." He turns his head back toward the sky. Closes his eyes and lets the sun he loves best warm his face, while the sea breeze ruffles his hair. It is the first time that I ever thought of my father as beautiful.

I didn't understand everything he was saying at the time, but it didn't matter. I understood that he was sharing something with me because he loved me.

Whenever I think of my father, try to remember his essence, I think of that moment.

My dad was an amazing person. Mom died when I was ten. Though he staggered, he never fell. Never left me to myself while he wallowed in his grief. The one thing I never had to doubt, whatever else was happening, was that my father loved me.

I wake up to someone touching me, and I spin off the couch, drawing my weapon as I open my eyes. It takes a few moments to register that it is Tommy. He doesn't seem alarmed. Just stands there, hands at his sides. I lower my gun.

"Sorry," he says.

"No, I'm sorry, Tommy."

"I finished with the sweep. The only thing I found is a tap on your phone. This is probably because you live alone. Unless you talk to yourself, the phone would be the only thing worth listening to."

"So, it's the phone and the car."

"Yes. Here's what I propose. I'll sleep down here, on your couch. Tomorrow when you leave, I'll follow you."

"Are you sure, Tommy? About staying here?"

"You're my principal now, Smoky. My job is to protect you, around the clock."

"I'd be lying if I said I didn't like it. Thanks."

"It's no problem. I owe you."

I look at him for a long time. "You know, Tommy, you don't really owe me anything. I was just doing my job.

I doubt that you feel anyone you guarded in the Service owed you for that."

He turns his eyes to me. "No. But *they* felt they did. Because it was about their life. You stuck by me at a bad time. Whether or not you feel I owe you, I do." He's silent for a moment. "I only wish I had been here when Sands came."

I smile at him. "Me too."

He nods. "I'm here for you now. Get a good night's sleep. You don't have anything to worry about." He looks at me, and his eyes have changed. They are stone. Ice. Frozen granite. "Anyone who wants you has to come through me."

I look at Tommy. Really look at him. I think about the dream of my father, about everything that has happened. Everything that could happen. I examine his dark, deep eyes. His handsome face. I feel a longing.

"What's the matter?" he asks, voice soft.

I don't reply. Instead, I shock myself to the core by leaning up and kissing him on the lips. I feel him stiffen. He pushes me away.

"Whoa," he says.

I look down, unable to meet his eyes. "Am I that ugly, Tommy?"

There is a long silence. I feel his hand on my chin, lifting it up. I don't want to see his face. Don't want to see the revulsion.

"Look at me," he demands.

So I do. And my eyes widen. No revulsion. Just tenderness, mixed with anger.

"You're not ugly, Smoky. I always thought you were one sexy lady. Still do. You want somebody right now. I understand that. But I don't know that this would lead anywhere."

I gaze at him, feel the honesty of his words. "Would you think less of me if I didn't care?" I ask him, curious.

He shakes his head. "No. But that's not the problem."

"Then—what?"

He spreads his hands. "Whether or not you would think less of me."

His words make me pause. And they make me feel good. I lean forward. "You're a good man, Tommy. I trust you. I don't care where it leads, or if it leads anywhere." I reach out a hand, touch his face. "I'm lonely and I was hurt, yes. But that's not why. I just want a man to want me right now. That's all. Is that wrong?"

His eyes regard me, still revealing nothing. Then he reaches forward and takes my face in his hands. Brings his lips down on mine. They are soft and hard at the same time. His tongue slips into my mouth and my response is instantaneous. My whole body arches into him, and I can feel his hardness through his slacks. He pulls back. His eyes look half hooded in pleasure, and sexy as hell.

"Upstairs okay?" he asks me.

I think if he hadn't asked, had just assumed and tried to take me up into the bed that I only ever shared with Matt, my answer would have been no. Part of me still feels like I should say no.

"Yes, please," I answer.

He gathers me into his arms in a single motion, carrying me like I'm a feather. I put my face against his neck and smell the smell of man. My longing intensifies at this. It has been missed, that scent. I want to feel someone else's skin against mine. I want to not be alone.

I want to feel beautiful.

We get into the bedroom, and he lays me down, gentle. He proceeds to undress as I watch. And, boy, it's worth watching, my body tells me. He's well-built without being overmuscular, the physique of a dancer. He has chest hair, which I find sexy, but not too much. Just right. When he slips off his pants, followed by his boxers, I gasp. Not at his cock—though I sure can't miss it. I gasp at the sight of a man, naked in front of me again. I feel an energy building inside me, a kind of formless wave, roaring toward some internal shore.

He comes over to me, sits down, and moves a hand to unbutton my blouse. I feel the doubts come again. "Tommy, I—the scars . . . they aren't just on my face."

"Shhh . . ." he says to me, his fingers continuing to unbutton. He has strong hands, I notice. Callused in places, soft in others. Tender and rough, like him.

He opens my shirt, sits me up to pull it off, and then removes my bra. He lays me back and looks at me. My fear disappears when I see the expression on his face. No revulsion, no pity. All I see is that awe men can have at times when you stand naked in front of them. That kind of "Really? All for me?" look.

He bends forward and kisses me again, and I feel his chest against mine. My nipples harden, turning into pulsing sunbursts of sensation. He kisses my chin, then moves down my neck, to my chest.

When he takes one of my nipples into his mouth, I arch and cry out. Jesus Christ, I think. Is that what months without sex will do to you? I grab his head and start speaking unintelligible things to him, feeling an urgency build. He continues kissing me, going from nipple to nipple, making me groan and mewl, while his hands undo my slacks and pull the zipper down. He sits up on his knees to pull them off me, taking my panties with them, and then pauses for a moment, looking down at me, slacks bunched up in one hand. His eyes are dusky, his face partly shadowed, and the look he's giving me is pure desire.

Here I am, I think. Naked in front of a more than handsome man. And he wants me bad. Scars and all. Tears come into my eyes.

Tommy looks concerned. "You okay?" he asks.

I smile up at him. "Oh yeah," I say, tears running down my face. "Just happy. You made me feel sexy."

"You are sexy. God, Smoky." He reaches a finger out and traces the scars on my face. Moves down, circling around the ones on my chest, my belly. "You think these make you ugly." He shakes his head. "To me, they reveal character. They show strength, and survival, and not getting beat. They show that you're a fighter. That you'll fight for life, to the death." His hand comes back up to my face. "They're not defects on the package, Smoky. They're proof of what was always there."

I reach my arms out to him.

"Come down here and show me that you feel that way. Show me all night long."

He does. It goes on for hours, a mix of the dark and the divine, and perception turns into a blend of unbearable emotions combined with sensation. I am insatiable, and I keep demanding, and he keeps providing, until the end, when the world recedes first to a dot, and then explodes into a near-blinding display that has me screaming in pleasure at the top of my lungs.

"Window rattling," Matt used to call it.

The sweetest pain of all is the lack of guilt. Because I know that if Matt is watching, he is happy. That he is telling me, a whisper in my ear: *Get on with your life. You're still among the living.*

As I fall asleep I realize that I know I will not dream tonight. The dreams aren't finished yet, but the past and the present are learning to live with each other. The present has hated the past, and the past has been an enemy of the future. Perhaps soon, the past will just be the past again.

Sleep claims me, and it is not a retreat, but a comfort.

40

WHEN I WAKE in the morning, I feel satisfied and sore. Like I slaked a thirst. Tommy isn't here, but when I cock an ear, I hear him downstairs. I stretch, feeling every muscle, and then bound out of bed.

I shower, regretful at having to wash his smell off me but feeling refreshed afterward. Great sex can be that way. Like a good marathon run. A shower always feels better if you get really dirty first.

I luxuriate in this feeling for a moment and then get dressed and head downstairs, finding Tommy in the kitchen.

He looks the same as he did before we went to bed, not a wrinkle in his suit. He is fully awake and alert. He has brewed coffee, and he gives me a cup.

"Thanks," I say.

"Are you going to be leaving soon?"

"In about a half hour. I need to make a call first."

"Let me know." He regards me for a moment, sphinx-like, until a smile plays on the edge of his lips.

I raise an eyebrow at him. "What?"

"Just thinking about last night."

I look at him. "It was great," I say, quiet.

"Yeah." He cocks his head. "You know, you never asked me if I was seeing anyone already."

"I figured if you were, last night wouldn't have happened. Was I wrong?"

"Nope."

I look down at my coffee cup. "Listen, Tommy, I want to say something about last night. About what you said. About not being sure if it would go anywhere or not. I want you to know I meant what I told you. If it doesn't go anywhere, it really will be okay. But..."

"But if it does, that's okay too," he replies. "Is that what you were going to say?"

"Yeah."

"Good. 'Cause I feel the same way." He reaches out a hand, strokes my hair. I lean into it for a second. "I mean that, Smoky. You're a hell of a woman. And I've always thought that."

"Thanks." I smile at him. "So what do we call it? 'A one-night stand with potential'?"

He drops his hand, laughs. "I like that. Let me know when you're ready to go."

I nod and walk away, feeling not just good, but something even more important: comfortable. However it goes, neither Tommy nor I will have to regret last night. Thank God.

I go back upstairs, nursing my coffee like it's the elixir of life. Which, with the hours I've been keeping, isn't far from the truth. It's only eight-thirty, but I feel certain that Elaina is an early riser. I dial the number.

Elaina answers. "Hello?"

"Hi. It's Smoky. Sorry about last night. How is she?"

"She seems happy. She's still not talking, but she smiles a lot."

"How is she doing at night?"

Silence. "She was screaming in her sleep last night. I woke her up and cuddled her. She was fine after that."

"Ah, jeez. I'm sorry, Elaina." I feel parent's guilt at this. While I was howling at the moon, Bonnie was screaming at the past. "You have no idea how thankful I am for this."

"She's a child who's been hurt and needs help, Smoky. That's never a burden in our home, and never will be." Her words are simple factual statements, meant from the heart. "Do you want to speak to her?"

My heart skips a beat. I realize that I do. Very much. "Please."

"Hang on for a moment."

A minute later, Elaina comes back on the phone. "She's here. I'm going to hand her the phone now."

Fumbling sounds and then I hear the faint sound of Bonnie breathing.

"Hi, honey," I say. "I know you can't talk back, so I'll just talk to you. I'm really sorry I didn't come get you last night. I had to work late. When I woke up this morning and you weren't here..." My voice trails off. I hear her breathing. "I miss you, Bonnie."

Silence. More fumbling noises, followed by Elaina's voice. "Hold on, Smoky." She speaks away from the phone. "You have something you want to say to Smoky, sweetheart?" More silence. "I'll tell her." Talking to me now: "She gave me a big smile and hugged herself and pointed to the phone."

My heart clenches tighter. I don't need a translation for that one. "Tell her I just did the same thing, Elaina. I have to go, but I'll be by this evening to get her. No more sleepovers if I can help it. Not for a while, at least."

"We'll be here."

I sit for a moment after hanging up, staring at nothing. I am aware right now of all the layers of emotion I am feeling, the obvious and the subtle. I have strong feelings for Bonnie. Feelings of protectiveness, tenderness, a burgeoning love. These are fierce, real. There are other feelings whispering around, though. Tumbling through me like dry leaves, padding on quiet, shadow feet. One is annoyance. That I can't just be happy about my night with Tommy. It is faint but has its own strength. The selfishness of a very small child who doesn't want to share. Don't I deserve some happy time, it whispers, petulant?

And there is the voice of guilt. It is a smooth voice, oil and snakes. It asks only one question, but it's a powerful one: How dare you be happy when she isn't?

Recognition shivers through me. I've heard these voices before, all of them. Being Alexa's mom. Being a parent is not a one-note thing, a single-act play. It's complex, and it contains both love and anger, selflessness and selfishness. Times you are breathless and overwhelmed at the beauty of your child. Times you wish, for just a moment, that there was no child at all.

I'm feeling these things because I'm becoming Bonnie's mom. This brings a new guilt voice, one of rebuke and misery: How dare you love her?

Don't you remember?

Your love brings death.

Rather than bringing me down, this voice makes me angry. I dare, I reply, because I *have* to. That's being a parent. Love gets you through most of it, duty gets you through the rest.

I want Bonnie to be safe, and have a home, and that feeling *is* real.

I dare the voices to respond. They don't.

Good.

It's time to go to work.

The door to the office flies open, and Callie enters. She's wearing sunglasses and clutching a cup of coffee.

"Don't talk to me yet," she growls. "I'm not well caffeinated."

I sniff the air. Callie always has the best coffee. "Mmm..." I say. "What is that? Hazelnut?"

She moves away, clutching the coffee close. One side of her mouth raises in a snarl. "Mine."

I walk over to my purse, reach inside, and pull out a package of small chocolate donuts. I see Callie's eyebrows shoot up. I wave the donuts. "Oh, look, Callie. Yummy chocolate donuts. Mmm, mmm, good."

Emotions war across her face in something just short of a nuclear conflict. "Oh, fine," she says, scowling. She grabs the cup on my desk, filling it halfway with her coffee. "Now give me two of those donuts."

I pull two out of the wrapper, moving them toward her as she pushes the coffee cup toward me. When the two meet, she snatches the donuts as I grab the cup. The hostages have been exchanged. She sits down at her desk, gobbling the donuts, while I sip from the cup.

Heavenly.

Callie sips her coffee and eats her donuts, and I feel her gaze on me. Thoughtful and piercing at the same time, even through the sunglasses.

"What?" I ask.

"You tell me," she murmurs, taking another bite from a donut.

Jesus, I think. Is that old myth true? About it showing if you got laid?

"I don't know what you're talking about."

She continues to look at me through her sunglasses, giving me a big, Cheshire-cat smile. "Whatever you say, honey-love."

I decide to ignore her.

Leo, Alan, and James all arrive fairly close to one another. Leo looks like he's been hit by a truck. James looks like he always does.

"Gather round," I say. "Time for a coordination meeting.

"Leo and James—where do we stand on the user name and password search?"

Leo rubs a hand through his hair. "We reached every company, and all are cooperating." He checks his watch. "I actually spoke to the last one a half hour ago. We should have all the results within an hour."

"Let me know the moment you have anything. Callie, where did we end up on the DNA?"

"Gene really put some feet to the fire, honey-love. He told me he'll have results by the end of the day. Meaning, if there is DNA and he's on file, we'll know who it is by dinner."

Everyone pauses at this, considering. The idea that we could have the face of one of our monsters before it gets dark. Could have one or both in custody before the day is over.

"Wouldn't that be a hoot?" Alan murmurs.

"No kidding," I reply. "In the meantime, when did Dr. Child say he'd be ready to see me?"

"Anytime after ten," Callie replies.

"Good. Callie and Alan—follow up with Barry and see what's happening with CSU processing the rest of the Charlotte Ross crime scene."

"Sure thing, honey-love."

"I'm going to see Dr. Child." I look around at everyone. "We are now officially hot on his trail, people. Let's keep moving. Speed and momentum are everything." I look at my watch and stand up. "Let's go."

It's time to cast another net.

I knock on Dr. Child's door before opening it. He's seated behind his desk, reading a thick file. He looks up when I poke my head in and smiles.

"Smoky. Good to see you. Come in, come in." He indicates the chairs in front of his desk. "Please sit down. I'll just need a moment to refer to my notes. Fascinating case."

I sit, and I watch him as he reads the papers in front of him. Dr. Child is in his late fifties. White-haired, with glasses and a beard. He looks like he is in his sixties. He always seems tired, and his eyes have a haunted look to them that never goes away, not even when he laughs. He's been peering into the minds of serial killers for almost thirty years. Will I look like that, I wonder, twenty years from now?

He's the only person I trust more than James and myself to have useful insights on what drives the monsters.

He nods to himself and looks up. Leans back in his chair. "You and I have collaborated before, Smoky. So you know that I tend to natter on. I imagine I'll do a fair amount of that now. Do you mind?"

"Not at all, Doctor. Please."

He steeples his fingers under his chin. "I'm going to address this as applying to a single individual. The 'Jack Jr.' persona is our primary, and dominant, personality. Do you agree?"

I nod.

"Good. What we have here can be one of two things. The first is possible, but, I feel, improbable. That he is faking all of it. That his claims of being a descendant of Jack the Ripper are a part of an act, designed to throw you off his trail. I feel this view is overly paranoid and unproductive.

"The second is the most probable and is highly, highly unusual. What we are talking about is a case of nurture versus nature. A kind of long-term brainwashing. Wherein someone spent a very long time imprinting our 'Jack Jr.' with the identity he has assumed. In my opinion, this would have to have started from a very young age to be this successful. It's probable that this was done by one, or both, of his parents.

"Most serial killers, we find, have similar histories. This usually involves abuse from a very young age. It could be physical, it could be sexual, often it is both. The result of this is rage, and it is a rage that they cannot express against their abuser, someone larger and stronger than they are, someone in a position of emotional trust and authority. The abuser is almost always a father or a mother. The abused loves this person and feels certain that the abuse must be justified. Caused by something they have done wrong.

"Rage must have an outlet. Without an immediate target, it is channeled by them, almost invariably in the same three ways. First, in violence against themselves: chronic bed-wetting. Then in violence against their environment: the setting of small fires. Finally, escalating in violence against living things: torturing and killing small animals. Once they are adults, this leads them to the logical conclusion: the infliction of harm against other human beings.

"All of this is, of course, an oversimplification. Human

beings are not robots, and no one mind is the same as the other. Not all of them wet their beds, set fires, or kill small animals. The abuse is not always from a father, or a mother. But over time, the trends that we have found make this oversimplification more or less accurate."

He leans back, looking at me.

"There are exceptions. They are rare, but they do exist. They are the argument for those that feel nature is the explanation. Killers who came from decent homes and decent parents. Bad seeds. No apparent reason or explanation for what they do." He shakes his head. "Why does it have to be one or the other? I have always felt, and many agree, that it can be both. Nature and nurture. Of course, nurture, as I said, tends to be the most prevalent and observable cause." He taps on the report in front of him. "In this instance, the variables abound. He says he wasn't abused physically or sexually. That he didn't set fires or torture small animals. That may not be true. Perhaps he is in denial. But if he's not, then he is something new. He is a serial killer created from scratch. Someone who has been indoctrinated so heavily and for so long into a belief system that it has become a certainty for him. If that is true, he would be a very, very dangerous man. He won't have the injuries to the psyche caused by sexual or physical abuse. He won't have the low self-esteem these things cause.

"He would be able to operate at an extremely high level of rationality. He would have no difficulty assimilating himself into society. Indeed, he might have been trained to do just that.

"Jack Jr. would be doing what he does with the idea that it is his destiny. What he was born to do. He wouldn't consider it wrong. Because he has been told just the opposite from the moment he could understand the spoken word."

Dr. Child looks at me. "He has fixated on you because he needs this to complete the fantasy. He stated as much himself, that Jack the Ripper must be chased, preferably by a brilliant detective. He has chosen you for this. An astute choice."

He leans forward, tapping the report again. "The truth about the contents of the jar he sent you, the fact that they were bovine and not human, as he seems to think, this could be your most potent weapon. It is a symbol of everything he believes. He has always accepted it as truth. If he were to find out that this symbol is a lie, and always has been ... it could shatter him. Could bring the world he's crafted tumbling down." He leans back. "He has been very smart, very organized, very precise. If he were to find out about the jar—he could unravel. Of course, there is another possibility we can't ignore. That he would reject that truth out of hand. That he would decide it was a lie, designed to unsettle him. In such a scenario, he would blame the individual who had delivered this 'lie.' He would likely have an overwhelming urge to harm that individual. Both scenarios have their uses, yes?"

I nod. "They do."

"Be aware that each one contains possible dangers. If what he has built his life on is removed with such suddenness—he could become suicidal. In this case, however, I can almost guarantee you that he would not want to die alone."

I get the message. An enraged Jack Jr., devoid of hope, might well turn into a suicide bomber. Dr. Child is telling us to be prepared for this possibility.

"What about Ronnie Barnes?" I ask.

He nods, looking up at the ceiling. "Yes. The young

man he claims to have found on the Internet and 'nurtured' himself. Very interesting—though not entirely unprecedented. Killing in teams isn't as rare as people might think. Charles Manson may have led the most famous group of killers, but he was not the first or the last."

"Right," I reply. "I can think of twenty cases off the top of my head."

"More than that; but, yes, that's my point. An estimated fifteen percent of serial victims are the result of team killings. And while this one has a twist, it does fit the scenario. Teams generally consist of two individuals, but have numbered more. There is always a dominant figure, someone with a particular energy and a specific fantasy. He—or she—inspires the others, emboldens them to put the fantasy into action. All involved have psychopathic traits, but it's been thought in some instances—and I agree—that without that central figure, the others might never have taken that extra step to committing actual murder." He smiles, and I get a glimpse of weary cynicism. "That's not to say that they were victims. It's not uncommon after arrest for the nondominants to claim that they were unwilling accomplices. But the evidence rarely bears this out."

"The Ripper Crew," I say.

Dr. Child smiles at me. "Excellent example. And a relatively recent one."

I was referring to the so-called Chicago Rippers of the 1980s. A psycho named Robin Gecht led a team of three other like-minded men. By the time they were caught, seventeen women or more had been raped, beaten, tortured, and strangled. Gecht's crew severed one or both breasts off their victims, which they used later for sexual purposes and ... dining purposes.

"Gecht never *personally* killed anyone, did he?" I ask.

"No, he did not. But he was the driving force behind it all. Very charismatic man."

"Similar," I muse. "But not the same."

Dr. Child cocks his head, interested. "Explain."

"It's just a sense of him that I get. Sure, Jack Jr. is the dominant. He's calling the shots. But in most cases of team killings, there's an interpersonal relationship between the killers. They give each other something. They may be twisted, but they're a *team*. Jack sacrificed Barnes, and it was all to get to me and confuse us." I shake my head. "I think the followers are a calculated means to an end. I don't think he needs them, emotionally, for his fantasy."

Dr. Child steeples his fingers, considering this. He sighs. "Well, that would fit with his dual victimology."

"You mean his other victim type being us."

"Yes. It certainly makes him more dangerous. He's a 'man with a plan' as they say. Mr. Barnes—and any others—would in that scenario be pawns. Plastic pieces to move on a chessboard. Not the worst news, but not the best either. Less emotional involvement means less chance of him tripping himself up."

Great, I think.

"How would he go about finding potential teammates?" I ask. "In your opinion."

"Obviously, the Internet has provided him with both anonymity and access." Dr. Child looks almost wistful. "It's the continuing irony: world-changing inventions, they can do great things or be used for great harm. On one hand, the Internet has broken down political boundaries. E-mails came out of Russia before the Iron Curtain fell. People from different places in the world can communicate in a heartbeat. Americans and Eskimos can find out that they aren't really so different from one another. On the other hand, it has provided an environment nearly free of constraint for the Jack Jr.'s of this world. Rape Web sites, pedophilia, sites devoted to displaying photographic grotesqueries such as execution victims or the bloody results of car crashes." He looks at me. "So, to answer your question, and based on the evidence he's provided thus far, he would look for converts by rooting around in the less-desirable areas of the Internet, specifically in areas where he could first observe. He'd need to be able to do nothing, in the beginning, but watch. He'd look for certain proclivities. Like all manipulators, he'd find key talking points, those things to ingratiate himself, to be authoritative about. However"—and he leans forward as he says this—"he would have to meet them face-to-face. Simple e-mail or chat rooms would not be sufficient. For various reasons. One would be simple security. It's far too easy to pretend an online identity. Our Jack is a risk taker, but he prepares before taking those risks. He'd want to ensure that the person he was talking to really was who and what they claimed to be."

"Why else?" I ask.

"Foremost is the proverbial two-way street. Those he was speaking to would be just as concerned about the truth of his identity. Most relevant, however, is that I simply do not think it's plausible for him to make them *act* on their fantasies without personal interaction on his part. No. If I were him, I would take my time, look around, and make my list. Next, I would verify their identity in some way. Then I would initiate online contact. This would be followed by face-to-face meetings. From there, you can pick your method of will-bending. Perhaps it begins on a small scale. 'Let's go peeping on a sorority house. Let's beat up a prostitute, but not kill her. Now let's murder a cat, and be sure to look into its eyes as it dies.' By building slowly, he would break down whatever flimsy morality they may have thrown up to regulate their behavior, to make them feel human. Once you've put one foot into hell, why not two? After all, and let's not forget: To them, hell feels like heaven itself."

"How long would something like that take? Conditioning a person, making them cross that line?"

He looks at me. "You're asking me how many other protégés could he have created, yes?"

"Basically."

Dr. Child spreads his hands. "That is an unknown. It depends on too many factors. How long has he been doing this? What pool does he draw from? If, for example, he were to choose recently paroled rapists to contact and mold...well, the jump from rape to murder is a short leap indeed."

I look into his tired eyes and take this in. How many years? How many Jack Jr. converts? We don't know. Can't know.

"One other thing bothers me about him, Doctor. You touched on it when you said he's a risk taker. This whole process of creating followers, it's a dangerous move. Any one of these 'protégés' could become a point of exposure." I shake my head. "It seems like a contradiction. On one hand, he's smart. Very smart, and very careful. On the other, he's taking huge chances. I don't get it."

Dr. Child smiles. "You haven't considered the simplest explanation for this contradiction?"

I frown. "Which is?"

"That's he's insane."

I stare at him. "That's it? 'He's insane'?"

"I'll expound some." His face gets serious. "But don't lose sight of that simple truth. It is the Occam's razor of my profession, and it has served me well, many times." He leans back. "As to specifics...I think there are two factors. One fits the fantasy. This twisted 'propagation of the species,' passing the Ripper torch, and so on." He pauses. "The other speaks to hungers."

"Hungers?"

"The thing that drives all serial offenders. The need to do what they do. It overcomes their cautions." He shrugs. "This process of contacting others, manipulating them, molding them, it is irrational. Aside from the broad strokes of his insanity, Jack Jr. has not *been* irrational. Unless there is a sensible motivation we haven't yet divined, then this deviation must be driven by something *other* than reason. Hungers. Some hunger is fed by doing this, and that satiation is both more satisfying and more important than his own safety."

"So basically—he's crazy."

"As I said."

I consider this. "Why the Ripper? Why the obsession with whores?"

"I believe one is the reason for the other. I feel the whores are the reason for the Ripper fantasy, not the other way around. Whoever it was that concocted this finely tuned travesty, well..." He shrugs. "They had a problem with women. Possibly driven by abuse or witnessed abuse. Ironically, the motivations and reasons behind this modern-day replica are probably very similar to the motivations and reasons behind the original Ripper. Woman-hate mixed with sexuality and denied desire. That old saw."

"So again—he's crazy. And whoever indoctrinated him was *really* crazy."

"Yes."

I look off, thinking. Predictable and unpredictable.

Driven by both reason and insanity. Great. Still, I felt we knew him just a little bit better now.

"Thanks, Dr. Child. You've been a big help, as always."

Those sad, tired eyes look at me. "It's what I do, Agent Barrett. I'll make sure you get my report. And please—be careful with this one. This is something new. While new may be interesting from a clinical standpoint..." He pauses, looks me in the eye. "New in reality is just another word for dangerous."

I feel the dragon stir at this, defiant. "Let me give you some perspective from my side of the fence, Doctor. How he does it and why he does it? Those might be new. But what he does?" I shake my head, grim. "Murder is murder."

41

UPDATE ME."

I'm in AD Jones's office. He's called me up so that I can report to him on the progress of the case. He stops me when I get to Tommy Aguilera.

"Hold on—Aguilera? He's a civilian now, isn't he?"

"He's good, sir. Really, really good." You have no idea, I think to myself.

"I know he's good. That's not the point." The look on his face is sour. Sucking-lemons sour. "I'll let it go this time, Smoky. In the future, if you're going to bring in outside people, I need you to clear it with me."

"Yes, sir."

"Go on."

I finish with everything, up to and through the visit with Dr. Child. He takes a moment to think before clasping his hands together on the desk. "Let me make sure I have it all. He's killed two women. Each time he does, he sends you video of it. He's got a partner. He's fixated on you, to the point of sneaking into your home and bugging your phone and car. He's initiated personal attacks on the rest of your team, and threatened future ones. He's reaching out to other potential serial killers in addition to the one he's working with. He is not who he thinks he is. Do I have it so far?"

"Yes, sir."

"You have fingerprints, you probably have DNA. You have his recon MO—and your hottest lead right now is searching for the other sites he's signed up for, if he has. That about it?"

"That's a pretty good summary, sir. I want to attack this in two additional ways, and I need your permission."

"What?"

"I want to take this to the media."

His eyes grow wary. We don't like the media, most of the time. We interact with them if forced to, or, sometimes, if we think it will be useful. I feel this is one of those times. I just need to convince him.

"Why?"

"Two reasons. The first is a point of safety. The bottom line is, while we're starting to get a picture of him, we can't predict when we're going to catch him. We need to get a warning out there. It's time."

He gives me a grudging nod. "What's the second reason?"

"Dr. Child said if he were to find out about the contents of the jar, it would shake him up. Badly. It might even push him over the edge. We need to do that, sir. He's been a cool operator up to now. This is the one piece of information we have that he doesn't. It's a good weapon. I want to use it."

"He might blow up, Smoky. I'm not talking about this sick bullshit he's been pulling. I'm talking full-on guided missile, coming straight at you."

"Yes, sir. That's possible. And then we'd catch him."

He gives me a look I can't read. Stands up and goes over to his window. His back is to me as he begins speaking. "His obsession with you…" He turns around. "I want you to be very, very careful. I"—he hesitates—"I don't want a repeat of Joseph Sands. Ever again."

I'm at a loss for words. Because I can feel the emotion radiating from AD Jones.

"I've known you since you came into the Bureau, Smoky. Since you were young and enthusiastic and still wet behind the ears. It matters to me what happens to you. Understand?"

I see the pain in his eyes. "Yes, sir. I'll be careful."

And the pain disappears, shoved back inside somewhere. He let me see it, wanted me to know it was there. I know it might be the only time he lets me in, in that way, and I am touched and thankful.

"What's the second thing?"

"If we locate a probable victim—I'm going to want to set a trap. And I'll have to do it fast."

"When and if that time comes, talk to me about it first."

"Yes, sir."

When I walk back into the office, Leo waves a piece of paper. "They finished the search," he says. "One name came up with that same user name and password combination."

Strange, I think. That they wouldn't vary it. "Give me the details."

He looks down at the page. "Her name is Leona Waters. She runs a personal site called"—he looks up at me, gives me a tired smile—"Cassidy Cumdrinker. She lives in the Santa Monica area."

"Do you have an address?"

"I printed it out." He hands it to me.

"What do you want to do, honey-love?"

"What's the word from Barry?"

"They found another exterminator receipt," Alan rumbles. "Same bullshit as the last time."

"So it's a definite MO."

"Looks that way."

"Anything else?"

"Nah. Their CSU is still going over it."

"Here's what I want. Callie and I are going to go and see Ms. Waters. I want to check things out, get the lay of the land. We'll figure out a plan from there. Alan, I want you to stay on Barry and follow up with Gene on the DNA. If anything changes, you call me."

"Got it."

"What do you want us to do in the meantime?" James asks.

"Look at dirty pictures," I say, pointing at the sex-party photos that they've been going through with the facial-recognition software. I snap my fingers. "Callie. Do you still have that contact on Channel Four?"

"Bradley?" She gives me a very unladylike smile. "Well...we're not still sleeping together, but we are on speaking terms."

"Good. I need you to get hold of him. We're going to go public with this. I want him over here pronto. I want coverage out on the six o'clock news."

She raises her eyebrows. "Already?"

I share my reasoning with her. She thinks about it, nodding her head. "It would rattle him—which would be good." She looks at me, pensive. "Of course, he might come after you then."

"He's already doing that. This way, we'd be ready for him."

"I'll call Bradley now."

* * *

The office is a beehive, but I am not needed, just now, as a participant. I use the time to check my e-mail. I have ordered everyone to check theirs every half hour; I haven't gotten to mine for a few hours.

I see something that makes me sit up straight in my chair. It is a subject heading, titled: *Greetings from the Dark-Haired Slut!*

I double-click on the message. The words at the top are the ones that I have become familiar with:

> Greetings, Agent Barrett!
> By now I assume that you have seen my
> latest work. Little Charlotte Ross. My oh
> my, what a little whore she was! She'd
> spread her legs for anyone, male or female.
> Alone or in groups. Interesting, is it not,
> that I was the only man she wouldn't spread
> them for willingly?
> Not that it mattered.
> Another whore gone. And you—you are
> still no closer. Are you feeling
> discouraged yet, Agent Barrett? Outclassed,
> perhaps?
> In that vein, please feel free to remove
> the tracking device on your car and the bug
> on your phone.

"Shit," I mutter.

> Who do you think you are dealing with,
> Agent Barrett? I applaud the effort, but
> did you really think you would catch me
> that way? I knew you would eventually find

them. You can send your Mr. Aguilera away,
or keep him there. Neither choice will lead
you any closer to me.

I am well on my way now. I am following
in the footsteps of my ancestor, carrying
out his sacred mission. Collecting my own
keepsakes to pass on to future generations.

I am looking at my next victim as we
speak. A sweet peach, she is. But then,
beauty is only skin deep. Look at you,
Agent Barrett. Scarred, yes, but inside,
the beauty of a born huntress. My victim—
to-be, she is attractive on the outside.
But inside?

Just another whore.

I have some other surprises in the works
for you as well.

I will be in touch. For now, stay busy,
busy, busy!

I know you will.

From Hell,

Jack Jr.

His smugness grates on me. Well, I have my own message to deliver, you psycho. One that will wipe that smug
smile I can't see, but know is there, off your face.

"I reached Bradley, honey-love," Callie calls to me.

I close my e-mail program.

"And?"

She smiles. "I think he nearly wet his pants. He'll be
here within a half hour."

"Good. Tell reception to direct him to the second-
floor conference room."

* * *

True to his word, Bradley Cummings arrives twenty-five minutes later. He looks the same as the last time I saw him. Craggy good looks, impeccable suit. Tall. Never one to be embarrassed, Callie had regaled me with tales of the adventurous jungle sex they'd had. "Quite satisfactory," she'd dubbed him.

He's kept it simple. Him and a cameraman.

"Thanks for coming, Brad."

"Callie gave me the short version on the phone. No self-respecting newsman would pass this up. How do you want to do it?"

"I'll give you all the details off-camera. Then you can do whatever Q and A on camera you need to go along with it."

"That sounds fine."

"Here's the thing, Brad. I need this on by six o'clock."

"Trust me, that's not going to be a problem."

"Good. The other thing is that I want to ensure a specific part of the information on this case is communicated by me to the camera. You'll understand when you see it. It's vital that I'm the one to say it, and no one else."

He gives me an uneasy look. "This is on the up-and-up, right, Smoky? The story?"

"If you mean, am I just using you, then yes, I am. But"—I hold a finger up—"every detail will be true. You'll be reporting the truth. But you'll also be doing two other things: warning future potential victims, and giving me a chance to piss this killer off. That's why I have to be the one to say it. Think of this guy as a hand grenade, Brad. I'm going to pull the pin." I shrug. "Whoever pulls the pin runs a chance of getting caught in the blast."

He looks into my eyes, searching for a lie. "Fine. I trust you. Lay it on me."

I spend the next twenty minutes giving him a run-down of what has happened in the last five days. He does his job well, jotting down notes, interjecting questions here and there. When I am done, he sits back.

"Wow," he says. "This really is ... something. I assume the thing you want to say concerns the contents of the jar."

"That's right. One of the reasons it's important that I be the one to say it and no one else is that it's going to piss him off. He'll probably fixate on whoever delivers that news."

"Right," he says, thoughtful. "Well, then, let's get to it."

Brad is deft on camera. His questions are sharp and pointed, without being an attack. He arrives at the crucial question.

"Special Agent Barrett. You stated that you have revealing information concerning the contents of the jar he sent to you. Can you elaborate?"

"Yes, Brad. We had the jar opened and its contents analyzed. We found that the flesh inside was not human. It was cow flesh."

"What does that mean?"

I turn so that I am looking right into the camera. "It means that he is not who he says he is. He is not a descendant of Jack the Ripper. It's most probable that he believes he is. I doubt he knew what was in that jar." I shake my head. "Sad, really. He's living a lie, and he doesn't even know it."

"Thank you, Agent Barrett."

Brad leaves more than happy. He promises to get the story on at six and eleven and just manages to keep from running out in eagerness.

"That went well," Callie remarks. "I'd forgotten how handsome that man is. Perhaps I need to give him a call."

"If you do, I don't want all the details this time."

"That's no fun." She pauses. "He's going to be enraged, honey-love. Jack Jr., I mean. This could push him over the deep end."

I give her a grim smile. "I sure hope so. Now let's go see Ms. Waters."

We take an agency vehicle, as I want to ensure that we aren't followed or tracked. While the cars belonging to other members of the team have been swept for bugs and tracking devices, it's always possible that he knows them by sight.

On the way to see Leona Waters, I call Tommy Aguilera and tell him about the e-mail.

"One of them must have been there last night. Or this morning. It also means they're well-informed about the people you know. People like me."

"Yeah. So I guess that's it, Tommy. I'll give you a call later, if you don't mind. About getting rid of the bug and the GPS tracker."

"You won't have to."

"Why is that?"

"Because I'm going to keep shadowing you, Smoky. I told you last night. You're my principal. The job isn't over until you catch him and I know you're safe."

I want to protest, but the truth is, part of me had hoped he would say something like this.

"I'll still be watching, Smoky."

* * *

The trip takes longer than it should, thanks to an accident on the freeway; a van had run itself into a guardrail. The accident was minor, but the rubbernecking, as always, was major. By the time we arrive, it's nearly two in the afternoon. Leona Waters lives in a very nice apartment building in a not-so-nice area. Santa Monica is a crapshoot of kinds. Many parts of it remain middle-class or even upscale, but much of it has decayed, like the rest of LA. This is the constant tale of this city, leading people to move farther and farther out to try and escape the cancer. It always seems to catch up.

We park and walk up to the front entrance. There are security doors, requiring residents to enter a pass code. A security guard sits at reception. I rap on the glass to make him look up. He gives me his best expression of bored irritation until I place my FBI identification against the glass. He flies out of his chair like it's an ejector seat, rushing over to let us in.

He sees the scars on my face and stops for a moment, staring openly. Then his eyes move to Callie. They crawl up and down her body in a flash, pausing for a noticeable half second on her bust.

"What's going on, ma'am?"

"Just an interview . . . ?"

"Ricky," he offers, licking his lips. He stands up a little taller. Ricky looks to be in his late forties. He has the run-down appearance of someone who used to be in shape but let himself go. His face is lined and tired-looking. Not someone enjoying his life.

"We're just doing an interview with one of your residents. No big deal."

"Do you need any help, ma'am? Which resident?"

"I'm afraid that's confidential, Ricky. You understand."

He nods, tries to look important. "Oh, yes, ma'am. Of course. I understand. Elevator's right over there. Let me know if you need anything." Sneaks another peek at Callie's boobs.

"I will, thanks." I won't, I think to myself.

We get in the elevator. "Revolting little man," Callie remarks as we ride up to the third floor.

"No kidding."

We exit. Arrows direct us to apartment number 314. I knock on the door, and a moment later it opens.

The woman who has opened it and I stare at each other, both at a loss for words. Callie breaks this silence.

"Have a sister I don't know about, honey-love?"

I don't, but it's a fair question. Leona Waters and I could be related. Our height is almost identical. She has my curves at the hips, and lack of them at the bust. The same long, dark, thick hair, and our faces have similarities. Same size nose. Different color eyes than mine. She's missing the scars, of course. Behind my amazement at this, I feel a sick unease. I think it's clear why Jack Jr. chose this particular woman.

"Leona Waters?" I ask.

Her eyes dart from me to Callie and back again. "Yes..."

I hold up my identification. "I'm Special Agent Smoky Barrett, with the FBI."

She frowns. "Am I in trouble?"

"No, ma'am. I'm the head of the Violent Crimes Unit in Los Angeles. We're hunting a man who has raped, tortured, and murdered at least two women. We think he plans to make you his next victim." I'm going right for the jugular, maximum shock value.

Her mouth drops open. Her eyes go wide. "Is this some kind of a joke?"

"No, ma'am. I wish it were. But it's not. Can we come in?"

It takes her a moment, but she gathers herself. She steps aside.

As we enter her apartment, I'm struck by its tastefulness. Subtle beauty, and very feminine. Very much a woman's home.

She indicates for us to take a seat on the couch. She sits across from us in a matching cushioned chair.

"So—is this for real? You say there's some freak out there who wants to kill me?" she asks.

"A very dangerous man. He's killed two other women already. He targets operators of amateur adult Web sites. He tortures them, rapes them, and murders them. Afterward, he disfigures their bodies. He thinks he's a descendant of Jack the Ripper."

I continue to deliver it fast and furious, so as to knock down any misgivings or hesitation on her part. This seems to have worked; she's gone from pink to pale.

"What makes you think he's picked me?"

"He has a pattern. He signs up as a Web site member. He's done this with each woman he's killed so far. He chooses a user name and password combination that ties into his Jack the Ripper theme. We found one of those combinations on your members' list." I point at myself. "He hates me, Ms. Waters. He's obsessed with me. Don't you see our similarity?"

She hesitates, looking me up and down. "Yes. Of course I can see it." She pauses. "Did he . . . did he do that to you?" She points at my face.

"Not him. Someone else."

"I don't mean to be unkind, but that's not very confidence-inspiring."

I give her a slight smile. Want her to see that I'm not

insulted. "That's understandable. But the man who did this caught me unprepared. That's what we're trying to avoid here. He won't know that we're on to him."

I see understanding break out on her face. "I get it. You want to set a trap for him, right?"

"Yes."

"With me as bait?"

"Not exactly. You are the bait—in that he thinks you'll be here. But I want to put an agent in place of you. I can't take any chances of endangering you as a civilian. It would require that you let us use your apartment. And you'd have to leave it for a little while."

Something passes through her eyes that I can't read. She gets up, walks away. She stands for a moment with her back to us. When she turns back around, her face is set in a resolute look.

"Do you know how old I am?" she asks.

"Um—no," I respond.

"I'm twenty-nine." She indicates herself with her hands. "Not too bad for twenty-nine, huh?"

"No. Not too bad."

"I got married when I was eighteen to the first man I had sex with. I thought he was the love of my life, just the greatest guy in the world. I would have done anything for him. Did, for a while. But then Prince Charming changed. And for the next seven years, he beat me. Oh, he never broke bones. Never left marks on my face. He was too smart for that. But he knew how to make it hurt. And he mixed in plenty of degradation." Her eyes are locked on mine. "Do you know what sex is with a man like that? It's rape. It doesn't matter whether you are married to him or not. He makes it rape." She shakes her head, looking off. "It took me a long time to grow up. Seven years. For the first six, it just never occurred to me to leave him.

The thought didn't enter my mind. He convinced me that what he was doing was my fault. Or his right."

"What happened to change that?" Callie asks.

We know better than to ask her where this is going or what it has to do with the here and now. Whatever she is saying needs to be said; in order to get what we want, we are just going to have to listen.

She shrugs, a hard flintiness entering her eyes. "Like I said: I grew up. I knew that he was smart about abusing me. I talked with a few cops. They told me it was going to be an uphill battle to prove it." She smiles. "So I hid a camera and got it on tape. One last time, I let him beat me, hurt me, degrade me. I turned it over to the cops and pressed charges. His attorney tried for entrapment on the video, but..." She shrugs. "The judge let the video stay. My husband went to jail, and I sold everything we owned and came to LA." She indicates the apartment. "This is mine. I know you probably don't approve of what I do for a living. I don't care. This is mine, and I'm out from under his thumb." She sits down, facing us. "The point is this: I promised myself that no man was ever going to control me in that way again. Not ever. So—if you want to use my apartment to catch this psycho, I'll cooperate. To the limit. But I won't leave my home." She sits back, arms folded. The picture of firm resolve.

I regard Leona Waters for a long time. She bears my scrutiny without a flinch. I don't like it. At all. But I can tell that she's not going to bend. I spread my hands in surrender.

"Fine, Ms. Waters. If I can get my boss to sign off on it, we'll do it your way."

"Call me Leona, Agent Barrett. So"—she leans forward, looking both fierce and excited—"how is this going to work?"

* * *

I am cautiously excited. Leona hasn't received any exterminator visits, meaning they haven't done their recon yet. It could happen at any time. Today, tomorrow. I'm convinced it will be soon.

The dragon thrashes inside me, smelling blood.

I had spoken to AD Jones, told him what I needed. After a lot of cursing, he agreed. Callie and I are still in Leona's living room, this time with cups of coffee she has offered us. We're waiting for the arrival of two agents and two LAPD SWAT officers. All would be arriving at staggered times. We didn't want to alert the killers if either happened to be watching.

Leona was in her home office, telling us she needed to answer some e-mail.

"You know," Callie says, "I don't like what she does, but I like Ms. Leona Waters. She's strong."

I give her a crooked smile. "Me too. I wish she didn't insist on staying. But I have to give it to her. She's brave and she's tough."

Callie sips from her coffee, thinking. "What do you think our odds are on this?"

"I don't know, Callie. I'm certain, after seeing her, that we're on track. She is on his list. I mean, look at her." I grimace in disgust. "He probably picked her so he could feel like he was raping and killing me."

"It is spooky, honey-love. It could almost make you a believer in the whole doppelgänger thing."

My cell phone rings. "Yeah," I answer.

Alan's baritone rumbles in my ear. "Just wanted to give you an update. Gene says DNA is going slower than expected. He'll have something by ten or so tonight."

"We have a hopeful lead here." I tell him about Leona Waters and the current plan.

"That could be good news," he says. "Maybe we'll catch the fuckers."

"Keep your fingers crossed. I'll keep everyone apprised." I hang up and check my watch. "Damn. Time went by fast." I look at Callie. "It's almost six o'clock."

"Time for the evening news," she responds.

"Time to piss this psycho off."

42

BRAD LOOKS HANDSOME and serious as he delivers his special report.

"Many will remember Special Agent Smoky Barrett from an incident last year. A serial killer she was chasing, one Joseph Sands, took her family from her in one brutal evening. She managed to escape but was left with her face disfigured and her family dead. Despite these personal tragedies, she has returned to her job.

"She is currently tracking a man known only as Jack Jr. He claims to be a direct descendant of Jack the Ripper..."

He lays out the basics without embellishment. He doesn't need to embellish. The truth is horrific enough. My face appears near the end of the report as I deliver the shocker about the jar. I look at myself without passion. I am becoming used to my scars. I doubt the viewers feel the same.

"The FBI is warning other women in this profession to take serious precautions." He rattles off a list we'd given him of precautions we thought they should take. He looks into the camera, dramatic. "Be vigilant and be careful. Your life could be at risk."

The segment ends. "He did a good job," Callie says. "You too, honey-love."

"You're trying to piss him off, aren't you?"

The voice comes from behind us. We'd been so engrossed in the report that we hadn't noticed that Leona had come out from her office.

"Yeah," I say. "I am."

She gives me an admiring smile. "You're something else, Agent Barrett. If I'd been through what you have..." She shakes her head.

"I don't know about that, Leona. You've been through a different version of it. You've kept going."

A knock comes at the door, ending any small talk. Leona tenses up.

"Stay there," I murmur to her, pulling my gun.

I go to the door. "Yes?" I say.

"Special Agent Barrett? It's Agents Decker and McCullough, along with two SWAT-team members."

I look through the keyhole. I recognize Decker.

"Hang on," I say. I open the door, wave them inside.

As per my instructions, they are dressed in civilian clothes. I note with some amusement that they're all wearing the same basic outfits: jeans and pullover shirts. Even dressed casually, they manage a vague uniformity. But none of them would be made for law enforcement at a glance.

"You've all been briefed?" I ask when everyone is in the living room.

A chorus of "Yes, ma'ams."

"Good. We're laying a trap here, gentlemen. Our unsubs have killed twice. They're sharp—real sharp. They operate with precision: little hesitation, lots of willingness to act. We know their current MO from the prior victims: One of them scouts things out in the guise of being a pest exterminator, and that's what we're hoping is going to happen here. Don't underestimate our unsubs, gentlemen. If one or both pull a knife, it's not to scare or intimidate—they'll use it. We need whichever one shows up taken alive so that he can lead us to the other perpetrator." I indicate Leona Waters. "This is Ms. Waters. We're certain that he's selected her as a victim."

I see them glance at her. Assessing. One of the SWAT guys is giving her an unprofessional, sexual once-over. I am both mortified and enraged. I step in front of him and jab a finger in his chest, hard enough to leave a bruise. "I expect every one of you to operate at a high level of professionalism. You should know, I asked Ms. Waters to stay somewhere else while we run this op. She refused and has volunteered to be here." I lean into the officer and let him see just how pissed off I am. I whisper, "If this woman gets hurt because you were thinking with your dick, I'll fucking eat you alive, understand?"

To his credit, the officer's look of apology appears genuine and ungrudging. He nods.

"What's the plan, ma'am?" This from Agent Decker, bringing us back to the business at hand.

I push away my anger. "We're going to keep it simple. One on the roof. One outside the elevator. Two in here with myself and Agent Thorne. The guy on the roof will alert us to anyone coming in from the street. Elevator guy will be able to confirm whether or not that same person exits onto this floor. Those inside are here for the takedown. You have the equipment we'll need?" I ask Decker.

"Yes, ma'am. Earpieces and throat mikes. Weapons."

"Including a sniper rifle for the roof work," says one of the SWAT officers.

I nod. "Good. I want to stress: It's important that you don't draw attention to yourself. We have evidence that one or both of our unsubs has been tailing me. If either of them suspects anything, they'll bolt." I look at each of them. "Any questions?"

They all say no. "Get in position then. Stay alert, but settle in for a long wait."

43

THIS, I THINK, is indicative of this job I do. It causes my life to be governed by outside influences, to race toward sudden leads. The irony isn't lost on me. I hate to be forced to do *anything*, yet I have chosen a profession that does just that on a regular basis. When you are hunting a killer, there is no schedule. The timetable is simple: The longer he is out there, the higher the death count climbs. You go until he's caught.

So I find myself here, sitting in the apartment of a woman who displays her sexual adventures for a living, willing to wait as long as needed in the hopes that either Jack Jr. or his partner will show.

I look over at Callie. She is sitting on the couch, feet up on the coffee table, watching a talk show on TV with Leona while both of them eat popcorn. This is one of the traits Callie has that I love and admire. She can live in the moment, relaxed, and yet spring into action like a whip crack. It's a talent I have never had.

I look at my watch. It's now nine-thirty. I check in with the SWAT officer on the roof, who I now know as Bob. "Anything anomalous, Bob?"

His voice crackles in my ear. "Not yet, ma'am."

I cock an ear, eavesdropping on the conversation between Callie and Leona.

"Let me ask you this, honey-love. What happens when you decide you want a man in your life again?"

"What do you mean?"

"I mean, do you change the lifestyle you're living?"

Leona ponders this. "It would depend. Lots of people meet in nonmonogamous settings. The odds are against it, but it does happen. I suppose if I didn't find that, I'd have to wait until I decided to quit before I went looking. I made a promise that I'd never make a huge and sweeping change of my life for a man. Never again."

"Interesting subset of problems though, don't you think?"

"It's unique to the lifestyle I follow, that's for sure."

I tune them out. Callie has a voracious interest in what makes others tick. She always has.

This is the schedule. The way it goes. And not just here. Everyone is still working back at the office. Everyone shares the burden and the responsibility. Everyone will share the guilt if he kills again before we catch him.

Bob's voice crackles in my ear, pulling me away from my boredom and musings. "Male, about six feet tall with dark hair, entering the building. Dressed in some kind of uniform. I can't make it out."

"Copy that," the guy at the elevator—Dylan—replies.

I look around at Callie and Agents Decker and McCullough. They nod, letting me know they've heard. Moments pass.

"Male matching that description just exited the elevator, heading toward the apartment," Dylan reports. "I confirm uniform, say again, I confirm he is in the uniform of a pest-extermination company."

"Copy that," I say. My heart pounds, and the dragon

stirs, excited. "Stay where you are to block possible escape, Dylan."

"Copy that."

"Bob, I'll let you know if he gets past us. I may call on you to take a shot."

"Copy that. I'm cocked and locked."

I look at Leona. "It's him."

She nods. She looks excited, wired. She doesn't, I notice, look afraid.

A knock comes on the door. I motion to Leona. She walks up to the door and looks through the peephole, one last double-check. Turns to me and shakes her head. She doesn't know him. I give her a nod.

"Who is it?" she asks.

"ABC Exterminators, ma'am. Sorry for the late hour, but the building owner called us out on an emergency basis. Something about rats. I need to come in and check out your place. It'll only take a few minutes."

"Um...okay. Hold on a moment."

She looks back at me. I motion her into her bedroom. I pull my weapon, as do Callie, Decker, and McCullough. I hold up a hand, giving a three-count on my fingers. One... two...on three, I throw the door open wide.

"FBI!" I yell. "FREEZE!"

My gun is about two feet from his face. I get a good look at his eyes and see the emptiness I'd been imagining. He drops the clipboard he was carrying and raises his hands above his head.

"Don't shoot!" he says. He sounds startled, the way you should with a gun in your face, but something in me feels uneasy, because his eyes aren't startled at all. They are busy. Looking, weighing, thinking.

"Do *not* move," I say. "Put your hands behind your head, and get down on your knees!"

He fixes his gaze on me, licks his lips. "Whatever you say ... Smoky."

I have a millisecond to be alarmed at his use of my name. He moves like a savage wind, stepping first to one side and then straight into me. His hands move in separate directions, one pushing my gun aside, the other slamming into my face. I am flying backward, seeing stars, and the millisecond passes.

I land on my back on the floor and struggle to get up. I've managed to hold on to my gun.

He is still moving, some kind of ultrapractical form of martial arts, all power and uniformly devastating. As with me, he moves into his targets, and all his punches and kicks are short and brutal. It's not flowery, but it's effective. I watch as Agent Decker gets elbowed in the jaw, note with dizzy interest that two of his teeth don't just fall out, they *shoot* out, like two bullets, and then I hear Callie, cold as ice, saying, "Move, and I'll fucking kill you."

Everything that had been in motion becomes still. Suspended. Because Callie now has her gun at his forehead. His eyes dart around in rage and then he is being body-tackled by Agent McCullough, and by Dylan as well, who's arrived from the elevator lobby to join in on the fun.

I register that I am bleeding, and that I am dizzy. Very dizzy.

"Honey-love, are you all right?"

I stand up, staggering. "I'm fine—"

And then I fall back down. I don't pass out, but I sit straight down on my ass.

The perp is screaming at me. "You stupid *whore*! Useless cow! You think this means anything? This means nothing! Nothing! I'll still—"

"Jesus *Christ*!" I yell. "Shut *up*—or I'll shoot you in the leg. Dylan, McCullough. Book him and gag him, please."

Dylan grins at me but slaps the cuffs on our guy and takes him out into the hallway to search him and read him his rights.

"How are you now?" Callie asks, concerned.

I shake my head, testing. "Not dizzy anymore. Okay, I think. How's my face look?"

"He did a number on your lips, honey-love. You have that 'I don't use collagen, I just beat my face against a wall' look."

This makes me jump to my feet, alarmed. "Decker!"

"Over here. I'm okay."

I see him standing. He's using a wall for support. He has a handkerchief against his mouth, which is soaked through with blood.

"Whoa," I say. "You need to see a doctor."

"I need to see a dentist," he moans. "Fucker knocked out two of my teeth."

"Callie."

She flips open her cell phone. "Calling the EMTs now, honey-love."

The door to Leona's bedroom opens, just a crack. "Is it safe to come out?" she asks, voice quavering. "Is everyone all right?"

I look around at her living room, taking in Decker and his bleeding mouth, the splintered coffee table, and it hits me. Adrenaline doesn't just shoot through me, it explodes.

"WE GOT HIM!" I yell.

Callie and Decker both jump and stare at me. Callie grins. Decker tries to.

"Everything is fine, Leona," I say. I look toward the doorway. "Everything is just great."

I crack my knuckles. My lips ache.

But the dragon is thrashing, roaring, and gnashing her teeth.

Feed me, she's hissing. *Let me crunch on his bones.*

I lick my upper lip and taste my own blood. That should keep her satisfied for now.

44

I'M ON MY way into the FBI building with Callie. We'd left a policeman with Leona, and our suspect is being taken to the Wilshire police station for booking. I came here to get Alan and to plan out our interrogation strategy. I have just punched the up elevator button when my cell phone rings.

"Smoky!"

I go on instant alert. It's Elaina, and she sounds terrified. "What's wrong, Elaina?"

"There are three men sneaking around outside the house. In the backyard. Young-looking."

A thrill of terror shoots through me. I think of Ronnie Barnes. Is this related? Did Jack Jr. create himself a little psycho army? Or am I just being paranoid?

Paranoid? With Jack Jr.? No way.

I think about what I had said to Alan, about how Elaina wasn't in any physical danger, and I am sick at the possible consequences of this misestimation.

I break into a run, forgoing the elevator, rushing up the stairs. Callie follows. "Elaina, what about the agents out front?"

Silence.

"Their car is there. I don't see them."

"Do you have a weapon in the house? A gun?"

"Yes. Upstairs, in the closet."

"Get it, lock yourselves in the bathroom. I'm getting Alan and it'll take us maybe fifteen minutes to get over there."

"I'm scared, Smoky."

I close my eyes for a moment, as I continue to run. "Call the cops, get the gun. We'll be there soon, Elaina."

I hang up, hating myself as I do it. But I do it to force her into motion. Moments later I burst through the door of our office. The look on my face has everyone's attention.

"Alan, Elaina has visitors!" I point at Leo and James. "You two stay here. James, coordinate with LAPD on the suspect they're booking for us. Callie and Alan, come with me. Move it!"

Alan is in motion already. His face is full of questions, his eyes are full of terror. His voice is steady, even as we rush down the stairs toward the parking lot. "How many?" he asks.

"Three. Creeping around the house. I told her to call the cops, get the gun, lock herself in the bathroom."

"Where the fuck are the agents who are supposed to be guarding Bonnie?"

"I don't know."

We run through reception, slamming through the front doors of the building, racing down the steps. Elaina and Bonnie, Elaina and Bonnie, the mantra cycles through my mind, over and over and over. On some level I register that I should be more afraid, but everything is about forward motion, not enough time to feel or think deeply. Callie hasn't said a word. She's following without question.

And then it happens.

"Die, *cunt*!"

We are in the parking lot, and the young man who screamed this is rushing toward me, a knife raised in his hands. His face is contorted, maniacal. His eyes are hungry. Time slows to a frame-by-frame. Six feet, I think, analytical. Running, knife raised, that means he'll be on me in about a half second—

I have blown a hole through his head before I really even finish this thought. The speed involved in pulling my weapon and firing is just too fast to track if I had to think about it. It's instinctive, a decisive lightning strike.

His head explodes, time restarts at normal speed, I'm whipping aside as he pitches forward, his body hitting the pavement with a dull thud that sends both gray matter and the knife flying.

"Holy fucking shit!" Alan yells.

I notice neither he nor Callie have pulled their weapons yet. I don't hold it against them. We have a special relationship, my steel blackbird and I.

My mind continues to move at the same blinding speed. "Callie, you're going to drive. Keep moving!"

I see Tommy running toward us. I don't stop. "We're okay!" I yell. "But there are unsubs at Alan's home!"

Tommy doesn't break stride, or nod, or do anything other than whip around and continue running at the same speed back toward his car. That Secret Service training, I think. Instant, unhesitating, decisive action.

We reach Callie's vehicle and pile in. She has it in gear and is burning rubber about two seconds later.

"Who the hell was that?" Alan asks.

Callie responds for me. "Blood brothers of Ronnie Barnes, honey-love," she murmurs, eyes fierce as she rockets out of the parking lot.

Alan doesn't respond. I see understanding dawn on his face, followed by fear. "Oh, no . . ." he whispers.

I don't respond. None is needed. He has the same mantra going on in his head as I do in mine: Elaina and Bonnie, Elaina and Bonnie, Elaina and Bonnie.

I'm sure for him, like me, it's turning from a mantra into a prayer.

45

ALAN CALLS ELAINA. "Babe? We're on our way. Did you call the cops—what? Shit! Stay there, honey! Right where you are." He puts a hand over the mouthpiece. "They're in the house. She can hear them creeping around." Talks to Elaina again. "Listen, babe. Don't speak back to me anymore. I don't want them to hear you. Keep the line open, put the phone down, and point the gun at the door. If you don't hear me, Smoky, or Callie, then you shoot whoever tries to come through it."

Elaina and Bonnie, Elaina and Bonnie, Elaina and Bonnie...

We're on Alan's street. Callie screeches up to the driveway and we pile out. Alan has put his phone away, has his weapon ready. We all do. I look around, see Keenan's car. I run up to it, and what I find fills me with rage and sorrow. Both he and Shantz are dead, holes in their foreheads.

Vengeance now, I think. Mourn later.

I move away from the car, up the driveway to the front of the house. I point at the door. It's been forced open, the jamb splintered. "Go in quiet," I whisper. "We need them alive if possible. Do you hear me, Alan?"

He stares at me for a moment, a long, cold, killer's stare. Then gives me a begrudging nod.

We enter through the front door, guns and eyes moving, checking for signs of the intruders. Callie, Alan, and I all look at one another, shake our heads. Nothing down here. We all stop as we hear motion upstairs. I point to the ceiling.

We move up the stairway. My heart is hammering away. I can hear Alan breathing and see sweat on his brow, even though it's cool inside the house. We're almost to the top when Elaina screams.

"Alan!" Her voice is filled with terror. I hear the *BOOM-BOOM-BOOM* of a handgun being fired.

"FBI!" I yell, and we hit the top of the stairs, silent no more. *"Drop any weapons you're holding and get down on your fucking knees!"*

BOOM-BOOM-BOOM! Again, more handgun fire, and now I can see where it's coming from. A young man with dark hair looks like he's jitterbugging as Elaina's handgun blows holes through him. She's on overkill, going to keep firing until she clicks on empty.

Two others turn to face us. One has a gun, one has a knife, I note in an instant. They seem surprised at first, then see me and hatred kicks in.

"It's her!" the one with the gun says. "That Smoky cunt!"

He raises his weapon to fire, the one with the knife rushes toward me, and now everything is moving frame by frame again.

I see Alan and Callie fire on the gunman, watch with a kind of detached approval as holes open up in his head and chest, spraying blood. I see his weapon discharge as he falls backward. Knife guy is heading toward me, and it's a replay of the parking lot, except that this time I shoot the hand holding the blade to take him alive. Watch as two of his fingers disappear, see his eyes widen and roll up into his head as shock hits him like a sledgehammer. He drops to his knees, mouth in an *O*. Vomits once, then falls forward, unconscious but trembling.

"*Elaina!*" Alan screams.

"*In here!*" she screams back, hysterical. "We're okay! We're okay! We're okay!" Both Alan and I rush forward into the bathroom.

I am weak-kneed with relief to see them there, in the bathtub, unharmed. Elaina is weeping, still gripping the gun in both hands, eyes wild. Bonnie is sitting at one end of the tub, arms wrapped around her legs, forehead against her knees, rocking back and forth. Alan and I bump into each other as he rushes to Elaina and I rush to Bonnie.

"You okay, sweetheart?" I ask, frantic, grabbing her head in my hands, searching for any signs of harm.

Alan is doing the same with Elaina, and Bonnie starts sobbing, throws her arms around me, and Elaina mirrors this with Alan. The sound of Alan and me saying, "Thank God, Thank God," echoes off the bathroom walls. It is the chaos of relief.

"Callie!" I yell out the door. "They're both fine! No one's hurt!" There is no reply. "Callie?"

The image slams into me, a thunderclap. His gun discharging...

"Oh no..." I whisper. I put Bonnie down, draw my gun, creep out of the bathroom.

I see her.

I am enclosed in a bell of silence. A stillness formed of shock.

Callie lies at the top of the stairs, on the carpet, hair fanned. Her eyes are closed.

A red stain spreads on her chest.

"911, Alan..." I whisper. Then I am screaming. *"911! 911! Motherfucking 911!"*

46

I **AM IN** Tommy's car, and we are racing toward the hospital. I am shaking, a whole-body shake, out of my control.

I can't think formed thoughts. Terror keeps shooting through me, huge bursts of adrenaline.

Alan has stayed behind with Elaina and Bonnie, and to make sure that our one living suspect is dealt with. He hadn't said anything to me, but he didn't need to. It showed in his eyes.

The fact that Tommy is talking to me pierces my haze.

"I saw the wound, Smoky. I know wounds. I can't tell you if she's going to be fine or not. All I can tell you is that it's not a guaranteed kill shot." He turns his head to me. "Do you hear me?"

"Yes, goddammit! I hear you!" It comes out as a scream. I don't know why. I'm not angry at Tommy.

"Go ahead and scream, Smoky. Do whatever you need to do." His voice is stoic. For some reason, this infuriates me.

"Mr. Cool, Calm, and Collected, huh?" I can't hold it back. Poison is inside me, bitter and galling and overpowering, and it's demanding release. "You think that makes you something special, being a fucking robot?"

No reply.

"Must not be too special! You got kicked out of the Secret Service, didn't you? Fucking loser!" He doesn't even blink. I start screaming at him. *"I fucking hate you right now! Do you hear me! You mean nothing to me! My friend is dying and you treat it like it's nothing so you mean nothing to me and I hate you and—"*

My voice breaks into a moan. The poison is gone. What's back now is my old friend, pain. I roll down the window frantically and proceed to puke into the street. An ache spikes through my head.

I sit back, depleted by my orgy of emotion. Tommy reaches over and opens up the glove box. "There's Kleenex in there."

I grab a few. Wipe my face.

We drive on.

"I'm sorry," I say in a small voice, about a mile later.

He looks at me, gives me a soft smile. "Don't worry about it for a second."

When I begin to weep, he puts a hand on my knee and keeps it there, as we continue to barrel toward the hospital.

47

THE HOSPITAL CHAPEL is quiet. I have it all to myself. Callie is in surgery and we have no word yet. Everyone is here. Leo, James, Alan, Elaina, Bonnie. AD Jones is on the way.

I'm on my knees, praying.

I've never believed in the literal God most people do. In someone up there, omnipotent, guiding the universe.

I do believe that there is *something*. Something that isn't much interested in us but likes to check in from time to time. See what the ants are up to.

I kneel and put my hands together because, perhaps, this is one of those times.

I have blood and bits of brain on me. I am covered in violence.

But I bow my head and I pray, a constant, desperate murmur.

"Okay, so Matt gets taken from me, and my daughter, and my best friend. I get carved up and horribly scarred and have nightmares that make me wake up screaming. I spend six months in pain, wanting to die. Bonnie is mute because of an unreal horror some psycho visited on her. Oh yeah, and Elaina, one of the best people I know, a woman I love, has cancer." I pause to wipe a tear from my eye with a shaking hand. "With all that, I've been dealing. Took me a little while, but I've been dealing." A tear I missed runs down my cheek. I clench my hands until they hurt. "But this. No. No way. This is too much. Not Callie. So, here's the deal. You ready?" I can hear the wretched-ness and pleading in my voice. "Keep her alive, and you can do whatever you want to me. Anything. Blind me. Cripple me. Give me cancer. Burn down my house, fire me from the FBI in disgrace. Make me insane. Kill me. But keep her alive. Please."

My voice cracks then, and so do I. Something inside me breaks. The pain of it makes me pitch forward, and I have to put my hands out to catch myself. I'm on all fours, and I watch as tears rain down on the chapel tile. "You want me to crawl?" I whisper. "You want to have someone, ten someones, rape and cut on me again? Fine. Just keep her alive."

There isn't any answer, or even the hint of one. This doesn't bother me. I didn't expect a response. I just needed to say it. Call it talking to God, begging Allah, or just envisioning a goal. Whatever. I needed to plead with the universe to spare Callie. I needed to show that I was willing to give up anything, everything, to save my friend.

Just in case it might make a difference.

I walk back out of the chapel to the waiting room. I'd taken some time to try and pull myself together, but I still feel jumbled and shocky and broken. I know that I should be here for my people right now. That's my func-tion. My place. What a leader does. "Any word?" I ask. I'm proud of myself. My voice is steady.

"Not yet," Alan replies, morose.

I look at them all. James looks grim. Leo is pacing

back and forth. Alan is as helpless as I've ever seen him. Only Elaina and Bonnie seem calm, which amazes me. They were the ones most recently victimized. You never know where strength is going to come from until it happens.

I smell the sterile smell of this place, hear the little "whooshing" sounds and beeps that always fill a hospital. So quiet. Like a library where people bleed and die.

I walk over and sit next to Bonnie. "How are you doing, honey?"

She nods, and then shakes her head in the negative. It takes me a minute to get it. *Yes, I'm fine, no, you don't need to worry about me,* that's what she's telling me.

"Good," I murmur.

The door to the waiting room bursts open, and AD Jones is there. He looks frantic.

"Where is she? Is she okay? What happened?"

I stand up, walk over to him. Clickety-clack on the hospital tiles, I notice with the part of me that's still dazed and numb. "She's in surgery, sir."

He regards me for a long moment. "What's her status?"

"The bullet entered the upper chest. Nine millimeter. No exit wound. She lost a lot of blood and they rushed her into surgery. That's all we know." Concise, I think. Crisp, clean, and efficient. I suppress a little bubble of hysteria. Tiny bubbles in the whine…

He looks at me, his face turning red. I'm appalled at the level of rage I see in his eyes, because it's not something I've ever associated with this man. It dampens the craziness that's percolating inside me. "How long has she been in surgery?" he snaps.

"Two hours."

He turns away from me, a sudden motion. Paces.

Whips back, stabbing a finger in my direction. "Listen and listen good, Smoky. I have two dead agents, and another one in surgery. None of you, and I mean *none* of you, is to be alone from this point forward. If that means some of you have to bunk together until this is over, that's what happens. You don't go to the bathroom or wipe your nose without having someone with you. Got it?"

"Yes, sir."

"No more casualties. Do you hear me, Smoky? *No more!*"

I take his rage, bend to the storm of it. This is his version of me in the car with Tommy. This is him venting about Joseph Sands. This is him caring. I empathize.

The storm passes, he deflates. A hand comes up to his forehead. I recognize the short struggle. The same one I'd had just moments before. He is the boss. Time to be the boss.

"Let's regroup while we're waiting. Bring me up-to-date."

I fill him in on the arrest of one half of the Jack Jr. duo. I recount the phone call from Elaina, the guy I killed in the parking lot. What happened at Alan's.

"Where's the guy you shot in the hand?"

"He's here," I say. "He's in surgery too. They're trying to reattach his fingers."

"Fuck him," AD Jones snarls.

Out of the corner of my eye, I catch Bonnie nodding in agreement. It dismays me.

"The other three?" he asks. "All deceased?"

"Yeah."

"By who?"

Who killed them, he means. This will have to be accounted for at some point. Every bullet. "I killed the guy in the parking lot. Elaina shot one of the guys in her house. Alan and Callie killed the other guy, the one with the gun."

AD Jones looks over at Elaina. His eyes have softened. "I'm sorry," he says. Sorry you, a civilian, had to kill a man, he's telling her. She understands.

"Thank you."

"And we think these are all little Jack Jr. protégés?"

"There's not much doubt of that, sir."

"What about the suspect you caught tonight? This is one of them? For sure?"

"It's not a hundred percent until either he or the evidence says he is, but—yeah . . . it fits."

He nods in approval. "That's good. Real good." He's quiet for a moment, mulling it all over. Looking at each of us. When he speaks again, his voice is softer. "Listen. We're all going to wait here and see if she comes out of this in one piece. We're going to hope she does. When it's over, whether she's fine or not, we're going to go back to work. Get mad first, get sad later."

There are no words of dissent. All I see is a kind of grim resolution. He seems to see it too, because he nods. "Okay, then."

Okeydoke artichoke, I think, another little hysterical bubble making it past my internal force fields. I feel unsteady and sit back down.

Someone's cell phone is ringing. Everyone checks, and then I see Tommy putting his to his ear. I'd almost forgotten about him. He is the outsider, and he has pulled away from all of us, settling in to wait.

"Aguilera." He frowns. "Who is this?"

I see a terrible calm come over him. There's nothing relaxed about it, nothing relaxed at all. No, he wants to kill whoever is on the other end of that phone. He looks once at me. "Hang on for a moment."

He walks over to me, holding one hand over the mouthpiece. "It's him."

I leap out of the hospital seat, followed by almost everyone else. The bubbles are gone, replaced by the bright white light of shock. "What? You mean Jack Jr.?" I feel as incredulous as I sound.

"Yep. He asked to talk to you."

A zillion different thoughts shoot through my head. This is a complete break in his routine; it doesn't make sense. "Any chance of a trace?" I'm asking Tommy as the resident expert on electronic surveillance.

"If it's not set up already, no."

I'm lost, for just a moment.

AD Jones sighs. "Talk to him, Smoky. Only thing you can do."

I hold out my hand and take the phone. After a single deep breath to steady myself, I put it to my ear. "This is Smoky."

"Special Agent Barrett! How are you?" He's using some kind of electronic device to change and disguise his voice. It sounds like I'm having a conversation with a robot.

"What do you want?"

"I thought, just this once, that we should speak. If not face-to-face, well, phone-to-phone. E-mails and letters are so impersonal, don't you think?"

"I think you've made this very personal, Jack. Plus you're a fucking liar."

He chuckles. The voice alteration makes it sound hideous. "You are talking about my little visitors, aren't you? Well . . . it's true. But it's not a matter of lying. I just got—bored. In many ways, playing my little games with you and yours is as satisfying as my work upon my whores."

I want to hurt him. To do something to break through that arrogant gloating. "Hey, Jack. Did you see my little spot on the news?"

A long silence. When he starts speaking again, I feel a kind of snarling satisfaction as I note that his voice has gone flat. "Yes, Smoky. I saw your lies."

I laugh, a short, mocking bark. "Lies? Why the hell would I lie? You just don't want to own up to it, fucker! That there is no 'legacy,' no Annie Chapman's uterus, no sacred mission. You're the liar, Jack. Your whole life is a lie! Jesus, you can't even follow the Ripper's MO! He killed *whores,* Jack, not cops. You can't seem to decide *which* you want more. At least the Ripper picked a victim type and stuck with it! What's the matter, can't face the truth? Can't face just how pathetic you are?"

I hear him breathing, hard, angry. Even this is modified; it sounds surreal.

"You still there, *Jack?*"

Another long pause, then—"Nice try, Smoky. Hurrah for you, and applause. Why would you lie? Why, for the simplest reason of all: psychological warfare. To destabilize me." He pauses, and I can almost feel his rage. "I never said I *was* the Ripper, you silly bitch. I said I am descended from him. But I've evolved. I'm beyond him. Why do I hunt you and yours as much as I hunt the whores? Because I'm that *good.* Because I *feel* like it. For the same reason I amuse myself making my little acolytes. Because I *can.*"

For a moment, just for a moment, I come close to taunting him with the knowledge that we've captured his buddy. I manage to reel this impulse back.

"No, because you're a fuckup, Jack. Evolved? I don't

think so. The original Ripper, he never got caught. But I'm going to catch you. Count on it."

A long silence follows. When he starts speaking again, the rage is gone. His voice is calm. Back in control.

"Speaking of the whores—how is little Bonnie?"

I'm fighting for control. I need to keep him talking. I decide to try a different tack. I lower my voice, making it even, reasonable.

"Jack. Why don't we stop pretending? You and I both know who it is you really want, right?"

He pauses. "And who would that be, Special Agent Barrett?"

"Me. You want me."

AD Jones makes cutting motions across his throat. "No! Dammit, Smoky!"

I ignore him. "Am I right?"

He laughs again. "Smoky, Smoky, Smoky..." His voice is patronizing. "I want all of it, dear one. I want the whores, and I want you, and I want everyone that you love. Speaking of that—how is dear Callie? Is she going to survive?"

My rage flares up, hot and ready. "Fuck you!"

"You have one day," he says, ignoring my anger. Dismissing it. "And then another whore dies. Oh, and you and yours can expect continued fun as well."

I get the sense that he's about to end the call. "Wait."

"No, I don't think so. I couldn't resist, just this once, but this is a chancy way for us to communicate. For me, that is. Don't expect it to happen again. The next time you hear my voice, it will be in person, and you'll be screaming." A short pause. "One other thing: If Agent Thorne does die, you might want to consider cremating her. Otherwise, I'll be tempted to dig her up and...play with her. Just like I've done with sweet Rosa."

He hangs up, leaving his words grating across my bones.

"What the fuck is wrong with you?" James asks. The anger in his voice shocks me, and I am dumbfounded at it, here and now, in this place. I look at him and am stunned at the force of the rage I see in his eyes. He's trembling. It's coming off him in waves.

"What are you talking about?" I ask, incredulous.

"You just had to fucking taunt him, didn't you? Couldn't resist." His words are swollen with venom. "He's after us, and you had to piss him off even more, had to egg him on. What you always do. Tell us we're fucking invincible and tell them the same thing, and it's all bullshit." He's picking up his pace, the words tumbling out of him, inexorable.

All I can do is stare at him.

"What? You don't remember? Don't remember going on TV back when we were trying to catch Joseph Sands? Talking about how he was a pathetic limp dick, goading him, hoping he'd take the bait?" He pauses, eyes bright, snarling. "Well, he took it, didn't he? He took it and he killed your family and he almost killed you, and now this psycho is hell-bent on doing the same thing to all of us—and you *just won't learn*! Keenan and Shantz are dead—have you learned yet? Does Callie have to die for you to get it?" He leans into me. "That sometimes, when you play tough guy, other people *die*?" He pauses and I get the sense of a rubber band being pulled back before being snapped, the trembling silence that occurs just before a roar. He speaks into this silence. "Didn't getting your husband and daughter killed teach you that lesson already?"

My mouth falls open at this, and in an instant I am poised to slap him. Not a light slap. A broad, full-body backhand across the face. Something to loosen his teeth and bloody his nose. I want to do it so bad I can taste it, like blood in my mouth. Two things stop me. One is the near-instantaneous flash of shame I see come into his eyes. The other is Bonnie. She's standing next to James, tugging on his hand, hard.

"Wha-what is it?" he asks. He sounds as dazed as I feel.

She motions for him to kneel down next to her. I watch him do this, as my body shivers and trembles.

She slaps him for me, flat of her palm against his cheek. And although she's only ten, and small for her age, the sound of the smack is like a whip crack in the waiting room.

James's eyes widen in shock, his mouth forms an *O,* and he stumbles back, landing in a sitting position on the floor. My mouth falls open. Bonnie gives me a brief look, nods, and walks back over to sit next to Elaina.

Everyone is silent. I can feel their stillness and their dismay. James stands up slowly, hand to his cheek, eyes filled with shame and pain and wonder.

I want to say something, but once again, two things happen before I can. Callie's daughter comes rushing through the door, and one very sweaty, exhausted surgeon appears as well. For a moment I'm torn between the two, but Marilyn solves this for me by moving toward the surgeon.

"First things first," he says, his voice heavy and tired. "Agent Thorne is alive."

"Thank God!" Elaina cries.

I want to stagger in relief, fall to my knees. But I don't.

The surgeon holds up his hands for silence. "The bullet just missed her heart. And it stayed in one piece. But it did bounce around a little. It ended up near her upper left shoulder, after, I'm afraid, brushing past her spine."

The temperature of the room seems to drop fifty degrees at the word *spine*.

"The spinal cord itself wasn't cut. But it was bruised, and there is some swelling. There was also quite a bit of internal bleeding."

"What's the bottom line, Doc?" AD Jones asks.

"The bottom line is that she lost a lot of blood and sustained a lot of trauma. She's still critical. She seems stable, but we're not out of the woods." He pauses, looks like he's searching for a better way to put what he's going to say next. "She could still die. Unlikely, but that's not off the table yet."

Marilyn asks the other question. The one we're all terrified of. "And the spinal cord swelling...?"

"The best bet, in my opinion, is that she'll be fine. The swelling should go down, with no lasting paralysis or damage. But..." He sighs. "We can't be sure, not one hundred percent. There's always the worst-case scenario of permanent paralysis."

Marilyn's hand flies to her mouth. Her eyes are all whites.

I speak into the silence. "Thanks, Doctor."

He gives all of us a tired nod and walks off.

"Oh no, oh Jesus..." Marilyn moans. "Not now. I just got to meet her, I..."

And the tears start. I move to her and hug her tight as she begins to weep in earnest.

My own eyes are dry. I'm too busy bending, bending but not breaking.

48

WE'RE BACK IN the office, a battered bunch. Elaina and Bonnie are at my house, since Alan's place has become a crime scene. Marilyn stayed at the hospital to wait for news of Callie. She wasn't put off a bit by our leaving.

"Get him" was all she'd said.

James is standing, looking out the window. He won't meet my eyes.

I want to go crawl into a hole, curl up, and sleep for a year. But I can't do that.

"You know what the thing is about stress, James?" I say, musing.

He remains silent. I wait him out. "What?" he asks finally, still looking out the window.

"Stress creates little hairline fractures. They start small, and they spread, and then they get big, and eventually the result is that something shatters." I keep my voice careful, nonaccusative. "Is that what you want, James? For me to shatter? To just break up and—blow away?"

His head whips around at this. "What? No. I—" He sounds like he's strangling. "I just, with Callie..." He clenches his fists, unclenches them, takes a deep breath.

Steadies himself. Now he looks at me directly. "I'm not afraid for myself, Smoky. I'm afraid for Callie. You understand?"

"Of course I do," I reply in a soft voice. "I was afraid for my family too. Every day. I had nightmares about something happening to them exactly like what *did* happen." I shrug. "But Matt told me the truth once. He said that I was doing what I loved. And he was right. I hate chasing these fuckers, but I love *catching* them, you know?"

He looks at me for a moment, then nods.

"And I thought a lot about exactly what you said in there, long before you said it. I agonized over it. Did Sands come after us, did he kill my family, because I goaded him? For a long time, I thought the answer was yes. But I realized later that that was bullshit. He came after us because I was coming after him. Because I do what I do. He was going to do it whether I talked trash about him or not. You follow?"

He doesn't reply.

"The point, James, is that it doesn't matter what I say or don't say to Jack Jr. He *is* coming after us, period. We're his prey now. You want to know his victim type?" I gesture around the room. "They're all right here."

He looks at me for a long time before responding. When he does, his response is to close his eyes once, and nod.

I smile. "Apology accepted," I murmur.

He looks off for a moment, clears his throat. Everyone else has been silent and watching. Tense. It's like we're all on a hot plate, just waiting to pop and sizzle and burn. The fine machine that is my team is grinding its gears, ready to fracture and explode. I know the real source of this anger is Jack Jr. But I worry that we're going to start taking that anger out on one another. I've always thought of myself as the spindle around which the spokes of the wheel turn. If I'm the spindle, Callie is the motion. The thing that makes the wheel move over whatever terrain, however rough. Her jibes and jokes, her teasing and relentless humor, it keeps us sane. Its absence is like the void of space, and we're ready to fill that void by lunging for one another's throats.

"You know what the first thing Callie ever said to me was?" I say without preamble. "She said, 'Thank heavens! You're not a midget, after all.'" I smile at the memory. "She told me that she'd heard I was four foot ten and just couldn't get a picture of how tall that was in her mind. She kept imagining me as a dwarf."

Alan laughs at this, a quiet, sad laugh. "You know what she said when she saw me? She said, 'Oh dear, it's a giant Negro!'"

"She did not!" I exclaim.

"She did, I promise."

We all stop talking as Alan's cell phone rings, and watch as he answers it and listens. "Yeah. No kidding? Thanks, Gene." He hangs up, looking at me. "The prints from our suspect in custody match the prints taken off the bed in Annie's apartment. We also have some of his DNA for comparison—"

"How did we pull that off?" I interrupt.

"He cut his lip as a result of that mix-up you guys had taking him down. Barry offered him a handkerchief to clean himself up with."

I smile, grim. "Smart."

Alan leans forward, looking at me. "He's one of the guys, Smoky. For sure, one hundred percent. Maybe not provable yet, but close enough. What do you want to do?"

They are all looking at me, the same question in their eyes. What do you want to do? The answer is simple.

We kill him and eat him? the dragon asks.

In a way, I think.

"One of us is going to do the interrogation of our lives and crack him wide, wide open, Alan."

49

WE'RE STANDING IN the observation room with Barry, looking through the one-way glass at Robert Street. He's seated at a table, cuffed at the wrists and ankles.

He's nondescript, which surprises me on some level. He has brown hair, and a hard face made up of planes and edges. His eyes are hot and angry, while the rest of him is relaxed. He's staring back at us through the mirror.

"Pretty cool cucumber," Alan says. "We know anything about this guy yet?"

"Not much," Barry says. "Name is Robert Street. Thirty-eight years old, single, never been married, no kids. Works as a martial-arts instructor in the Valley." He looks at me, nodding to indicate my swollen lips. "But you already found that out."

"Do you have an address on him yet?" I ask.

"Yeah. He lives in an apartment in Burbank. With the match to the prints found in your friend's place, we'll be able to get a warrant. I have someone on that now."

"Who should do the interview?" Alan asks. "You said 'one of us'—so who's it going to be? You or me?"

"You. No question." It's a no-brainer for me. Alan is the best, and the man inside that room holds the key to finding the real Jack Jr. To ending all of this.

He gives me a long look and nods, turning to watch Robert Street through the glass. He watches him for long moments. Barry and I are patient, we wait him out; we know that we are disappearing for Alan, that he is fixing himself firmly into the zone, studying Street like a hunter studies game.

Getting ready to crack him like a walnut.

We need to break him, for all kinds of reasons. The truth is, we don't have him, not yet. The fingerprints at Annie's apartment could be explained away. A good defense attorney might argue that the prints got there when he moved the bed doing his whole pest-control thing. Which, while fraudulent and compelling in its own right, doesn't add up to murder, per se. We have his DNA but no results back yet. What if it's Jack's DNA under Charlotte Ross's fingernail and not Street's?

More than all of this, we need him to lead us to Jack Jr.

Alan looks at Barry. "Can you let me in?"

Barry takes him outside and, not long after that, I watch Alan enter the interview room. Robert Street looks up at him. Cocks his head, examining. And smiles.

"Wow," he sneers. "I guess you're the bad cop, huh?"

Alan saunters over, the picture of someone with plenty of time on his hands, and pulls up a chair so that he's seated directly in front of Street. He straightens his tie. Smiles. Watching, I know that every move is calculated. Not just the moves, but their speed. How close they come to Street. The pitch of his voice when he speaks. It's all an act, with one end in sight.

"Mr. Street, my name's Alan Washington."

"I know who you are. How's the wife?"

Alan smiles, shaking his head, and waggles a finger at him. "Smart," he says. "Trying to get me rattled and angry right out of the box."

Street yawns in exaggerated boredom. "Where's that cunt Barrett?" he asks.

"She'll be around," Alan says. "You popped her pretty good in that apartment."

This elicits a nasty smile. "Glad to hear it."

Alan shrugs. "Hey—between you and me? I feel like popping her one myself, sometimes."

Street's eyes narrow. "Really?" He sounds doubtful.

"Can't help it. I'm old-school. I was raised, women have a place." He grins. "And it's under me, not over me, if you know what I mean." He chuckles. "Hell, I've had to slap the wife around every now and then. Just to make sure she remembers where she stands."

Alan has Street's full attention now. The monster's gaze is full of fascination, desire warring with doubt. He wants Alan to mean what he's saying, and this need is overcoming his distrust.

The days of rubber hoses and "good cop bad cop" are long gone. There is an established science of interview and interrogation, tried and proven. It is a dance based on psychology, involving a certain art mixed with tremendous observation. Step one is always the same: Establish a rapport. If Street liked bass fishing, Alan would become an instant sports-fishing enthusiast. If he was a gun nut, Alan would draw him out with a knowledge of weapons. Street likes to hurt women. And so, for now, Alan does too. And it will work. I have seen it work on hardened criminals. I have even seen it work on cops who know this technique and are trained in it. It's human nature, irresistible and inevitable.

"What would the FBI think about that?" Street asks.

Alan leans forward, full of menace. "She knows to keep her mouth shut."

Street nods, impressed.

"Anyway," Alan says. "You hit Smoky pretty good. Some of the other guys too. They said you were doing some fancy martial arts in there. You teach, right?"

"That's right."

"What style?"

"Wing chun. It's a form of kung fu."

"No shit? Bruce Lee, huh?" He smiles. "I got a black belt in karate."

He looks Alan up and down, gauging his size. "Are you any good? Do you take it seriously? Or is it just for show?"

"I spar twice a week, do my kata daily, and have for the last ten years."

I look at Barry. "Alan doesn't know a karate chop from a roundhouse kick."

Street nods. A little dip of man-to-man respect. Alan is connecting with him. "That's good. You have to keep yourself sharp. A big man like you, you could be pretty lethal."

Alan holds his hands open, a "hey, I try" gesture. "I have my moments. What about you? What year did you start with kung fu?"

I see Street pause, thinking. Doing what Alan wants without knowing it. "I don't remember the exact year...I was five or six. We were living in San Francisco."

Alan whistles. "Long time. How long does it take— average—for a guy to go from nothing to competent in kung fu?"

Street considers. "That's hard to say. It depends on the person. But as a general rule—four to five years."

Alan is using innocuous questions to create a baseline. He's using a technique called neurolinguistic interviewing, which involves asking the subject two types of questions. One type asks him to remember something. The other requires him to use his cognitive process. Alan is noting Street's body language as he does this, what changes take place when he thinks of information as opposed to remembering it. This is primarily in the eyes, and Street has the classic mannerisms. When Alan had asked him for an actual memory—what year did he start learning kung fu?—Street's eyes had looked to the right. When he had asked him a thinking question—to calculate how long it would take for someone to become proficient—Street's eyes had looked down and to the left. Alan now knows that if he asks Street a "remember question" and Street's eyes look down and to the left, he's probably lying, as he is thinking rather than remembering.

"Four to five years. Not too bad." Alan motions with a hand behind his chair. It is a signal, and I respond to it by tapping on the window. Alan grimaces. "Sorry. Give me a second."

Street doesn't reply, and Alan gets up and leaves the room. A moment later, he is in the observation room with us.

"He may act cool," he says, "but he doesn't know squat about body language and interrogation. I'm going to roll right over him."

"Be careful," I say. "We want him to point us to Jack Jr. You don't know yet how loyal he'll be."

Alan looks at me, shakes his head. "It won't matter." He turns to Barry. "You got that file folder?"

"Right here." Barry hands him a file folder filled with various papers, all of them either unrelated to Street or blank. The name ROBERT STREET is clearly printed on the front of the folder.

The folder is just a prop. Alan is about to change the tone and pace of the interview. It will now become confrontational. In our society, file folders are equated with important information, and the fact that this one is filled with documents will imply to Street that we have a lot of evidence against him. Alan will go in and deliver what's called the "confrontational statement." It's a key point in this type of interrogation, and can be dramatic. Some suspects become so demoralized that they'll actually faint when they're given the confrontational statement.

Alan watches Street for a few more moments and then heads toward the door. A moment later he reenters the interview room. He acts like he's reading through the folder. He closes it and holds it so that Street can see his name on it. Alan stands this time, he doesn't sit. He takes a wide stance, legs shoulder-width apart. Everything about him says he is dominant, in control. Confident. All of it is purposeful and calculated.

"Here's the thing, Mr. Street. We know you were involved in the murders of Annie King and Charlotte Ross. We have you pretty cold on this. Fingerprints found at Annie King's apartment have been matched to your prints. We're comparing DNA evidence from Charlotte Ross's apartment to some of your DNA right now, and I'll bet we get a match. We also have the MO you used prior to committing the crimes—the signed receipts you left as an 'exterminator.' We have some pretty good hand-writing experts who should be able to tie those to you. We got you. What I want to know is—are you willing to talk to me about this?"

Street looks at Alan, who towers over him, exuding confidence and power, the picture of the alpha male. His eyes widen a bit, and I can see that his breathing has quickened. Then they narrow again, and he smiles. Shrugs.

"I would—if I had any idea what you were talking about."

Street smiles wider, the Cheshire cat. He thinks he still holds a trump card. That we don't know there are two of them.

Alan is quiet. Staring at him. In an abrupt motion he turns to one side, picks up the interview table, and moves it against the far wall. He then puts his chair directly in front of Street. He sits down, close.

Threatening.

"What are you doing?" Street asks. There is a hint of nervousness in his voice. Some sweat on his brow.

Alan looks surprised. "I just want to make sure I'm getting everything, Mr. Street."

He looks through the meaningless file folder again and frowns. Shakes his head. Acting, acting, acting. He puts the folder down on the floor next to his chair and moves the chair closer to Street, invading his personal space. I watch as he positions one knee just inside Street's knees, creating a subconscious threat to his manhood. The killer swallows. The sweat on his forehead is more noticeable now. He, however, is unaware of these physiological reactions. All he knows is that Alan has filled his world and that he is getting very uncomfortable.

"See, there's a loose end."

Street swallows again. "What?"

Alan nods. "A loose end." He leans even closer now. Pushes his knee in a bit farther. "You see, we know you haven't been acting alone."

Street's eyes open wide. His breathing accelerates. He belches, without being aware of it. "What?"

"You have an accomplice. We were able to figure it out from the video of Annie King's murder. A difference in height. And we know he's the real Jack Jr., not you."

Street looks like a fish on a hook, mouth opening and closing. His eyes are fixed on Alan. He belches again. His hands come down in a protective cupping of his crotch. All of this is reflexive; he remains unaware. Alan leans in closer.

"Do you know who he is, Robert?" Alan asks.

"No!" Eyes down and to the left. Lying.

"Well, Robert...I think you do, Robert. Robert, I think you know who he is and where we can find him. Robert, is that true?" Alan uses repetition of his name to create both an undercurrent of accusation and a feeling of there being nowhere to hide. It's like going "hey—YOU" again and again.

Street stares at Alan. He is covered in sweat.

"No."

"What I can't figure out? Why you'd be protecting him." Alan leans in farther. Rubs his chin in thought. "Maybe..." He snaps his fingers. "You know, when two male serial killers are working together, a lot of times they're fucking each other. Well—the dominant one is doing the fucking. That the case here? That why you're protecting him? 'Cause you like catching while he's pitching?"

Street's eyes pop wide open. He's quivering in rage.

"I'm no fucking fag!"

Alan leans in, till they're almost nose to nose. Street is shivering. He belches again. "That's not what the little girl said. Bonnie? Remember her? She said that one of you was gobbling the other one's johnson like he was at a sausage-eating contest."

Street is apoplectic. "She's a *lying little cunt!*"

"Gotcha," Barry says.

Alan doesn't let up. "You sure? She said that one of you was sucking the proverbial golf ball through the garden hose. She gave a lot of detail. Details a girl her age wouldn't have."

"She's *lying!* She probably knows about cocksucking because her mother was a whore! We never touched each—"

He stops, realizes what's happened. What he's said.

"So you *were* there," Alan states.

Street's face goes red. Tears are running down his cheeks. I don't think he realizes this. "Fuck it! Yeah—I was there! I helped kill that cunt! So what? You'll never catch him. He'll get away, you'll see. He's too *smart* for you!"

"That's a confession from one of them," I say.

Barry nods. "He just bought himself a one-way ticket to the gas chamber."

Alan moves back, just a bit. He keeps his knee where it is, threatening. Street is unraveling before our eyes.

"You know, Robert, we have guys on their way to your apartment now. Robert, I'm betting there's something there that'll help us find out who he is, isn't there, Robert?"

Street's eyes go to the right. Remembering. Then: "No! Nothing! Fuck you! Stop saying my fucking name over and over!"

"Did you see that?" Barry murmurs, excited.

I had seen it, and a thrill had gone through me when I did.

When he'd said no, the eyes had gone down. Down and to the left.

He's lying.

There is something in his apartment he doesn't want us to find.

50

WE ARE STANDING in Street's apartment. Barry and I had watched as Alan continued to break Street down, inch by subtle inch. He was unable to get him to give up Jack Jr.'s identity, but he had given up everything else. How Jack had contacted him, how they picked their victims, other facts. He'd signed a confession and was a sweat-soaked, broken, blubbering mess by the time Alan left the interview room. Alan had destroyed him.

The dragon approved.

My cell phone rings. "Barrett."

"It's Gene, Smoky. I thought you'd want to know that Street's DNA is a match to the DNA found on Charlotte Ross's fingernail."

"Thanks, Gene. That's good news."

He pauses. "Is Callie going to be okay?"

"I think so. We'll have to wait and see."

He sighs. "I'll let you go."

"Bye."

"Place is clean," Alan notes.

I look around. He's right. Street's apartment is not just clean—it's spotless. It's the clean of the obsessive-compulsive. It's also devoid of personality. There are no pictures on the wall, not of Street or family or friends. No paintings or prints. The couch is functional. The coffee table is functional. The TV is small.

"Spartan," I murmur.

We wander into the bedroom. Like the living room, it is spotless. The bedsheets are tight, the corners military-sharp. He has a single computer on a small desk facing the wall.

And then I see it. The one thing that's out of place here, that doesn't fit. A small locket, arranged with precision next to a college textbook. I bend over to get a closer look. It's a woman's locket, gold on a gold chain. I pick it up and open it. Inside is a miniature photo of a striking older woman. Someone's mother, I think.

"Pretty," Alan remarks.

I nod. I put down the locket, open the textbook. It's a basic college English text. Inside is an inscription: *This book belongs to Renee Parker. It might not look like much, but it's actually MAGIC—ha ha!* ☺ *It's my magic carpet. So don't touch, boobie heads!*

It's signed and dated.

"That's . . . what? Twenty-five years ago?"

I nod. My heartbeat is quickening. This is it. This is the key.

This will show us his face.

I touch the book, running my fingers across the inscription.

Perhaps it really will end up being magic.

51

I STAND AND listen to Alan. He's excited. I have the sense that everything is moving faster and faster, heated molecules coming to a slow but inexorable boil.

"We got a hit on VICAP with the name Renee Parker. A doozy."

VICAP stands for Violent Criminal Apprehension Program. Conceived by an LAPD detective in 1957, it didn't become operational until 1985, when it was established at the National Center for the Analysis of Violent Crime at the FBI Academy. The concept is brilliant. It's a nationwide data center, designed to gather, collate, and analyze crimes of violence. With an emphasis on murder. Any and all information on both solved and unsolved cases can be supplied by any member of law enforcement participating, at whatever echelon. Taken as a whole, this mountain of information enables a nationwide cross-referencing of violent acts.

He refers to the papers in his hand. "It's an old case—twenty-five years ago. A stripper in San Francisco. Found strangled in an alleyway, and—get this—some of her organs were removed."

My tiredness disappears in a flash. I feel as though I

have just snorted caffeine. "That has to be him. Has to be."

"Yeah, and it gets better. They had a suspect at the time. They couldn't find enough evidence to make it stick."

I jump up. "Leo, you'll stay here to act as a contact and coordination point. James and Alan—let's go to San Francisco. Now."

"Don't have to tell me twice," Alan says, and we are moving toward the door, filled with a second wind concocted of adrenaline, excitement, and a little bit of fury.

We get outside and I see Tommy, sitting in his car. Still and watchful.

"Give me a second," I tell Alan and James. I walk over to the car. Tommy rolls down the window.

"What's happening?" he asks.

I tell him about the VICAP hit. "We're going to San Fran now."

"What do you want me to do?"

I give a smile, reach over and touch his cheek, once. "Get some sleep."

"Sounds good," he replies. Mr. Laconic, as always. I turn to walk away. "Smoky," he says, stopping me. I look back at him. "Be careful."

I have time to see the worry in his eyes before he rolls up the window and drives away.

For some reason, Sally Field at the Oscars jumps into my mind.

"He likes me, he really, really likes me," I murmur in falsetto.

Hysterical bubbles.

52

THIS DREAM IS new. The past and the present have merged, have become one thing.

I am asleep in my bedroom when I hear a noise. Sounds of sawing, squishy sounds. I get up, heart beating fast, and grab my gun from the nightstand.

I pad through my door, weapon drawn, hands trembling at the thought of someone in my house.

The noises come from the living room. Cackles have been added to the sibilant squishes.

When I enter, he is there. I cannot see his face, for it is obscured by the bandages around his head. His lips are visible, and they are huge, bloated, red. His black eyes are flat and dead, like bits of burned skin.

"Do you see?" he whispers, snakelike.

I can't see what he's pointing to. The back of the couch is hiding it. A certainty begins to rise in me that I don't want to see.

But I must.

I move forward, forward, forward.

"Do you see?" he whispers.

And I do.

She is lying on the couch. He has opened her from sternum to crotch, exposing her organs. Cemetery earth cakes her hair. And one grime-covered finger points at me.

"Your fault..." she croaks.

She is Alexa, and then she is Charlotte Ross, and then she is Annie.

"Why did you let him kill me?" Annie's face asks me, as she points, accusing. "Why?"

The man with the bandaged face cackles. "Do you see?" he whispers. "Their dirty fingers. They point at you, forever."

"Why?" she asks.

"Do you see?" he whispers.

I jolt awake. The cabin of the jet is quiet and shadowed. James and Alan are dozing.

I look out the passenger window to the cold, dark night and shiver. Dirty fingers. No need to search for symbolism there.

I feel them always, pointing at me from the grave. The ones I did not save.

I'd called Jenny Chang at SFPD from the plane, and she is waiting for us.

"I'm not your friend anymore," she says, tapping her watch to indicate the early hour.

"Sorry, Jenny. Things are pretty fucked up." I fill her in on Callie. Her lips tighten into a straight, angry line.

"No further word on her yet?" she asks.

"No," James replies.

"Christ..." she says, staring off.

I hold up my briefcase. "But we got a good hit from VICAP."

The detective in her comes out, sharp and interested. "Tell me."

I give her the gist of it.

"Twenty-five years ago. I came on the force when I was twenty-two. That's before my time. Who was the primary on the case?"

"Detective Rawlings," Alan says.

Jenny stops still. Looks at Alan. "Rawlings? Are you sure about that?"

"Yeah, I'm sure. Why?"

She shakes her head. "Because things may really be looking up for you now. Rawlings is a first-class fuckup. Always has been, from what I hear. He's boozing it up, counting time till retirement."

"And how is that good for us?" I ask.

"It makes it a lot more probable that he missed something back then. Something you guys wouldn't miss."

At SFPD, Jenny taps a pencil on the desk while waiting for the phone to be answered. "Rawlings? This is Jenny Chang. Yeah, I do know what time it is." She frowns. "It's not my fault you're a drunk."

I give her a pleading look. I need the guy to come in, not hang up on her. She closes her eyes. I get the idea she's counting to ten.

"Look, Don. I'm sorry. I got woken up out of bed too. Made me cranky. The head of NCAVC Coord LA is here, about an old case of yours. A"—she consults a pad in front of her—"Renee Parker." A look of surprise crosses her face. "Sure. Okay. See you in a few." She hangs up the phone, musing.

"What?" I ask.

"The moment I said her name, he stopped complaining and said he'd be here right away."

"I guess this one meant something to him."

* * *

Don Rawlings shows up within the half hour. I can tell just by looking at him that Jenny was right on target. He's about five foot nine, with a large gut, rheumy eyes, and the florid face of a dedicated drinker. He looks aged before his time.

I stand up and shake his hand. "Thank you for coming, Detective Rawlings. I'm Special Agent Smoky Barrett, head of NCAVC Coord in Los Angeles. That's James Giron and Alan Washington, who also work in my unit."

He squints at my face. "I know you. You're the one whose home got broken into." He grimaces. "Every cop's nightmare."

I notice he's holding a folder in his hand. "What's that?" I ask.

He plops it down on the desk as he takes a seat. "That's a copy of the file on Renee Parker. I've kept it all these years. Pick it up in the early hours sometimes when I can't sleep."

Rawlings's face undergoes a change when he speaks about Renee Parker. The eyes become more alert. His mouth grows sad. I was right. This case had meant something to him.

"Tell me about it, Detective."

His eyes go distant. Empty, with no horizons. "Takes a little bit of backstory, Agent Barrett. Detective Chang here probably told you I'm an alcoholic fuckup. And she's right. But I wasn't always that way. Once upon a time, I was where she is now. The best homicide guy here. First grade." He looks at Jenny, smiles. "Didn't know that, did you?"

Jenny raises an eyebrow. "I had no idea."

"Yeah. Don't get me wrong, now. When I started on the force I was young, and I was a real prick. A racist, a homophobe, with a hair-trigger temper. I used my fists on more than one occasion where it might not have been needed. But the streets have a way of teaching you the way things really are.

"I stopped being a racist the day a black cop saved my life. Perp came up behind me. This cop tackled me out of the way and shot the perp down at the same time. We were fast friends for years, till he died. Killed in the line of duty."

Those sad eyes grow even emptier and more distant.

"I stopped being a homophobe after a year in homicide. Death does that to you. Tends to give you a perspective on things. There was a young man who was—well, flamboyant about his homosexuality. He worked a roach coach near the station, and he picked up on my hate real fast. Little fucker would tease me, do all kinds of things just to make me uncomfortable."

A faint smile ghosts across his lips. Disappears, torpedoed by sadness.

"God, he made me crazy. Well, one day a group of guys beat that young man to death because he was a homosexual. And wouldn't you know it, I caught the case." He gives me a sardonic grin. "How's that for karma? During that case I got to see two things, and I was never a gay hater again. I got to see his mother scream and pull her hair out and just die inside right in front of me. I watched her world end because her boy was dead. Then I went to his funeral, looking for suspects. You know what I saw there? About two hundred people. You believe that? I don't think I even *know* two hundred people. Not who would come to my funeral, that's for sure." He shakes his head in disbelief. "And they weren't just people from the community, there because he was gay. They were people whose lives he'd touched. Turns out he volunteered all over the place. Hospices, drug-rehab centers, crisis counseling. That young man was a saint. He was good. And the only reason he was dead was because he was gay." He clenches a fist. "That was wrong. I just couldn't be a part of it. Not anymore."

He waves a hand. "Anyway. So . . . yeah. Here I was, new to the homicide bureau, and a new man. No longer thinking words like *faggot* or *nigger*. I was different, I was dedicated, life was good.

"Now jump forward five years. I was about three years past my peak and sliding down the other side fast. I'd started to drink; I was fucking around on my wife. I thought a lot about eating my gun. All because of those damn dead babies." His eyes grow haunted, haunted in a way I recognized. I'd seen that same look in the mirror. "Someone was killing babies. I'm talking toddlers or younger. Snatching them, strangling them, and tossing them out on the sidewalks or the streets. All it took was six of them and no suspects, and I was dying inside." He peers at me. "You know that feeling, I'll bet, doing what you do."

I nod.

"Imagine that it's six dead babies you're letting down. That you not only haven't caught the guy doing it, you don't even have any suspects. I was fucked."

Just a year ago, I'd have looked at Don Rawlings and would have to have suppressed a sneer. I would have considered him weak. Someone blaming the past for the present, using it as an excuse. I can't forgive him entirely for giving up, but I don't feel that need to sneer at this moment. Sometimes the weight of this job is just too much. What I feel now is not superiority but compassion.

"I can imagine," I say, looking at him. I think he sees that I mean it, and he continues his tale.

"I was already fucking up and not caring about it. I did anything I could to try and get those dead babies off my mind. Drinking, sex—anything. But they'd keep showing up in my dreams. Then I met Renee Parker."

A genuine smile, one belonging to a younger Don Rawlings, appears.

"I ran into her when her boyfriend got killed. He was a small-time dealer, pissed off the wrong guy. She was a stripper who'd only just started shooting up. You see it all the time and learn to write it off real fast. But there was something different about Renee. There was someone home. Some life in there, right near the surface." He looks up. "I know what you're thinking. Cop, stripper, end of story. But it wasn't like that. Sure, she had a great body. But I didn't think of her like that. I saw her, and I thought maybe this was my chance to do something good. To make up for the babies.

"I got her story. Went to LA to act, ended up dancing topless to make ends meet. Met a scumbag, he said, 'Hey, try a little bit of this, you won't get hooked.' Nothing original there. But there was something original with her. This kind of desperation in her eyes. Like she was still hanging on to the edge of the cliff and hadn't fallen off it yet.

"I grabbed her and I slammed her into rehab. When I was off duty, I'd go see her. Hold her while she was puking. Talk to her. Encourage her. Sometimes we'd talk all night. And you know what? She was my first female friend." He looks at me. "You know what I mean? Think male-chauvinist stereotype. Women are for marrying or fucking. You understand?"

"I've known a few in my time," I say.

"Well, that was me. But this twenty-year-old girl, she became a friend. I didn't think about fucking her, and I didn't want to marry her. I just wanted her to be okay. That's all I wanted." He bites his lip. "You see, I was a good detective. I was never on the take; I usually caught the bad guy. I never hit a woman. I had rules, right and wrong. But I was never really a decent man. You understand the difference?"

"Sure."

"But what I was doing with Renee, it was decent. Selfless." He runs a hand through his hair. "She came through it and got out of rehab. I mean, really came through it. One of the ones who was going to make it. I lent her some money and she got her own apartment. She started working a job. A few months later, she even started night school. Taking drama classes. Said if she never made it as an actress, she could always be a waitress, but she wasn't ready to give up on her dream yet.

"We'd hang out every now and then. Go to a movie. Always as friends. I never wanted anything else. It was the first time it was more important to me to have a friend than a piece of ass. Best of all, the babies went away. I stopped drinking, made up with the wife."

He falls silent, and I know what's coming, can hear it like a phantom freight train. I already know the end to this story. Renee Parker, firecracker, saved from herself, gets murdered in a hideous fashion. What I didn't know until now is what that meant to the people around her.

For Don Rawlings, it was a point where fate turned on a dime and began hurtling into the black. The point where the dead babies came back and never left.

"I got the call at four in the morning. Didn't know who it was until I got out there." His eyes look like ghosts in the fog. Lost and howling and doomed to wander. "He'd burned her good. The ME said she had almost five hundred separate cigarette burns on her. Five hundred!

None of them fatal." His hand trembles on the desk. "He'd tortured her and raped her. But the worst was what he did after. Cut her open, took out some of her organs, and dropped them next to her body. Just dropped them there on the concrete, to rot with her.

"It's hard to remember that feeling. How I felt when I saw her there. Maybe I just don't want to. What I do remember is one of the uniforms looking down at her and saying, 'Oh yeah, I know her. Stripper, used to work over in the Tenderloin. Great tits.' That was it for him, all the explanation he needed. He looked down at Renee, remembered her tits, and labeled her. Not a human being, or a bright girl who was turning her life around. Just a stripper." He traces a finger over an imperfection in the desk. "They had to pull me off him. Not that it mattered. Can you believe this—that little bastard went in and pulled the file, years later. Under *profession,* he whited out *waitress* and wrote in *stripper/poss. prostitute.* Even sent it in as a correction to VICAP."

I'm appalled. I suppose it shows on my face, because he looks at me and nods.

"Believe it." He sighs. "So anyway, I kept my past relationship with her quiet so I could stay as the primary on the case. I wanted to catch this guy. Had to catch him. But he was good. No prints, not a damn thing. We didn't have DNA back then, so"—he shrugs—"I went looking where you always do when you come up dry on the physical evidence."

"Who knew her, who'd been around her," I say.

"That's right. She was going to night school. Turns out she'd met a guy there. Been seeing him for a week or two. Good-looking kid named Peter Connolly. But right off, I knew something wasn't right with him. Something about the way he talked when I questioned him, like he was making fun of me. Getting away with something. On a hunch, I flashed his photo around at the strip joint she used to work at. Sure enough, people remembered him. The times they placed him there matched what Renee's schedule had been. Then it got better. Turns out Peter had a little drug problem. He'd attended rehab. Can you guess? At the same place and at the same time that Renee had been cleaning up. Now my antennae are way up. Once I found out he'd enrolled in college only a week after she had, I knew, I knew, he had to be my guy."

He falls silent and doesn't start speaking again.

"I can guess where this goes, Don," I say in a gentle voice. "No evidence, right? You couldn't connect him to the crime. Sure, he'd been at the strip club, rehab, and the college. But all of that could be explained away."

He nods. Bereft. "That's right. It was enough to get a warrant for his place, but nothing turned up. Not a damn thing. His past was clean." He looks back up at me, and his eyes are filled with frustration. "I couldn't prove what I knew. And there weren't any more killings. No other scenes. Time went on; he moved away. I started dreaming again. Sometimes it was the babies. Most of the time it was Renee."

No one here feels superior to Don Rawlings now. We know that everyone has that point. Where they can no longer bend without breaking. He no longer seems pathetic or weak. Instead, we recognize him for what he is: a casualty.

Whoever said "time heals all wounds" wasn't a cop.

"The reason we're here," I speak into the silence, "is because VICAP matched the MO of our unsub to your unsolved case. He has killed again." I lean forward. "After listening to you, I'm certain our killer and yours are one and the same."

He studies my face like someone does when they don't trust in hope. "You having any better luck than I did?"

"Not in terms of physical evidence. But we did find out one thing that, combined with your suspect of twenty-five years ago, might break this case."

"What's that?"

I explain to him about Jack Jr. and the contents of the jar. Cynicism begins to fall away from his face, replaced by excitement.

"So you're saying this guy was indoctrinated in this idea of being Jack the Ripper's great-great-grandkid, or whatever, and that it started when he was young?"

"That's what I'm saying."

He leans back in his chair with a look of amazement. "Man oh man oh man ... I never had any reason to check out his mom back then. The dad was long gone and in the wind ..." Don has the look of someone in shock. Reeling. He gathers himself up and taps on the case folder he'd brought with him. "That info's in there. Who his mom is, where she lived at the time."

"Then that's where we're going," I say.

"Do you think ..." He takes a deep breath, draws himself up. "I know I'm not much these days. I'm an old, drunk has-been. But if you let me go with you to see the mother, I promise I won't fuck it up."

I've never heard someone sound as humble as he does right now.

"I wouldn't have it any other way, Don," I say. "It's time for you to see this through."

53

CONCORD IS LOCATED north of Berkeley in the Bay Area. We are headed there to see Peter Connolly's mother, a woman named Patricia. The driver's license on file says that she is sixty-four years old. We have opted to show up on her doorstep, rather than telegraph our coming or our suspicions. Mothers have sent their sons on killing sprees before. In this case, who knows?

I am in the zone. It is that place I get to near the end of a hunt, when I know, at a primal level, that we are zeroing in on our quarry. All senses heighten to an almost painful level, and I feel as if I am running full tilt across a piano wire over a chasm. Sure-footed, invincible, unafraid of falling.

I look at Don Rawlings as we drive, and I see a spark of it there as well, though perhaps mixed with more desperation. He has dared to hope again. For him the price of failure might be more than a disappointment. It could be fatal. In spite of this, he looks ten years younger. His eyes are clear and focused. You can almost see what he was like when he was still honed sharp.

We are junkies, all of us who work in this profession. We walk through blood, decay, and stench. We toss and turn with nightmares caused by horrors the mind has trouble encompassing. We take it out on ourselves, or our friends and family, or both. But then it comes toward the end, and we arrive in the zone, and it is a high like no other. It's a high that makes you forget about the stench and blood and nightmares and horrors. And once it is behind you, you are ready to do it again.

Of course, it can backfire on you. You can fail to catch a killer. The stink remains, but without the reward that cleanses it away. Even so, those of us who do this thing continue, willing to take this chance.

This is a profession where you work on the edge of a precipice. It has a high suicide rate. Just like any profession where failure carries such a terrible weight of responsibility.

I think of all these things, but I don't care. For now, my scars have no meaning. Because I am in the zone.

I have always been fascinated by books and movies about serial killers. Writers and directors so often seem dedicated to the idea that they must lay out a path of bread crumbs for their hero to follow. A logical array of deductions and clues that lead to the monster's lair in the blazing light of an *aHA!*

Sometimes this is true. But much of the time it's not. I remember a case that was making us crazy. He was killing children, and after three months we didn't have a clue. Not a single, solid lead. One morning I got a call from the LAPD—he had turned himself in. Case closed.

With Jack Jr., we have exhausted the gamut of physical evidence and the search for the esoterics of "IP numbers." He has costumed himself, planted bugs and tracking devices, enlisted confederates, been brilliant.

And in the end, the resolution of it all will probably come down to just two factors: a piece of cow flesh and a twenty-five-year-old unsolved case gathering dust in VICAP.

I have learned to need only one truth over the years, and it provides all the order I require: Caught is caught and caught is good. Period.

Alan's cell phone rings. "Yeah," he says. His eyes close, and I am fearful, but they open again, and I can see his relief. "Thanks, Leo. I appreciate you calling me." He hangs up. "She's not awake yet, but they've upgraded her condition from critical to stable. Still in ICU, but the surgeon told Leo specifically that death wasn't on the table anymore, unless something really unexpected happens."

"Callie'll pull through. She's too damn stubborn," I say.

James says nothing, and silence rules again. We keep driving.

"Here it is," Jenny murmurs.

The home is old and just a little shabby. The yard's uncared for but not quite dead. The whole place has the same feel: on its way out but not yet gone. We get out of the car and walk up to the door. It opens before we can knock.

Patricia Connolly looks old, and tired. As tired as she looks, her eyes are awake.

With fear.

"You must be the police," she says.

"Yes, ma'am," I respond. "As well as members of the FBI." I show her my credentials and introduce myself and the others. "Can we come in, Mrs. Connolly?"

Her brows knit together as she looks at me. "You can as long as you don't call me Mrs. Connolly."

I hide my puzzlement. "Certainly, ma'am. What would you prefer I call you?"

"Ms. Connolly. Connolly is my name, not my late husband's. May he burn in hell." She opens the door wide for us to enter. "Come on inside."

The interior of the house is clean and neat, but devoid of personality. As though it is cared for only through force of habit. It feels two-dimensional.

Patricia Connolly ushers us into her living room, indicating for us to take seats. "Do any of you want anything?" she asks. "I only have water and coffee, but you're welcome to either."

I look around at my crew, who all shake their heads in the negative. "No thank you, Ms. Connolly. We're fine."

She nods, looking down at her hands. "Well, then, why don't you tell me why you're here."

She continues to look at her hands as she says this, unable to meet my eyes. I decide to follow my instincts. "Why don't *you* tell me why I'm here, Ms. Connolly?"

Her head snaps up, and I see I was right. Her eyes glint with guilt.

Not ready to talk yet, though. "I have no idea."

"You're *lying,*" I say. I'm startled at the harshness of my own voice. Alan's face registers surprise.

I can't help it. I'm done fucking around. I am filled to the brim, and the anger inside me is overflowing. I lean forward, catching her eye. I stab a finger at her. "We're here about your son, Ms. Connolly. We're here about a mother, a friend of mine, raped and gutted like a deer. About her daughter, tied to her mother's corpse for three days." My voice is rising. "We're here about a man who tortures women. About an agent, another friend of mine, laying in the hospital, maybe crippled for life. We're—"

She jumps up, hands against her head. *"Stop it!"* she screeches. Her hands drop to her sides. Her head falls forward. "Just . . . stop it." As suddenly as she has reacted, she deflates. It's like watching an air balloon sink to earth. She sits back down.

Patricia sighs, a long exhalation that seems to signal the letting go of something older than this moment. "You think you know what you're here about," she says, looking at me, "but you don't. You think you're here about those poor women." She looks at Don Rawlings. "Or about that poor young lady from twenty-some years ago. They are part of it. But you're here about something a lot older than both of those things."

I could interrupt her, tell her about the cow flesh in the jar and Jack Jr., but something tells me to let her speak at her own pace.

"It's funny how you miss the most important things in people sometimes. Even in people you love. Doesn't seem fair. If a man is cruel inside, someone who's going to turn into a wife beater or worse, there should be something you can see that would tell you that. Don't you think?"

"I've thought the same thing many times, ma'am," I reply. "Doing what I do."

"I suppose you would," she says as she regards me. "Then you also know that's not how it works. Not at all. In fact, many times it's just the opposite. The ugliest people can be the most decent. The charmer can be a killer." She shrugs. "Appearance is no index, no index at all.

"Of course, when you're young, you don't worry about things like that. I met my husband Keith when I was eighteen years old. He was twenty-five and he was one of the most handsome men I had ever seen. And that's no exaggeration. Six feet tall, dark hair, face of an actor. When he took his shirt off...well, let's just say he had the body to go with the face." She smiles. A sad smile. "When he showed an interest in me, I was bowled over from the word *go*. Like many young people, I was convinced my life was boring. He was handsome and exciting. Just what the doctor ordered." She pauses her narrative, looking at all of us. "This was down in Texas, by the way. I'm not native to California." Her eyes look faraway. "Texas. Flat and hot and boring.

"Keith pursued me, though it wasn't a marathon pursuit. More of a sprint. I made him run just far enough to let him know I wasn't completely pliable. I didn't know it at the time, but he saw through me like I was made from glass. He always knew he had me. He just put up with it, went through the motions, because it amused him. He could have grabbed me and told me to come with him right away, and I would have said yes. He knew it, but he took me on the requisite few dates anyway.

"He was good at what he did. Good at pretending not to be a monster. He was a perfect gentleman and as romantic as anything I'd ever seen in the movies or read in the books. Kind, romantic, handsome—I thought I had found my perfect man. The one every young woman is certain they deserve and are destined to find." Her voice and smile are both bitter.

"Now, you have to understand, my home life was difficult. My daddy had a short temper. It's not as if he beat on my mother every day, or even every week. But it happened every month. I'd been watching him backhand her or punch her for as long as I could remember. He never laid a hand on me, but in later years I understood that this wasn't because he didn't want to hit me. It was because he knew if he touched me, it would be for a reason other than violence." She raises her eyebrows. "You understand?"

Unfortunately, I do. "Yes," I say.

"I think Keith understood too. I'm sure of it. One

night, just a month after he met me, he asked me to marry him."

She sighs, remembering. "He picked the perfect night to do it. There was a full moon, the air was cool without being cold. Beautiful. He brought me a rose and told me he was going to California. He wanted me to come with him, to marry him. He said he knew I needed to get away from my daddy, and he loved me, and this was our chance. Of course I said yes."

She closes her eyes and is silent for a span of moments. I get the idea she is remembering that as the point where she took a wrong turn and plunged into darkness, forever.

"We left four days later, in secret. I didn't say good-bye to my parents. I packed up what little I had and snuck off in the middle of the night. I never saw either of them again.

"That was an exciting time. I felt free. Like life had gone my way. I had a handsome man who wanted to marry me, I'd escaped the dead end that I'd been born to, I was young and headed toward the future." Her voice drops to a monotone. "It took us five days to get to California. We got married two days later. And the night of our honeymoon is when I found out that the future I had headed into was a place made in hell."

Her face has gone expressionless. "It was like the opposite of Halloween. Instead of being a human wearing a monster mask, Keith was a monster wearing a human mask." She shivers. "I was a virgin when I married him. He stayed sweet, right up to the point he carried me across the threshold of that cheap hotel room. Once the door closed, the mask came off.

"I'll never forget that smile. Hitler might have smiled like that when he thought about Jews dying in one of his horrible camps. Keith smiled and then he backhanded me across the face. Hard. It spun me around; blood flew out of my nose. I landed facedown on the bed. I was seeing stars and was still trying to convince myself that I was dreaming." She purses her lips, grim. "No dream. A nightmare, maybe. 'Let's get a few things straight,' he said to me while he started tearing my clothes off. 'You're my property. A breeder. That's all you are to me.' I think it was his voice, more than what he was doing, that scared me. It was calm and flat and—normal. It didn't fit with what he was doing, not at all. He put me on my knees and…you couldn't say he had sex with me. No. I don't care that we were husband and wife. He raped me. Tied a gag around my mouth to cover up my screams while he raped me.

"The whole time, he kept talking in that calm voice. 'We're going to spend a few days in here teaching you your place, breeder. You're going to learn to do what I say without hesitation or question. The penalty for disobedience, no matter how minor, is going to be more pain than you can bear.'"

She is quiet for a long time. We wait out her silence, respecting it. I'm in no immediate rush. There's no longer any doubt she's leading us toward what we need to know.

When she begins to speak again, her voice is almost a whisper.

"It took him three days to break me. He cut on me. Burned me with cigarettes. Beat me. By the end of it, I would do anything he said, no matter how disgusting or degrading." Her mouth twists in self-loathing. "Then, the final lie was exposed. He took me from that hotel room to this house." She nods. "That's right. He had this home all along. He hadn't lived in Texas. He'd been out hunting. Hunting for someone to bear him a child."

"Peter." I say it as a statement.

"Yes," she says. "My sweet little boy." She gives the "sweet" a sardonic twang. "Keith kept me tied up at night to keep me from running away from him. Beat me, used me. Made me do things. Then I got pregnant. That was the only peaceful time I had. While I was pregnant he didn't lay a hand on me. I was important to him, I was carrying his child." She puts a hand to her forehead. "I used to thank God it wasn't a daughter. He would have killed her at birth. Now I know that having a son was just as bad, in its own way."

She takes a moment to compose herself before continuing. "He made me have the baby at home, of course. Delivered it himself. Gave me a rag to clean up with while he marveled and cooed at little Peter. Once I was cleaned up and had slept a little, he handed Peter back to me. And that's when he gave me his ultimatum." She rubs her hands together, an unconscious gesture of nervousness. "He told me that he would give me a choice. He could kill me now and raise Peter himself, or I could stay and raise Peter with him. He said that if I stayed, he would never raise a hand against me again. He'd even sleep in a separate bed. But if I did stay, and I ran...he said he would hunt me down and that it would take me weeks to die." Her hands have a death grip on each other. "I believed him. I should have said yes and killed myself and Peter right then and there. I still had hope then. I still thought things would change." Her eyes, her face, her mouth, all are bitter.

"So I agreed. He was good to his word. He never hit me again. He slept in his own room, I in mine. Of course, Peter slept in a room with him. Just to ensure that I wouldn't steal him away at night. He was devious and careful like that. Peter started to grow, and by the time he was five, I had almost begun to make myself believe that things were better. Life was normal. Not wonderful, but livable. What a silly girl I was then. Things became bad again soon enough. And even though he wasn't abusing me anymore, what he did start doing was much, much worse." She pauses now. She gives me a weak smile. "I'm sorry, but I need a cup of coffee before I go on. Are you sure none of you wants a cup?"

I sense that this would make her more comfortable. "I'd love one," I say to her, smiling.

Jenny and Don concur, while Alan asks for a glass of water. Only James abstains.

"You believe all this?" Alan whispers to me while Patricia is in the kitchen.

"I think so," I say after a moment. I look at him. "Yeah. I do."

She comes back in with our drinks on a tray and passes them out. She sits back down and looks at Alan. "I heard what you said."

He looks surprised and flustered. Either one is a rarity for Alan. "I'm sorry, Ms. Connolly. I didn't mean any offense."

She smiles at him. "None taken, Mr. Washington. One thing you get from living your life with an evil man, and that's the ability to spot a good one. You're a good man. Besides, it's a fair question." She turns around in her chair so that her side is facing us. "Do you mind pulling the zipper on the back of my dress down, Agent Barrett? Just halfway should do it."

Brows knitted, I stand up. I am hesitant.

"It's all right. Go ahead."

I pull the zipper down. I have to close my eyes, for a moment, at what I see.

"Quite a sight, isn't it?" Patricia asks. "Go on, pull it open, let them see."

The area of Patricia's back that is revealed is a mass of ancient scar tissue. The part of me that is not horrified, that is clinical, observes that these scars were made in different ways, at different times. Most likely over a period of years. Some are circular burn scars, made by cigarettes. Some are long and thin. Cuts. I can guess that many are whip marks. Everyone looks; no one lingers. This provides proof of her story, gives it three dimensions. It is a terrible sight. I pull her dress closed and zip her back up.

The silence that follows is somber and uncomfortable. It's Alan who breaks it.

"I'm sorry for what happened to you," he says. "And sorry I questioned your story."

Patricia Connolly smiles at him. It is a smile that hints at the girl she used to be. "I appreciate your kindness, Mr. Washington." She folds her hands in her lap. Takes a moment to gather herself.

"You need to understand that I didn't know what he was doing until later. By then it was too late. Keith started to spend hours at night in the basement with Peter. He'd always keep it locked. At first, Peter would come back upstairs looking as though he'd been crying. Within a year, he'd come back up smiling. A year after that, he had no expression, no expression at all. Just a look in his eyes. He looked arrogant. By the time he was ten, the arrogance went away. He seemed like any normal ten-year-old boy. Bright, funny. He could make you laugh."

She shakes her head.

"I see all of this in retrospect, of course. At the time, those changes he went through, they didn't quite register. They settled in the back of my mind and festered there.

"Through all of these years, Keith kept his word. He didn't touch me. Didn't try and sleep with me. It was as if I didn't exist for him. Which was fine with me. Except—except—"

The emotion that grips her has arrived with the suddenness of a summer thunderstorm. Tears begin to run down her face.

"Except that was selfish, so, so very selfish. He'd left me alone, sure. But that was because he was busy with Peter. And me, I never questioned or pried, or tried to do anything. I just gave my son over to him." Her voice is filled with self-loathing. "What kind of a mother was I?"

The storm passes. She wipes her eyes with the back of a hand.

"Because when I look back, I saw the changes in my son. I saw his father's smile, that smile he'd given me years back in that hotel room on our honeymoon night. I sensed that coldness in him." She is silent for a long time once again. Heaves a deep sigh. "When he was fifteen, it happened." Her eyes grow distant again.

"So many years of not being beaten or raped. Years where I had time to look inside myself, think without distraction. In some ways, it was like being trapped in a tower. But that isolation began to bring me back to myself. So I decided. Then I began to plan. I was determined that it was time for me and my son to be free. At some point, the sorrow inside me had begun to change to anger. I started to plan Keith's murder."

Her face grows blank. "I decided to keep it simple. I would invite him to my bed. Something he wouldn't expect. I'd let him do what he wanted with me. And then I'd use the knife under my pillow. I would kill him, and then my son and I would leave this place and go home to Texas. Have a real life." She looks at me, sad. "I suppose there are those who are good at killing, and those who aren't. Or maybe it's not that I was bad at killing. Maybe it's just that he was so very, very good at it. I didn't know that at the time, of course, but I'd learn soon."

She fingers a small gold chain around her neck.

"He was surprised, that much was true. I told him I missed him being in my bed. I saw the lust light up in his eyes like a fire. I was prepared for him to be rough with me; that's the only way he could enjoy it. He almost ripped my clothes off my body when he took me into my bedroom." She continues to finger the gold chain. "I let him go on for a good, long time. It was as terrible as it had ever been, but what was a last few hours of that if I had a chance to end it forever?" She nods. "I wanted him good and tired. By the time he was done, one of my eyes was black. I had a fat lip and a bloody nose. He rolled his sweaty body off mine, onto his back, and closed his eyes while he sighed in satisfaction." Her eyes grow wide as she relates what happened next. "Who would have known a human being could move that fast? Then again, perhaps he wasn't truly a human being. The moment his eyes closed, my hand went under the pillow and came out with the knife. It couldn't have been more than a second that passed before I had the point racing toward his throat." She shakes her head again, in disbelief. "He caught my wrist an inch before that knife would have plunged into him. Caught it and stopped it dead. He was always so strong, stronger than anyone I'd ever known.

"He held my wrist there, and smiled that smile, and shook his head at me. 'Bad idea, Patricia,' he said to me. 'I'm afraid you're going to have to go.'" Her hands tremble a little. "I was so afraid. He took the knife away and then he beat me. He beat me good and long and hard. Knocked out some teeth. Broke my nose and my jaw. I could hardly keep conscious. I was going to pass out when he leaned forward and whispered in my ear, 'Get ready to die now, breeder.' And then everything went black."

She grows silent. I am mesmerized by the motion of that gold chain as she twists it back and forth.

"I woke up in the hospital. I hurt so much. But I didn't care, because I knew one thing: If I was still alive, that meant he was dead. I looked over and Peter was sitting next to my bed. When he saw I was awake, he reached over and took my hand. We just sat there for an hour, not saying anything.

"The sheriff told me what had happened a few hours later." Tears come to her eyes. "It was Peter. He had heard my screams. He burst into the room just as Keith was about to cut my throat. He killed him. He killed his father to save me."

She hugs herself, looks lost. "Do you have any idea of the kinds of emotions that go through you at something like that? After all those years and what I'd been through? The relief was almost unbearable. And then to find out that my son was my son, that in the end he chose me over his father." Tears continue to run down her cheeks. "I was certain I had lost him forever. Excuse me for a moment."

She stands up and totters over to a shelf where a box of tissues sit. She brings the box over, extracting one to wipe her eyes with as she sits back down.

"I'm sorry about that."

"Don't be," I say to her. I mean it. What this woman went through, it's unimaginable. Some would look at her with contempt for putting up with that abuse over so many years. For not being strong. I like to think I'm wiser than they are. Patricia dabs her eyes with the tissue and pulls herself together.

"I healed up, and we came home. It was a good time. Peter doted on me. Dinner was no longer an hour of silence, where no one spoke. We were..." Her voice trails off. "We were a family." Her face falls, the grimness and bitterness seeping back in like a black mask. "It didn't last long."

Her hand goes back to the gold chain again. Twisting, turning. "He still went down into the basement every night. He'd spend hours down there. I'd never been allowed inside, didn't know what he did in there. But I was scared. It was something he had done with his father, and part of me knew nothing good could result from it.

"Months went by with me worrying about that basement. But I didn't do anything about it. I was—what is that term for ignoring a truth you don't want to be true?"

"I think you mean denial," James says.

"That's it. I was in denial. Can you blame me? Keith, my longtime living nightmare, was dead. I had my son back. Life was good." She rubs her forehead with a hand. "But I suppose that something inside me had toughened up somewhere along the way. Too much time went by, too many nights where I couldn't get that basement out of my head. One day when he was at school, I decided it was time to go down and look.

"Keith had always kept his key to the basement door hidden under a lamp in his bedroom. He thought I didn't know, but I did. So that day I went and got it, and I went to the basement door and unlocked it.

"I stood for a long time at the top of the stairs, looking down into the darkness. Wrestling with myself. Then I turned on the light and I went down those stairs."

She stops speaking for so long that I am afraid she has lost sense of the here and now, that she is trapped in that past moment. I almost reach out to touch her arm when she begins speaking again.

"I waited for him to come home from school. When he came in the door, I told him that I'd gone into the basement. What I'd found. I told him that he'd saved my life and set me free, and that he was my son. So I wouldn't tell. But I told him I could no longer let him live under my roof.

"I wasn't sure if he would believe me, at first. About not telling what I'd found, I mean." Her smile is bemused. "I suppose there was something, some part of him, that loved me. I don't know if it was because I was his mother, or if it was because he felt that he needed something he could hold on to, something that would remind him he was still a human being. Whichever it was, he barely said a word. He packed up his things, grabbed a few items from the basement, kissed me on the cheek, and told me he loved me and understood—and walked out the door. I haven't seen him since. It's been almost thirty years."

Tears are running down her cheeks again. She looks up at Don Rawlings. "When I read about that poor girl and saw that Peter was a suspect, I knew he had to have done it. It fit, you see. With what I found in the basement." She wrings her hands. "I know I should have said something. Should have come forward. But I...he'd saved my life. He was my son. I know none of those things makes it right. It seemed right at the time, somehow. Now..." She sighs a sigh that seems to contain decades of exhaustion. "Now I'm old. And I'm tired. Tired of all the pain and secrets and nightmares."

"What did you see in the basement, Patricia?" I ask her.

She looks into my eyes, fiddling with the gold necklace.

"Go and see for yourself. I haven't opened that door for nearly thirty years. It's time to open it now."

She pulls the necklace I have been watching her twist up over her head. Attached to it is a large key. She hands it to me.

"Go ahead. Open that door. It's time to let the sunlight in."

54

I BELIEVE WHAT Patricia has said. That no one has entered through this door for a long, long time. The lock resists the turn of the key. It probably hasn't been opened for almost thirty years. Alan works on it, alternating between being a picture of concentration and cursing like a mine worker.

"Ah..." he says, followed by the click of the lock. "Got it."

He stands up and swings the door wide. I see a set of wooden stairs, leading down into darkness. For the first time, the question occurs to me.

"Patricia, this is California. This house didn't come with this basement. Did Keith put it in?"

"His grandfather did." She points to the left side of the door. "Do you see the discoloration on the wall there? Keith said a fake shelf on hinges used to hide the door. I don't know why he ever took it off." She is standing back, away from the opening to the basement. Afraid. "You'll find that the stairway leads down to a walkway. The basement is not actually right underneath the house. Keith said his grandfather built it that way on purpose. Due to the earthquakes."

"Have you been down there since the '91 quake?" Jenny asks.

"I haven't been down there since that day. Light is on the wall to the right. Be careful." She heads back to the living room at a fast pace. Not a run, but close.

Jenny looks over at me, eyebrows raised. "That's not good, Smoky. There's a reason we don't have basements in California. Reasons called 'seismic events.' It might not be safe down there."

I think about what she's saying. But only for a minute. "I can't wait, Jenny. I need to see what's in that basement."

She looks at me for a second, and nods. "Me too." A faint smile. "But you go first."

I head down the stairs, followed by everyone else. The clopping sound of shoes on wood is muffled the farther down we go. I assume it is the dirt around and above us, natural soundproofing. It is cool down here. Cool, quiet, and alone.

It's as Patricia said. At the bottom of the stairs, we find ourselves in a narrow hallway of concrete. Approximately twenty feet away, I can see a shadow in the shape of a door. It takes just a few moments to reach, and I see a light switch outside it. I turn on the light and all of us enter.

"Wow," James says. "Will you look at all that?"

It is a large room, about five hundred square feet. Nothing about it is decorated or distinct. It's a thing of gray concrete, stark lighting, and utilitarian furniture.

What had drawn James's remark was what he saw against the far left wall.

I walk toward it, amazed. The wall is covered, ceiling to floor, with life-size professional diagrams of the human body. All precisely labeled, starting first with the ex-

terior, a fully fleshed body. Then skin removed, showing
the muscular system, followed by more diagrams showing the internal organs in detail.

I move closer to this wall, and in doing so notice a far
wall, which had been obscured by the bad lighting. What
I see on that other wall sends a jolt through my system.

"Everyone," I say, "look at this."

This wall had been painted white, so as to emphasize
the black of the lettering on it:

The Commandments of the Ripper:

*1. Most of humanity are cattle. You are of the ancient
predators, the original hunters. Never let the morality of the
cattle deter you from the mission.*

*2. It is never a sin to kill a whore. They are the spawn
of the devil, and a boil upon the skin of society.*

*3. When you kill a whore, and you have moved from
the shadows, kill her in the most ghastly way possible, as a
lesson to her fellow whores.*

*4. Feel no guilt if you exult in the murder of a whore.
You are from the ancient line, and you are a meat-eater.
Your bloodlust is natural.*

*5. All women have it in them to become whores. Take
a woman only to pass on the line. Never allow them to
confuse your mind or heart. They are breeders, nothing
more.*

*6. If the teachings are passed on, they may be passed
on only to a son, NEVER a daughter.*

*7. Each Ripper must find his own Abberline. You
must be hunted if you are to keep your senses honed, your
skills sharp.*

*8. Until you find your Abberline, you must keep your
work hidden from view.*

9. Die rather than be caged.

10. The descendants of the Shadow Man are fearless. They satiate their needs without hesitation or compunction. Always strive to exemplify this. To seek out the calculated risk, the gamble that makes your blood sing.

11. Never forget that you descend from him—the Shadow Man.

"God damn," Don whispers.

I'm inclined to agree.

"Look over here," Alan says.

There are three rows of shelving in the room.

"More anatomy. All kinds of texts on Jack the Ripper." He peers closer, pulls something off one of the shelves, opens it up. "I thought so." He looks at me. "Journals." He flips through the pages, stopping at one. He holds it out for me to see.

Taped inside are a series of black-and-white photographs, stretched out over a number of pages. They show a young woman bound to a table and gagged. The walls in the photo look like this room. I stop for a moment, walk around the shelves.

"Alan," I say. He moves to me and I point to the table in front of us, then to the photo.

"Damn," he says, his face tightening. "That's right here."

The series of pictures show the rape, torture, and evisceration of the young woman. They all have a ghastly "how to" look to them. As though the masked man in the photographs is delivering a seminar on suffering and depravity.

"Jesus," I say. "How many of these are there?"

"Close to a hundred, I'd guess."
I flip past the pictures to one of the written entries.

>*Peter is showing himself to be of the line, even at eight. He watched as I murdered the whore, taking photos and asking intelligent questions throughout. He was especially interested in the mechanics of the evisceration. I am happy to note that his vomiting problem, which has been gone for a year now, shows no signs of resurfacing.*

I move along to another entry.

>*I brought Peter along on the hunt this time. It wasn't a school night, and I feel it's important that he begin to be more personally involved. He is ten, after all. I was pleased. He is gifted.*
>
>*Side note—he was embarrassed when I stripped the whore down and he noticed that his penis had gotten hard. I explained the mechanics of this to him and forced the whore to pleasure him with her hand. He was fascinated and seemed to enjoy this. He thanked me afterward.*

And more:

>*Peter asked me today how old I was when I killed my first whore. I hesitated to tell him the full truth of it. He is so filled with the strength of our line, I was afraid of revealing my father's weakness to him. I feared he might begin to doubt the nobility of our blood. In the end, I told him all: How my father had hidden the secret of our lineage from me. How I had only discovered the truth through my own research of our genealogy. About my father's weak denials when I confronted him with what*

*I had found. How he and my mother had attempted to
make me think I was crazy. I needn't have worried about
Peter. The look of adoration he gave me when I told him
my tale of perseverance, of my search for truth and of the
vengeance I exacted on my father, is something I will
cherish forever.*

"Christ," Alan mutters. "It's just like Patricia said. He
started warping the kid early."

"Never had a chance," James remarks. "Not that it
matters now. It's been too long. He's unsalvageable."

I don't respond. My ears are filled with a roaring noise,
and I am dizzy. Electric shocks dance through my body. I
have flipped to the last page in the book, and the signature I see there has my mind spinning in terror, rage, disbelief, shame, and betrayal.

Maybe it's just a coincidence, I think to myself.

I know it's not.

I look up at the commandments painted on the wall,
reading number seven again: *7. Each Ripper must find his
own Abberline. You must be hunted if you are to keep your senses
honed, your skills sharp.*

"Smoky?" Alan's voice is sharp, concerned. "What's
the matter?"

I don't say anything. Just hand him the journal, pointing at the signature I had seen. *Keith Hillstead,* it was
signed.

Hillstead.

Son Peter.

I knew who Jack Jr. was. And he knew me.

Intimately.

55

MONSTERS WEARING HUMAN masks, and acting their parts to perfection.

Peter Hillstead has fooled everyone, including me. Worse, he has been with me in my moments of greatest vulnerability.

But there is something even more terrible, something that makes me want to vomit as I realize it. He has not only fooled me, used me, and violated me—he has also helped me. To his own ends, true, but still ... The thought that some part of me is better for having met him makes me want to scream and puke and shower for a year.

"I know who he is," I say, answering Alan's question.

Shocked silence, followed by a babble of voices. Alan shushes them all.

"What are you talking about?"

I point at the signature on the final page of the journal. "Keith Hillstead. His son's name is Peter. My shrink's name is Peter Hillstead."

Alan looks doubtful. "That could be pure coincidence, Smoky."

"No. I can be a hundred percent certain if I can see photos of Keith and Peter Hillstead. But the ages match up."

"God damn," James mutters.

I head toward the stairs. "Come on."

Patricia is still in the living room. "Ms. Connolly? Do you have a picture somewhere of Keith Hillstead? And of your son?"

She tilts her head, looking into my eyes. "You've found something, haven't you?"

"Yes, ma'am. But if I could see pictures of Keith and Peter, I could be sure."

She lifts herself out of her chair. "I found out after he left that Peter had taken all the photos I had of him. I do have one of Keith. It's buried at the bottom of a drawer, but I kept it to remind me what evil looks like. Hold on for a moment."

She heads toward her bedroom, returning with an eight-by-ten photograph. "Here it is," she says, handing it to me. "Handsome as the devil. Which makes sense, I suppose, since he and the devil were such good friends."

When I look at the photograph, a chill runs through me. Any remaining doubt evaporates. I see those electric blue eyes, as shocking and beautiful in this portrait as Peter's are in real life. "They look almost exactly alike." I nod to James. "I'm sure now. Peter Hillstead is Keith Hillstead's son."

"So, you mean...we know who he is? The man who killed Renee?"

Don Rawlings is asking this question. Hope is trying to dawn in his eyes, but he is fighting it, reining it in, like a man trying to lasso a sunrise. Even with the turmoil churning inside me, I manage to give him a smile.

"That's right."

I watch ten years of age melt away from him. His eyes become even clearer, his face determined. "What do you want me to do?"

"I need you and Jenny to process the hell out of that basement. And this house. If we can find fingerprints to match up to Peter's…" I don't have to elaborate. They understand. We know who Jack Jr. is, but knowing and proving it in a court of law are two different things.

"We're on it," Jenny replies. "Where are you guys headed?"

"Back to LA to catch this fucker."

I feel a touch on my arm. In the blitzkrieg of excitement, I had almost forgotten that Patricia Connolly was there.

"Promise me something, Agent Barrett?"

"If I can, Ms. Connolly."

"I know Peter is a bad man now. He was probably doomed the moment his father made him set foot in that basement. But if you have to kill him…promise me you'll make it quick."

I look at Patricia and I see what I might have become. Had I continued to sit in my bedroom, staring at my scars in the mirror. If I had not killed myself, I would have become as she is: a ghost, made of smoke, chained by memories of pain. Waiting for one good gust of wind to blow her away into nothing.

"If it comes to that, Patricia, I'll do my best."

She touches my arm, this woman of gray, and sits back down in her chair. I imagine she will be found dead in that chair one day, having dozed off and never awoken.

"Can you give us a ride to the airport, Jenny?"

"You bet."

I look at James and Alan. "Let's go and end this."

56

I'M ON THE phone with Leo as we hurtle through the air, halfway back to LA.

"Are you serious?" he's asking me.

I have just finished filling him in on what we found at the house in Concord.

"I'm afraid so. I need you to start putting together a warrant. It needs to cover his office and his home. Flesh it out, and when we arrive I'll fill in the details."

"Right."

"Dig up a photo of Hillstead. Then I want you to have the photographs that have been culled from the sex parties compared against that, and only that."

"I'm on it."

"Good. Let everyone know what's happening. I have to call AD Jones. We should be back in a little over an hour."

"See you then, boss."

I hang up and dial into reception. They connect me with Shirley. "I need to speak to him now, Shirley. Wherever he is, whatever he's doing. It's important."

She doesn't ask or argue. Shirley knows I do not cry wolf. Within the next thirty seconds, I'm on the phone with AD Jones.

"What's happening?" he asks.

I give him the whole story. Concord. Keith Hillstead. The basement and what we found there. Ending with the revelation about Peter.

Stunned silence. Then I have to hold the phone away from my ear for a moment as he rants and raves and curses.

"So the primary shrink for our agents in LA for the last decade—is a serial killer? That's what you're telling me?"

"Yes, sir. That is what I'm telling you."

A moment of silence, then: "Tell me the plan." His outbursts are over. Time for business.

"SFPD is processing the scene in Concord. Hopefully we'll find Peter's prints in that house. Even better, in the basement."

"Prints? After nearly thirty years?"

"Sure. There's a case of prints being developed off porous paper after forty years. I also have James putting together a warrant for his home and office, which I'll finish once we arrive. Once we have the warrant, I want to hit the search like gangbusters."

"What do you want to do with Hillstead?"

I understand his question. We don't have the evidence needed to arrest him, much less convict. "I'll have him pulled in and detained for questioning while we do the searches. Between that and the house in San Francisco we should be able to turn up something that we can make a formal arrest with."

"Bring me the warrant when you get here. I'll walk it through personally."

"Yes, sir."

He hangs up. I look at James and Alan. "It's all a go. Now we just need to get this damn plane to fly faster."

* * *

When the plane lands, we hit the ground running. Ten minutes later, we are speeding down the 405 freeway. I call Leo again.

"We're in the car on our way there. Do you have the basics of the warrant ready for me?"

"All you'll have to do is fill in some specifics and print it off."

"Good."

My cell phone rings after we've pulled up to the FBI building and are heading toward the entrance.

"This is Agent Barrett."

"Greetings, Agent Barrett." The voice is clear and undisguised.

I motion for everyone to be silent.

"Hello, Dr. Hillstead."

"Bravo to you, Smoky. Bravo. I have to say, I wondered if Renee Parker would ever come back to haunt me. I broke one of the commandments with her—I hadn't found you yet, but I displayed my work regardless. I just couldn't *help* myself. I thought after twenty-five years... ah well. Best-laid plans. And giving Street the locket and book, well... he begged me for *something*. And he really did deserve a token. He was such a good student. Very enthusiastic." He chuckles. "Of course, I played around with the idea of trying to pin her murder on him, but here we are. Ah well."

His voice is the same, but its tone and the way he uses it are different. He speaks with a kind of sick frivolity and a properness I never heard from him in his office.

"You know?" I ask.

"Of course I know. I just stated that I have wondered

about Renee, did I not? It wouldn't have been prudent of me to wonder and not prepare for this eventuality. Of course, this changes the game for good."

"How is that?"

"Why—you know my identity. You know who I am. That means the end of me. Me and mine have always existed in the shadows, Agent Barrett. We don't aspire to the light, nor do we thrive in it. Such a shame too. Do you know how many years I had to sit and listen to you people whine, while I searched for my Abberline? The endless hours of pretending to care, and worse—having to truly help these weak and broken worms, just so I could continue my search?" He sighs. "And find you I did. Perhaps I did *too* well."

"It doesn't have to be that way, Dr. Hillstead. I can bring you in."

He chuckles. "I don't think so, Smoky. We'll address that in a moment. First, I have a confession to make to you. Do you remember that night with Joseph Sands, my dear?"

I am calm. His words don't anger me. "You know I do, Peter."

"Did you ever read the file? In full, I mean? Including the notes regarding his ingress into your home?"

"I read the file. Minus the ballistics report you had removed, of course. Why?"

Silence. I imagine I can hear him smiling. "Do you remember if there were any signs of forced entry?"

I am about to tell him that I am bored of this. That I want to know where he is. Something stops me. I think about what he said and try to recall what I had read. I remember. "There weren't any signs of forced entry."

"That's correct. Would you like to know why?"

I don't respond.

I think of Ronnie Barnes, the dates. Barnes died on the nineteenth and Sands killed my family on the nineteenth.

"For the most obvious reason, Smoky. He had a key. Why force a lock if you can just walk in the door?" He laughs. "You're allowed one guess as to how he acquired that key." A pause. "Why—from *me,* dearest Smoky. From me."

I can see my reaction in James's and Alan's eyes. Alan takes one step away from me, and looks very, very cautious. I'm not surprised. I have been stricken speechless by the need to murder that runs through me, replacing the blood in my veins.

My head is filled with the roar of shotguns. My eyes are burning, and the rage—it is that same rage I felt tied to the bed as Joseph Sands hurt and destroyed my Matt.

My Matt and my Alexa, the loves of my life. The scars that disfigured my face and body, that twist my heart and nearly crippled my soul. Months of nightmares, waking screaming, oceans of tears. Funerals and gravestones, the smell of cemetery dirt. Cigarettes and despair and the kindness of strangers.

This monster, smiling at the other end of this phone, he has left a legacy of ruination. Don Rawlings. Me. Bonnie. He has crumbled our hopes in his hands like bread, feeding the crumbs to things that slink through the dark. He's fed on our pain like a ghoul at a grave.

He is not all the evil in the world. I know this. But for now he is the source of it in mine. He is my rape, Matt's screams, the look of surprise as my bullet killed Alexa. He is the dead babies Don Rawlings dreams of, the end of my childhood friend, Callie lying in the hospital, and the gray exhaustion of his mother as she withers away, an ancient rose.

"Where are you?" I whisper.

I can hear his smile. "Touched a nerve there, I think. Good." He pauses. "It was your last test, Smoky. If you could survive Sands, then you truly were my Abberline." His voice sounds almost gentle.

Wistful.

"Where are you?" I repeat.

He laughs. "I will tell you where I am, but first I need to introduce you to someone. Say hello to Agent Barrett."

I hear the phone come up against an ear. "S-Smoky?"

I am jolted, a shock from a car battery.

Elaina. Everything has moved so fast, Keenan and Shantz haven't been replaced yet. I curse myself, *stupid, stupid, stupid!*

"I have her here with me, Smoky. Along with someone else, someone smaller. Someone who can't talk on the phone because, well—she can't talk these days." He laughs. "Can you say déjà vu?"

I am drowning. I'm surrounded by air, but I can't breathe. Time is now moving to the beat of my heart, one long, slow *lub-a-dub* after another. This isn't fear I'm feeling, it's terror. Soul-drenching, gut-grinding, hysterical, babbling terror. I'm surprised that my voice is calm when I speak.

"Where are you, Peter? Just tell me, and I'll come to you." I don't ask him not to harm them. I wouldn't believe him anyway.

"Here are the rules, Smoky. I'm at my home. Elaina is naked and tied to my bed. Little Bonnie is snuggled in my arms. Sound familiar? If you are not here in twenty-five minutes, I will kill Elaina, and things for Bonnie will get very familiar indeed. If I see any police or SWAT team personnel, or even suspect they are here, I will kill them both.

You may bring your team, but otherwise, this is between you and me. Do you understand?"

"Yes."

"Good. Time starts—now."

He hangs up.

"What the hell is going on?" Alan asks.

I don't answer. I look at Alan. His eyes are intense, worried, ready. Alan was always ready. Especially when it came to being a friend. I feel my own breathing, in and out, in and out.

A great, disconnected calm has settled over me. I'm on a beach, alone, with a seashell pressed to my ear. It gives off that faint, seashell roar. Is this shock? I wonder.

I don't think so. I don't think so at all. This is Hillstead, getting what he's wanted all along.

Me as him. Ready to murder without thought, regret, or moral quandary. Ready to feel about killing like I would about pulling a weed.

I put my hands on Alan's shoulders, look up into his face. "Listen to me, Alan. I'm going to tell you something, and I need you to be ready for it. I need you to hold it together. I'm going to take care of it."

He doesn't speak. It all comes out in his eyes, the beginning of alarm, the start of understanding.

"He's got Elaina and Bonnie," I say.

My hands are still on his shoulders and I feel the muscles spasm, feel his whole body shake once, hard. His eyes never leave mine. "He's got them, and he wants me, and we're going to where he has them. Once we're there, whatever it takes, we make him dead and them okay." I grip his shoulders, really dig into them. "Do you understand me? I'm going to take care of it."

He looks at me for a long time. James is quiet, waiting.

"He's going to try to take himself out and take you with him," Alan says.

I nod. "I know. I guess I'll have to be faster."

He reaches up, takes my hands. He holds them for a moment. God, he has big, hard hands. Even so, his touch is soft. "Be faster, Smoky." His voice cracks.

He drops my hands and steps away. Pulls out his gun, checks the clip, and starts moving toward the car.

"Let's go," he says.

Bending, not breaking.

But we break? the dragon asks. *We crunch his bones?*

It's a rhetorical question; I don't reply.

I dial Tommy on the way over.

"You still following me?" I ask.

"Yeah."

"Things have changed." I bring him up to date.

"What do you want me to do?"

"I want you to go to his address and wait. If you see him come out by himself, that means he got past us."

"And?"

"And if that happens, I want you to take him out."

A long pause. Then he replies, in his usual way. "You got it."

"Thanks, Tommy."

"Hey, Smoky. Don't get shot." He pauses. "I still want to see if it's going to go anywhere." He hangs up.

We pull into the driveway. Everything looks normal. Nice and quiet, the picture of suburbia. As I turn off the car, my cell phone rings.

"Barrett."

"You got here ahead of time, Smoky. I'm so proud! Now, let me inform you of how this is going to work. You're going to come in through the front door. Your friends are going to stay outside. If anything other than just those two things happen, I will kill Elaina and young Bonnie. Clear?"

"Clear."

"Well, enter, then, enter!"

The signal ends. I pull out my gun, checking it once, letting it find a place in my hand. Dark, sleek, black steel bird of death. I can almost feel it hum.

"I go in, you stay out. Those are his rules."

"I don't want to hear that shit," Alan says. Desperation gives his voice an edge.

I look at him. Really look at him. "I'm going to take care of it, Alan." I let him see the dragon, hear her. I hold up my gun. "I won't miss."

He looks at the gun. Licks his lips. His face is both grim and helpless, a war in futility, a rage of fear. But he swallows and nods. I glance at James. He nods as well.

What else is there to say? I turn away from them, gun hand at my side, and walk up the path to Hillstead's front door. I put a hand on the knob and turn it. My heart is pounding in my chest, my blood is shooting through my veins. I am both afraid and exhilarated. I enter his home, shutting the door behind me.

"Come on upstairs, Smoky dear," I hear Hillstead say. His voice is coming from the second floor.

I move up the stairs slowly. My neck is sweating. I get to the top.

"In here, Agent Barrett."

I move into the bedroom, gun raised. What I see does what it is calculated to do: It freezes me with fear.

Elaina is tied to the bed. She is naked, hands and feet

bound. Bile rises in my throat as I see he has already cut on her. He has carved a game of tic-tac-toe into the skin of her stomach. He has slashed a line above her breasts. I look into her eyes and I'm relieved by what I see there. She's terrified, but she's still defiant. This means Hillstead hasn't gotten down to it yet. He hasn't broken her.

Peter sits at the foot of the bed, in a padded chair. Bonnie is on his lap. He's holding a knife at her jugular. She, too, is defiant, but her eyes contain something additional that Elaina's do not: hate. If she could kill this man who murdered her mother, she would.

"Déjà vu, is it not, Agent Barrett? You'll notice I haven't touched Elaina's face yet." He chuckles. "I thought I'd incorporate various elements of your own pain and psychosis here. We have the destruction of something lovely, a recurring area of difficulty you seem to have. We have the scarring and disfigurement. And finally, perhaps best of all, we have your daughter Alexa, the human shield."

I bring up my gun, but he moves Bonnie's head to block his own. The knife tip presses harder and a dot of blood appears at her throat.

"Now, let's not be hasty," he says. "I have a chair for you too. Sit down. Take a load off, as they say." His face reappears, and he smiles. "It will be just like old times."

Crunch his bones! the dragon snarls.

Hush, I tell her. I need to concentrate.

I look around, see the chair he's indicated. It's facing him, of course. As he said, just like old times. I go over and sit down.

"Planning to analyze me some more, Peter?" I ask.

He laughs and shakes his head. "We're past that now, both of us. I have no more opinions to give you about yourself."

"So what do you want, then?"

His eyes twinkle. It's a hideous sight, in the context of the moment. "I want to talk to you, Smoky. And then I want to see what happens."

I look at his knees. I could shoot them out, in the space of a single blink. Gun up, *bam-bam,* finish it with a shot to the head. Just breathe in and exhale, three squeezes, bye-bye, Peter.

I start the motion, even as I'm thinking it. The gun barrel rises, and I *know* that it's lined up right, know it in a visceral place. I know on a less-than-conscious level how many pounds of pressure will be required to pull the trigger. I know how many inches I'll have to move the barrel after the first shot in order to shoot out the other knee. This is all *nonthought,* unconscious advanced calculus.

Except that it's not.

Because the hand that grips the gun . . . *trembles.*

And then it doesn't just tremble—it *shakes.*

I close my eyes and lower my hand. Peter laughs out loud.

"Smoky! Perhaps I spoke too soon! Perhaps we have therapy to do yet."

I feel panic coming. It's riding in, slow, like a dark wave on some night beach. I glance at Bonnie's face and am startled to see that she is looking right at me. Her eyes are filled with trust.

I blink, and her face blurs. Blink again. She becomes Alexa.

Angry eyes. No trust there.

Alexa knows better, after all.

My ears are filled with a faint ringing.

Ringing? No . . . I cock my head, listening. It's a voice. Too far away and faint to make out.

"Smoky? Are you with us?"

Hillstead's voice brings back Bonnie's face.

I realize with a shock that I am losing my mind. Right here, right now. Right when I'm needed most.

Dear God.

I clear my throat and force myself to speak. "You—you said you wanted to talk. So talk, then." It doesn't sound convincing, but at least it sounds sane.

I'm drenched in sweat.

He pauses. "Do you think," he starts, "that I regret the situation I find myself in? If you do, then you'd be wrong. My father, he taught me to hold to a standard. One of his favorite sayings was: 'It's not how long you live—it's how excellently you killed while you were alive.'" He squints at me. "Do you understand? Being true to my heritage, to the example of the Shadow Man, is not just about killing whores and taunting the FBI. It's about a certain...*flair*. It's about the character of murder, not just the act." His voice is proud. "We cut you with the finest silver and drink your blood from designer crystal. We strangle you with silk while dressed in Armani." He peeks out from behind Bonnie. "Any fool can murder. My ancestors and myself? We make *history*. We become immortal."

Buy time, I think. Because I hear that faint voice in my head again, and I know—I *know*—that whatever it's saying is important.

"You don't have any children," I say. "So it stops with you. So much for immortality."

He shrugs. "These genes will surface again. Who's to say that he didn't cast his seed in other places? Who's to say I didn't?" He smiles. "I was not the first, I doubt I'll be the last. Our race will survive."

A single, terrible thought occurs to me. Is it possible that I don't *want* to save Bonnie? That some part of me thinks that that wouldn't be fair to Alexa?

My hand shakes in my lap, spasms around the gun butt.

The voice in my head is still faint but has become more urgent.

I frown at Hillstead. "Race? What race?"

"The original hunters. The predators who walk on two legs."

"Ah, right. That bullshit."

I miss a breath as his knuckles tighten on the knife at Bonnie's throat. But then they relax and he chuckles.

"The point of it all, Smoky-mine, is this: It doesn't matter that you caught me. In the end, I was true. That's all that counts. Far truer than my father—he never found his Abberline. And my acolytes?" I get the sense of a bird preening, self-satisfied. "*That* is a definite original." He peeks at me again. "Besides, I have an offer or two to make you. A little bit of final fun."

For the first time since my gun hand shook, the voice in my head goes quiet. Unease creeps in. "What kind of offer?"

"Some scars for a life, Smoky. I want to leave my mark on you and give you something in return."

"What the fuck are you talking about?"

"If I were to tell you, take your gun and shoot yourself and I'll let Bonnie and Elaina go, would you believe me?"

"Of course not."

"Yes. But—if I were to tell you, take a knife and cut your face and I'll let Elaina go . . . ?"

My unease increases. I start to sweat again.

"Ahhhhh . . . see? That's the fun part of dealing in these kinds of stakes, Smoky. You'd *have* to think about it, wouldn't you?" He laughs. "The possibilities abound. Do nothing, continue as we are, perhaps you get them out of this, perhaps they both die. Cut yourself, perhaps

I'm lying and we continue as we are...but then you'll only have cut yourself trying. Not exactly death, now, is it? Or cut yourself, and perhaps I *do* let her go—and the very chance of this happening means scenario number two is worth considering. Worse still, for you, it *is possible* that I'm telling the truth. It's believable that I'd trade Elaina for the joy of making you scar yourself further, isn't it? Particularly when I keep this little cutie as a shield?"

I still haven't replied. The unease has become nausea, a greasy roiling in my stomach. He's not wrong. I would think about it. Hillstead's made the stakes horrible but bearable. As with any gamble, I could lose, but the prize if I won...worth rolling the dice?

Probably, yeah.

No, no, no! the dragon cries. *Crunch his bones!*

Shut up, I say.

The other voice remains quiet. It's still there, it's just silent. Waiting.

"Are you making that offer, Peter?" I ask.

"Of course I am. There's a knife between the cushion and arm of the chair."

I transfer the gun to my lap and reach with my fingers along the side of the cushion. I feel it. Cold steel. I fumble until I find the handle, grab it, and draw the knife out.

"Look at it."

I do. It's a hunting knife. Made to cut flesh.

"Scars," Hillstead murmurs. "Reminders. Like... rings on a tree, marking times gone by." One eye peeks out from behind Bonnie's head and fixes on me. I see it moving, can almost feel it on my face. Like soft hands tracing my scars. Loving them, in a way, I realize. "I want to put my mark on you, my Abberline. I want you to see me when you look in the mirror. Forever."

"And if I do?"

"Then I will let you use that knife to cut Elaina free. Whatever else happens, she will walk out of here, alive and well."

Elaina is trying to talk through her gag. I look over at her. She is shaking her head. *No,* her eyes are saying. *No, no, no . . .*

I look at the knife. Think about my face, the road map of pain it's become. It's meant the loss of everything. That's what my scars have been reminders of. Perhaps the scar he wants will be a reminder of saving Elaina. Perhaps it will just be another scar. Perhaps we'll all die here and I'll be buried with it as an unhealed wound.

Perhaps I'll put the gun to my own head and pull the trigger. Would my hand shake then? If it was me I was shooting at?

The world spins, Bonnie becomes Alexa, Alexa becomes Bonnie, and oceans roar inside my head. I feel both peaceful and terrified.

Losing my mind, yes, sir. No bout adout it.

I turn away from Elaina's eyes.

"Where?" I ask.

That peeking eye widens. I see the edge of it crinkle. He's smiling.

"A simple request, Smoky-mine. We'll keep the one side free of scars. I like to think of you as beauty in one profile, beast in the other. So, on the left. One single line, from below your eye to the corner of that beautiful mouth."

"And if I do this, then I get to cut Elaina free?"

"So I've said." He shrugs. "I could be lying, of course."

I hesitate, and then I bring up the knife. There was never any question. Why delay?

Don't delay, do it today! the crazy-me cackles. *Cut yourself now, and we'll throw in an Easy-Bake oven—free!*

I put the tip under my left eye, feel its coldness. Funny, I think. Nothing feels quite as cold, quite as unfeeling as a knife when its edge is against your flesh. A knife is the ultimate soldier, it will follow any order and doesn't care what use it's put to so long as it gets to *cut*.

"Make sure it's deep," Hillstead says. "I want to see bone when you're done."

Joseph Sands wanted me to touch his face. Peter Hillstead wants me to touch my own, and I am, I am cutting, deep and decisive. The pain is exquisite. The blade is razor-sharp; it slices me open with a yawn, bored, no heavy lifting involved. The line is long and there is blood, lots of it, running down my face. A rivulet runs over my lips. I taste the fine wine of me.

The dragon screams.

Hillstead is captivated. That one eye is wide. Taking it all in, drinking it down. Feeding his needs.

I give him a moment to appreciate it.

I point the knife at him. "So? Can I cut Elaina loose?"

His eye is still wide. Blood drips from my chin and the eye follows it.

"So beautiful..." he breathes.

Drip, drip, drip. He's captivated by my blood-brook.

"Peter." The eye pulls itself away from my gore, reluctant. "Can I cut her loose?"

A crinkle. He's smiling again. "Well..." he says, drawing it out. "No. I don't think so. No."

I fill with despair and contempt at the same time. "So predictable," I say. "If you were going to be original, you would have let Elaina go. Not doing it—that's what I'd expect."

He shrugs. "Can't please everyone."

"You can still please me."

"How?"

"By dying, Peter. By dying."

Bold words, I think, but I'm still afraid of my gun.

He laughs. "Fair enough, Smoky. Now we will truly get down to it." One hand grips the back of Bonnie's neck. The other has the knife, still at her throat. "You gave me what I wanted. Time to end this."

I drop the knife. He follows it as it falls to the floor, clattering.

I follow it too, mesmerized by the shine of it, by the slick of my blood on its oh-so-keen edge.

I squint. Cock my head. The voice in my head is back, and it's nearer.

I don't look at him as I answer. "How is this going to end, Peter?"

"Why, the only way it can, Smoky. One way, or the other."

I glance at him. I exist on two levels. One part of me looks at Hillstead, listens to him, responds. The other strains, strains, strains to hear the voice.

"What does that mean, 'One way, or the other'?"

The eye crinkles.

"I'm going to cut Bonnie's throat, Smoky. I'm going to count to ten, and then I'm going to slice her from ear to ear, give her a wide, wet, weeping grin. Unless you kill me first, of course." The knife wiggles. "Whatever happens, in the end, I feel certain you'll shoot me and I will die. So, 'one way'? You shoot me *before* I get to ten, Bonnie lives. 'Or the other'?" He glances at my gun hand. "Alexa all over again. Bonnie dies, another daughter lost. You still kill me . . . but too late, too late."

And now I hear the voice.

Mommy.

"All you have to do, Smoky-mine..." His head appears. He's grinning. "Is let me help you one last time."

Listen to me, Mommy. You can do it. It's okay.

I am emptying out inside. Becoming still, still, still.

"Fuck you."

"I don't think so." He smiles even wider. "Make no mistake about it, Smoky. I'm going to give you ten seconds, and then I'm going to kill her. I'm going to take my knife and slice her pretty little throat wide open. The only chance she has is you taking your shot. Of course, you might miss and kill her, just as you did with Alexa. You might murder another child with your gun."

Blood drips from my face. Bonnie's eyes fill my mind.

But it's Alexa who fills my soul.

Everything beautiful about her comes to me. All at once. Every moment of seeing her smile, holding her close, smelling her hair. Every tear I ever wiped away, every angel kiss she ever gave me. Memories of her have been coming back to me lately, it's true. But these are ten thousand times more vivid. Ten million times stronger.

All gone, gone forever.

"Come *on*, Special Agent Barrett. I'm counting the seconds down now."

I am swimming in an ocean of tears, and it has no horizon.

So, the question once again: Will my hand shake if I point the gun at myself? I could end it that way. Quick. Easy.

An end to the memories. I want that more than anything—to un-know my past.

"You were my Abberline, Smoky. You should be happy—you are the best of the best. No one has caught any of us, dating all the way back to my ancestor. I applaud your ploy with the flesh in the jar. An obvious lie, but I will admit—you made me angry. And catching Robert, well...he was sloppy, so I won't call it genius on your part. But you are gifted, Smoky-mine. So very gifted."

I can barely hear him. There is a roaring in my ears, threatening to drown out the world. It's me, pounding my fists against myself until they're bloody. Me, screaming forever. Me, howling and crusing and dying and—

Mommy!

The roaring stops.

Silence.

I see her out of the corner of my eye. But I cannot look at her. No.

I'm too ashamed.

It's okay, Mommy. It's okay. You just need to remember the important thing.

What? That I failed you? That I killed you? That I lived and you didn't? That—worst of all—life went on?

Shame fills me, roots its snout into every part of me. Burrows down into the depths of me.

This is pain, absolute and infinite.

Here we are, I think. Finality. The place where I lose for good. Fade to black.

I begin to pass out.

Before I can, Alexa smiles.

It is a blazing sun. A golden juggernaut of light.

No, Mommy. Remember the love.

It's as if someone hit a pause button. All the pain, all the shame, stops. Suspends.

Now there is stillness.

A moment of time is passing, and I'm watching it go by. *Lub,* my heart begins to say, and then, *a dub,* it finishes, a single beat.

Standing there, right in front of me, is Alexa. No longer blurred, a shadow, or a brief moment in a dream.

My beautiful Alexa, shimmering.

"Hi, Mommy," she says.

"Hi, baby," I whisper.

I know she is not really there. I also know she is as there as there can be.

"You have to choose, Mommy," she says, her voice soft. "Once and for all."

"What do you mean, sweetheart?"

She leans forward and grabs my hands in hers. Tenderness washes off her, rolls over me. So beautiful it makes me wince.

"To *live*, Mommy."

Truth, in my experience, arrives without fanfare, but it arrives in an instant and changes everything forever. Real truth is always simple.

This truth is no different.

A choice between life or death is a choice between Alexa and Hillstead.

Between Matt and Sands.

Alexa smiles, nods . . . and disappears.

And just like that, from one heartbeat to the next, I'm sane. With that truth, my madness leaves me.

Time begins again.

Hillstead is still jabbering away, but I can't hear what he's saying. I feel as though I am in a chamber of silence. A world where everything else moves at its regular rate but my own thoughts are dreamy, like doing tai chi at the bottom of a swimming pool.

Bonnie's eyes have not left mine from the moment I entered the room. Full of terror, full of trust. I look at her now, now that I am sane. I really see her.

She's beautiful, Mommy.

"Yes, she is, honey," I murmur.

Hillstead's eyes narrow. This time I can hear him. "Who are you talking to, Smoky-mine? Losing it for good now? Better pull it together. Just three more seconds before little Bonnie starts smiling below the chin."

This shot I must make to save her, it will be difficult. Approximately one quarter of Hillstead's head is visible. The rest is hidden behind Bonnie.

The calculations begin whirring away inside me, spinning slow at first, then picking up speed.

The dragon senses her time is coming and she purrs.

The voice of Alexa comes to me again, fitting the rhythm of the whirring like wind fits a rainstorm. *Don't worry, Mommy. Just feel it. It's in you, you just have to trust in it.*

"I don't know, Alexa," I tell her. "Two inches, an inch and a half. I just don't know. I could kill her."

I feel her ghost arms wrap around my waist from behind. One hand reaches up to touch my heart. *It's there, Mommy. You stopped trusting it, but she needs you now. And I don't mind that you need her. You asked me that in your dream, but you woke up before I could answer you. Love her, Mommy. I don't mind.* Alexa's face appears in my mind; Matt's brown eyes, pixie smile, mailman's dimples. I'm not afraid to look at her now. The hands pull away and I feel her receding behind me. Before she goes, she whispers one final thing: *Don't you understand, Mommy? You're not perfect. Do what you feel, and it'll be the best you can do. Your best is all you'll ever have to give.*

The dragon snarls, and the whirring becomes a scream, building in me like a hummingbird aflame, growing into a hawk, and then an eagle, and—

My hand stops shaking.

I raise the gun and pull the trigger without thinking about doing it.

I don't hear the *crack* of the shot. It is all visual for me. I see Bonnie's face jerk back as Hillstead's head explodes and the knife falls from his hands, and I know that I have killed her with him.

I feel a scream begin to build in me, my hands go to my head, but then Bonnie is moving toward me, hobbling with her bound feet.

She turns her left cheek to me and I see Hillstead on the floor, a bullet hole through one eye, and I understand.

I had made the shot. It was close, my bullet had grazed Bonnie's cheek, but it had found its mark. She was fine. He was dead.

My hand is trembling as I holster my weapon. James and Alan come rushing up the stairs, followed by Tommy. Alan is weeping as he unties Elaina and gets a blanket around her, while James and Tommy ask me if I am hurt. I don't reply.

I look down at him, dead on the floor. The man who provided Sands with access to my home, who was ultimately responsible for the death of my family, the scars on my face. I think about the swath of destruction his actions left behind him.

In the end, he proved his own point.

Death is always just a step away.

But then again, so is life, and all of its champions.

57

CALLIE ASKED THAT three people be here for this.
Me, Marilyn, and Elaina. Bonnie is here by default, which
seems fine with Callie.

Two days after Peter Hillstead died, Callie woke up.
It's been another two days since that, and the doctor is
preparing to test her feet for sensitivity. Callie is doing
her best to cover it, but I can tell that she is terrified.

She looks terrible. Pale, tired. But she is alive.

Now we'll find out if she's going to walk again.

The doctor holds one of those instruments everyone
has seen but can't name—like a revolving spur on the end
of a handle. He is poised to run those sharp points across
the bottom of her feet, and he looks up at Callie. "Ready?"

Elaina grips her hand on one side of the bed, I on the
other. Marilyn stands to Elaina's left. Bonnie looks on, a
worried expression on her face.

"Tickle me, honey-love."

He runs the spur across the sole of her left foot. Looks
at her. "Did you feel that?"

Her eyes widen with fear. Her voice is small. "No."

"Don't panic," he tries to reassure her. I can tell this
is not working, because her hand is crushing mine.

"Let's try the other foot." He runs the spur across it, we wait...

And then a twitch. The big toe moves. Callie holds her breath.

"Did you feel that?" he asks again.

"I'm not sure..."

"That's okay. The toe moving is an excellent sign. Let's try it again." He runs the spur across the bottom of her foot. This time, the toe twitches immediately.

"I—I felt it!" Callie exclaims. "Not a lot—but I did."

"That's very, very, very good, Callie," the doctor says, soothing. "Now I want you to try something else for me. I want you to try and move that toe for me, the one that twitched."

Callie's hands are sweating. I can feel the smallest tremble.

"Come on," Elaina soothes. "Try it. You can do it."

Callie is looking down at her big toe, an intensity of concentration that an Olympic runner couldn't match. I can feel her mental strain as something palpable.

The toe moves.

"I felt something that time!" Callie says, excited. "More of a...connectedness. Does that make sense?"

The doctor smiles. It is a big smile, a huge smile. None of us have allowed ourselves to relax into relief yet, but I can feel the possibility building. We need to hear the words from his mouth. "Yes. That makes a lot of sense. And it is very good news. There is only a five percent chance that you'll experience some impairment. Nothing that physical therapy can't handle, but I don't want you to worry if it happens. If that occurs, it'll be a matter of re-training your body to accept the messages between brain and legs." He pauses. "But I feel confident in saying this: You are not going to be paralyzed."

Callie's head goes back against her pillow and she closes her eyes, the room is filled with a chorus of "Thank God"s; it's a hurricane of relief.

Then we all stop.

Because we hear the wail.

It is the sound of someone releasing something crippling and huge and awful, a keening, and we all turn to see where it is coming from.

Bonnie. Little Bonnie is against the door of Callie's room, face red, tears practically bursting from her eyes, fist against her mouth. Trying to hold in a volcano of grief that is demanding release.

I am shocked into speechlessness. I feel as though someone has cut my heart in half with a straight razor.

Of us all, it is Bonnie who feared for Callie the most, and the sheer unexpectedness of this makes her grief all the more overwhelming. That, and my understanding of it. If Callie had been crippled, he would have won, in Bonnie's eyes. She is wailing for her mother, for me, for Elaina, for Callie, and for herself.

Callie's voice cuts through the air, a soft arrow. "Come here, honey-love," she says, with a gentleness that makes me want to stagger.

Bonnie rushes over to her bedside. She takes Callie's hand and closes her eyes and weeps against it as she rubs her cheek across the knuckles, over and over and over. Cherishing Callie's life and crying for her own world, all at the same time.

Callie murmurs to her, wordless, while the rest of us remain mute.

We couldn't speak if we wanted to.

* * *

Callie had asked to see me alone, for just a few moments.

"So," Callie says, after a space of silence. "I suppose just *everyone* knows about me and Marilyn now?"

I grin. "Pretty much."

She sighs, but it doesn't sound like a sigh of regret. "Ah, well." She's quiet for a moment. "She loves me, you know."

"I know."

"But that's not why I asked you to stay in here with me," she says.

"No? Then why?"

"There's something I need to do, and... well, I'm not quite ready to do it with Marilyn yet. Maybe never."

I look at her, puzzled. "What?"

She motions me closer. I sit on the edge of the bed. "Scoot in a little bit closer."

I do. She reaches out with her hands and gently grabs the sides of my arms, pulling me into her, until she is hugging me.

It takes me a moment to get it, and then I do, and I close my eyes and hug her tight.

She's sobbing. Silent and wordless, but with everything she has.

So I hug her and let her cry, and I don't feel sad.

These aren't those kind of tears.

58

IT IS FIVE O'CLOCK, and James and I are the only ones left in the office. This is a rare moment. All the monsters have been put to bed, for now. We can leave on a schedule. I plan to take advantage of it.

I watch as my report prints out. The last page will come, and that single piece of paper will stand for the end of the Jack Jr. case. All its blood and misery and life snuffed out too soon.

But not really. The things he did, and how those things affected us and others, will resonate and echo for years to come. He cut with a broad sword, indiscriminate and deep. Scar tissue may be nerveless, but it's still visible, and sometimes during the wee hours, it can tingle like a phantom limb.

Like Keenan and Shantz. That limb does not just tingle, it aches.

"Here are my notes," James says, startling me. He drops them on the desk.

"Thanks. I'm almost done."

He stands there, watching the printer as well. It's another rare moment: James and I sharing a comfortable silence.

"So I guess we'll never know," he says.

"I guess not."

We share the dark train, and so we both share the same wonder, without needing to put specific words to it.

Was there someone before Peter Hillstead's father? Was there a deadly grandfather, or great-grandfather? If you could follow it back, before the days of true forensics and cross-referenced computerized data, would you take a trip across the ocean and find yourself in gaslamp-lit cobblestone streets?

Running from a faceless man holding a gleaming scalpel and wearing a top hat?

Would you finally put a face on a legendary terror?

Probably not.

But we'll never know for sure.

It is the ability to let questions like this go unanswered, to walk away from them without looking back, that lets us keep our sanity.

The last page prints out.

EPILOGUE

I HAD ANNIE buried next to Matt and Alexa. That way Bonnie and I can visit our families together.

It's a beautiful day. That California sun, the kind my dad loved best, is out in all its glory, tempered by a cool breeze that keeps you from getting too hot.

The grass in the cemetery hasn't been cut yet this week, and it waves every so often, all thick and lustrous green. Looking across the cemetery, where the gravestones go as far as the eye can see, I can imagine this as the bottom of the ocean, covered with seaweed and row after row of wrecked ghost ships.

I see other people, single or together, young or old. They are visiting their own wives or husbands, sons or daughters, brothers or sisters. Some died peacefully. Some died in violence. Some were comforted, while others died alone.

Some graves have no visitors. They grow old and cracked with neglect.

Though it is filled with memories of death and haunted by ghosts, it is a peaceful place. And this is a perfect day.

Bonnie has been planting flowers on Annie's grave by

hand. She finishes, standing up and brushing the dirt off her palms.

"You done, honey?" I ask her.

She looks at me, nods. Smiles.

Elaina has started chemo. Alan is still coming to work. I've accepted that the outcomes of both are beyond my control. All I can do is love my friends and be there for them.

James had his sister's body reinterred. Leo bought a new dog, a Lab puppy he's been talking about for days. Callie is healing well, becoming grumpier and grumpier about her confinement to a hospital bed, a good sign. Her daughter continues to visit her, and Callie seems to be coming to a grudging acceptance that she now has to bear the title of Grandmother. She doesn't seem to mind.

Tommy and I have seen each other a few more times. Bonnie likes him. We're taking it easy, seeing where it leads.

It turns out that Peter Hillstead had been responsible for the death of at least twelve women over the years. Most were perfect crimes—in fact, we know about them now only because of his journals. He kept meticulous notes, just like his father. And like his father, he'd hidden his victims, picking women who wouldn't be missed, destroying their corpses when he was done with them. There was no evidence left of their passing, just—shadows. We still have no idea what other monsters he corresponded with and encouraged, beyond those we know about, or even if he did. I have learned to accept that this, too, is beyond my control. If they crawl out of their caves, I'll be here to slap them down.

It turns out that Robert Street had known Hillstead for almost three years. He had participated only in the two most recent murders. To be honest, I don't really care. Hillstead is dead and gone, and Street will soon take his own place on death row.

Hillstead had used his position as a doctor and as an authorized therapist for agents to gain access to personnel records, which is what we think led him down the road to Callie's daughter. The Bureau had done a thorough background check on Callie; Marilyn hadn't escaped their scrutiny.

He'd seemed omnipotent at times in his ability to find out everything about us. In the end, it turns out that he was just smart.

We were smarter, something I remain grimly smug about. I recognize the danger of this. The dark train is my own arrogance, one that could carry me off a cliff if I don't watch it. For now, I let it ride. Dragons are prideful, after all.

The Hillsteads have the profilers in some kind of foaming-at-the-mouth tizzy. Something new and unheard of in a serial killer, blah, blah, blah.

I don't think he was all that different from any of the other killers I've hunted and caught. He made a mistake, just like they all do. However "perfect" he may have been, it was Renee Parker—his first—who reached out from the grave in the end, pulling him down into the earth with her. This brings me a feeling of tremendous satisfaction.

The real ghosts of this world are just that, I have thought many times since: the consequences of our actions. The footprints of change we leave in our passage through time.

Consequences. They can haunt or harm us. They can also exalt us, and be a source of comfort in the night. Not all ghosts wail or weep. Some just smile.

Bonnie still isn't speaking. She doesn't scream in her sleep every night, but neither is every night peaceful. She is a beautiful child, smart, thoughtful, generous with her love. She is an artist as well, a painter. She churns them out, things beautiful and dark, and I recognize that for now they are her substitute for the spoken word.

We've settled into a routine. Not quite mother-daughter, not just yet. But we are making progress, and I am no longer terrified. I am happy with the First Rule of Mom, ready to let it take me wherever it wants to go.

The ghosts of Matt and Alexa visit me in my dreams, and they are a comfort. I no longer have the nightmares.

"You ready to go?"

Bonnie takes my hand as an answer.

She is mute, and I am scarred, but the day is beautiful, and the future no longer terrible. I have her and she has me, and from there grows love.

And from love—life.

We leave the cemetery hand in hand, watched by our ghosts.

I can feel them smiling.

ABOUT THE AUTHOR

Cody McFadyen lives with his family in California.
Shadow Man is his first novel.

Don't miss the next
novel of suspense
featuring
Smoky Barrett

THE FACE
OF DEATH

Available as a Bantam hardcover
in June 2007

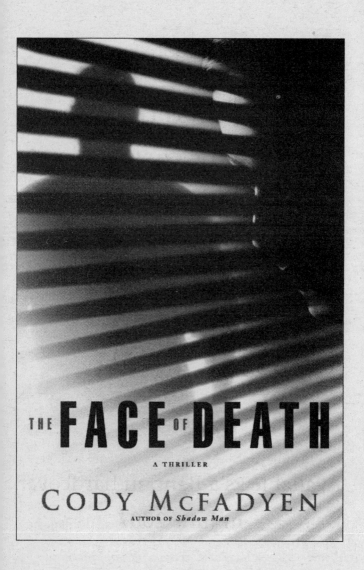

THE FACE OF DEATH

A THRILLER

CODY McFADYEN

AUTHOR OF *Shadow Man*

THE FACE OF DEATH

On sale June 2007

THE MUSIC AND SUNLIGHT work, at least in my bedroom. We go through Matt's closet without me feeling too sad.

We pack away his shirts and slacks, his sweaters and shoes. The smell of him is everywhere—the ghost of him. It seems like I have a memory for every piece of clothing. He'd smiled wearing this tie. He'd cried at his grandfather's funeral in this suit. Alexa had left a jam handprint on this shirt. These memories seem less painful than I had expected. More rich than depressing.

Doing good, babe, I hear Matt say in my head.

I don't reply, but smile to myself.

I think about Quantico and that possibility, too. *Maybe it would be good to leave this place behind.*

If I do, it needs to be about choice, not retreat. I need to embrace my ghosts and lay them down, because they'll follow me wherever I go. That's what ghosts do.

We get through the closet and the bedroom and then the bathroom, and I float through it all, the pain there but tolerable. *Bittersweet, waitress, heavy on the sweet.*

We file down the stairway carrying the boxes, move into the garage, then up into the attic above the garage, dropping the boxes off and pushing them back into corners where I know they'll sit in the dark and gather dust.

Sorry, Matt, I think.

They're just things, babe, he replies. *The heart doesn't get dusty.*

I guess.

By the way, Matt says, out of nowhere, *what about 1forUtwo4me?*

I don't answer. I stand on the ladder, in the attic from the waist up.

"Smoky?" Callie calls from the doorway of the garage.

"Be there in a sec."

Yes, I think. *What about 1forUtwo4me? What's the plan there?*

I had learned, doing what I do, that good men and women can still have secrets. Good wives and husbands can still cheat on each other, or have secret vices, or turn out not to have been so good after all. And, I had learned, it all comes out once you die, because once you're dead, others are free to root through your life at their leisure and you can't do a darn thing about it.

Which brings me to 1forUtwo4me. It was a password. Matt had explained the concept of picking secure passwords to me once after a family e-mail account had been compromised.

"You want to include numbers with letters. The longer the better, obviously, but you want to pick something you can memorize and not have to write down. Something that'll be mnemonic. Like . . ." He'd snapped his fingers. "One for you, two for me. That's a phrase that sticks in my mind. So I change it a little and add some numbers and come up with 1forUtwo4me. Silly, but I'll remember it, and it'll be hard for someone to guess by accident."

He'd been right. It was like gum on your shoe. 1forUtwo4me. I'd never have to write it down. It would always be accessible.

A few months after Matt died, I'd been sitting at his

computer. We had a home office, and we each had our own PC. I was feeling numb and looking for something to awaken an emotion inside of me. I scrolled through his e-mail, dug through his files. I came upon a directory on the computer labeled "private." When I went to open the directory, I found that it was password-protected.

1forUtwo4me, there it was, trotted out before I had to really think about it. My fingers had moved to the keyboard. I was about to type it out. I stopped.

Froze.

What if? I'd thought. *What if private really does mean private? Like, private from me?*

The thought had been appalling. And terrifying. My imagination went into overdrive.

A mistress? Porn? He loved someone else?

Following these thoughts, the guilt.

How could you think that? It's Matt. Your Matt.

I'd left the room, tucked away Mr. 1forUtwo4me, and tried not to think about it.

He popped up every now and then. Like now.

Well? Truth or denial?

"Smoky?" Callie calls again.

"Coming," I reply and clamber down the ladder.

I still feel Matt.

Waiting.

1forUtwo4me.

Packing away the past, it occurs to me, is messy stuff.

We're standing in the doorway of Alexa's room. I can feel discomfort looming in the not-far-off. Pain is a little sharper here, though still tolerable.

"Pretty room," Elaina murmurs.

"Alexa liked the girly-girl stuff," I say, smiling.

It is a little girl's dream room. The bed is queen-sized, with a canopy, and it's covered with purples of every possible hue. The comforter and pillows are thick and lush and inviting. *Lie down and drown in us,* they say.

One quarter of the floor is covered in Alexa's stuffed animal collection. They range from small to big to huge, and the species run the gamut from the identifiable to the fantastic.

"Lions and tigers and heffalumps, oh my," Matt used to joke.

I take it all in, and a thought comes to me. I wonder at the fact that it never occurred to me before.

Bonnie has slept with me since the day I brought her home. I don't think she's ever entered this bedroom.

Be accurate, I chide myself. *You never brought her in here, that's the truth. Never asked her if she might want a king's ransom of stuffed animals, or a purple explosion of bed sheets and blankets.*

Time to fix *that,* I think. I kneel down next to Bonnie. "Do you want anything in here, sweetheart?" I ask her. She looks at me, her eyes searching mine. "You're welcome to whatever you want." I squeeze her hand. "Really. You can have the whole room."

She shakes her head. *No, thank you,* she's saying.

I've put away childish things, that look says.

"Okay, babe," I murmur, standing up.

"How do you want to handle this room, Smoky?" Elaina's gentle voice startles me.

I run a hand through Bonnie's hair as I look around the room.

"Well," I start to say—and then my cell phone rings.

Callie rolls her eyes. "Here we go."

"Barrett," I answer.

Sorry, I mouth to them.

A deep voice rumbles. "Smoky. It's Alan. Sorry to bother you today, but we got a situation."

Alan is overseeing the unit while I'm on vacation. He's

more than competent; the fact that he's felt the need to call me raises my antennae.

"What is it?"

"I'm in Canoga Park, standing in front of a house. Scene of a triple homicide. *Bad* scene. Twist is, there's a sixteen-year-old girl inside. She's got a gun to her head and says she'll only talk to you."

"She asked for me by name?"

"Yep."

I'm silent, processing.

"Really sorry about this, Smoky."

"Don't worry about it. We were just about to take a break, anyway. Give me the address and Callie and I will meet you there soonest."

I jot down the address and hang up.

The man had gotten it wrong: Death *doesn't* take a holiday, apparently. Par for the course. As always, I was living my life on multiple levels: Make this a home, decide if I was going to leave this home and go to Quantico, go stop a young woman from blowing her brains out. I could walk and chew gum at the same time, hurrah for me.

I look at Bonnie. "Sweetheart—" I begin, but stop as she nods her head. *It's okay, go,* she is saying.

I look at Elaina. "Elaina—"

"I'll watch Bonnie."

Relief and gratitude, that's what I feel.

"Callie—"

"I'll drive," she says.

I crouch down facing Bonnie. "Do me a favor, sweetheart?"

She gives me a quizzical look.

"See if you can figure out what we should do with all those stuffed animals."

She grins. Nods.

"Cool." I straighten up, turn to Callie. "Let's go."

Bad things are waiting. I don't want them to get impatient.

"All tucked away," Callie muses as we pull onto the suburban street in Canoga Park.

She's talking to herself more than to me, but as I look around, I understand the observation. Canoga Park is a part of Los Angeles County. Los Angeles doesn't provide a lot of distance between the suburbs and the city proper. You can be on a street lined with businesses, drive two blocks, and find yourself in a residential neighborhood. It was a casual transformation; traffic lights gave way to stop signs and things just got more *quiet*. The city hustled nearby, never stopping, always there, while the homes were here, *tucked away*.

The street we turn onto is in one of those neighborhoods, but it has lost that quiet feeling. I spot at least five cop cars, along with a SWAT van and two or three unmarked vehicles. The obligatory helicopter is circling above.

"Thank God we still have daylight," Callie remarks, looking up at the helicopter. "I can't stand those blinding spotlights."

People are everywhere. The braver ones are standing on their lawns, while the more timid peek out from behind window curtains. It's funny, I think. People talk about crime in urban areas, but all the best murders happen in the suburbs.

Callie parks the car on the side of the street.

"Ready?" I ask her.

"Born ready, bring it on, pick your cliché," she says.

As we exit the car, I see Callie grimace. She places a hand on the roof of the car to steady herself.

"Are you alright?" I ask.

She waves away my concern. "Residual pain from getting shot, nothing I can't handle." She reaches into a jacket pocket and pulls out a prescription bottle. "Vicodin, today's mother's little helper." She pops the top and palms a tablet. Downs it. Smiles. "Yummy."

Callie had been shot six months ago. The bullet had nicked her spine. For one very tense week we weren't sure she was going to walk again. I thought she'd recovered fully.

Guess I was wrong.

Wrong? She carries her Vicodin around with her like a box of Tic-Tacs!

"Let's see what all the shouting is about, shall we?" she asks.

"Yep," I reply.

But don't think I'm going to let this go, Callie.

We head over to the perimeter. A twenty-something patrolman stops us. He's a good-looking kid. I can sense his excitement at being a part of this law enforcement cacophony. I like him right away; he sees the scars on my face and almost doesn't flinch.

"Sorry, ma'am," he says. "I can't let anyone in right now."

I fish out my FBI ID and show it to him. "Special Agent Barrett," I say. Callie does the same.

"Sorry, ma'am," he says again. "And ma'am," he says to Callie.

"Don't sweat it," Callie replies.

I spot Alan standing in a cluster of suits and uniforms. He towers above them all, an imposing edifice of a human being. Alan is in his mid-forties, an African-American man who can only be described as *gargantuan*. He's not obese—just *big*. His scowl can make an interrogation room seem like a small and dangerous place for a guilty man.

Life loves irony, and Alan is no exception. For all his size, he is a thoughtful man-mountain, a brilliant mind in a linebacker's body. He combines meticulous precision with near-infinite patience. His attention to detail is legendary. One of the best testaments to his character is the fact that Elaina is his wife, and she adores him.

Alan is the third member of my four-person team, the oldest and most grounded. He told me when Elaina had been diagnosed with cancer that he was considering leaving the FBI so that he could spend more time with her. He hasn't brought it up since, and I haven't pushed him on it, but I am never really unaware of it.

Callie popping pills, Alan thinking of retiring—maybe I should leave. Let them rebuild the team from scratch.

"There she is," I hear Alan say.

I start to catalogue the various reactions to my face and then let it go. *Take it or leave it, boys.*

One of the men steps forward, putting a hand out to shake mine. The other hand, I note, grips an MP5 submachine gun. He's dressed in full SWAT regalia—body armor, helmet, boots. "Luke Dawes," he says. "SWAT commander. Thanks for coming."

"No problem," I reply. I point to Alan. "Do you mind if I have my guy fill me in? No offense intended."

"None taken."

I turn to Alan and push aside all my own internal chatter, letting the simplicity of action and command take over. "Hit me," I say.

"A call came into 911 about an hour and a half ago from the next-door neighbor. Widower by the name of Jenkins. Jenkins says that the girl—Sarah Kingsley—had stumbled into his front yard, dressed in a nightgown, covered in blood."

"How did he know she was in the front yard?"

"His living room is in the front of the house and he

keeps his drapes open until he goes to bed. He was watching TV, saw her out of the corner of his eye."

"Go on."

"He's shook up but he musters up enough courage to go out and see what the problem is. Said she was unfocused—his word—and mumbling something about her family being murdered. He tries to get her to come into his house, but she screams and runs off, reenters her own home."

"I take it he was wise enough not to follow her?"

"Yeah, the heroics only went as far as his own front yard. He ran back inside, made the call. A patrol car happens to be nearby, so they come over to check it out. The officers"—he checks his notepad again—"Sims and Butler, arrive, poke their heads in the front door—which was wide open—and try and get her to come back out. She's unresponsive. After talking it over, they decide to go in and get her. Dangerous maybe, but neither of them is a rookie, and they're worried about the girl."

"Understandable," I murmur. "Are Sims and Butler still here?"

"Yep."

"Go on."

"They enter the home and it's a fucking bloodbath from the get-go."

"Have you been inside?" I interrupt.

"No. No one's been in there since she got hold of a weapon. So they go in, and it's obvious that something bad happened, and that it happened recently. Lucky for us, Sims and Butler have dealt with murder scenes before, so they don't lose their heads. They give anything that looks like evidence a wide berth."

"Good," I say.

"Yeah. They hear noise on the second floor, and call out for the girl. No answer. They proceed up the stairs, and find her in the master bedroom, along with three dead bodies. She's got a gun." He consults his notes. "A 9mm of some kind, per the officers. Things change fast at that point. Now they're nervous. They're thinking maybe *she's* responsible for whatever happened here, and they point their weapons at her, tell her to drop the gun, etc., etc. That's when she puts it to her own head."

"And things change again."

"Right. She's crying, and starts screaming at them. Saying, quote, *'I want to talk to Smoky Barrett or I'll kill myself!'* End quote. They try and talk her down, but give it up after she points the gun at them a few times. They call it in and"—he opens his arms to indicate the overwhelming presence of law enforcement around us—"here we are." He nods his head toward the SWAT commander. "Lieutenant Dawes knew your name and got someone to get ahold of me. I came here, checked things out, called you."

I turn to Dawes, study him. I see a fit, alert, hard-eyed professional policeman with calm hands and brunette hair in a crew cut. He's on the short side, about 5'9", but he's lean and coiled and ready. He radiates calm confidence. He's a SWAT stereotype, something I always find comforting whenever I encounter it. "What do you think, Lieutenant?"

He studies me for a few seconds. Then shrugs. "She's sixteen, ma'am. A gun's a gun, but . . ." He shrugs again. "She's sixteen."

She's too young to die, he's saying. *Definitely too young for me to kill without it ruining my day.*

"Do you have a negotiator on-site?" I ask.

I'm asking about a hostage negotiator. Someone trained in talking to unbalanced people carrying guns. *Negotiator* is a bit of a misnomer, actually; they usually operate in three-man teams.

"Nope," Dawes replies. "We currently have three negotiating teams in L.A. Some guy decided today was the day he was going to jump off the top of the Roosevelt Hotel in Hollywood—that's one. There's a dad about to lose custody of his kids who decided to put a shotgun to his head—that's two. The last team got T-boned in an intersection this morning on their way to a training seminar, if you can believe that." He shakes his head in disgust. "It was a truck that hit them. They'll live, but they're all in the hospital. We're on our own." He pauses. "I could handle this all kinds of ways, Agent Barrett. Tear gas, nonlethal ammo. But tear gas is going to fuck up what sounds like a murder scene. And nonlethal ammo, well . . . she could still shoot herself even after getting hit with a bean bag." He smiles without humor. "Seems like the best plan involves you going in there and talking to a crazy teenager holding a gun."

I give him my best sucking-lemons sour face. "Thanks."

He gets serious. "You gotta wear body armor and have your weapon out and ready to fire." He cocks a head at me, interest sparking in his gray eyes. "You're some kind of *super shooter*, right?"

"Annie Oakley," I reply.

He looks doubtful.

"She can put out candle flames and shoot holes through quarters, honey-love," Callie says to him. "I've seen her do it."

"Me, too," Alan growls.

I'm not trying to brag, and this is not bravado. I have a unique relationship with handguns. I really *can* shoot out candle flames, and I really *have* shot holes through quarters thrown into the air. I don't know where this gift came from—no one in my family even *liked* guns. Dad was gentle and easygoing. Mom had an Irish temper, but she still covered her eyes during the violent parts of movies.

When I was seven, a friend of my father's took me and my dad to a shooting range. I was able to hit what I wanted with minimal instruction, even then. I'd been in love with guns ever since.

"Okay, I believe you," Dawes says, raising his unencumbered hand in a gesture of surrender. His face grows serious. His eyes get a little distant. "Targets are one thing. Have you ever shot a person?"

I'm not offended by him asking this. Since I *have* shot and killed another human being, I understand why he asks, and know that he's right to ask. It *is* different, and you can't know just how different until you've done it.

"Yes," I respond.

I think the fact that I don't offer any further details convinces him most. He's killed, too, and knows it's not something you feel like bragging about. Or talking about. Or thinking about if you can help it.

"Right. So—body armor, gun out, and if it comes down to a choice between you and her, do what you gotta do. Hopefully, you can talk her down."

"Hopefully." I turn to Alan. "Do we have any idea—at all—why she's asked for me?"

He shakes his head. "Nope."

"What about her—any details on who she is?"

"Not much. People here are into the 'good fences make good neighbors' philosophy. The old guy, Jenkins, did say that she was adopted."

"Really?"

"Yeah. About a year ago. He's not close with the family, but he and the dad talked to each other from their driveways every now and then. That's how he knew who the girl was."

"Interesting. She could be the doer."

"It's possible. No one else had anything substantial to offer. The Kingsleys were good neighbors, meaning they were quiet and minded their own business."

I sigh and look toward the house. What had started out as a beautiful day was turning into a bad one fast.

I turn to Dawes.

"If I'm acting as negotiator, that means I have command for now. Any problems with that?"

"No, ma'am."

"I don't want anyone getting trigger-happy, Dawes. No matter how long it takes. Don't go behind my back and start rappelling from the roof or anything cute."

Dawes smiles at me. He's not offended. This is standard fare. "I've been to a few of these, Agent Barrett. Contrary to popular belief, my guys aren't itching to shoot someone."

"I've worked with our own SWAT, Lieutenant. I know all about getting pumped up for a call."

"Even so."

I study him. Believe him. Nod.

"In that case—do you have some body armor I can borrow?"

"You don't have your own?"

"I did, but it was recalled. Mine and four hundred others in the same lot—faulty composition resulting in them being overly brittle, or something like that. I'm waiting for a replacement."

"Ouch. Good catch on their part then, I guess."

"Except that I had reason to wear it three times before they figured out that it might not actually stop a bullet."

He shrugs. "Vest won't protect you from a head shot, anyway. It's all a roll of the dice."

With that encouraging observation, Dawes goes off to get my Kevlar.

"He seems calm enough," Alan observes.

"Keep an eye on things anyway."

"They'll have to go through both of us," Callie says. "I'll flash them a little leg, Alan will terrify them, end of problem."

"Just worry about what to do once you're inside," Alan says. "You ever done any negotiation?"

"I've taken the class. But no, I've never dealt with a 'situation.'"

"Key is to listen. No lies unless you're sure you can get away with them. It's about rapport, so lies are a deal breaker. Watch for emotional triggers and give them a nice, wide berth."

"Sure, simple."

"Oh yeah, and don't die."

"Very funny."

Dawes reappears with a vest. "I got this off a female detective." He holds it up, looks at me, frowns. "It's going to be big."

"They all are unless I get them custom."

He grins. "No height requirement, I take it, Agent Barrett?"

I grab the vest from him with a scowl. "That's Special Agent Barrett to you, Dawes."

The grin fades. "Well, be careful in there, Special Agent Barrett."

"If I was going to be careful, I wouldn't go in there at all."

"Even so."

Even so, I think. *What a great turn of phrase. Short and sweet, but fraught (another great word) with meaning.*

You could die in there.

Even so.